Praise for

AMANDA STEVENS

"The sinister world of Amanda Stevens will feed
the dark side of your soul...and leave you
hungry for more."
— *New York Times* bestselling author Christina Dodd

"Breathless, chilling and unforgettable.
When you crack open an Amanda Stevens book,
prepare to be thrilled."
— *USA TODAY* bestselling author Patricia Kay

"*Just Past Midnight* is a taut and suspenseful tale
guaranteed to keep readers on the edge of their
seat. The twists and turns are diabolical,
unpredictable and chilling."
— *Romantic Times BOOKreviews*

"Ms. Stevens shows her magic of writing tales to
snare the reader. She weaves intrigue,
believable characters, legends and emotion
together seamlessly for an engrossing read."
— *Best Reviews* on *Secret Sanctuary*

D1014111

AMANDA STEVENS

the dollmaker

MIRA®

MIRA

ISBN-13: 978-0-7783-2428-7
ISBN-10:   0-7783-2428-1

THE DOLLMAKER

www.MIRABooks.com

Printed in U.S.A.

For Leanne, Lucas and Steven

I am deeply grateful to my editor,
Denise Zaza, and everyone at MIRA Books
for their encouragement and support and
for helping me turn a dream into reality.
Many thanks to my agent, Helen Breitwieser,
for her advice and enthusiasm, and most of all,
for not allowing this story to fade away. Thanks
also to Carla Luan and Heather MacAllister for
their tireless brainstorming and critiquing and to
Leanne Amann for her innovative PR strategies.

Prologue

~⦅⦆~

The doll was getting to him. Even though Travis McSwain wasn't a man easily spooked. She was so lifelike that anyone glancing through the shop window might mistake her for a pretty, little, blond-haired girl.

But up close, the eyes gave her away. They looked like pieces of turquoise. Travis had never seen real eyes that color.

He didn't like staring at her for too long because his mind kept playing tricks on him. Earlier, when he'd packed her up to bring her into the city, he could have sworn those glass eyes followed his every move. They gave him the chills so bad he'd had half a mind to chuck her in the swamp. But he needed the money and so here he was.

The shopkeeper glanced up from her inspection. "She's stunning. Absolutely breathtaking. If you'll just give me a few more minutes we can discuss your payment terms."

"Take your time," Travis muttered, but he wished to

hell the woman would hurry up. The sooner he got rid of the doll the sooner he'd breathe a lot easier.

Something about that porcelain face creeped him out. It was almost as if Travis had seen her before, in a dream maybe, but he didn't know how that could be possible. She was one of a kind.

He'd gone up to the old Sweete place looking for work, and when he spotted the doll through the front window, he'd decided to snatch her, because that's what he did. He took things that didn't belong to him. It was some kind of sickness, he reckoned.

Before his Pentecostal mother went off the deep end, she used to weep and pray for his immortal soul, but his daddy had favored another approach. Whenever Travis got caught using the five-finger discount, the old man would take a belt to his hide, work him over good until his back and butt cheeks resembled raw steak.

But after the first time Travis got sent off to juvenile detention in St. James Parish, Cletus McSwain's attitude had changed. He'd pretty much washed his hands of his son. "One of these days you'll pinch from the wrong person, boy, and end up with a bullet right between the eyeballs. And when that happens, I'll be damned if I shed a tear over your sorry ass."

Well, that was fair. Because Travis sure as hell hadn't done much crying when the pious old bastard got swept off a shrimp boat and drowned in the Gulf. And now here Travis stood, right as rain, while his daddy swam with the fishes down in Terrebonne Bay.

Sometimes you just had to laugh at how things worked out.

Travis leaned an elbow on the counter and tried to assume a casual air as the shopkeeper continued to study the doll. But every once in a while, when the woman wasn't looking, his gaze would dart to the front window. He didn't like to put much stock in his old man's predictions, but ever since he'd taken the doll, Travis had a real bad feeling that maybe, just maybe, he'd gotten in over his head this time. Boosting cars was one thing, but jacking that doll was starting to feel a little like kidnapping.

A shiver snaked up his spine. It was like the damn thing was hexed or something.

He fingered the mojo bag he carried around in his pocket. *It's just a toy.*

But the doll was more than a toy. Everyone in Terrebonne Parish knew that Savannah Sweete's dolls were one of a kind and worth a lot of money. And someone was going to want it back.

He cast another glance at the window. Rain was coming and the gloomy twilight deepened his unease. He was letting his nerves get the better of him, but he couldn't seem to help it. New Orleans did that to him. He hadn't been back since Katrina, and the landscape had changed so much he'd hardly recognized the place, driving in. But the soul of the city—the Vieux Carré—remained the same. Travis didn't know if that was a good thing or not.

Earlier, he'd walked around for a little while before his appointment with the shop owner, and he'd been struck by how normal everything seemed. Normal for the Quarter, anyway. It was still early, but the strip joints on Bourbon Street were already open, giving passersby free peep shows from the doorways. Travis's attention had been captivated by a tall, leggy blonde undulating to a country and western song. Her back was to the door, but when she glanced over her shoulder, her dark eyes fastened like laser beams on Travis.

She was incredibly limber, and her ass and thighs were as tight as the skin on a snare drum. She smiled and curled a finger in his direction, inviting him in for a closer inspection, and Travis had been sorely tempted. But then she turned slowly to face him, and anger washed over him when he realized he'd been standing there gawking at a transvestite.

A throaty voice had said from the doorway, "Come on in, sugar, she don't bite. Her name is Cherry Rose. You like what Cherry Rose got down there, no?"

"No," Travis muttered, and turned away.

"Hey, don't be like that!" the voice called after him. "Come on back here, baby. Cherry Rose make a real man out of you."

Some of the tourists on the street overheard and started laughing, and Travis's fist itched to connect with the he-bitch's red mouth. But Bourbon Street drag queens were notorious for strapping switchblades to their thighs, and when they got all hopped up on speed, they'd as soon cut a man's balls off as look at him.

So Travis had hurried away. But as he crossed the street he'd glanced back and noticed someone standing on the sidewalk, staring after him. Not the dancer or the hawker in the doorway, but a strange-looking woman wearing silver earrings and a flowing green skirt.

Something about the way she gazed at him startled Travis, and he'd paused for a moment to stare back at her. Then he lost her in the noisy crowd on the street and moved on.

He thought about the woman now and wondered

where she'd gone off to, wondered if he might be able to find her once his business with the shopkeeper was settled.

Then again, maybe he ought to leave well enough alone and get his ass on home, where he could tell what was what. But after taking that doll, Terrebonne Parish might not be the safest place for him right now.

Suppressing a shudder, he said impatiently, "Don't mean to rush you, ma'am, but I ain't got all night."

The woman looked up with an apologetic smile. "I'm sorry for making you wait, dear, but I rarely come across workmanship of this quality. The freckles across the nose...the tiny birthmark on her left arm...that kind of attention to detail is a Savannah Sweete trademark. I just can't get over how meticulous she is."

"Uh-huh."

"However..." The woman's tone sharpened, as if she was readying herself to get down to business. She was an old broad with steely blue eyes and cottony hair. Her glasses were the shape of cat's eyes, and as she spoke, she kept slipping them off and chewing on one of the stems.

Travis frowned. "What's wrong? You don't like her so much all of a sudden?"

"No, it isn't that. As I said, the doll is beautiful. But there are some fairly convincing imitations making the rounds these days. A few of Savannah's former students have mastered her technique, and I know of one or two who have actually tried to pass off their work as hers." The woman paused, her gaze dropping to the doll. "Do you have the certificate of authenticity?"

Travis had thought that might be a problem, but he was prepared to bluff his way through it. After all, bullshitting was second nature to him. Just like stealing. "If you're the expert you claim to be, you should be able to tell just by looking at her that she's the real deal." He reached out and flipped one of the doll's golden curls with his fingertip. "You said yourself you've never seen such quality."

The woman slid the glasses up her nose and bent back over the doll. "I'm ninety-nine percent certain she's genuine, but if you could obtain her paperwork, the value would double."

"Sorry, but I'm offering her as is. You don't want her, I'll go elsewhere. I figure there's plenty of shops and private collectors out there who'd like to get their hands on a fine piece like this."

"Perhaps. But you have to understand my position. My livelihood hinges on my reputation. If you could at least tell me how and where you acquired her…?"

Travis didn't like the sound of that. The last thing he needed was for the old biddy to call the cops. "Why do you need to know that?"

"As I said, I have a reputation to consider. I have to be cautious."

This wasn't going as well as he'd hoped. The woman was playing hardball and he now had two options. Stay and haggle or take the doll and walk. By this time tomorrow he'd probably have another buyer, but he didn't much like the notion of driving all the way back home, knowing those glass eyes would be watching him another night.

"Okay, it's like this. The doll belonged to my girlfriend's kid. The little girl up and died suddenly, and my old lady can't have a reminder like that lying around the house. She asked me to get rid of it for her.

Considering everything she's been through, I don't see how I can worry her about the paperwork. You understand."

"Of course I do. How awful to lose a child. And one so beautiful." She stroked the doll's smooth cheek. "I have two little granddaughters. I can't imagine anything more tragic—"

"So we got us a deal or what?"

The shopkeeper's attention lingered on the doll. She couldn't seem to tear her gaze away. "Cut ten percent off the price we discussed on the phone and we'll call it a day."

"Sounds fair enough."

She smiled, satisfied. "Good. If you'll wait here, I'll write you a check."

Travis's hand snaked out to curl around her wrist. "Like I said earlier, I'm partial to cash."

The woman's eyes flickered. He could see suspicion working its way back to the surface, but she wanted the doll so bad she was willing to ignore her instincts. She shook off his hand and gave a curt nod. "I'll be right back."

She reappeared a few moments later and handed him an envelope. "It's all there—the amount we agreed on earlier, less ten percent. But feel free to count it, Mr...."

Travis pocketed the envelope with a grin. "I trust you. Besides, if you short me I know where to find you."

The woman's hand fluttered to her throat and she turned a little pale, as if suddenly realizing that she'd just struck a bargain with the devil.

Lady, if you only knew.

She followed him to the door and after he stepped outside, he heard the click of the dead bolt behind him. Glancing over his shoulder, he saw the woman's silhouette in the window, but she quickly shut off the light and pulled the shade.

Travis stood on the sidewalk for a moment, deciding whether he wanted to go straight home or stop off somewhere for a drink. It wasn't often he had spare change in his pocket. Might as well do a little celebrating.

Across the street, a shadow darted into a doorway, and his heart raced. For a moment he thought it was the woman he'd seen earlier on Bourbon Street, but as he peered into the shadows, he couldn't make her out.

He was seeing things, probably. A guilty conscience could make a man jumpy.

Whatever the hell was wrong with him, he couldn't wait to get out of New Orleans. Too many weirdos hanging around to suit him. He'd leave the city before having that drink. Maybe stop off at a little place he knew on the way home, buy a bucket of shrimp and have a few beers. Later he'd make a liquor store run with Desiree, and the two of them could sit out on his back porch getting shit-faced as they watched heat lightning over the Gulf.

It all sounded good.

Hunching his shoulders against a light rain, he headed east toward Bourbon Street. At the corner of Chartres and St. Louis, a group of tourists had stopped to watch an old black man tap-dance beneath a balcony. The rat-a-tat-tat of his shoes resonated in the darkness, and for some reason the sound made Travis feel lonely.

He stopped to stuff a couple of bills into a beat-up

coffee can, then quickly moved on, discomforted by the man's toothless grin. The old geezer looked to be pushing eighty. He should have been tucked away somewhere in a rest home instead of busting his hump on a street corner in the rain. But that was New Orleans for you. The old didn't die here. They were just forgotten.

"You don't get yourself straightened out, that'll be you someday, boy," he could hear his daddy goad him.

Travis didn't want to think about his father or the future or even what he was going to do with himself beyond the next drunk. He tuned out the echo of the old man's taps as he neared the cathedral and turned up St. Peter.

The street was nearly deserted here except for a woman who stood in the glow of a shop window. She wore a green skirt, and when she moved her head, light sparked off her silver earrings.

Travis slowed his steps. She was the same woman he'd seen earlier on Bourbon Street.

Their gazes connected as he approached, and a shiver slid up his spine. She had the palest face he'd ever laid eyes on. He knew he'd never seen her before tonight, but there was something eerily familiar about her features. He couldn't put his finger on what it was.

She smiled, and the skin at the back of his neck crawled. Who the hell *was* she?

Spooked by that smile, Travis decided to keep on walking, but as he passed her, she said in a low voice, "Can I trouble you for a light?"

Not exactly an original line, but curiosity got the better of him and he reached in his pocket for a lighter. Turning, he shielded the flame with his cupped hand as she lifted a cigarette to her lips. They were nice lips. Not too full, not too thin. It was only when she smiled that something seemed off about her mouth.

She took a pull and slowly exhaled the smoke, then handed the cigarette to Travis. He didn't know what he was supposed to do with it, but when he took a drag, she didn't seem to mind.

"So what are you doing out here all by your lonesome?" he asked.

"Killing time."

"Kind of dangerous to be here alone. Nothing but freaks in the Quarter."

She smiled. "Really? I hadn't noticed."

That smile. Travis wished she'd stop doing that. It wasn't a nice smile and it kind of ruined the mood for him. He glanced away.

"Do you like to party?" she asked.

"Doesn't everybody?"

"My place is just back there." She nodded toward a narrow alley that ran between two buildings. "Got a nice little courtyard where we can sit and watch the rain. Come on," she said, and started walking. "I'll buy you a drink."

Her smile might not do anything for him, but the way she walked sure as hell did. Travis followed her into the alley. He didn't know if she was a hooker or just some bitch out for a good time, but at the moment, he didn't really give a shit. The money he'd made from the doll was burning a hole in his pocket.

She was a few steps ahead of him, humming something under her breath.

"What's that you're singing?"

"It's an old song. Something my mother used to

sing to me at bedtime." She glanced over her shoulder. "Do you like it?"

"Yeah, it's nice." He hurried to catch up with her. "My mama didn't believe in music. Or dancing."

"How sad for you." She paused to adjust the strap on her sandal, and when she lost her balance, she grabbed Travis's arm to right herself.

He stared down at her in the darkness. She laughed softly, and the next thing Travis knew, he had her backed up against the brick wall.

She laughed again, a breathy sound that spiked his heartbeat. But when he tried to kiss her, she turned her head so that his lips only grazed her pale cheek. He moved to her ear, then nuzzled her neck as he put a hand on her narrow waist, letting his thumb slide up beneath her breast. She was small there, too, but he didn't mind. "What's your name?"

After a slight hesitation, she said in a husky whisper, "Madeline."

"That's a nice name." Travis figured she'd made it up on the spur of the moment, but he didn't care if she had. After tonight, they'd never see each other again, anyway. "You smell good, Madeline."

He again tried to kiss her, but she gave him a playful shove. "Take it easy, okay? We've got all night. Don't you want that drink first?"

He rubbed up against her, grinding his hips against hers. "You know what I want."

"Sure I do, baby." Her hand slid between them and she ran it up and down his fly. "But it'll cost you."

"How much?"

"A hundred and fifty." Her hand squeezed him. "You got that much?"

He fished in his pocket for the money and handed it to her in the dark. "For that kind of dough, you better be something special."

"Oh, I am." She slipped the folded bills into her bra. "I'm very special. You've never been with anyone like me before, honey."

Reversing their positions, she pushed him up against the wall, then wet a finger in her mouth and traced his lips. "You want it fast or slow?"

"Right now, I want you on your knees," he said, and unzipped his pants.

"Patience, baby. Good things come to those who wait." Her fingers closed around him as she slid her other hand over his shoulder.

Travis let his head fall back against the brick wall, his breath quickening as he swelled in her hand. An instant later, he felt a sharp sting in the side of his neck, and pushed her away. "What the hell was that?"

She smiled in the dark. "You're going to need something for the pain."

"Pain?" His voice rose in fury as he lifted a hand to his neck. "What did you do to me, you fucking bitch?" Light from an apartment overhead filtered into the alley, and he could see her eyes staring back at him. He hadn't noticed before how blue they were. And then in a flash, it came to him where he'd seen that face before.

Fear and revulsion rose in his throat a split second before his muscles collapsed. He tried to stay on his feet, tried to grab her around the throat, but he had no control over his limbs. He fell to his knees, his gaze locked on hers. His mouth gaped open, but no sound came out.

"You took something of mine and now I'm going to have to do some very bad things to get her back."

With a foot on his chest, she shoved him backward. Paralyzed, he fell to the dirty pavement, his gaze fixed on those blue eyes.

She removed a scalpel from her bag and knelt beside him. "This is going to be a little crude and messy, I'm afraid, but I can't have the police tracing you or the doll back to me."

A fresh wave of terror washed over Travis. He wanted to get up and run. He wanted to scream for help. He wanted to fight for his life.

But he could only lie there helplessly as she lowered the blade and began to cut off his fingers.

One

Twilight always fell anxiously over the Big Easy, especially when it rained. That's when the ghosts came out. A wisp of steam rising from the wet pavement. The murmur of voices from a hidden courtyard. Something dark and stealthy moving in the shadows, and suddenly you were reminded of a past that wouldn't stay buried.

New Orleans was like that. A city of memories, Dave Creasy always called it. A city of secrets and whispers and the kind of regret that could eat a man up inside. Like the wrong woman, she'd get in a man's blood, destroy his soul, make him feel alive and dead at the same time. And on a hot, rainy night—when the ghosts came out—it could be the loneliest place on earth.

Welcome back, a voice whispered in Dave's head as he lifted his face, eyes closed, and listened to the rustle of rain through the white oleanders that drooped over a crumbling brick wall along St. Peters.

It was strange how the city could still seduce him.

He'd been born and raised in New Orleans, and like everyone else he knew, there'd been a time when he couldn't wait to get out. Now he couldn't seem to stay away. The ghosts wouldn't let him.

A car slowed on the street in front of him, and a child stared out at him from a rain-streaked window. She looked a little like Ruby, and Dave watched her until the car was out of sight, the pain in his chest as familiar now as his heartbeat. Then he started walking.

Around the next corner, a neon half-moon sputtered in the gathering darkness. He wanted to think of the light as a beacon, but he knew better. The Crescent City Bar could never in a million years be considered a haven. Not for him, at least.

As he entered the room, an infinitesimal chill slid over him. *Welcome back,* that taunting voice whispered again.

The bar was nearly empty. A handful of zombielike patrons sat with heads bowed over drinks, the only acknowledgment of their coexistence a mingling of cigarette smoke that drifted up from the tables. The old wood blades of the ceiling fans rotated overhead, barely stirring warm air that reeked of sweat, booze and despair.

Welcome back, welcome back, welcome back.

Dave took a seat at the end of the bar, where he could watch the door. He hadn't been a cop for nearly seven years, but old habits died hard.

From the other end, the hulk of a bartender watched him with open suspicion. He was tall and tough, with skin the texture of leather. Jubal Roach had to be at least sixty, but the forearms underneath his rolled-up shirtsleeves bulged with muscle, and his sullen expression reflected, as Dave knew only too well, a still-murderous disposition.

Dave's old partner had once warned him about Jubal's temper. They'd stopped in for a beer after their watch one night and the surly bartender had copped an attitude from the get-go. Back in the day, Dave hadn't been one to turn the other cheek.

"Man, let it go," Titus had said in a nervous whisper. "You don't want to tangle with that S.O.B. Once he start in whaling on you, he like a big 'ol loggerhead. He ain't gonna let you go till it thunders. Or till you dead."

It was good advice. Too bad Dave hadn't had the sense to heed it.

He and Jubal played the staring game for several more seconds, then, with a hardening of his features, the older man ambled down to Dave's end of the bar.

"Jubal." Dave greeted him warily, mindful of the nightstick and brass knuckles the bartender kept under the counter. "How's it going?"

"Dave Creasy. Been a while since I saw your ugly mug in here. Kinda thought you might be dead."

Kinda *hoped* was the inference. "I bought a place in St. Mary Parish awhile back."

"Same difference, you ask me." Jubal got down a glass and a bottle of whiskey. "The usual?"

"Nah, I'm on the wagon these days."

"Since when?"

Eight months, four days, nine hours and counting. "Since the last time I got thrown in jail for disorderly conduct."

Jubal's gold tooth flashed in the light from the Abita Purple Haze sign over the bar.

Dave touched the area over his left eye. His memories of that night had faded, but the scar hadn't. It had taken him two days to get out of the drunk tank, another five before he'd stumbled into the nearest emergency room with a raging fever. The infection had laid him flat for nearly two weeks, and by the time he got out of the hospital, fifteen pounds lighter, a jagged scar was the least of his worries.

"You're lucky you didn't lose your eye," the young intern had scolded him. "However, at the moment, I'm more concerned about your liver. You have what is known as alcohol hepatitis, which can be treated but only if alcohol consumption is stopped. Otherwise, this condition is likely to cause cirrhosis, Mr. Creasy," he'd stated bluntly. "If you don't stop drinking, there's a good chance you won't make it to your fortieth birthday."

Dave wasn't particularly worried about dying, but he would prefer not to go out the way his old man had. So he'd stopped drinking…again, started going back to AA, and he'd moved down to Morgan City to work part-time for his uncle while reopening Creasy Investigations. Marsilius had found him a little house on the bayou where he could live and set up shop until he was able to afford office space in town. The only problem with that arrangement was that his uncle now considered it his moral duty to keep Dave on the straight and narrow.

As if testing Dave's resolve, Jubal poured a shot of Jack Daniel's and slid the tumbler across the bar. "First one's on the house. For old times' sake."

"No thanks, but I'll take a cup of that coffee I smell brewing."

"Suit yourself." Jubal filled a cup and passed it to Dave. "If you're not drinking, what brings you in here?"

"I'm meeting someone." Dave lifted the cup and took a sip of the strong chicory blend. The coffee was hot. It scalded his tongue and he swore as the front door swung open. And in walked Angelette Lapierre.

She stood in the doorway taking stock of the room just as she always did. That was Dave's first memory of her, the way she'd planted herself on the threshold of the captain's office, her gaze sweeping the room as the group of homicide detectives huddled over a map had looked up with a collective indrawn breath.

Dave had been married back then and in love with his wife, but he couldn't help noticing Angelette. Dark-haired, dark-eyed, she'd had that dog-in-heat quality that drew men to her side and made any woman unfortunate enough to be in the same room dislike her on sight.

Dave had tried to ignore her, but later in the crowded squad room, he'd glanced up to find her watching him, and her slow smile had sent a shiver down his backbone. Something that might have been a warning glinted in her sultry eyes that day, and Dave would later wish that he'd taken heed of it.

But instead, he'd told himself there was no harm in looking. What Claire didn't know wouldn't hurt her.

Claire.

Dave winced at the memory. He didn't want to think about her at that moment. He didn't want to think about her ever. She was a part of his past. One of the ghosts that came out to haunt him on rainy summer nights.

But he couldn't help himself. He closed his eyes briefly as an image of his ex-wife appeared in his head. She wasn't as curvy or as beautiful as Angelette, but her appeal was far more dangerous because she was the kind of woman you could never get out of your system. No matter how much you drank.

As if she was reading his mind, Angelette's expression hardened. Her gaze seemed to pierce right through him, and then she blinked and the daggers were gone. The familiar smile flashed, dazzled, even as her chin lifted in defiance.

Same old Angelette.

She wore a blue dress, transparent from where she stood in the doorway. Jubal leaned an elbow on the bar and swore under his breath. Together he and Dave watched her walk with fluid grace to the stool next to Dave's, a whiff of something seductive preceding her.

Still smiling, she placed her purse on the bar and crossed her legs, letting that blue dress skate up her slender thighs.

"I don't want no trouble," Jubal warned.

She tossed back her dark hair and laughed. "I don't want any trouble, either."

"You start throwing beer bottles like you did last time, I'm calling the law on both of you."

"I am the law, remember?" She laughed again, but her amusement didn't quite reach her eyes. "Just relax, okay? Dave and I kissed and made up a long time ago. Didn't we, Dave?"

"If you say so." He was all for letting bygones be bygones, but when Angelette leaned over to brush her lips against his, he couldn't help tensing.

Her gaze lit on the scar above his eye. "Wow. Did I do that?"

"Better than a tattoo."

"Speaking of tattoos…I got myself a new one. Remind me to show it to you sometime."

Dave let that one go. He might not be the sharpest tool in the shed, as Marsilius frequently pointed out, but he'd learned his lesson with Angelette.

Not getting the response she wanted, she turned to Jubal. "Double whiskey."

There was something about Angelette that Dave hadn't remembered from before. She'd always had an edge. Had always been able to give as good as she got. An ambitious female detective had to know how to handle herself in a man's world. But it wasn't that. It wasn't her years as a cop that had given her face a brittle veneer. It was selling out. Being on the take for too long had chipped away at her sensuality and left in its wake something hard and unpleasant and faintly decadent.

Dave cradled his cup, gratified to note that his hands no longer trembled. He hadn't felt this steady in years. "So how did the anger management classes go?" He knew the question was likely to set her off. Angelette didn't like being called on her bullshit—by him or by the judge who'd ordered her into the classes—but Dave couldn't resist goading her a little.

She surprised him. Instead of rising to the bait, she gave an airy wave with one hand as she lifted her drink with the other. "Oh, I finished up months ago. You're looking at the new and improved Angelette. What do you think?"

"Not bad."

One brow lifted as her eyes seemed to challenge him. *Not bad? There was a time when you couldn't keep your hands off me, you bastard.* "You're not faring too badly yourself. You've put on a little weight, but it suits you. I was never all that partial to scrawny guys. A girl has to have something to hang on to, right, Jubal?" She gave the bartender a wink.

The older man glared at her with open suspicion. "You want another drink?"

"Oui, bien sûr." She waited for him to pour the whiskey, then picked up her glass. "Let's move over to a booth." She slid off the stool, and as she turned, her full breasts brushed up against Dave's arm for a split second before she moved away.

He got up and, taking his coffee with him, followed her to a back booth. By the time he sat down, she'd already finished her second drink.

"Maybe you ought to ease up on the hooch."

"What is that? A friendly piece of advice from one drunk to another?" Her face was flushed and her voice sounded strained as she folded her arms on the table.

Something was wrong. Dave could feel it. Her eyes wouldn't quite meet his. Instead, she watched the steam rising from his cup that drifted up between them.

"What did you want to see me about?"

Her gaze darted to the front door, and Dave noticed that she'd chosen a booth where they both had a view of the entrance. He'd taught her that. The things she'd taught him didn't come in so handy these days.

"I'm seeing someone. I wanted you to hear it from me first." She ran a fingernail around the rim of her empty glass and Dave could tell she wanted another drink. He knew that feeling, that hunger. It was like a needy old friend you could never get rid of.

He waited for a moment, thinking he might feel a twinge of regret at her news, but no. Not even a flicker of relief. He just didn't care anymore. "Is it serious?"

"Who knows?" Angelette shook out a cigarette and

lit up. The smoke mingled with the steam from his coffee, softening her features and making her face seem almost vulnerable, but Dave knew better than to believe in a mirage. "We're taking things slow for now. Something you and I should have done, I guess." She propped an elbow on the table, letting the Camel smolder between her fingers. "Never was anything slow about you, Dave."

"Most men wouldn't take that as a compliment."

"But you're not most men, now are you?" She gave him a dark smile. "We both liked it fast, didn't we? And often."

Her lowered voice conjured images best left in the past. Seedy motel rooms. The hood of his car. A deserted road with the smell of the river drifting in through the open windows.

"We were good for a while, baby. You can't deny that." She reached for his hand, but Dave pulled his away.

"Tell me about your new guy. Anyone I know?"

"It's Lee Elliot."

Dave was caught off guard by the name. The conservative Orleans Parish district attorney hardly seemed suited to Angelette's free spirit, but then Elliot came from old money and that would most definitely appeal to her.

"Are you impressed?"

"Have to say that I am. Does he know about the payoffs?"

"I'm clean these days, Dave. I swear. So I'd appreciate it if you'd just keep your mouth shut about the past. I kind of like the idea of a stable relationship for a change and I don't want you ruining this for me."

"I wouldn't do that. Besides, I don't exactly operate in Elliot's circle."

"No, but Claire's sister does."

"I don't talk to Claire's family. You know that."

"I thought things might be different now."

"You mean because I'm not seeing you anymore?"

Angelette took a quick drag on her cigarette. "I did wonder."

"Claire and I are over," Dave said slowly. "We've been over for a long time. You know she's remarried." And wasn't it pretty damn remarkable how he was able to say it without punching a wall or shattering a window?

But the outbursts of temper and the drunken brawls were behind him. Dave had accepted his life for the way it was, and he'd finally figured out there was no profit in dwelling on what he'd lost.

He could almost hear his AA sponsor coaxing him: *Say it with me, Dave. God, grant me the serenity to accept the things I cannot change, courage to change the things I can, and wisdom to know the difference.*

A nice sentiment, but it didn't mean shit when you were lying facedown in a gutter.

"You said there were two reasons why you wanted to see me. What's the other?"

Angelette's gaze flashed to the door again. Dave wondered if she was expecting someone. Her nerves were right beneath the surface and he couldn't help wondering why. "This conversation is going to stay between us, right?"

"Sure."

She waited a moment longer, then slid the empty glass aside. "Have you been following the Losier case?"

"The murdered Tulane student? Hard not to. Her picture's been plastered all over the news for weeks." Nina Losier's girl-next-door looks had captured the public's attention, but after nearly a month with no arrests and nothing new to report, media interest was starting to wane. A sure sign the investigation was going nowhere. Dave had learned that lesson the hard way.

Angelette blew a stream of smoke from the corner of her mouth. "The father is looking to hire a P.I. I told him about you."

"Since when does NOPD recommend a private dick for an active investigation?"

"Since it's not my case." She grinned, but her eyes were sober as she gazed across the table at him. "Let's just say the official investigation has run into some problems."

"What kind of problems?"

"There's a lot about this case that hasn't been released to the public. Nina Losier was from a wealthy family in Baton Rouge. Her father has a lot of political clout and NOPD has been pressured to keep certain aspects of the investigation out of the news."

"Like what?"

"Like the fact that when Nina wasn't in class, she sometimes danced at a strip club on Bourbon Street. The Gold Medallion." Angelette paused. "That's where Renee Savaria worked, isn't it?"

Dave suddenly realized how badly he wanted a drink. It hit him like that sometimes. Everything would be going along fine, and then *bam*. A face, a memory… even a name could smash his control all to hell.

The Savaria homicide was the last case he'd worked before his resignation. He'd been knee-deep in the investigation when his daughter went missing. Snatched in broad daylight as she rode her new bicycle up and down the sidewalk in front of their home.

Images were already flashing in Dave's head. The kind of visions that had made him reach for a bottle—or his gun—on more sleepless nights than he cared to remember.

Ruby had been seven when she was taken. Just seven years old.

"If Nina Losier comes from the kind of background you say she does, how'd she end up stripping on Bourbon Street?"

"You make it sound like she was an anomaly, but rich girls slumming to embarrass their powerful daddies is nothing new in this town."

"What about leads?"

"One dead end after another, just like the Savaria case. I remember how frustrated you were back then. You told me once it was like beating your head against a stone wall. Then all of a sudden you turned up a new lead. You thought you were getting close to a breakthrough when Ruby went missing. Maybe you were getting a little too close."

For a moment Dave felt as if the air had been squeezed from his lungs. He'd never told anyone about those phone calls, not even Angelette. She couldn't know about the missing page from the dead woman's diary, either. No one knew about that except Dave and Renee Savaria's murderer.

He'd destroyed evidence in a homicide investigation in order to save his daughter's life, but Ruby hadn't been returned as promised. Instead, her trail had grown cold while Dave collaborated with a killer.

A muscle in his jaw began to throb. Seven years and the guilt was still as fresh and deep as the day he'd answered Claire's frantic phone call.

Angelette's eyes searched his face. "I always wondered if there was a link between Renee Savaria's murder and Ruby's kidnapping. I think you did, too."

Dave looked down at his hands. They weren't trembling, but his fingers had curled so tight, his knuckles whitened. "It doesn't matter what I thought. It's all in the past."

"A guy like you lives in the past."

"Not anymore."

"I call bullshit on that."

Dave shrugged.

"After you left, the active investigations on your desk fell through the cracks. Nobody wanted to get tainted by your bad karma. So the Savaria case has been sitting in the cold case files all this time, and the way I see it, that old unfinished business has been eating away at you for too damn long. Maybe it's time for a little closure."

Dave wanted to believe it was as simple as that, but Angelette never did anything without demanding something in return. "What are you really after, Angie?"

"Nothing. I owe you one, that's all."

"Now why don't I believe you?"

She looked hurt. "Hey, I'll be the first to admit I haven't exactly conducted myself like a Girl Scout in the past, but I'm still a cop and, believe it or not, I'd like to see justice done. Renee Savaria and Nina Losier got in over their heads at that club. Drugs, prostitution…God knows what else. But that doesn't mean they deserved what happened to them. And your little girl sure as hell didn't deserve what happened to her."

He didn't say anything. He couldn't.

Angelette leaned toward him. "What if I tell you I can put a copy of the case file in your hands? Would you be willing to at least take a look?"

"You sure you want to risk your career over this one?"

"You let me worry about my career. I know what I'm doing. You game or not?"

"I'll take a look at what you've got, but I'm not promising anything."

"Fair enough. You don't like what you see, you walk away and that's that. We don't mention it again." She gathered up her purse and stood. "Give me a call when you decide something. Or better yet, drop by the Monteleone on Saturday night. Graydon Losier is making an appearance at Lee's fund-raiser. I'll see that you get an introduction."

She started toward the door, then turned back. "One other thing I forgot to mention." She leaned over the table to slowly grind out her cigarette. "I've been hearing some talk around town. Claire and Alex Girard… they've split up. Not that you give a shit about your ex-wife, right, Dave?"

Two

The Dollmaker had been working steadily ever since he returned home from New Orleans a few hours ago, but he wasn't happy with his progress. For one thing, the smile was all wrong. The shape of the jaw, the angle of the nose…everything about her eluded him tonight.

His hand tightened on the knife, but instead of slicing away the offending features as he usually did, he took a step back from his work and drew a calming breath. He was letting anger and fear interfere with his concentration, and for him that could be a very dangerous thing. He needed to get his emotions under control before he did something rash. Something he might live to regret.

He sucked in more air, but the breathing exercises weren't working this time. The voice inside his head kept needling him.

She's gone, you fool! And it's all your fault. You lost her!

"I didn't lose her," he muttered. "She was taken."

Because you were so careless!

He couldn't deny that. Leaving her alone had been imprudent, to say the least, but he'd been called away on an emergency and hadn't taken the time to lock her up before he rushed out. When he came home hours later, she was missing.

Snatched in broad daylight from her home.

A part of him wanted to appreciate the irony even as his conscience continued to berate him. He'd flown under the radar of the local authorities and even the FBI for so long, he'd become too complacent, even a bit reckless at times. It had all been so easy until now, and he wondered if he should regard this as a test. How he conducted himself could be crucial.

"It's all right," he whispered. "I know where she is. I'll get her back."

By this time tomorrow she would be home where she belonged. In the meantime, he had plenty to do to keep busy.

With an effort, he relaxed his grip on the knife. Everything would be okay if he just kept his cool. After all, there was no way now that she could be traced back to him. He'd seen to that. And even if someone came sniffing around, he wouldn't draw attention. He'd learned at an early age the advantage of maintaining a low profile. Nothing in his appearance or lifestyle would ever arouse suspicion. He even wore contacts in addition to his glasses to subdue the color of his blue eyes so they wouldn't be remembered. He was the very epitome of decorum.

Everything was fine. The party would go off without a hitch. All he had to do was close his eyes and remember Maddy's face.

If only it were that simple. But even with the old photograph he'd squirreled away years ago, he'd always had a difficult time reconstructing her winsome features.

Not that he wasn't talented enough. He was quite gifted, in fact, and he'd learned from a master. But for the Maddy doll and for the others in his private collection, each and every detail had to be perfect. Such precision could be maddening without a live model, but he wouldn't give up. *Couldn't* give up. For Maddy's sake, he had to keep trying. He owed her that much.

Closing his eyes, he waited for the shivering to pass, and then, wielding the sculptor's knife as precisely as a scalpel, he set to work remolding the delicate features one sliver at a time until the lovely little face seemed to take on a life of its own.

"You're in there," he whispered. "I can feel you…."

He kept at it for a long time, refusing to stop even when his fingers became so cramped that every stroke of the blade was agony. Clay molds and sketches cluttered the studio, and as the evening hours turned into early morning, the disorder subtly wore on his nerves. Even the orchid he'd placed on the corner of his worktable drooped from neglect, and that wasn't like him.

Ever since the doll had been stolen, his regimen had been severely disrupted. Normally he nurtured his orchids just as he pampered himself. He was accustomed to showering several times a day when his schedule permitted, and he kept his clothes pristine, his hair trimmed just so. He strove for nothing less than perfection in his personal appearance and in his surroundings. But until he had her back—one way or another— he wouldn't be able to eat or sleep, much less indulge himself in his time-consuming routine.

He stepped away from his workbench and stud-

ied the doll's features yet again. Better. Almost there…
but not quite…

Something was missing.

He caught a glimpse of himself in the mirror that
hung on the wall across the room, and froze, arrested
as he always was by the sight of his own reflection. The
man who stared back at him still seemed a stranger.
Brownish-blond curls. Blue eyes rimmed with thick
lashes. A rather weak jawline, but the mouth was good
and the complexion was to die for. Not a single blem-
ish or mole to mar his smooth skin. No morning
shadow, either. He almost looked airbrushed.

But his new glasses would take some getting used
to. They gave him a bookish air that wasn't to his liking, but for now the look suited his purposes.

Unable to resist, he walked over to the mirror for a
closer scrutiny. Turning first one way then the other,
he frowned. His nose was still not right, but the carti-
lage was too weak for another surgery. He supposed he
would have to make do with what he had.

He removed his glasses because his eyes looked
bluer without them, and when he smiled a certain
way, his dimples flashed sweetly. He'd practiced that
smile for years.

Yes, when he smiled *in just that way,* he could almost catch a glimpse of her….

"You're in there," he whispered to his reflection. "I
can feel you."

He lifted the blade to his face, the compulsion to
peel away the flesh until he found what he needed almost irresistible. After all, he was no stranger to the
knife. His body had been carved and mutilated so badly
that his distaste for his own appearance sometimes

forced him to use a sponge and gloves to clean himself in the shower. But no matter how often he washed, he couldn't scrub away the scars. He couldn't rinse away the memories.

"Why did you have to die?" he whispered.

Because you let me.

His voice became petulant. "But I was just a child."

You should have found a way to stop him.

"I've stopped him now."

Too late.

"It's not too late. You're not dead. You're just…hiding."

Then come and find me.

He leaned closer, searching and searching his reflection until the ringing of his cell phone jarred him. He didn't want to answer it. He hated disturbances while he worked, but his concentration was already broken. Fetching the phone from his jacket pocket, he checked the caller ID and, recognizing the number of the nursing home, didn't bother to answer.

Tossing the phone aside, he returned to the unfinished doll and placed a gentle hand on her sculpted head. "I have to go out for a while, but I'll be back soon, I promise."

Leaving the door to the studio open, he hurried up the steps to the kitchen to fix a tray. He toasted bread and poured a bowl of cereal, then, once he had the dishes and silverware arranged just so, carried everything back down the steps and placed the tray on his worktable while he unlocked and slid open a hidden compartment in one wall. He bent down to peer inside.

The lights were out. He couldn't see anything in the shadowy room, but he knew she was already awake because he could hear her whimpers. The sound irritated him. So did her persistence.

I want to go home.

She must have said it a hundred times already. They all did. And his answer was always the same.

You can't go home. Not until after the party.

Slipping the tray through the opening, he waited a moment, hoping to catch a glimpse of her, but when she didn't appear, he shut the compartment and locked it without a word, then hung the key on a peg near the door.

If he'd learned anything in the past seven years it was that even the most stubborn girl would eventually eat when she got hungry.

Three

⟿⦿⟾

The dark clouds piling up over the Gulf of Mexico brought an early twilight to the city, but Claire Doucett barely noticed the sporadic raindrops that splashed against her cotton blouse as she hurried along the sidewalk. Her gaze was fastened on a group of teenage girls in front of her, and as they stopped to admire something in a shop window, she paused, too, her heart beating a painful staccato inside her chest. Their backs were to her, but when the one in the middle turned just so… dear God, she looked like Ruby.

At least the way Claire imagined her daughter would look at fourteen. The way she appeared in the age-progressed photo created by a forensic artist at the National Center for Missing and Exploited Children.

She would be tall like her dad, but with Claire's thin stature and her grandmother Lucille's golden ringlets.

The girl in front of her shook her head and her blond curls shifted against her narrow back. She wore shorts and flip-flops, and her legs were long and tanned and gorgeous. Her laughter drifted back to Claire, sending a fine chill along her spine, and her heart started to beat even harder. There was something so sweet and innocent and familiar about that sound.

Claire closed her eyes and tried to conjure Ruby's laugh. It was getting harder and harder to do. After seven years, the memories were sometimes elusive.

But, no, there it was…the image of a two-year-old Ruby at the zoo, tugging on Claire's hand as she laughed up at her. "Bears, Mama!"

Even as a toddler, Ruby had been such a happy child. Sweet and tenderhearted, and yet so willful and stubborn at times that Claire's patience had been sorely tested.

"That child would argue with a fence post," Claire's mother used to say with an exaggerated sigh.

"Yes, and I wonder who she gets that from," Claire would counter.

Secretly, Claire had been grateful that her daughter inherited more of Lucille's disposition than hers. Claire was too much like her moody father, although she hoped to God she never succumbed to the same demons that had driven him to suicide when she was just a baby.

Even in her deepest despair after Ruby's kidnapping, Claire had never contemplated taking her own life, and for one good reason—she'd never given up hope that her daughter would someday come home to her. The flame had grown dimmer with each passing year, but on days like today, the glimpse of a familiar face on a crowded street could rekindle her faith, and she'd find herself indulging in the same old fantasy.

Ruby was still alive and she'd been happy and healthy all these years. A childless couple had seen her riding her bike on the sidewalk that day and had been enchanted by her blond curls and sunny smile.

They'd taken her home with them, loved her as if she was their very own, and in time, Ruby had responded to their kindness and affection. In time, she'd adjusted to her new home, and for the past seven years, she'd led a perfectly normal life. Maybe she no longer even remembered her real family. Her real mother.

Claire blinked back unexpected tears.

The fantasy was just that. Nothing more than a wishful daydream that had helped sustain her through some of her darkest days. And the girl on the street in front of her wasn't Ruby. The likelihood of her daughter still being alive was miniscule. To even consider for a moment that Ruby might have been in New Orleans all this time, that fate would have miraculously brought them together on this very street, was ludicrous.

And yet…

Claire whispered her daughter's name. The sound slipped through her lips as a plea.

The girl turned, as if responding to the soft entreaty, and Claire saw her clearly for the first time. The girl's face split into a broad smile, and Claire's breath caught. Everything around her seemed to still. The noise from the street faded, and the palm fronds and banana trees in a nearby courtyard stood motionless in the heat, as if nature itself was holding a breath.

And then Claire exhaled in a painful rush. It wasn't Ruby. Of course it wasn't Ruby. But for that one fleeting moment when their gazes touched, Claire had a glimpse of what it might be like to see her daughter's face again after all these years.

The girl's attention moved past her and she waved

at someone behind Claire. Someone who had called out her name.

Megan. The girl's name was Megan. Not Ruby.

Claire glanced at her reflection in a store window, saw the pinched look on her face, the whitened knuckles where her hand gripped her purse strap, and slowly she let out another breath.

Ruby was dead and she wasn't coming back. She'd been taken from the sidewalk in front of their home while riding her bike, the victim of an abduction that had never been solved. Claire knew the statistics. Her daughter had probably been dead within the first twenty-four to forty-eight hours after she'd been grabbed, her body discarded in some remote field or shallow grave, where she had been lying all these years. Alone.

Claire put a hand to her mouth. Tears scalded her eyes, but she held them back as she scoured the street in front of her. The girl and her friends had scurried beneath an awning to get out of the drizzle. Claire deliberately turned and started walking in the opposite direction.

"Did you hear about the body they-found in the Quarter?" Charlotte LeBlanc asked casually when she and Claire met a few minutes later at their designated rendezvous.

"I saw it on the local news before I left the house this morning. Do the police know who did it?"

Claire's sister was an assistant D.A. for Orleans Parish and usually had an open pipeline to the police department, but she shook her head. "They think it was probably drug-related. So far they haven't even been able to identify the body. Poor bastard was sliced up pretty bad. All his fingers were missing."

Claire shuddered. "I don't know how you do it, dealing with that kind of violence on a daily basis. I think it would start to get to me after a while."

"I think it would, too, but I'm not you. And someone has to keep the baddies off the street." Charlotte snapped open her umbrella as the drizzle turned into a full-fledged shower and the gray clouds over the Gulf vibrated with lightning. Within a matter of moments the city was soaked and dripping, and as they walked along Decatur, Charlotte tried to hold the umbrella over both of them.

"Here, let me," Claire said as she took the handle. "I'm taller."

"Okay, but just make sure I'm covered. I'm wearing silk. *Damn.*" Charlotte swore as she stepped in a puddle. "And these shoes are brand-new."

Claire glanced down at her sister's high heels. The delicate footwear had obviously not been designed for wet weather, but certainly looked elegant and sophisticated on Charlotte's dainty feet.

Claire felt a stab of envy. She couldn't remember the last time she'd splurged on a pair of expensive shoes. As a matter of fact, she couldn't remember the last time she'd enjoyed any indulgence whatsoever, but with her divorce nearly final, she had to keep her belt tightened. Now was not the time for extravagant purchases.

Although Charlotte would argue that designer shoes were not an extravagance, but a necessity. Image was everything and nothing screamed success like a good pair of shoes. Unless, of course, it was her gorgeous leather handbag, the one that had come with a four-figure price tag in roughly the same amount as Claire's new central air-conditioning unit.

Her grandmother's old house was going to be the death of her yet, Claire thought as she and Charlotte side-stepped crates of watermelons and cantaloupes stacked in front of a small grocery store. The old Uptown house was a classic money pit with the never-ending repairs and the exorbitant utility bills. Little wonder that she'd worn the same sandals and carried the same battered tote for two summers in a row. But then, an ar*tist*, as Charlotte teasingly called her, didn't need to worry about her image the way an up-and-coming assistant D.A. did.

Claire wondered if any of the people they passed on the street would ever guess that she and Charlotte were sisters. They were so different in so many ways. They shared the same mother, but their looks and temperament had come from their respective fathers.

Charlotte was a petite brunette and as charming and vivacious as her handsome father, A. J. LeBlanc, who had sweet-talked his way into their mother's heart and bed and then absconded with her life savings two days after she'd told him she was pregnant.

Charlotte's abandonment issues aside, her father's Creole heritage had blessed her with a honey-colored complexion and beautiful almond-shaped eyes the color of fine Burmese jade. Claire had always thought her sister resembled a porcelain figurine, but when she got angry, those green eyes would glitter like a knife blade.

In contrast, Claire was tall, thin and fair, an introvert whose propensity for brooding had come from her bookish father. William's suicide, followed by A.J.'s betrayal, might have made some women a little gun-shy in the romance department, but not their mother, Lucille. A string of live-in lovers had followed, until her latest paramour, Hugh Voorhies, had swept her off her feet eight years ago. That was an endurance record for Lucille.

"Damn, Claire, pay attention, will you? I'm getting soaked."

"Sorry." Claire repositioned the umbrella to make sure that her sister was protected. The rain stirred a myriad of scents along the street—stale wine, flowers and damp brick. And from a restaurant doorway, spicy sausages and fresh-baked bread.

"I'm starving," Charlotte grumbled. "Tell me again why we're out walking in the rain instead of having an early dinner somewhere."

"Because now that I've increased my hours at the gallery, I don't have much time for shopping. Mama's birthday is next week and I want us to get her something special." Claire was a glassblower and shared a space in the Warehouse District with several other artisans. They took turns manning the gallery and using the studio and furnaces in the back, but because Claire needed the money, she'd started working additional shifts in the showroom.

"If time's that tight, maybe we should just run into Canal Place and pick out a nice scarf or a bottle of perfume," Charlotte said. "Or some gold earrings. Lucille loves jewelry."

"Let me remind you that your idea of accessories is quite different from our mother's."

"You're right. Better forget the gold earrings. Subtlety has never been Lucille's strong suit." Charlotte smiled and her eyes crinkled charmingly at the corners. Even with her hair all windblown and damp, she was still the most beautiful woman Claire had ever seen. "So what do you have in mind?"

"There's a place on Chartres that has one of a kind dolls. I saw an ad for it in the paper recently."

Charlotte made a face. "Please, not another doll! She already has forty gazillion lying around the house. She doesn't need another one."

"It isn't a matter of need," Claire gently chided. "It's what she wants, and I think a fiftieth birthday warrants something special, don't you?"

"Well, when you put it that way. I've got a little cash stashed away, but what about you? Now that you're single again, money must be tight."

"I'll manage. My pieces are selling pretty well these days. Besides, if we find something special, Hugh's agreed to chip in half. All you and I have to do is split the difference."

Charlotte's mouth dropped in astonishment. "How on earth did you talk Hugh Voorhies into coughing up that kind of cash? The man's so tight he squeaks when he walks."

"I know, but he's crazy about Mama. He likes to complain about her dolls, but he'd do anything to keep her happy."

"Ain't that the damn truth? I'd really love to know that woman's secret. I'm serious," Charlotte said when Claire chuckled. "Think about it, Claire. She smokes like a furnace, cusses like a sailor, dresses like a cheap whore and yet she *always* has some man crazy over her. I can't even get a date for my boss's fund-raiser on Saturday night. How does she do it?"

"She's Lucille."

They waited for traffic to clear, then crossed the

street and turned up Conti. Claire could smell the river behind them. The rain had cooled the air, and the lights coming on in the early twilight looked like a turn of the century French painting. It was the kind of soft, dreamy afternoon that made her glad she'd come back to New Orleans after the flood. Not that she would ever seriously consider living anywhere else. She was third generation. Her grandmother had been born and raised in the same house that Claire now owned.

"I've been giving the matter a lot of thought," Charlotte said as she looped her arm through Claire's. Her silk blouse clung damply to her small breasts, but she didn't seem to care anymore. "I'm Lucille's daughter. I must have inherited a little of…whatever it is that she's got, so why am I still alone?"

"You're asking me? The sister with two failed marriages?"

"Don't say that. Your second divorce isn't final yet."

"Yes, but the waiting period is merely a formality."

"It doesn't have to be. Just say the word and Alex would move back home in a flash."

Claire looked away, shook her head. "It's too late for that."

"It's never too late. And a man like Alex Girard doesn't come along every day. Take it from me, the world is full of losers, but then…I guess you already know that, don't you? Having been married to the biggest asshole of all time."

"Charlotte."

Claire's rebuke brought her sister's chin up in defiance. "Well, I'm sorry. I know we're not supposed to talk about Dave Creasy, but I can't help it. I'm never going to forgive him for what he did to you. *Never.*"

"It's ancient history. Let it go."

Charlotte's mouth thinned. "If only that were true. But he's the reason you could never fully commit to Alex. Don't even bother to deny it, because I know you better than you know yourself."

"Then you must also know that I don't want to talk about either of my ex-husbands," Claire replied in exasperation. "I just want to spend the rest of the day shopping with my sister."

"Okay, I'll make you a deal then. I won't mention he-who-shall-remain-nameless for at least, oh, another twenty-four hours if you'll agree to come with me to the fund-raiser on Saturday night."

"Why in the world would you even want me there? I'm terrible at parties."

"I know you are, but that's kind of the point. Now that you're single, you need to get out more. You spend way too much time puttering around alone in that old house. It's just not healthy. But…" Charlotte's expression turned contrite. "I do have an ulterior motive. If I show up at the fund-raiser by myself, people will know I couldn't get a date. If I bring you, they'll think I'm a good sister trying to help you through a rough patch."

"You're shameless."

"And desperate," Charlotte freely admitted. "So what do you say? Will you go? Claire?"

But Claire barely heard her. Mignon's Collectibles was just across the street, and her gaze was fixed on the doll in the front window. Attired in a pink ruffled dress and black patent leather Mary Janes, she was seated at a tiny table decorated with a miniature tea set.

The doll's face was so cleverly sculpted and painted that Claire had to stare for several moments before convincing herself that she wasn't seeing a beautiful child seated at the table.

A child who looked exactly like Ruby.

Claire's heart started to race as she stared at the doll. She tried to tell herself that the sighting of the teenager earlier had triggered her imagination. Ruby was already on her mind.

But the golden hair. That sweet smile. The little ruffled dress…

She put a trembling hand to her mouth.

"Claire, are you all right? You're as pale as a ghost. What happened? Are you sick? I knew we should have stopped for something to eat—"

"That doll," Claire said hoarsely. She couldn't look away from it.

Charlotte turned toward the store. "The one at the little table?"

"Charlotte, it's *her.*"

"You mean the one you want to get Lucille?"

Claire grabbed her sister's arm. *"Don't you see it?"*

Charlotte frowned at Claire's harsh tone. "For God's sake, see what?"

"That doll looks just like Ruby."

"Ruby? Oh, honey, no. It's just the hair. All those blond curls—"

"It's not the hair," Claire whispered. "Look at her face. Her smile. Even the dress. It looks like the one Mama made Ruby for her birthday. She had it on the day she disappeared."

Fear flickered in Charlotte's eyes as she glanced back at the shop window. "It's just a pink ruffled dress. They all look the same—"

"No, they don't!" Claire said desperately. "Mama

had that fabric special ordered. It can't be a coincidence."

Charlotte turned slowly toward her sister. "Claire, what are you saying?"

"I'm saying that doll is the spitting image of my missing daughter. That dress is identical to the one she had on when she disappeared."

Charlotte bit her lip. "We both know that's not possible. It's just a doll. It's not Ruby. Claire, wait!"

But Claire had already dashed into the street. Oblivious to the traffic, she kept her gaze fixed on the shop window. The closer she got, the harder her heart pounded. The doll *did* look like Ruby. It wasn't her imagination.

"Claire!"

Behind her, she heard Charlotte scream her name at the exact moment she spotted the oncoming car out of the corner of her eye.

It happened so quickly, Claire didn't have time to panic. The squeal of brakes barely registered a split second before the impact knocked her off her feet. She landed with a metallic thud on the hood and rolled off, hitting the pavement with such force the breath was knocked from her lungs.

She lay on her back, so stunned she couldn't move, as a crowd began to gather around her. Charlotte reached her first and dropped to her knees beside her.

"Someone call 911!" She grabbed Claire's hand. "Oh, God, Claire, are you all right?"

Claire tried to answer, but she couldn't speak. She could do nothing but stare up at the sky as raindrops splashed against her face.

Four

~~~⟡~~~

Mignon Bujold had planned to close the shop early so that she could drive out to Jefferson Parish and surprise her little granddaughter with an early birthday present. The big day wasn't until Sunday, but Mignon would be attending a huge doll show in Baton Rouge all weekend long, and if she didn't see Piper today, the child would have to wait until Tuesday for her gift. And if past experience was any indication, the exhibition would be so hectic, Mignon might not even get the chance to call. She'd hate for Piper to worry that her grandmaman had forgotten her birthday entirely.

Thinking about the goodies she'd bought for her youngest granddaughter, Mignon smiled in anticipation. She loved both of Lily's children dearly, but the oldest, MacKenzie, was such a tomboy that Mignon couldn't spoil her with all the girlie things she so adored. But four-year-old Piper was a real little princess. She lived for her grandmother's lavish gifts.

Mignon fingered the silver ribbon on the package. The Mori Lee dress and the Queen Tatiana doll were both extravagances, but at least she hadn't succumbed to her initial temptation and given the child the Savannah Sweete doll. She might be a doting grandmother, but she was also a savvy businesswoman, and she'd recognized what a gold mine that doll would be the moment she first set eyes on her.

And Mignon's instincts were dead-on, as usual. Not only had a bidding war erupted between two private collectors, but the electronic newsletter she'd hastily sent out to her mailing list had generated a steady stream of customers all afternoon. Business had been so brisk that she might not be able to close early, after all. But it couldn't be helped. She was not one to turn away customers, especially with the shop just now starting to show a profit since the devastation of the flood.

When the store finally emptied just after five, Mignon headed for the door to lock up. But a commotion on the street drew her to the window, and she stood staring out at the revolving red and blue lights that reflected off the wet pavement. The area was suddenly crowded with policemen, paramedics and rubberneckers gawking at a woman who lay motionless on the street in front of a light blue sedan.

Good heavens, Mignon thought, and hastily crossed herself. First that ghastly murder only a few blocks away last night, and now this.

The woman had obviously been struck while crossing the intersection. Mignon could see one of the patrolmen taking a statement from the distraught driver of the vehicle, while another officer stood nearby, talking into a radio.

At least the poor woman hadn't been the victim of

a hit-and-run like the one that had put Savannah Sweete in a wheelchair all those years ago.

Ever since Mignon acquired the doll in the window, Savannah Sweete had been on her mind. She'd met the artist once, but it had been so long ago, she doubted that Savannah would even remember. However, for Mignon, the encounter had been the highlight of her career. She'd been a devoted fan for years and, along with the rest of the doll-collecting community, had been shocked and distressed to hear of Savannah's accident.

Mignon remembered the doll maker as beautiful and gregarious, but from everything she'd heard, the accident had turned her into a recluse. And even though her dolls were still exquisitely sculpted and painted and remained highly coveted, the artistry in her creations had never been quite the same. Mignon would bet her teacher's retirement fund that the doll in the window had been sculpted before the accident. She was that perfect.

Turning away from the sirens and flashing lights, Mignon sent up a prayer for the victim as she reached for the sign in the window. Before she could flip it to Closed, however, the bells over the door tinkled, and she chided herself for not being quicker. She could always turn the customer away, of course, but that wouldn't be good business. So instead, she shrugged off her impatience and plastered a welcoming smile on her face.

Most of her regulars were women, but there were enough male collectors in the area that she wasn't too surprised to see a man walk through the door. What did take her aback was his appearance. She'd rarely encountered anyone so…arresting.

The round, wire-rimmed glasses perched on a rather delicate nose gave him a scholarly appearance, even as the full lips hinted at an unexpected sexuality. Blondish-brown curls fell across a high forehead, and a white orchid adorned the lapel of his dark jacket. But rather than detracting from his subtle masculinity, the exotic flower somehow suited him.

He gave a courteous little bow as their gazes met, and Mignon's grandmotherly heart fluttered with awareness.

"Hello," she said with an indrawn breath. "Can I help you?"

"Yes, I hope so. I'm interested in one of your dolls."

His cultured voice sent another shiver up her spine. "Let me guess, you've come to see the latest Queen Tatiana collection."

"No, as a matter of fact, I'm interested in the Savannah Sweete in the window."

Ah, a collector. And one who knew his stuff. "She's a beauty, isn't she? Savannah Sweete is undoubtedly the most talented doll artist working today, but I suppose I could be a bit biased. She's a native Louisianan and we do tend to brag on our own."

"How much is she?"

"I'm sorry, she's already sold."

One brow lifted. "Really? I would have assumed since you have her so prominently displayed—"

"I haven't had a chance to remove her from the window yet."

He sighed. "I don't suppose you would consider another offer."

"No, I'm sorry. A deal is a deal. But I could show you something else. The Queen Tatiana—"

"I'm only interested in the one doll."

Mignon gave him another apologetic smile. "Then I can't help you."

She expected him to turn and leave, but instead he took a step toward her. Mignon saw something in his eyes then that the glasses had previously masked. A coldness that made her shiver.

"You'll have to excuse me," she said. "I was just about to close up."

"I won't keep you. If you could just tell me from whom you acquired the doll…?"

Mignon frowned. "I'm afraid I can't divulge that information. Now if you'll please excuse me—"

"Then perhaps you'd rather talk to the police."

The police? Oh, dear Lord…

Her hand flew to her chest. "What do you mean?"

"The doll was recently stolen from my private collection."

Mignon's heart sank. She'd known something was fishy about the doll when the other man couldn't produce the certificate of authenticity. She should have listened to her gut, because her greed and carelessness had brought this strange man to her shop. And now Mignon's instincts were warning her again. But she wouldn't let him see her fear. She somehow knew that would be a mistake.

Her voice sharpened. "You can prove ownership? You have the certificate of authenticity or a receipt of some kind?"

"I have something better than that." He reached in his pocket and pulled out a photograph of a child who bore a striking resemblance to the doll.

Mignon's eyes fastened on the picture. For a moment she couldn't tear her gaze away, and her uneasiness faded. "What a beautiful child. Your daughter?"

"A childhood friend." His lips curled grotesquely, in a smile that made Mignon's skin crawl. And his eyes... they were so...empty. They didn't even look real.

"I'm sorry," she said, and was annoyed when she heard her voice tremble. "If the doll really does belong to you, then perhaps this *is* a matter for the police...."

She trailed off when he whirled and headed for the door. He'd forgotten his picture, but Mignon didn't call him back. She slipped the photograph into her pocket and kept silent, glad to be rid of him.

But instead of leaving, he locked the door, drew the shade over the window and slowly turned back to face her.

He was still smiling.

Mignon backed away from him, but when she saw what he held in his hand, she spun and tried to run. He was so much younger and so much quicker, however. He grabbed her and pulled her roughly to him. She started to whimper.

"Stop it! Stop that racket this instant, do you hear me?"

Mignon nodded and swallowed a sob. "Don't hurt me. Take the doll and whatever else you want, but please don't hurt me."

"Hush, now," he crooned as one hand feathered over her hair. "It's okay."

His voice turned so soothing and liquid that for a moment Mignon wondered if he would let her go. Maybe he wouldn't hurt her, after all. Maybe she would still be able to give little Piper her gifts.

The needle sank into her neck, and almost immediately, her knees buckled.

Slipping from his arms, she fell to the floor.

She didn't make a sound because she couldn't. She lay with her eyes open, watching him move about the shop.

He found packing materials and a box in the storeroom, and when he came back, he was surprised to see that she'd managed to crawl over to the counter. She had a strong constitution for someone her age. She'd even pulled off the telephone, but she hadn't mustered enough muscle coordination to punch in a number. He could hear the drone of the dial tone as he peered down at her.

Kicking away the phone, he squatted beside her. Spittle ran out the side of her mouth as her eyes pleaded for mercy. He smiled and patted her head, then got back up to finish his tasks.

Lifting the doll from the window, he wrapped her in several layers of plastic, placed her carefully in the box and sealed the flaps with packing tape. And all the while, he sang softly as he worked. "'You are my sunshine, my only sunshine....'"

Once he had the doll protected, he came back over and stood looking down at the old woman. Ignoring the terror that gleamed in her pale eyes, he grabbed her ankles and dragged her to the back of the shop.

Five

From the window in her hospital room, Claire watched the flashes of lightning as the storm rolled in from the Gulf. Her door had been left ajar and hospital noises drifted in, but she tuned out the sounds. If she closed her eyes and concentrated hard enough she could hear the rain.

She imagined the patter of it through the palm fronds and banana trees in the courtyard behind her house. She could smell the musty scent of wet dirt and ancient brick, and she pictured herself standing beneath the eave of the house, her palms turned up to the sky.

When she was a child she used to catch rainwater in a fruit jar. Her mother could never understand her fascination, but to Claire there had always been something soothing about the rain that fell in New Orleans. Something spiritual about the way the trees would begin to whisper in the sweltering heat and the sky would darken suddenly, as if a curtain had dropped over the landscape. And then the rain would come.

"You're gonna get wet, Mama," Ruby would later tell her.

"I don't mind. Come out here with me. Take my hand, that's a girl. Now hold your face up like this and close your eyes. What do you feel?"

"It tickles."

"Feels good, too, though, doesn't it?"

"I like the rain, Mama."

"I like it, too, baby."

Claire turned from the window, letting the memory of her daughter drift away as she stared up at the ceiling. Ruby had vanished seven years ago without a trace. And now a doll that looked exactly liked her had turned up in a shop window in the French Quarter. It couldn't be a coincidence. The resemblance was too striking. Someone who knew Ruby, or at least had seen her, had sculpted that doll. There was no other possible explanation for such an uncanny likeness. The artist had captured perfectly the shape of Ruby's face, her expression, even the precocious half smile that had been the child's very essence.

Claire's eyes filled with tears as she thought about the implication of the doll's existence. After all this time, was it possible that she might find out what had happened to her daughter?

She was afraid to let even a tiny glimmer of hope back into her heart. She'd been disappointed so many times in the past. What if it *was* just a coincidence? If she'd learned anything in the last seven years, it was to take things one step at a time. The first thing she had to do was get out of the hospital.

Feeling helpless and trapped by her injuries, she brushed away frustrated tears. She had a concussion and a gash on her left hand that had required twelve stitches. After the doctor patched her up in the emergency room, he'd used tweezers to pick out the bits of glass and gravel that were embedded in her palms and the backs of her arms. Then he'd sent her to X-ray, and afterward she'd been transferred to a room on the second floor, where she was supposed to spend a quiet night.

But people had been drifting in and out of her room all evening. Doctors, nurses, her family. She found it impossible to rest, especially once the painkiller started to wear off. Every bone in her body ached, and she knew the cut on her hand was going to give her problems in the studio. She wouldn't be able to work the glass properly, which meant that until she healed, she would have fewer pieces on display in the gallery. The loss of income would be a blow to her already dwindling bank account, but she couldn't worry about that now. Her immediate concern had little to do with her physical discomfort or her financial problems.

She didn't want to stay in the hospital until morning. She wanted to go back to the Quarter, back to that shop. But every time she tried to leave, she'd been discouraged by one of the nurses who came in periodically to check on her, or by Charlotte, who'd barely left her side since the accident happened. The extent of her injuries couldn't be determined until all her test results came back, they insisted.

And then her mother had burst into the room, and Claire's remaining energy had been expended trying to calm her down. Lucille meant well, but she could be both physically and emotionally exhausting under the best of circumstances. Claire had been relieved when Charlotte finally dragged her off for a cup of coffee in the cafeteria.

The quiet had been welcome at first, and Claire had even managed to doze off. But the sound of a siren had roused her with a start, and now she was wide-awake and getting more anxious by the moment.

Slipping out of bed, she walked stiffly to the bathroom and washed her face with cold water, then took stock of the damage. A bandage covered the cut on her hand, and when she tugged up her hospital gown, she discovered a bruise the size of a basketball on her left hip and thigh where the car had struck her.

In spite of how she looked and felt, she would have checked herself out of the hospital, no matter how vehemently Charlotte and the nurses argued, if she thought she could even make it to the elevators. But considering the way her legs trembled from the short walk to the bathroom, the prospect of escape tonight seemed doubtful. By the time she made it back to her bed, she was shaking all over and perspiring.

Sitting on the edge of the bed, she eased herself under the covers and collapsed against the pillow just as the door opened and a nurse came bustling into the room, her dark eyes striking against her pale skin.

"You should have pushed the call button for help," she scolded.

"I'm okay."

"Your family is in the waiting room just down the hall." The nurse picked up Claire's wrist and timed her pulse. "They asked me to let them know when I'm finished so they can come back in. But if you'd rather, I can tell them you need your rest."

"Have you met my mother? She doesn't discourage so easily."

"Oh, I've met her all right." The nurse strapped the blood pressure cuff around Claire's arm and pumped it up. "Everyone on this floor has met her by now. She's a real pistol, that one."

"To say the least."

The nurse noted Claire's vitals on the chart, then looked up with a smile. "Anything I can get for you? Do you need something for pain?"

"I don't want to take anything else just yet."

"That's up to you. But if you get too uncomfortable, let me know. And if you need help getting up to go to the bathroom, push the call button. I don't want to come in here and find you collapsed on the floor."

Claire nodded.

"You've missed dinner, but I could find you a tray if you're hungry."

"No, thanks, I couldn't eat a bite."

"Okay. I'll be back in a little while to check on you." The nurse paused at the door. "What's the verdict? Shall I send your mother back in?"

"If you must."

The nurse grinned. "To tell you the truth, I'd be afraid not to."

"There's no point in you two staying here all night," Claire told her mother and sister a little while later. "You should just go home and get some sleep."

"I'm not going anywhere." Charlotte folded her arms as she stared down at Claire. "I have a feeling the minute my back is turned, you'll try to get up out of that bed. You heard what the doctor said. You have a concussion. You need to rest quietly for at least twenty-four hours."

"I can rest at home."

"Claire, listen to your sister." Her mother bent over the bed and tucked the sheet around Claire's shoulders. "We're not going anywhere, so you just lie there and let us take care of you."

"But you know I don't like to be fussed over."

"Like it or not, that's what happens when you get hit by a car." Lucille Doucett patted the nest of blond curls piled on top of her head, then her hand came down to rest on a hip bone sharp enough to slice meat.

After Charlotte had called her from the emergency room, Lucille had dropped everything to rush straight over to the hospital, barely taking the time to smear on lipstick and slide her feet into the three-inch high heels she always favored. But her hair and clothes were a mess. The neck of her T-shirt was stretched out of shape and her jeans were a size too small even on her slight frame. She hadn't gained weight since she'd bought them; she wore them that way on purpose, with the legs rolled up to show off the gator tooth that hung on a gold chain around her left ankle.

"You're still trembling, honey. Are you cold?" She unfolded the blanket at the foot of the bed and pulled it up.

Claire sighed in resignation. "No, Mama, I'm fine. I just want to get out of here so I can go back to the shop and find out about that doll."

Lucille and Charlotte exchanged a glance over Claire's bed, and she frowned. "Please don't look at each other like that. I'm not crazy."

"No one said anything about you being crazy, hon."

"No, but you're both thinking it." Claire turned to Charlotte. "I never should have let you talk me into getting into that ambulance."

"Well, it's not like you had a choice in the matter. You weren't even conscious when the paramedics arrived. You're hurt, Claire. A lot worse than you want to admit."

"But what if something happens to the doll before I can get back to the store? What if she's sold—"

"Hush now." Lucille rubbed Claire's arm. "Don't worry about that tonight. You just do as the doctor said and get some rest."

Claire turned her head toward the window and watched the lightning. "You don't believe me, do you, Mama?"

"What a thing to say. Of course I believe you."

"Then why are you and Charlotte still here? Why haven't you gone to that shop to see the doll for yourself?"

"Because my main concern at the moment is you, baby girl."

"But if you really believed me, you'd be moving heaven and earth to find out where that doll came from."

"Claire, honey—"

"I'm not crazy, Mama, and I'm not imagining things. The doll in that window was the spitting image of Ruby. Charlotte saw her, too."

Her sister's gaze wavered and she looked away.

Claire said angrily, "Why are you acting this way, Charlotte? Just tell Mama what you saw."

"I can't." Charlotte's cheeks were flushed with emotion. "I can't tell her what you want me to because I didn't get a good look. And I don't see how you did, either. All I could tell was that the doll had curly blond hair. She wore a pink ruffled dress. She might have looked a little like Ruby, but even if she was the spitting image as you claim, it doesn't mean—"

"That Ruby's still alive? I know that. But it has to mean *something*."

Charlotte let out a long breath. "Maybe it does, I don't know. But I hate seeing you get your hopes up like this. It's been seven years."

Claire glanced back out at the rain. "I know how long it's been. Right down to the day, the hour, the very minute that I first noticed her missing."

"I know you do." Charlotte bit her lip. Tears shone in her eyes. "I know how much you still miss her. I miss her, too. Not a day goes by that I don't think about her."

"Then stop fighting me on this. There's a doll out there that looks like my missing daughter. Help me find out why."

When Charlotte didn't answer right away, Lucille rushed to fill the silence. "Claire, you know we'd do anything for you, don't you?"

"Will you go look at the doll with me?" Claire clutched her mother's hand. "Mama, you have to see her. She looks exactly like Ruby, right down to that little pink dress you made for her seventh birthday. You remember it, don't you? The one with the little white flowers?"

"Of course I remember it. I worked my fingers to the bone on all that embroidery."

"She loved it so much. I couldn't get her out of it."

Lucille sniffed. "She called it her twirly dress. We had to go out and get her a new pair of shoes to go with it. Man, was that kid headstrong when she set her mind to something."

Claire laughed softly.

A deep voice said from the doorway, "Is this a private party or can anyone join in?"

The room went still as Claire's gaze connected with Alex Girard's. He stood at the door, one hand propped on the frame as a lazy smile encompassed all three women. He looked lean and tanned, like someone who might belong to a country club. His suit was charcoal, his tie silver and his tasseled loafers were polished and buffed. That was one thing about Alex. Even on a cop's salary, he always made sure he was well put together. He didn't leave the house if he wasn't.

Claire found herself staring at him almost as if he were a stranger. They'd been married for nearly six years, but somehow she always found something about him that she hadn't noticed before. He was an attractive man, but his dark eyes made her think of one of those fun house mirrors that didn't always reflect reality. He was in his late thirties and already starting to look a little like his father.

He wouldn't want to hear that, Claire thought. Nor would he believe it. Like every other cop she'd ever known, he had a formidable ego.

"What are you doing here, Alex?"

He straightened from the doorway and came to stand at the foot of her bed. "My wife gets herself hit by a car, where else am I going to be?"

Claire was on the verge of reminding him that, for all intents and purposes, she was no longer his wife, but she didn't want to start an argument in front of her mother and sister, so she said instead, "How did you know I was here?"

He grinned. "I'm a cop. I know everything."

One look at Charlotte's guilty face, however, confirmed Claire's suspicion. "You didn't have to come all the way over here. I'm fine."

"I wanted to see that for myself." He nodded to her mother. "Hello, Lucille."

"Alex."

"Haven't seen you in a while. How've you been?"

"Can't complain. And you?"

"Same old same old. Stabbings, shootings, a sliced-up tweaker in the Quarter. Just a routine week in the Big Easy."

"If you're that busy maybe we shouldn't keep you."

Anger flashed like quicksilver in Alex's gray eyes. For some reason, his charm had never worked on Claire's mother, and he couldn't understand why. "Maybe you wouldn't mind giving me and Claire a moment alone."

"That's up to Claire."

"It's okay, Mama."

Charlotte came over and took Lucille's arm. "You could use a cigarette anyway, couldn't you, Mama? And I wouldn't mind having another cup of coffee."

Lucille said something under her breath, but she gathered up her purse and followed Charlotte to the door.

Before she stepped out, she glanced over her shoulder. "I won't go far, Claire. You need anything, you holler, hear?"

"I will."

After she and Charlotte disappeared into the hallway, Alex came around to stand at the side of Claire's bed. "What was that all about?" He jerked his head toward the door. "Lucille acts like she's afraid to leave you alone with me."

"It's not that. She's just worried about me."

"Well, I'm glad to hear it." He sat on the edge of the bed. "I know she's never been my biggest fan, but I'd hate her to think that you're afraid of me."

"She doesn't think anything of the sort. But I still don't understand why you're here, Alex. You could have called to find out how I'm doing."

His amiable smile faltered. "Like I said, I wanted to see for myself that you're okay."

"I appreciate your concern, but I'm not your responsibility anymore."

"Not my responsibility?" His lips pinched together as he stared down at her. "You think I can just turn off my feelings because you want me to? You think I'll stop caring just because you're divorcing me?"

"We both agreed to the divorce."

"Because you left me no other choice. It's not what I want and you know it."

Claire stared at the ceiling. Why was she letting him get to her like this? Their marriage was over. The decision had been made and it was time to move on. Time to pull the plug on all her guilt. "I don't want to do this. Not now."

"I don't want to do this, either. I didn't come down here to fight with you, Claire. It scared the hell out of me when I heard what happened to you."

"I'm sorry you were worried."

"Nothing to be sorry about. I'm just glad you weren't seriously hurt." He took her hand and squeezed it. "Why don't you tell me what happened?"

"Are you asking as a cop?"

"Just humor me, Claire."

She slipped her hand from his. "Didn't Charlotte fill you in on the details?"

"Her account was pretty sketchy. She said you stepped in front of a car, but I have to believe there's more to the story than that."

"Not really. It was an accident. I wasn't looking where I was going and I ran out in front of a car. It was my fault."

"What about the doll she said you saw in a shop window?"

Claire heard the edge in his voice and turned her head to the window so that she wouldn't have to see his face. Raindrops ran down the glass in tiny rivers. She watched one of the streams split in two and slide off in separate directions. "You don't really want to hear about the doll," she said quietly.

He sighed. "No, I probably don't, but why don't you tell me about it anyway?"

Claire kept her gaze focused on the window. "She looks exactly like Ruby."

"Claire." He said her name so tenderly her eyes welled with tears. "Why are you doing this?"

"I'm not doing anything." Her voice trembled in spite of her resolve. "You asked about the doll and I'm telling you what I saw."

"You can't keep tormenting yourself this way."

"That's not what I'm doing, and even if I am, it's no longer your concern. Just forget it, Alex."

"Like hell I will." He got up from the bed and strode over to close the door. When he turned back, Claire could see the anger and frustration on his face. "Let me ask you something. When was the last time you spotted a kid that you thought looked like Ruby?"

Claire remembered the girl she'd seen on the street earlier, and lifted her chin. "This is different."

"Different than what? The one you saw on the playground that you took pictures of? Different than the time you followed another little girl and her mother home from the mall? You thought she looked exactly like Ruby, too. So you got out of your car and beat on their front door until the poor woman became so frightened she called the cops. If I hadn't gotten wind of the situation, you would have been hauled in and booked."

Claire listened to everything he said, and then she shrugged. "I don't care what you think, this is different. I know what I saw."

He shook his head, at a loss. "I don't know what to do anymore. I don't know how to help you."

"You could try believing me."

"That's the one thing I can't do. I can't feed this obsession of yours, Claire. I won't. Because I know how it's going to turn out. You'll get yourself all worked up again and then your heart's going to be ripped open like it always is. I've seen it happen over and over, and this time won't be any different. It's been seven years. Seven damn years. You can't spend the rest of your life grieving like this. You have to find a way to get over what happened." He rubbed the back of his neck as he walked toward the window. "I don't know, maybe you need to see someone."

"I've been to a therapist. It didn't solve anything."

"Then maybe you need to find a different one. You have to do something."

"I'm not crazy, Alex."

"You will be if you keep this up. I don't want you ending up like your old man."

She gasped. "I would never do that!"

"I don't want to believe it, either, but sometimes I have to wonder." He stared out at the weather, his frustration collecting on his face like raindrops on the windowsill. "I see divorces in the department all the time. They're as common as dirt. Cops just can't seem to stay married. But most of the time it's because of another woman or the lousy pay or because the wife gets sick of her man rolling around in the gutter before he comes home to her." He shoved his hands into his pockets. "But none of those things were ever our problem, were they? What did us in was that what you had was never going to be as important as what you lost."

"That's not fair," she said. "My daughter was kidnapped. That's not something you ever get over."

"I'm not talking about Ruby."

The nerves in Claire's stomach tightened and she closed her eyes briefly. "Don't say it."

His face went white with suppressed fury. "You mean I'm not even allowed to mention the son of a bitch's name? Well, I don't know why that should surprise me. From the moment he showed up on your doorstep the night we got married, I never stood a chance, did I, Claire?"

"That's not true. Our problems had nothing to do with him. I haven't even seen him in years."

"When's the last time you dreamed about him?"

She looked away, silent.

"You can't even deny it, can you?" Alex scrubbed a hand down his face and drew a long breath. "Believe it or not, I didn't come over here to start something with you, Claire. I just want to help you. That's all I've ever wanted."

"Then let me go," she whispered.

"I wish I knew how to do that. I really do."

Six

The child was enchanted by the dolls.

And the Dollmaker was enchanted by her.

Earlier, when he first got back from the city, he'd prepared a dinner tray and brought it down to the studio, deliberately leaving her door open to see if she would venture out. Then he'd gone over to his worktable, where he'd mounted a mirror on the wall so that he could watch the room behind him as he pretended to sketch.

After a few moments, he saw her hovering in the doorway. She was such a slight child. Waiflike, with her long, wavy hair and big brown eyes. He couldn't take his own eyes off her.

She remained in the doorway, her gaze darting about the studio as she searched for a way out. His workbench was against the far wall, and the mirror was slanted in such a way that he could watch her discreetly. She didn't see him at first as she took a tentative step into the room, her head turning first one way and then the other.

When she spotted him, her eyes widened and she started to retreat back into her dim little room. But she must have noticed that his back was to her, and her gaze flew to the outside door. She paused, as if trying to gauge the distance, and then, casting another furtive glance in his direction, she hurried over and twisted the knob.

The door was locked, of course. He'd made certain of that.

She tried the knob several times before finally giving up. Turning, she looked back at him, not knowing what to do.

He couldn't get over how tiny she was. Much smaller at seven than Maddy had been. She wore blue jeans with elastic in the waist and a little yellow T-shirt with a mermaid on the front.

Her clothes were all wrong. Too casual for a little girl's birthday party, but that didn't matter. He would make her a new dress, something pink and frilly and utterly feminine. What mattered to him now were her features. The upturned nose, the heart-shaped mouth, the exquisite cheekbones. She was perfect. Or at least she would be very soon.

Several moments went by before the child saw the dolls. And then, for just a split second, the fear left her face and her brown eyes lit with wonderment. He couldn't blame her. They *were* wonderful. Beautiful and charming, and he loved them, too.

Dressed in their finest, they were seated around a small, rectangular table, one at the end and two on either side. At the far end, the sixth chair stood empty. For now.

The Dollmaker had set the table with Maddy's best tea set, and he'd made her favorite cake with strawberry icing. Her presents were piled on either side of her chair, as if waiting for tiny fingers to rip off the colorful bows and tear away the tissue paper.

The child stood transfixed by the scene. Her expression was rapt, and he swiveled around to watch her, but the movement startled her and she backed away.

"No, don't go," he said softly. "They've been waiting for you."

Sliding off his stool, he walked over to the little table and knelt beside the doll with the turquoise eyes.

"This is Maddy. Today is her birthday."

The little girl said nothing, but she didn't try to run away. She was captivated by the dolls.

He went around the table and made the introductions, and when he finished, he motioned to the empty chair at the end. "Come join the party."

The child shook her head. "I want to call my mama."

"In a little while perhaps."

"I want to go home."

He sighed, his shoulders sagging dejectedly. "Please don't be tiresome about this. Remember what happened the last time?"

The little girl flinched as fear crept back into her eyes, and her bottom lip trembled. Slowly she nodded.

"Then come sit down and have some cake."

She walked over to the table and sat down at the empty space. A tear spilled over and ran down her cheek. She scrubbed it away with her knuckles.

"You'll feel better after you eat." He cut a piece of the strawberry cake and placed it on the table in front of her. Then he cut pieces for everyone at the table and one for himself. He sat cross-legged on the floor and ate, his gaze never leaving the child's face.

At that moment he felt happier than he had in a long time. All that business in New Orleans was behind him now. Maddy was home safe and sound, and all was well in the private little world he'd created.

In spite of her tears, the child's company made him almost euphoric. He loved having her companionship. He always did. But he couldn't keep her here much longer. Once the doll was finished, he would have to send her away.

He wouldn't worry about that now, though. He didn't want to spoil the party. Besides, even after she was gone, a part of her would remain with him always. Just like the others.

And when they were all finally together, the way they were meant to be, no one would ever take them from him again.

Seven

After Alex left, Claire managed to convince Charlotte to go home for the night, but Lucille wouldn't budge. "No kid of mine ever spent the night alone in a hospital, and I don't see any reason to start now."

"But, Mama, I'm fine. There's no point in wearing yourself out."

"Claire, terrible things can happen in a place like this." Lucille's eyes, small and unblinking, were dead serious. She sat in a chair next to the bed, shoes kicked off, feet propped on the mattress. Her toenails were painted bright red. The lacquer matched the lipstick she'd reapplied after her last cigarette, but the crimson had already started to bleed into the deep crevices around her mouth, giving her a grotesque appearance in the harsh lighting.

"Nothing is going to happen to me in the hospital, Mama."

"You don't know that. You're at their mercy once they get you all doped up on morphine."

"They didn't give me any morphine."

"Well, they gave you something for pain, didn't they?" Lucille brushed stray ashes off the front of her T-shirt. "I ever tell you what happened to my cousin Corinne?"

"She got a staph infection from a contaminated needle."

"That's right, she did. The nurse dropped the syringe on the floor, picked it up and stuck it right in Corinne's arm. Didn't bother to wipe it off or nothing. Took twenty years, but that infection finally killed her." Lucille's birdlike eyes gleamed knowingly. "Now don't you think Corinne wished someone had been watching out for her that day?"

"Yes, Mama."

Lucille nodded in satisfaction. "You just close your eyes and get some rest. You don't need to worry about a thing. I'll be right here all night if you need me."

Twenty minutes later, she was snoring softly, her head thrown back against the chair, mouth open. Claire wanted to wake her and send her home, but Lucille would swear she wasn't a bit sleepy, she was just resting her eyes.

Turning off the light, Claire sat in the dark for a while, trying to sort through her emotions. Her nerves vibrated like a taut rubber band as the antiseptic walls closed in on her. A nurse had brought her something for the pain after Charlotte left, but the medication wasn't working.

Slipping out of bed, Claire walked over to the window to watch the storm. Thunder rumbled overhead and the rain came down hard, blurring the city lights like a soft-focus filter.

And then just like that it was over. The storm moved

farther inland, the rain stopped and moonlight broke through the clouds. The dripping treetops glistened and the lights from passing cars painted the glossy streets with misty streaks of color.

After the rain, ditches and backyards would come alive with the sounds of crickets and frogs, but inside Claire's hospital room, all was silent except for Lucille's soft snoring.

Climbing back in bed, Claire reached for the remote to the TV. Turning down the volume, she surfed until she finally found a cable news channel. She watched images from a car bombing in the Middle East and a mud slide in Southern California, but her attention was caught by the scrolling text at the bottom of the screen.

An Amber alert was in effect for a seven-year-old Alabama girl who'd been missing for nearly a week. The FBI and local authorities were still combing a wooded area near her home, but so far no trace of the child or her abductor had turned up. No eyewitnesses had come forward; no one had seen anything. It was as if the little girl had gotten off the school bus one afternoon and disappeared into thin air.

Claire watched the scroll until the broadcast finally switched to a video feed from Linden, Alabama. They ran footage of the search, an interview with the local sheriff and a tearful plea from the mother for her daughter's safe return.

"That poor woman."

Claire hadn't realized that her mother was awake, but when she turned her head, she saw the sheen of her eyes in the light from the television screen. Some of Lucille's hair had come loose from the bun, and the strands coiled around her face like tiny gold wires.

"I hope they catch that son of a bitch," she said in a fierce whisper. "I'd like to get ahold of him myself."

"I know, Mama."

"It's an abomination, men preying on little girls like that. They ought to fry every last one of them."

Claire switched off the TV. She couldn't watch anymore, and she didn't feel like talking. The room fell silent, but her mind raced with images that had plagued her for years. Ruby was dead. In her heart, Claire knew that to be true. But what torment had the child suffered before she drew her last breath?

Claire squeezed her eyes closed, trying to shut off those terrible questions, but it was no use. Another mother's agony, coming on the heels of seeing that doll, had reawakened her worst fears.

When Ruby first went missing, Claire had made the same plea to her daughter's abductor. Before the camera started rolling, she'd agonized over what to say, worried herself sick that she might not be able to make it through the broadcast without breaking down. Dave had wanted to go on camera in her place, but the reporter who conducted the interview encouraged Claire to make the appeal because it would have a more visceral impact coming from the mother. So she'd gone on air and begged for her daughter's safe return, pleaded with the kidnapper to spare Ruby's life. And it hadn't made any difference.

For weeks afterward, Claire worried that she'd come across badly or unsympathetic, and that's why whoever had Ruby didn't respond. Both Dave and the FBI agent assigned to the case told her that such an appeal was a long shot, anyway. It wasn't her fault. But Claire had wondered for ages if she should have said or done something differently. Sometimes she still wondered.

After the interview, she'd been so emotionally drained, she'd walked away from the reporter and collapsed in Dave's arms. He'd held her for a long time, as if he'd never let her go. He was so strong back then, a rock in times of crisis, but that was before the guilt had eaten him alive. That was before the alcohol had destroyed the man Claire had fallen in love with.

In the weeks and months following Ruby's disappearance, he'd become someone Claire barely recognized. A drunken stranger who'd shoved his gun in her face one night and demanded to know what she'd done with their daughter.

Claire could picture him the way he was at that moment, with hate and despair twisting his once familiar features. She would never get that image out of her head. That he'd suspected her even for a moment, even under the influence of alcohol, was something she hadn't been able to live with. She'd packed her bags and walked out the next day.

Drawing the covers over her shoulders, Claire slid down in bed and closed her eyes. The room was quiet, the air was cool and the pain medication she'd finally had to succumb to had started to numb the ache in her joints.

She'd always told herself it was the not knowing that still tore her up all these years later. If Ruby had died of a terrible disease or in some tragic accident, Claire would have been racked with grief. Her life would never have been the same, but eventually she might have been able to move on. If she could have buried Ruby…if she could have known in her heart that her child was at peace, maybe she could have drawn some comfort from her faith.

The not knowing was the worst.

Or so she'd always thought.

But on this dark, drenched night, as Claire huddled under the covers, dread settled like a shroud over her hospital bed. She'd never considered herself clairvoyant or even particularly intuitive, but she could feel the tug of something that might have been a premonition. A presage that warned of an evil she could hardly imagine.

And suddenly she realized how wrong she'd been. The not knowing wasn't the worst. Her ignorance had kept her sane all these years.

She dreamed about Ruby that night, the same nightmare that always came back in times of stress.

In her dream she was standing at her grandmother's kitchen sink shelling crawfish. She and Dave and Ruby lived in the tiny apartment over the garage, but Claire had come over that day to use her grandmother's stove because the one in the apartment was too unreliable and she wanted to make Dave's favorite meal for dinner.

The vision was so real that Claire could feel the crusty shells of the crawfish beneath her fingers as she watched out the window for Ruby. She'd gotten a new bicycle for her seventh birthday and was riding up and down the sidewalk in front of the house. Claire called through the open window for her to come inside, but Ruby ignored her. Each time she rode up the street, she took longer and longer to get back.

Putting away the crawfish, Claire washed her hands at the sink and then went outside to call her in. The late afternoon shadows from the oak and pecan trees slowly crept toward the street.

She could see the gleam of Ruby's red helmet off in the distance and she started running after her. Somehow she knew that she had to reach her daughter before Ruby got to the end of the street. Something terrible waited for her there. If Claire didn't get to her first, she would be lost forever.

Claire screamed her daughter's name, but Ruby just kept on pedaling. Claire could barely see her now. She was only a dot in the distance. But she was still on her bike. Claire could reach her in time. She tried to run faster, but her legs were suddenly so heavy she could barely lift them.

And then the dream shifted. She saw herself at the end of a narrow alley, the kind in the Quarter that led back to sun-dappled courtyards. She smelled roses and damp moss, and somewhere nearby water splashed against stone. Someone brushed up against her back, but when she glanced over her shoulder, no one was there.

A door appeared in front of her and she heard Ruby sobbing inside the room. Slowly, Claire reached for the knob. When she drew back the door, a shaft of sunlight spilled into the darkened space. A little girl sat at a small table, her head buried in her arms. Claire called out her daughter's name and the child lifted her head. But it wasn't Ruby. It was the little girl from the news.

Claire started toward her, but Alex's voice said from behind her, "She's dead, Claire. Leave her be."

She turned to search for him in the narrow alley, but he was hidden in the shadows. And when he stepped into the light, she saw that it was Dave. His lips moved, but he made no sound at all. When he realized that she didn't understand him, he lifted a hand and pointed behind her. Claire turned slowly back to the door. The little girl was gone, and in her place was the golden-haired doll from the shop window.

Clare glanced over her shoulder at Dave. He reached out to her now, as if to stop her, but she shook her head and walked through the door. She glided across the room and picked up the doll. The porcelain felt warm and soft in her arms, like human flesh, but when the doll slipped from her grasp and hit the stone floor, the fragile face shattered into a million pieces.

Eight

❧❧❧

Dave took the *Sea Ray* out at dawn the next morning to test the overhauled Chevy engines for his uncle. The boat had been in dry dock for over two weeks, a financially disastrous situation during peak season, but Marsilius had used the opportunity to update some of the equipment.

The old thirty-foot sports cruiser now offered a television, stereo, microwave and a fully stocked refrigerator, along with the two-burner stove, full head and stand-up shower. The cabin area could comfortably accommodate four guests for overnight trips out to the steel reefs where the bright vapor lights from the oil rigs beamed down to the water's surface, attracting schools of bait fish that in turn lured in the yellowfin, mackerel and amberjack.

Marsilius had night fishing down to a science, but Dave had been trying for years to get him to invest in a smaller boat for the anglers who liked to fish the marshes and oyster beds in the basin. His uncle was set in his ways, though, and wasn't looking to expand his business. He had Dave to relieve him when his knee acted up, and Jinx Bingham's boy to run the bait and tackle. No sense fixing what wasn't broke, he always said.

Throttling back the engines, Dave glided through a glimmering channel and dropped anchor in the bay to watch the sunrise. Mist hovered over the marshes and islets, and clung like wet silk to the treetops.

Pouring a cup of coffee from his thermos, he sat down to enjoy the solitude. He couldn't help but think about the past this morning, or the case that Angelette Lapierre had dropped in his lap. She'd faxed a copy of the file to his office, and he'd sifted through the reports and made a few calls before going down to New Orleans late last night. But he needed more time to study the case before he made a decision about taking it on. He didn't want to give the grieving family false hope until he figured out Angelette's angle. She'd used the similarity to the Savaria case to draw him in, but Dave couldn't figure out why she'd bother. She said Nina Losier's parents were looking to hire a private detective, and she'd told them about him, but that alone set off an alarm for Dave. He and Angelette hadn't exactly parted on good terms. Aside from the fact that she'd tried to kill him when he broke things off with her, he didn't trust her and never had. Maybe at one time her edge had been a big part of her appeal, but now Dave knew only too well the cost of getting mixed up with Angelette Lapierre. And that was one mistake he wasn't looking to repeat.

But a young woman had been brutally murdered and her parents wanted justice. That was a hard situation to walk away from, especially for Dave, and he had a feeling that was exactly what Angelette was banking on.

As the boat rocked gently in the current, Dave tipped back his head, propped up his feet and tried to let the peaceful setting lull him. Sunrise in the Gulf was always spectacular, a fiery palette of crimson and gold splashed across a deep lavender canvas. As the mist slowly burned away in the early morning heat, the landscape turned a deep, earthy green. Violet clumps of iris jutted through a thick carpet of algae and duckweed, and purple water lilies opened in the green-gold light that filtered down through the cypress trees.

Off to his right, a flock of snowy egrets took flight from the swamp grass, and a second later, Dave saw the familiar snout and unblinking stare of a gator glide past his boat. The vista was at once beautiful and menacing, a shadowy world of dark water and thick curtains of Spanish moss.

Dave had been born and raised in New Orleans, but he loved the Cajun Coast, with its teeming bayous and maze of channels where an outsider could get lost for days. Even when he'd still lived in the city, he had come down every chance he had to help Marsilius with the charters. After he and Claire were married, she would come with him, and when he was finished working for the day, they'd take the boat back out to watch the sunset. Sometimes he would rest on deck while she cooked dinner in the galley, but most of the time he would sit below and watch her.

Her face had mesmerized him. Even the menial tasks she'd performed dozens of times drew a fierce scowl of concentration to her brow, and Dave always wondered what went through her head then. He'd call out her name to make her glance up, so that he could see her quick smile. She had a shy, intimate way of looking at him that made him want to drop whatever he was doing and take her in his arms, no matter where they were.

Sometimes they would stay out on the water until well after dark, and make love on the boat. Afterward Claire would sit between his legs, his arms wound around her as they watched the stars shimmer through the treetops.

When Ruby got older they'd brought her along a few times, but she didn't take to the water. Too many bugs to suit her, and she didn't like getting her hair all tangled on the breeze.

"You're a little city girl," Dave would tease her.

To which Ruby would proudly respond, "I'm just like my maw-maw."

Claire had always been a little befuddled by how Ruby emulated her grandmother, and Charlotte had been downright horrified. But Dave got a kick out of it. Lucille was earthy and she looked like a hot mess most of the time, but she had a good heart. And she was the only one in the family who still gave him the time of day.

He stirred restlessly. The reminiscing had shattered his fragile peace. Loneliness started to creep up on him, and deep inside, he felt the familiar tug of a dangerous thirst. Maybe he'd been hiding out in the swamps and bayous of St. Mary Parish for a little too long. His trips to New Orleans—two days ago and again last night—had reminded him of a life he'd been trying for years to convince himself he didn't miss.

Finishing off the coffee, he started the engines and

headed back in. Marsilius's place on the bayou was an old weathered building covered in license plates and sheet metal that glinted in the early-morning sunshine. The ramshackle bait and tackle shop also sold sandwiches and snacks, and as Dave tied off at the private dock, he spotted Latrell Bingham dumping bags of ice into the washtubs Marsilius used to chill soft drinks and beer. The kid looked up, grinned and waved to Dave, then went back to his work.

Dave lived just down the road in an old two-story bungalow with screened-in porches and trellises of climbing roses. It wasn't much to look at from the outside, but the place suited him fine. Except for at night, and then he missed the noises of the city. The scream of a siren heading across Canal Street toward the hospital, or the music and drunken laughter spilling from the bars and strip clubs on Bourbon Street. But what he missed most of all was the hum of alcohol as it coursed through his bloodstream, numbing the pain and guilt, giving him a split second of peace before the rage took over.

The bayou gave him too much time to think. Sitting out on his porch after dark, with the moon glinting off the water and the croak of bullfrogs and crickets echoing up from the swamp, Dave would start to remember the way Ruby's eyes crinkled at the corners when she smiled, and how she'd cling to his neck when he galloped her off to bed. The way Claire would look up at him when he returned, and quietly put away her book.

He remembered everything, and yet at times, it seemed to Dave that he had a hard time calling up their faces and the sound of their voices. The old demons would start to prod him then. Alcohol had always given him a moment of clarity along with the peace. If he stopped at one drink or even two, he would be able to remember them properly. The problem was, he'd never known when to quit. A couple of whiskeys would turn into a two-day bender that left him shaky and sick and wondering why he didn't just hole up somewhere and die.

He didn't want to go back to those days, no matter how lonely the nights were out here. New Orleans was temptation. New Orleans was Claire and Ruby and a life Dave was never going to get back.

Stepping up on the porch, he fished his house key from a flowerpot and let himself in. The shades were drawn and the house was still dim and cool. He'd converted the small living space off the entrance into his office, and the only other rooms on the bottom floor were an eat-in kitchen and a half bath out back. His current setup didn't allow for entertaining, but that didn't matter much to Dave because he rarely had company. And whenever someone did stop by—usually Marsilius or one of the neighbors—they always sat out on the porch, where they could catch a breeze off the water.

Rolling up the old-fashioned shades to allow in some light, Dave walked into the kitchen to put on another pot of coffee before heading upstairs to shower. By the time he came back down, the sweet smell of chicory filled the house. He dug through the coat closet off his office until he located the box of files he wanted, and then carried it out to the porch. Settling down in a padded rocker, he lifted the lid from the box and removed one of the folders.

Before he left the department, he'd made copies of the Savaria case files, and thumbing through the reports and statements now was like sifting through a pile of bad memories. So many things had gone wrong in Dave's life that he didn't spend a lot of time dwelling on the loss of his livelihood. But he'd loved being a cop. It was the only thing he'd ever wanted to do. If someone had told him that he'd end his career by destroying evidence in a homicide investigation, he would have called that person a liar. But he'd done that and worse. His daughter, his wife, his job—all gone in the blink of an eye because of one bad decision. One weak moment that had changed the course of his entire life.

The day Ruby had gone missing, he'd let Angelette talk him into drinks after their watch, and the next thing he knew, they were checking into a seedy motel off the old Airline Highway. The tension had been building between them for months, and a part of him had known it was only a matter of time before he succumbed.

What he'd wanted from Angelette didn't have anything to do with the way he felt about Claire, but she wouldn't believe that. No woman would. Dave had still loved Claire then as much as he ever did. Maybe even more. But Angelette was like a poison in his bloodstream, and he only knew one way to get her out of his system.

Afterward, he'd left her fuming at the motel while he drove home to his wife and kid. And he liked to think that if things had turned out differently, he would never have put himself in that situation again. But he couldn't be sure. Back then he'd been reckless with the things he cared about the most.

Claire's call had come as he'd peeled out of the parking lot, and all he could think on his frantic drive home—and for days, months, years afterward—was that his daughter had been kidnapped while he'd been holed up in some motel room with another woman.

He'd never told Claire about that day, but she knew. When she hadn't been able to reach him right away, she'd sensed something was wrong. He could see it in her eyes. He could hear it in her voice every time she spoke to him. Claire knew, and she blamed him for not being there to protect their daughter. She knew and she would never be able to forgive him.

And because of his moral frailty they'd lost their daughter forever.

Pain seared through his chest and he glanced up from the file to stare off across the water, letting the glide of a blue heron capture his attention, giving him a moment's reprieve before the suffocating guilt settled back in his lungs. And with it came the longing.

All he had to do was walk over to Marsilius's place and take a bottle of beer out of the tub. For a moment, Dave let himself imagine the twist of the bottle cap between his fingers, the taste of the icy liquid in his throat and the soothing numbness that would come later when he moved on to the hard stuff. His need was so great that he actually got up from his chair and opened the screen door.

Marsilius stood on the other side. Dave hadn't even seen him come up, but now he felt annoyed and relieved at the same time by his uncle's unexpected appearance.

Peering around Dave, Marsilius glanced at the papers scattered on the floorboards, where the folder had slid from his lap when he stood. "You going some-where?"

"Just got up to let you in," Dave lied. He moved back so that Marsilius could step up on the porch. "What's up?"

"Thought I'd come over and make sure you're okay."

"Why wouldn't I be okay?"

Marsilius shrugged, but his blue gaze was direct and slightly accusing. "You were out pretty late last night. Must have been after two when I heard you come in."

"You keeping tabs on me?"

"What if I am?"

"Well, you can relax." Dave let the spring snap the screen door closed. "Not that it's any of your business, but I drove into New Orleans to visit a sick friend."

"A sick friend, huh?" Marsilius looked as if he wasn't buying it. "This sick friend wouldn't happen to be named Jim Beam, I don't reckon."

"I wasn't drinking, Marsilius."

"Never said you were." But Dave saw a flicker of relief on his uncle's face as he took out a white hand-kerchief and mopped the back of his neck. He sat down heavily in the rocker and stretched out his bad knee. "Gonna be a hot one today. Barely eight o'clock and it must be close to ninety."

"It's the end of July. What do you expect?"

"Heat gets to me worse every year, seems like. Maybe I'll sell my place and head north one of these days."

North to the Creasy clan was anything above I-10. "You're not going anywhere, old man. You'd freeze your ass off up north."

Marsilius grunted as he leaned over and absently rubbed his knee. He was a big, muscular man with grizzled hair and a broad face weathered from the years he'd spent under a sweltering Gulf Coast sun. He wore faded jeans, a Mardi Gras T-shirt from twenty years back and a pair of old Converse high-tops he'd bought at the Salvation Army.

Dave pulled out a lawn chair, but didn't sit. "You want some coffee?"

"I wouldn't say no." Marsilius folded his hands behind his head and stared up at the drowsy ceiling fan. "I heard the boat go out earlier," he called after Dave. "How's she running?"

"Purring like a kitten." Dave poured the coffee, then carried both cups out to the porch. Marsilius had picked up one of the folders from the box and was glancing through the contents. "That's private business," Dave told him.

"Saw the name on the box and couldn't help myself." Marsilius exchanged the folder for the coffee. "Why you hanging on to those files anyway, son? That was a bad time for you back then. You're not doing yourself any favors by dwelling on that old business."

Dave sipped his coffee. "I haven't had a look at those files since I've been sober. Thought I might have missed something. Besides, some new information has come to my attention."

Marsilius frowned. "What kind of information?"

"Have you seen the news reports about that murdered Tulane student?"

"It was all over the news a few weeks back, but what's that got to do with Renee Savaria?"

"They both worked at a strip joint on Bourbon Street

called the Gold Medallion. The owner's a greaser named JoJo Barone. He goes all the way back to your old vice squad days. You wouldn't happen to remember anything about him, would you?"

"Nothing more than what I told you seven years ago."

"I wasn't exactly thinking clearly seven years ago. Refresh my memory."

Marsilius shifted his weight to accommodate his knee as he looked out over the bayou. Dave followed his gaze, and for a moment they both seemed to get caught up in the sway of the Spanish moss that fell, like an old woman's knotted hair, from the water oaks in the yard. The motion was hypnotic in the silent heat. Then another heron took flight from the marsh, breaking the spell, and Dave watched until it was out of sight before turning back to his uncle.

"Well?"

"All I remember is that JoJo had a lot of irons in the fire back then. Besides the skin club in the Quarter, he ran a couple of massage parlors out on Chef Menteur Highway. Had a bunch of Haitian drug dealers for clients, low-life badasses that used to necklace Aristide's political opponents back in the early nineties. Bastards like that have antifreeze in their veins. I saw one of 'em bite the head off a chicken one night and drink the blood like it was pop."

"Did you ever bust JoJo?"

"We ran him in two or three times, but he had the juice on some pretty high-up officials back then. They always got a little nervous whenever JoJo was in custody, so the charges had a way of disappearing."

"Did you ever spend any off-duty time at his establishments?"

Marsilius's features tightened as if Dave might have hit a sore spot. "Chef Menteur Highway was always a place where a guy could get into trouble pretty damn fast. I never went out there unless I had to. And anyway, JoJo didn't hire the usual crack whores you saw hanging out in the Quarter. His girls were quality and they didn't come cheap. Where would a cop get that kind of coin?"

Dave laughed.

Marsilius didn't. He was like a lot of cops Dave had known over the years. He hadn't been above taking a little something under the table now and then in exchange for muscle or protection, but he didn't like getting called on it. "Where you going with this, Dave?"

"Maybe nowhere. But now that I've got a clear head, I'm starting to remember some things."

"Like what?"

Like a diary entry with initials and an address on Chef Menteur Highway, Dave thought.

The discovery of Renee Savaria's diary was the first break he'd had in her case for weeks, and it had come seemingly out of the blue when her roommate called him at the station and asked to meet at a bar on Magazine Street. She was a dancer at the Gold Medallion, too, but that day she'd traded her G-string and pasties for dark glasses and a black head scarf. She'd sat huddled in the back booth of the bar, fear dripping from every pore as she sipped a whiskey sour and chain-smoked Lucky Strikes.

She'd never told Dave how she came to be in possession of the dead woman's diary, but she did nervously confess that someone had ransacked her apartment looking for it. And she was getting the hell out of New Orleans before they came after her. She'd claimed she didn't know anything about Renee's murder, but she was convinced that whoever tore her place up looking for the diary was someone who would kill to get his hands on it.

She'd turned the diary over to Dave that day and he'd never heard from her again. He'd been in the tedious process of sifting through the entries when Ruby had gone missing. Two days later, he'd gotten the first phone call.

"If you want your daughter back alive, you better listen carefully to what I have to say."

Even at the memory, Dave's chest tightened painfully, and he had to wonder if Marsilius was right. Maybe he wasn't doing himself any favors by dragging up a seven-year-old homicide. But now that he was sober, he was starting to remember a lot of other things. Like the helpless rage that had engulfed him when he'd realized that his daughter's disappearance had nothing to do with Renee's death. The crimes were connected only by Dave's gullibility. While he'd been played by Renee Savaria's killer, Ruby's abductor had gotten clean away.

The pain in his chest intensified, and he absently rubbed his hand up and down his arm as he watched a pelican dive-bomb the surface of the water, rising a moment later with a sliver of glistening silver in its beak. Dave felt a little like that flapping mullet. Hopelessly trapped by the things he'd done in his past.

Beside him, Marsilius waited for a response, but Dave wasn't sure how much he wanted to tell him. Not that he didn't trust his uncle; he did. But if the calls Dave had already made generated some heat, he didn't want anyone else caught in the middle.

"Those murders were seven years apart," Marsilius finally said. "JoJo may not have the connections he once did…hell, no one does since Katrina. But you'll need more than that to go after him."

"Maybe I'm not after JoJo."

His uncle looked glummer by the moment. "Who you after, Dave?"

"Right now I'm just asking a few questions."

"Why?"

"It's what I do for a living, remember?"

"For a paying client, maybe, but not just for the hell of stirring things up. Why complicate your life? You've got things good these days. You don't need NOPD breathing down your neck."

"Who says they will be?"

"What, you think they're going to be happy to see you back in town? You were a mean drunk, Dave, and you burned a lot of bridges. Everyone understood what you were going through so they were willing to cut you some slack up to a point. But let's face it, you didn't exactly leave behind a pile of goodwill when you cleaned out your desk. You start nosing around in an active investigation, somebody might use that as an excuse to mop up the floor with your ass."

"By somebody, you mean Alex Girard."

Marsilius set his cup on the porch and straightened slowly. "There's a lot of bad blood between you two, and he's got the upper hand these days. Like I said, Katrina changed things in New Orleans. Most of the old alliances were swept away in the floodwaters, and the way I hear it, he's been cozying up to some of the new power brokers in town. He's got ambition and he's got muscle. That makes him a dangerous man in my book.

You get crossways with him again, you could end up losing your P.I. license. Then where will you be?"

Dave grinned. "Maybe I'll buy myself a boat and give you a run for your money, old man."

Marsilius wasn't the least bit amused. "You watch your back, boy, you hear me? You keep asking questions, you might find out the hard way there's a hollow point out there somewhere with your name on it."

Nine

The sun was already blazing when Claire took a cab into the Quarter. She'd been sleeping when her mother had left the hospital. Claire had awakened to find a note from Lucille propped against a cup of water on the bedside table.

> Running to the house to get cleaned up and get a little work done. I'll be back this afternoon to take you home.

Claire had waited until the aide who'd brought her breakfast came in to clear away the tray, and then she'd climbed out of bed, dressed and left the room. She'd used her cell phone to call a cab, then waited in the air-conditioned lobby for the car to pull up outside.

As she'd pushed open the glass doors, the heat had hit her in the face like a blast from the studio furnace. The trees lining the avenues stood droopy and motionless, and the sprinklers that kept the lawns green in the summer sprayed a steady mist over shady beds of impatiens, begonias and maidenhair fern.

As her cab crossed the tracks on Canal Street, the driver seemed overly concerned about Claire's health. He kept an eye on her in the rearview mirror and asked more than once that she please not be sick in his car. Luckily, Claire managed to oblige him, but as she climbed back out into the smoldering heat, a wave of dizziness washed over her and she had to seek refuge underneath a balcony until the dark spots stopped dancing before her eyes.

The sidewalk was damp from the rain the previous evening, and as the concrete dried in the sun, heat radiated up from the surface like a steam sauna. The air was thick and heavy, and the stench of stale wine and beer hovered over the gutters, turning Claire's stomach until she had to retreat deeper under the balcony, where cool air wafted from an open shop doorway.

As she waited for the nausea to pass, she stared across the street at the store window, but from where she stood, the glare on the glass made it impossible to see inside. The cool air from the doorway helped revive her, and a moment later, Claire left the shade and crossed the street. Stepping up on the curb, she felt her heart begin to hammer, and she had to draw in several deep breaths to keep the vertigo at bay.

And then she was there, in front of the window, and it felt as if the sidewalk had melted away beneath her feet. Her knees trembled and she put a hand against the glass to steady herself.

The doll was gone.

The beautiful little inlaid table was still set with the miniature porcelain tea service, just as it had been the day before. But the tiny chair was scooted back, as if the doll had gotten up and walked away of her own accord.

The shock and disappointment were so staggering that Claire could do nothing but stare at the empty chair, her chest rising and falling as she gulped the hot air deep into her lungs.

The doll was gone.

The first clue that had surfaced in over seven years was gone.

The last link she had to her missing daughter...was gone.

After the night's rain, the morning sky was a clear, fragile blue, the exact shade of a bowl Claire had made for Charlotte one Christmas. She kept the bowl on a table in the window of her apartment so that when the sun shone through, the glass became incandescent and warm to the touch, a living, breathing entity that seemed to glow with an inner soul. It was like having a piece of Claire with her always, and thinking about her sister now caused guilt to well in Charlotte's chest as she stared out the window at the hot July morning.

Through the maze of buildings, she could see the shimmering glide of the Mississippi River, and she imagined herself on a fancy houseboat, sipping mint juleps beneath a striped umbrella as the current carried her out to sea. Away from New Orleans. Away from her family. Far, far away from what she had done last night.

That she imagined herself on a houseboat instead of a yacht was a testament, Charlotte supposed, to the lingering power of a childhood fantasy. When she was little, her mother used to drive them out to her cousin's place in Metairie, and the houseboats moored along the lake had fascinated Charlotte. Back then she could think of no greater adventure than to live on the water and to wake up each morning with a new destination. It wasn't until years later that she realized the houseboats rarely left their moorings, and that the view, breathtaking through it might be, was as static as the alley she saw out her own bedroom window.

The grass is always greener, her mother used to warn her, and as often as not, Lucille had been right. But for some reason Charlotte could never bring herself to admit it. Nor did she ever feel the need to temper her fantasies, no matter how many disillusionments she encountered.

Hitching the sheet over her breasts, she shifted her position at the window. When she turned a certain way, the river disappeared and she could see Alex's reflection in the glass. He had his back to the window as he stood in front of the bureau, knotting his tie. Charlotte glanced over her shoulder and their gazes met briefly in the mirror before she looked away.

Tiny shivers whispered along her bare skin, and even now, with guilt and shame niggling at her conscience, she couldn't say that she was entirely sorry for what had happened. She'd been attracted to Alex Girard for as long as she could remember. He was nearly a decade older, but age had never mattered to Charlotte. She'd always had a thing for mature men. What did matter was that he was still technically married to her sister.

"You've been standing at that window for ten damn minutes," he said. "What are you looking at?"

"You can see the river from here."

"Just enough so that they call it a view and charge twice as much rent." He came over to stand behind her, casually resting his hand on her bare shoulder as he propped his other arm against the window frame.

He'd just come from the shower, and Charlotte could smell the soap on his skin and the starch in his shirt. She wanted to turn and bury her head against that snowy crispness, tug loose his tie and slide her hand up under his shirttail. His stomach beneath was flat and hard from the hours he spent at the gym. He took a lot of care with his appearance, and Charlotte appreciated the effort.

Absently, he massaged her shoulder. "Man, would you look at that traffic? Seeing all those cars out there, it's hard to believe what a ghost town this place was after the flood. Of course, eighty percent of the city was underwater. Nothing going in and out but gators and moccasins."

Charlotte glanced up at his profile. She felt a pull of desire every time she looked at him, so she hastily averted her gaze. This morning she wouldn't have the excuse of fear and loneliness driving her toward irresponsibility. This morning she wouldn't be able to blame anything but her own selfish needs.

"You rode out the storm here in town, didn't you? I can't even imagine what that must have been like."

Alex squinted against the glare of sunlight that spilled through the window. "It was bad. Worst damn thing I've ever been through, but half of what you heard on the news was bullshit. Like the reports about cops leaving the city in droves. Never happened."

"The first thing I learned when I went to work in the D.A.'s office was never to trust the media," Charlotte said with a shrug. "But they got one thing right. New Orleans is never going to be the same."

"No, probably not. But I've never seen much point in looking back. You can't change the past. All you can do is play the hand you got dealt and move on."

"Sometimes it's not that easy, Alex."

"And sometimes it is," he insisted. "It's all a matter of persective. Take this window, for instance. If you're the glass half-empty type, you'd look out and see nothing but the memory of flooded streets and piles of garbage. But me? I prefer to be a little more optimistic. I look out that window and see opportunity."

"Now you sound just like a politician," Charlotte teased. "You can't expect people to forget so soon. New Orleans has always been a city that lives in the past. It's who we are."

"And maybe that's been our problem all along. Like I said, I don't see much profit in looking back. I don't believe in regrets." His voice softened as he turned and traced a finger down her jawline. "That goes for what happened last night, too. I'm not sorry and I don't want you to be, either."

She kept her gaze trained on the window, as if the sunshine flooding through the glass could burn away her desire for him as easily as it melted the early morning mist over the river. "I can't help it. I shouldn't have come here, Alex."

"Then why did you?"

"Because I could tell that you were hurt and upset when you left the hospital last night. I just wanted to make sure you were okay."

"One thing you gotta know about me. I'm not a man who takes well to charity. I don't need your pity. That's the last thing I want from you."

"I don't pity you, but I do understand what you're

going through. Last night you were hurt and vulnerable, and I was lonely. We let things get out of hand. It never should have happened."

"Is that really the way you feel?" His eyes moved over her face. "If you don't want to see me again, that's fine. If the earth didn't move or we didn't click, or you can't stand the way I hog all the covers in the middle of the night, then tell me straight up. I can handle the truth. But don't give me any bullshit about guilt and regrets. We didn't hurt anybody."

"What about Claire?"

"Claire doesn't give a damn what I do."

"Are you going to tell her?"

The question obviously hit a nerve that was still raw and exposed. Alex winced as he turned back to the window. "No, I'm not going to tell her. Are you?"

Charlotte clutched the sheet to her breasts, the lingering passion she'd felt earlier dissolving now in the tawdry light of the morning after. "I don't want her to know. I can't stand the thought of her being hurt because of something we did in a weak moment."

"You need to lighten up." His voice was becoming irritated, but Charlotte didn't think he was so much annoyed with her as he was with his own conscience. "It's over between Claire and me. It has been for a long time. I was just too stubborn to admit it. I kept clinging to the way I wanted things to be instead of facing how it really was."

"Because you loved her," Charlotte said softly. "You still do. That's plain to anyone."

"Maybe I do, but I'm damned if I know why."

"Because she's Claire."

"Right." His eyes were suddenly cold and remote as

he stared out at the traffic. "She's Claire. The woman I let walk all over me for the past six years."

Charlotte flinched. "Don't talk about her that way. You don't know what she's been through."

He gave a bitter laugh as his eyes cut sideways at her. "*I* don't know what she's been through? That's a joke, right? Because I'm the one who used to wake her up from the nightmares, remember? I'm the one who was right there beside her when she went through the house looking for Ruby. I'm the one who held her for hours when she couldn't stop shaking. So don't tell me I don't understand what she went through, okay? I was with her every step of the way. And it still wasn't enough."

"I'm sorry." Charlotte put a hand on his arm. "I shouldn't have said what I did. You know as well as I do what a terrible time she's had. I'm just defensive when it comes to my sister."

He shook off her hand and walked back over to the mirror to adjust his tie. His movements were jerky with anger. "We're all defensive when it comes to Claire. But you and Lucille aren't doing her any favors by feeding into this latest obsession of hers."

"You mean the doll?"

"I mean the doll, I mean that kid she saw in the park, I mean everything. She's got to find a way to let this thing go or it'll eat her alive."

Maybe it already has. Because when she remembered her sister the way she once was, Charlotte realized all too painfully that the Claire she knew now was nothing but a shell. She'd never been outgoing like Charlotte, or as openly demonstrative as Lucille, but she'd adored her daughter, loved her more than life itself. And there was a time when she'd been quietly, ec-statically happy. With Dave.

Charlotte supposed if she searched her memory banks hard enough she might be able to remember why Claire had fallen so hard for Dave Creasy. He'd once been handsome enough, before the booze destroyed his looks. Charming, too, and maybe even a little cocky when he'd first made detective. But he'd never had Alex's sophistication or ambition. He'd never been the kind of man Charlotte would ever envision for herself, but he and Claire had once been good together. Then Ruby had disappeared and Dave had gone off the deep end. But even before that, he'd done some things to her sister that Charlotte would never be able to forgive.

In light of her current situation, she realized her attitude was probably hypocritical, and she thought there might be some truth in the old saying that everyone had the propensity to become what they hated the most. She'd despised Dave for his moral failings, and now here she was, standing naked in her brother-in-law's bedroom.

Alex picked up his keys and wallet and stuffed them in his pockets. "I have to get to the station. There's juice in the refrigerator and plenty of clean towels in the bathroom. Stay as long as you want. Just lock up when you leave."

He started for the door, then turned back and walked over to where she still stood at the window. He bent to kiss her forehead, the affectionate peck of a friend— or worse, of a brother—before he straightened and ran his knuckles down the side of her face.

"Don't beat yourself up over what happened, okay? Claire never has to know."

But I know.

And Charlotte wondered if, years later, she would look back at some point and be able to recall that this moment was the beginning of her own moral decline.

She turned and stared into the blinding sunlight until she heard the front door close behind Alex. She was still standing at the window a few moments later when the phone on the nightstand rang, and she heard the message machine in the living room pick up. Alex's recorded greeting came on, and then a moment later, the caller said impatiently, "You're a hard man to reach these days. If I didn't know better, I'd think you're trying to avoid me."

Something in the voice, a hint of familiarity, caused Charlotte to turn away from the window and walk across the bedroom. She stood listening unabashedly to the message as she tried to put a face to the caller's voice.

"I'll make this real short and sweet. Dave Creasy is back in town and he's been sniffing around the Losier case. A guy like that could really fuck up an investigation, so I suggest we pay him a little visit. The sooner the better, if you get my drift."

Claire stood in front of the shop window and tried to convince herself that the doll had only been put away for the night. The collectibles featured in such stores were usually quite valuable, and the owner might have felt it would be too risky to leave such a costly piece so prominently displayed overnight.

The other possibility, of course, was that the doll had already been sold, but that was a bridge Claire would cross when she had to. In the meantime she could do nothing but wait until the shop opened. The hours posted on the sign that hung in the door were Ten to Six, Tuesday through Saturday. Since it wasn't quite nine yet, she had over an hour to kill.

Claire's first instinct was to remain in front of the shop until someone arrived to open the door, but her stomach was still queasy and she felt weak-kneed and shaky. If she remained on her feet much longer, she might pass out and find herself right back in the hospital.

Keeping to the shady side of the street, she walked over to St. Louis Cathedral to wait. The sanctuary was quiet and cool, the glare of the hot summer sun muted by the small windows.

Someone had left a pink rose on the pew where she sat, and absently she picked up the stem and held the petals to her nose. The fragrance made her think of the dream she'd had last night, and the shattered face of the doll.

Shuddering, Claire glanced around. Coming on the heels of that nightmare, the quiet of the cathedral was a little too unnerving, and after a few minutes, she got up, placed the rose on the bench and left.

Outside, she used her cell phone to call her mother and let her know that she'd already left the hospital. Lucille wasn't thrilled by the news, and when they finally hung up, Claire knew she hadn't heard the last of it. But a scolding from her mother was the least of her worries. She wasn't scheduled to work in the gallery until the following day, but she'd been counting on spending several hours in the studio. Now that would have to wait until her hand healed.

As she walked past the hotels and bed and breakfasts along St. Peters, Claire couldn't stop worrying about what she would do if the doll had been sold or if the owner refused to give her the information she needed. What recourse would she have, since no one, including Charlotte, seemed inclined to believe that the doll looked like Ruby? Maybe if she showed the shopkeeper a picture of her daughter, the woman would be moved enough to help Claire.

And what if the doll was still there? What if in the bright light of day, she *didn't* look like Ruby? Would Claire then be forced to concede that Alex was right? That her refusal to let go of the past was slowly driving her crazy?

By her watch, it was straight up ten when she arrived back at the shop, but the Closed sign was still in the window, and when she tried the door, it was locked.

Shielding her eyes with her hands, Claire tried to peer through the crack at the edge of the blind, but the interior of the shop was so dim and the sun outside so bright that she couldn't see anything.

And then, as she started to turn away, she saw something move inside the shop. A shadow wavered, and Claire quickly lifted her fist to rap on the door.

"Hello? Hello? Is someone in there?"

She put her face back up to the window and peered inside. Someone stared back at her.

Ten

"Claire, what the hell are you doing?"

At the sound of the voice behind her, Claire whirled. "Alex!" She put her hand on her heart. "You scared me half to death. I wasn't expecting anyone to sneak up on me like that."

"I wasn't exactly sneaking, but I'm not surprised you didn't hear me. the way you were banging on that door. What are you trying to do…wake the dead?" He'd draped his suit coat over one arm and rolled up his shirtsleeves in the heat. Claire could see a fine sheen of perspiration across his brow.

"I'm trying to get someone to let me in. The store should be open by now, but the door's still locked." Lifting the damp hair off her neck, she twisted it up and pinned the strands with a clip she found in her purse. "What are you doing here, anyway?"

"Just checking up on you. I swung by the hospital on my way to the station, and when I saw your clothes gone, I figured I'd find you here." Slowly he removed his sunglasses and put them in his pocket, but Claire still couldn't tell what he was thinking. She'd never been very good at reading Alex. He kept a lot of himself hidden. After six years of marriage, sometimes it still seemed that she barely knew him at all.

It hadn't been like that with Dave. They'd grown up in the same neighborhood, and even as a kid, he'd worn his heart on his sleeve. From the very first date, Claire had always known where she stood with him…until Ruby disappeared, and then everything fell apart. He'd become someone Claire didn't know anymore, someone who even scared her at times.

Alex had never frightened her, and in his own way, he loved her as much as Dave ever had. Maybe more. But Claire also knew that even if they stayed together for another twenty-five years, he would never understand her the way Dave had.

She glanced across the street, where the drowsy sway of asparagus fern hanging from a second-story balcony caught her attention. Through the thick curtain of green, she caught a glimpse of a couple embracing in the morning heat, and a moment later, laughter drifted down to the street.

Claire deliberately turned away. She didn't know why Dave was on her mind so much this morning.

Alex flung his jacket over one shoulder. "So where is this doll that has you so worked up?"

Claire tried not to let his tone irritate her. He probably didn't even realize how condescending and impatient he sounded at times, or how annoying it was when he got that placating look on his face.

"I don't know where she is. That's what I'm trying to find out. It's after ten. The shop should be open by now."

He glanced at his watch. "It's just a few minutes past. Maybe whoever opens up is running late this morning. Probably got stuck in traffic or something."

"No, I saw someone in there right before you walked up," Claire said. "I kept on knocking. Maybe if you show your badge, we can get in."

Alex took her by surprise when he walked over and peered through the glass. "I'm not opposed to flashing my badge, but I don't see anyone in there."

"I spotted someone there just a minute ago."

Alex still had his face to the window. "Are you sure you didn't see your reflection in the glass?"

"Yeah, that's probably it. Because, Lord knows, I'm so crazy I can't tell the difference between another person and my own reflection."

He swung back around and Claire saw him take a breath, as if he was having a difficult time hanging on to his temper. His fingers drummed impatiently against his thigh as his gaze scoured the street. Except for a brief moment when he'd met her eyes directly, he didn't seem to want to look at her this morning.

"I'm sorry, Alex. I shouldn't be snapping at you like that. It's not your fault the doll isn't here. But I really don't know why you keep coming around like this. Every time we're together, all we do is fight. Why can't you just let it go?"

"Damned if I know, Claire." His voice sounded tired. "I never ran across anything or anyone I couldn't give up if I didn't think it was worth my time. But I don't seem to have it in me to walk away from you."

"You'd be so much happier if you did," she said softly.

"Oh, I know I'd be happier, that's not the issue.

Thing is, though, I'm not the kind of guy who likes to lose."

"You make it sound like our marriage was a game."

"Not a game, Claire, a farce."

Now it was she who had to hold in her anger. Down the street, the spires of the cathedral glistened in the hot white light, and she concentrated on the glare. "You shouldn't have come here."

"I shouldn't do a lot of the things I do, but that never seems to stop me." He walked back over and glanced in the shop window. "I still don't see anyone in there. If you ask me, it's time to give up the ghost."

"You do what you have to do, Alex, but I'm not leaving until I see her."

He turned at that. "Do you hear yourself? You keep saying *her.* Do you even realize you're doing it?"

"It's just a figure of speech. It doesn't mean anything."

"That doll is *not* Ruby."

"I know that."

"Are you sure?"

Claire frowned. "Yes, I'm sure. Have you been talking to Charlotte?"

His gaze faltered and he looked off down the street. "Why?"

"Because she seems to think I'm confusing the doll with Ruby, too. I'm not. I know in my heart that my daughter is dead. But I also know that the doll means something. It's not a coincidence she looks so much like Ruby."

"So what are you going to do, Claire? Buy the damn thing and take it home with you? Because I have to tell you, there's something a little morbid about that."

She didn't say anything for a moment. The anger inside her was too strong. She didn't want to lash out at Alex again, but *damn* him for not understanding. Damn him for making her feel guilty about clinging to the memory of her daughter.

"Maybe you should be asking yourself what you'll do," she said. "What if the doll looks as much like Ruby as I say she does? What if even you can't deny the resemblance? Won't it be a police matter then?"

"Come off it, Claire. You don't think NOPD has enough to worry about without investigating dolls?"

"I'm serious."

"I know you are, and that's what scares the hell out of me." He pinched the bridge of his nose. "This heat's starting to give me a migraine," he muttered.

The heat wasn't the cause of his headache and they both knew it. "The doll is a clue, Alex."

"A clue to what? You said yourself Ruby is dead."

"I still want justice. I still want to know what happened to her."

"Bullshit. Maybe you can lie to yourself, but I know how your mind works. You've already decided somewhere in that thick head of yours that the doll is going to lead you to Ruby. That's not going to happen."

"I'm not deluded," she said angrily.

"You may not be deluded, but you're still grasping at straws." He moved toward her in the shade and placed his hands on her shoulders. His eyes were level and unblinking and they stared straight into Claire's. "I'm worried about you. You could have been killed yesterday, and now here you are again. You keep putting yourself through this same shit over and over, and it never ends well. This time won't be any different."

"Maybe it won't. But I'm not giving up until I find out for sure."

"And so you're going to stand out here in this heat until you keel right over from exhaustion. Is that it?"

"If I have to."

He shook his head in disgust. "Have you seen yourself in a mirror this morning? You look like hell. You're as pale as a ghost and your hands are trembling like an old woman's. You need to get out of this heat. At least go with me down the street to get something cold to drink."

"You go if you want to."

"Claire—"

"Just leave me alone, Alex. Please."

"Damn it." He dropped his hands from her shoulders and turned to stare at the traffic, his mouth a thin, straight line. Then he started walking away. "Wait here."

"Where are you going?"

"Next door. Maybe someone there knows something about when this place normally opens."

Claire wished she'd thought of that. "Alex?"

He glanced over his shoulder.

"Thanks."

His face tightened. "Don't thank me. It's not like I'm doing you any favors. I'm just prolonging the inevitable, is all."

He disappeared into the neighboring shop, and Claire stepped back into the deeper shade of the doorway. Putting her face to the glass, she tried to peer through the sliver at the edge of the blind again, but Alex was right. The interior was so dim she could barely see anything. Maybe she really had glimpsed her own reflection earlier.

But in the split second before Alex showed up,

Claire had been certain that someone stood on the other side of the door, staring back at her. She hadn't seen a face, at least not clearly, but she'd glimpsed a silhouette that seemed distinct from the other shadows in the shop. And even now she still had a strange feeling that someone was in there.

Leaning a shoulder against the wall, she fanned herself with her hand. Alex was right about something else, too. If she waited out here much longer, the heat might do her in.

A young woman came toward her down the street, and Claire watched her curiously, wondering if she might be the one to open up the shop. But before she reached Mignon's, she turned down a narrow alley that ran between the two buildings.

Claire left her spot in the doorway and walked over to stare after her. At the back of the alley, the woman knocked on the door of the adjacent building, and a moment later, someone let her inside.

The alley was like any number of passageways that ran between narrow buildings in the Quarter, many of them leading back to the hidden courtyards for which New Orleans was so famous. At the rear, a wrought-iron fence ran between the two buildings, and the smell of wet brick and damp moss mingled with the scent of the yellow roses spilling over the scrollwork.

As Claire stood gazing after the young woman, she thought again of her dream last night and wondered if she might have glimpsed the alley a split second before the car hit her. Maybe the image had been stamped on her subconscious, only to surface hours later in her sleep.

Her grandmother would have claimed the dream was

a sign. In spite of her devout Catholic upbringing, Maw-Maw Doucett had been a big believer in omens and presages, and had been buried, at her request, with the silver dime she'd always worn on a string tied around her neck.

Claire was more inclined to think that the shock of seeing the doll and the trauma of the accident had produced her strange visions. She entered the alley without hesitation, sidestepping a puddle left from the night's rainstorm.

But as she slowly walked down the weathered pathway, she couldn't get the dream out of her head. The sound of a child crying from behind a closed door. Dave's silent warning as he stepped out of the shadows. And then the shattering of that porcelain face—a face that looked so much like Ruby's—against the stone floor.

She might not share her grandmother's faith in dreams and second sight, but Claire was Southern enough to believe that there were things in this world that couldn't be easily explained, things that couldn't be seen or felt, but were no less real and true. As she neared the end of the alley, a chill swept through her, and for one brief moment, she had the strangest sensation that her grandmother was somewhere behind her, calling her back before it was too late.

The feeling was so strong that Claire couldn't resist glancing over her shoulder. She could hear voices from the street, and from somewhere nearby, music drifted through an open window. The sky overhead was clear and blue, the air all around her as still as an indrawn breath.

But there was no one behind her. She was all alone

in the alley. Her grandmother was dead and so was Ruby. Yet at that moment it seemed to Claire that she felt them both. The tug on her hands was as real to her as the pounding heartbeat in her chest.

She didn't retreat, though. Instead, she walked to the back of the alley and peered through the iron gate into a courtyard that looked lush and cool after the night's downpour. No one was about, so Claire turned away.

The rear entrance to the collectibles shop was set in the brick wall directly across the alley from the door the young woman had disappeared into earlier. Claire lifted her hand and rapped loudly enough for anyone inside to hear her. When no one responded, she tried the knob. To her surprise, it turned in her hand, and she pushed open the door. "Hello? Is anyone here?"

Even with light spilling in, the back of the shop was dim and shadowy, and it took Claire's eyes a moment to adjust. Then she stepped inside and glanced around. The space was apparently used as a storage area and workroom. One side was equipped with a sink, microwave and an old refrigerator, and on the other side, shelves were crammed with cardboard boxes and packing materials.

And scattered across the surface of a worktable was a grotesque tableau of doll heads, torsos, and a pile of glass eyes.

The mangled dolls were creepy and unnerving in the gloomy light, and when the door closed behind Claire, she jumped in spite of herself.

The room was *cold*. Someone had turned down the thermostat, and at first the frigid temperature was a relief from the relentless heat outside. But as Claire lingered just inside the door, she had to rub her hands up and down her arms to ward off a chill.

Strings of crystal beads covered the entrance to the shop, and tinkled softly in the air that flowed from a nearby vent.

"I'm sorry to bother you," Claire called as she moved nervously toward the beads. "I've been waiting outside for your shop to open. Your sign says ten. It's after that now."

No one was there. Whoever she'd spotted earlier must have stepped out and left the door unlocked. If the person came back, Claire could be in big trouble for trespassing. But now that she was finally inside, it would take more than the prospect of jail to deter her from searching for that doll.

Nervously, she parted the beads and entered the shop. The place was small and cramped, but the owner had utilized every square inch to display her collectibles. Dozens and dozens of dolls were lined up on the shelves, and unlike their broken counterparts in the back, the showcased pieces were perfect in appearance, from their frilly dresses to the exquisite handpainted faces.

Claire's mother had been an avid collector for as long as she could remember. Lucille had never been able to afford the one of a kind dolls that commanded hundreds, sometimes thousands of dollars, but she'd always kept her eye out for bargains, and she'd dragged her daughters with her to flea markets and yard sales for years. From the hours they'd spent at shows and exhibits, Claire recognized the more common Madame Alexanders and Queen Tatianas. The expensive and truly collectible dolls were locked in cases.

As she made her way around the crowded shop, she had to resist the temptation to keep looking over her shoulder. She knew that she was alone, but all those glass eyes staring back at her became a little unsettling.

Ignoring the flutter of nerves in her stomach, she bent to explore the lower shelves of a display case, but had already concluded her search was pointless. The doll she'd seen the day before was nowhere to be found. As she stared at a collection of antique French dolls in velvet dresses and elaborate wigs, she tried to beat back her helpless frustration. She'd looked in every case, searched along every shelf. The doll was gone, and there was nothing more she could do until she spoke with the owner or someone who worked here.

She started to turn away from the case, then froze. For one split second, a dark silhouette had been reflected in the glass. Claire's heart slammed against her chest as she spun toward the back room.

The crystal beads swayed in a draft as panic tightened her chest. But in the next instant, she realized that the owner had probably returned and might be as frightened as she was.

"Is someone there?" She took a step toward the beads. "I'm not here to steal anything. I just need some information about a doll I saw in your window yesterday."

Silence.

Claire braced herself as she waited for an irate owner or employee to come charging into the shop to confront her. No one came. No one made a sound, but she could feel someone's presence. It was one of those strange sensations that couldn't be explained, but she knew someone was in the workroom, on the other side of the beaded curtain, waiting for her to make the first move.

She stood very still, wondering what she should do.

And then a knock sounded at the front door, and she jumped.

"Claire? Is that you in there?"

Alex's voice was muted from the street, but she had no trouble detecting his irritation. At the moment, she didn't care how angry he was, she was so relieved he was there.

"I'll be right out!"

Parting the curtain, she peered into the workroom, saw nothing out of place and hurried through, leaving the glass beads tinkling behind her as she rushed toward the door.

Relief washed over her as she stepped into the alley. She didn't know why she was so shaken. Maybe because she'd entered the shop illegally. If the wrong person had found her inside, the situation could have gotten sticky. But it was more than that. Something inside the shop had badly frightened her.

Claire couldn't stop trembling, even though Alex was headed toward her down the alley and she knew that she was safe. But the sense of danger lingered, and she could almost hear her grandmother whispering in her ear. *Listen to your instincts, Claire.*

A breeze drifted through the alley, stirring the wrought-iron gate that opened into the courtyard. A white flower lay on the cobblestones just outside the fence, and Claire walked over to have a closer look.

Against the damp darkness of the worn pavers, the snowy petals of the orchid looked fresh and pristine, as if someone had dropped it only moments earlier while hurrying through the courtyard gate.

Eleven

From the shopkeeper next door, Alex learned that the owner of the collectibles store, Mignon Bujold, was attending a doll show in Baton Rouge for the next four days and the shop would be closed until she returned on Tuesday morning. Why she'd left the back door unlocked was anyone's guess, but the neighbor seemed to think it was just an oversight. The locks on some of the old buildings in the Quarter were tricky, and if Mignon had been in a hurry to leave on Thursday, she might have failed to engage the dead bolt properly.

Alex had a quick look around the alley and the shop, but the entry hadn't been forced and nothing on the inside appeared to be amiss. In spite of Claire's contention that she'd seen someone inside earlier, he insisted there was little he could do but alert the neighborhood patrol to keep an eye on the premises until someone could get in touch with Mignon Bujold.

Claire went home after that and spent the remainder of the day intermittently resting and puttering around the house, until her mother showed up late that afternoon with an overnight bag and a determined expression. She'd come to make sure that Claire didn't overdo her first day out of the hospital, and she wouldn't take no for an answer. Claire knew better than to argue, so gave in gratefully and settled on the sofa in the living room, while Lucille went through the house cleaning like a buzz saw.

After a supper of boiled shrimp and dirty rice, they carried glasses of sweet tea out to Claire's front porch and watched twilight fall like a silky blanket over the city. Trails of pink clouds lingered just above the treetops, and as the color began to fade, the sky softened to gray. It started to mist, and the early evening air smelled of rain and flowers and freshly cut grass.

"We're in for another downpour later," Lucille predicted as she rocked back and forth. "See the way those thunderheads are piling up over the Gulf?"

"I don't mind the rain," Claire said.

"I know you don't. Charlotte used to climb the walls when she had to stay cooped up inside, but you'd just sit out on the porch like we are now, and watch it rain all day long. You two girls were as different as night and day when you were little, but you both took after your daddies. William was just like you, Claire. He could sit and watch the rain for hours. I never understood one thing about that man, but I sure did miss him after he was gone. I used to lie in bed at night and ask myself over and over what I might have done that drove him to do such a terrible thing."

"It wasn't your fault, Mama. It was just something inside him."

"I know that now. He was one of those people that couldn't ever find any peace. When he'd get that far-off look in his eyes, you just knew he was studying on something bad, something that kept eating at him until he couldn't take it anymore. I used to worry about how much you were like him. Always so quiet and gentle and keeping everything bottled up inside the way you did. But you're stronger than your daddy ever was. Sometimes I think you're the strongest person I know."

"Thanks, Mama, but I don't feel very strong right now." A strange mood had gripped Claire ever since she'd left the collectibles shop that morning. She'd felt nervous and edgy all day, and she couldn't seem to shake the notion that something bad was about to happen.

"You're just out of sorts because of the accident. A trauma like that can take the wind right out of your sails. Give yourself a couple more days to get over it."

Claire rested her head on the back of the rocking chair. "I don't have a couple of days. I'm going back to work tomorrow."

"Honey, you can't work with your hand all messed up like that."

"I can't blow glass, but there's still plenty I can do in the gallery. And I need the hours. Especially now that I have a hospital bill to pay."

Lucille gave her a sidelong glance. "Your divorce isn't final yet. You could probably file a claim on Alex's insurance."

"I can't do that. It wouldn't be right. And besides, I've always had someone looking after me. You or Dave or Alex. I'm thirty-three years old, Mama. It's high time I learn to take care of myself."

"You make it sound like you've been freeloading on the rest of us, but that's just not so. You're always doing for everyone else, Claire. Look at the way you took care of Maw-Maw before she passed away. I never could have done what you did. I didn't have the stomach for it."

"That's not true. You're taking care of me right now," Claire said.

"It's different when it's your own kid. Don't matter how old they get, they're always going to be your babies."

Claire stared out at the street, where the mist swirled like ghosts under a streetlight. "Can I ask you something, Mama?"

"What is it?"

"Why don't you like Alex?"

Lucille stopped rocking and stared at her in the gathering darkness. "What in the world brought that on?"

"I don't know. It's just been something I've always wondered about."

"Why didn't you ever say anything?"

"Maybe I didn't want to know before. But it bothered me that you couldn't warm up to him."

Lucille went back to rocking as she gazed out over the street. "What difference does it make now?"

"It doesn't. I'm just curious, that's all."

Her mother was silent for a moment. "I never thought it was my place to say anything, but since you're asking, I guess I don't need to hold back. He had his eyes set on you from the get-go, Claire, you just couldn't see it. And he wasn't above manipulating a tragic situation to get what he wanted. From the moment he found out Dave was out of the picture, he didn't let the shirttail touch his back before he made his move."

"But he didn't take advantage of me, Mama. He was a good friend to me. Someone I could lean on during the worst time of my life."

"He made sure of that, didn't he?"

"What do you mean?"

"He spent more time consoling you than he did out looking for Ruby."

"He was just trying to help."

"Help himself, you mean."

"He's a good man, Mama, and he was a good husband to me."

"Then why are you divorcing him?"

"It's complicated."

"That's what people always say when they can't face the truth. Or don't want to. But you and I both know why that marriage fell apart." Her gaze met Claire's. "You're divorcing him because he's not Dave Creasy."

"That's crazy, Mama."

"You can lie to yourself, honey, but you can't lie to me. I know you wanted things to work out with Alex, but it just wasn't meant to be. You tried your best, but you can't help how you feel. And no matter how much Alex loved you, he couldn't take being second best. No man could. Sooner or later things were bound to go south."

"It wasn't like that," Claire said. "Alex and I were happy for a while. We just drifted apart."

But even as she denied it, she felt something that might have been the truth tearing at her heart, and the weight of an old loneliness pressing down on her. Sometimes she thought that crushing loneliness must be a little like being buried alive.

A couple walked by on the sidewalk, their forms not much more than shifting silhouettes in the misty darkness. Their hands were linked, their bodies pressed closely together, and as Claire watched them pass beneath a streetlight, moments from her past flashed in her mind like photographs. She thought it strange how memories could lie dormant for years, and then when they came back suddenly, it was as if they'd been there all along. Not forgotten or lost, but lingering on the edges of consciousness, the pain softened by time and experience, but never extinguished. Never completely gone.

"Only one man's ever made you happy, Claire."

"Let it be, Mama. I don't feel much like resurrecting old ghosts tonight."

"You're the one who brought it up."

"We were talking about Alex, not Dave."

"Dave is your past, Claire. Alex is just a mistake."

Claire watched the couple on the street until they were out of sight. The mist turned into a drizzle and the temperature started to drop as the rain clouds moved in from the Gulf.

They sat in silence, and after a while Lucille began to doze off. In the dim light from the streetlamp, her face looked soft and peaceful, until her elbow slipped off the arm of the chair and she woke with a start.

"Why don't you go on to bed, Mama? You couldn't have gotten much rest last night. You must be all worn out today."

"I'm a little tired, I guess, but what about you? You're not ready to turn in?"

"Not just yet. I think I'll sit out here and watch the rain for a while. If the weather gets bad, I'll move inside."

Lucille got up and came over to drop a kiss on the top of Claire's head. "Don't stay out here all night, now. You need to get some rest, too."

"I won't. I'll see you in the morning."

"Good night, Claire."

"Good night, Mama."

The door closed softly behind Lucille, and Claire turned back to the street. A few cars went by, their tires sloshing on the wet pavement, but the pedestrians had all scurried inside. The sidewalks were empty and glistening as raindrops pattered against banana leaves, and a cooling breeze whispered through the oak and pecan trees. A dog barked excitedly in a neighbor's backyard and then fell silent.

The hair at the back of Claire's neck lifted suddenly; she didn't know why. She saw nothing unusual, heard only sounds she'd listened to on countless other rainy nights.

But something was different. Something had shifted in her quiet little world, and as she sat alone on her front porch, she felt the darkness closing in on her.

Claire opened her eyes. A noise had awakened her, but she didn't know if it was real or imagined. She lay in that fragile half-sleep state and listened to the night. The wind had risen since she'd gone to bed, and the live oak outside her bedroom raked against the side of the house as rain slashed across the windows.

Even on a calm night, the house was full of sounds. Claire had never minded the creaks and groans of settling wood, but since Alex moved out, she hadn't been sleeping well. Everything seemed to wake her these days. Maybe it was because she'd never lived alone before.

She'd married Dave right out of high school, and they'd lived in her grandmother's garage apartment until splitting up after Ruby disappeared. Claire had stayed on in the apartment for a while before moving in with her ailing grandmother. A year later, Maw-Maw was dead and Claire had found herself married to Alex. She was never quite certain how it happened. Her life back then had seemed like a dream she couldn't wake up from. One moment she'd been married to Dave and they'd had a beautiful little girl they both adored, and then in the blink of an eye, it had all been stolen on a hot, clear afternoon.

Her daughter's kidnapping had been the defining moment of Claire's life. Nothing before or after was ever going to be as important. That was the real reason her marriage to Alex had collapsed. There were times when the weight of her memories had pushed her so deeply into sadness that only the past seemed real to her. Alex had been patient up to a point, but Claire couldn't blame him for his resentment.

She closed her eyes and tried to go back to sleep. But it was no use. She was wide-awake now. She fluffed her pillow, tugged up the covers, then sighed in resignation.

Rolling over, she stared at the empty space that was Alex's side of the bed. She pictured him lying there beside her, his brown hair mussed in sleep, his bare chest rising and falling with each breath. She used to stare at him while he slept, wondering why she couldn't love him the way he deserved to be loved. He was a good man, a good husband. He was everything she needed, everything she should have wanted…but he hadn't been able to make her forget.

She put a hand on his pillow, remembering the way his skin had felt beneath her palm. Remembering the way he would open his eyes, his gaze deepening as he reached for her in the dark. Remembering how, in those first months of marriage, she'd thought too many times of Dave's touch.

And Alex had known. He'd pretended not to, of course, but he knew. How could he not? And in time his jealousy had turned into a festering bitterness.

Claire flopped onto her back and stared at the ceiling. The lightning created interesting patterns in the plaster. She tried to picture that same delicate design in a piece of glass. It was a trick she used to lull herself to sleep. She imagined herself slowly turning the blowpipe in the furnace, capturing a bit of honeylike glass on the end and continuing to work it evenly so that it didn't drip off. Step by step, she went through the arduous process, keeping the glass centered as she worked, adding layers and colors and using wet newspapers to control the shape.

Claire was so deep into the imagery that the sound of shattering glass almost didn't register. And then she bolted upright in bed, her heart pounding in terror.

The sound hadn't been imagined or dreamed this time. Something had been knocked over and broken.

Someone was in her house.

She tried to convince herself that her mother had probably gone downstairs for a glass of water, or even some warm milk, if the storm had awakened her, too. There was nothing to worry about. No need to panic.

Claire listened for a moment, hoping that she would hear Lucille's footfalls on the stairs. But when no sound came, she swung her legs over the side of the bed and sat on the edge, one ear turned toward the door.

Another sound came to her then, softer than the first and followed by a stealthy, waiting silence, as if someone somewhere in the house stood listening for her.

It was dark in her room, but Claire didn't turn on the light. Instead, she picked up the phone and lifted it to her ear. Then almost immediately lowered it. Was she really going to call 911? What if her mother had gone downstairs for some reason? What if the police responded to Claire's call, only to discover Lucille in the kitchen having a midnight snack?

Besides, Claire didn't want word of a distress call getting back to Alex. He'd rush over, thinking that he had to protect her, and another argument would ensue. She wasn't up to dealing with that tonight.

Sliding open the nightstand drawer, she pulled out the pistol that Dave had given her years ago after she'd been mugged on Canal Street. She'd never liked having a gun in the house, especially after Ruby came along, and she'd always meant to get rid of the thing. But now there it was, loaded and ready, a comforting weight in her hand as she disengaged the safety.

Rising, Claire walked quietly to the door and drew it open. Lightning flashed in the window behind her and a clap of thunder caused her to jump as she slipped into the corridor. She walked down the hall to the spare bedroom and opened the door a crack.

Her mother lay on her back, one arm flung over her face, and Claire could hear her soft snores. Closing the door, she turned and crept toward the stairs, holding the gun in her right hand, barrel pointed upward, as she pressed herself against the wall. Her heart hammered in her chest as she waited at the top of the stairs for an adrenaline rush that would give her enough courage to go downstairs and explore.

It never came. Claire counted to ten, then reached for the banister and slowly descended, certain with every step that someone would jump out of the darkness and grab her.

By the time she reached the bottom, her hand shook so hard she could barely grip the weapon. She couldn't allow fear to make her careless. If she didn't get her nerves under control, the gun would be more of a danger to her than to an intruder. He could easily overpower her, take the weapon away from her and use it on her and her mother.

As quietly as she could, Claire began to search the house. The living room was clear, as was the kitchen, dining room and hall closet. That left the small, glassed-in space off the living room that Claire had recently turned into a sunroom. The French doors were closed, but Claire could see into the room through the panels of leaded glass.

As she pulled back one of the doors, a wet draft blew in from an open window. The breeze caught the curtain and dragged it across a nearby table, drawing Claire's gaze to a shattered vase on the tile floor.

"Claire?"

The light came on in the room behind her and she whirled. "Mama? I thought you were asleep!"

"I was, but the storm woke me up." Lucille padded across the room. "Why are you prowling around in the dark with a gun?" She sounded more curious than upset.

"It's nothing. I heard something and came down to investigate. I think the wind must have knocked over a vase." Claire felt a bit foolish as she dropped the gun to her side. "You were in here smoking earlier. Did you leave the window open?"

Lucille rubbed her arm as she stared at the shattered vase. "I guess I must have. Damn, if I'm not getting forgetful in my old age…"

"No harm done. I'll clean up the glass in the morning."

Claire went over to close the window, and stood listening to the rain run off the roof and gutters, and splash against the front porch as she stared into the soggy darkness. A car was parked down the street, and as lightning flared, she saw a man behind the wheel. She couldn't see his face clearly, but for a moment it seemed that he was sitting there watching her house.

"Claire, what's wrong?"

"Nothing, Mama."

She closed the window and locked it, then turned to follow her mother out of the room.

A moment later, she was back, staring at the table by the window. A picture of Ruby was missing.

The Dollmaker hugged the picture frame to his chest as he listened to the rain drum against the roof of his car. The windows had fogged in the humidity and the interior became as dark as a closet. A familiar fear crept over him and he quickly rolled down the glass, letting the cool rain splash away his panic as he watched the house.

The lights were off, and he wondered if she'd gone back to bed. He was tempted to get out of the car and go find out, but she'd be alert now and he didn't want to create a situation that might force his hand. It was too soon for her to see him.

In a flash of lightning, he peered lovingly at the photograph. He shouldn't have taken it. She would miss it sooner or later, but it was so much like the one he'd lost, he hadn't been able to resist. And when he'd found the open window and crawled through, that photograph was the first thing he saw.

As if it was meant to be.

Even so, he never should have come back here. Not so soon. Someone was bound to remember a strange vehicle in the neighborhood. But that one glimpse of her as she'd stood silhouetted in the window made the risk worthwhile. For a moment, he could have sworn their gazes locked in the rainy darkness, and his heart had raced with excitement. He wondered if she felt it, too. That timeless bond that had drawn him back here almost against his will.

Ever since he'd seen her peering through the window in the collectibles shop earlier that day, he couldn't stop thinking about her. When he first heard her knock on the door, he'd tried to ignore her, hoping that she would go away and leave him to search for the photograph he'd left behind. But instead she nearly caught him when she came through the back way. He hadn't expected that. He'd barely had time to hide in the shadows before she stepped through the door.

At first he couldn't understand why fate had brought her to the shop at such an inopportune moment. But as he watched her move about the crowded space, peering into one display case after another, his apprehension faded and he became mesmerized by her gentle grace.

And then she'd turned in such a way that a shaft of light from the window fell across her face. He saw her eyes clearly for the first time, and the shock had been so great, he'd taken a step toward her without thinking. The beaded curtain stirred between them and he knew that she could sense his presence.

Somehow he'd managed to get out of the shop without being seen, and he'd waited for her in the courtyard. When she walked over to pick up the orchid, she was so near he could have reached through the rungs of the iron fence to touch her. His heart had beaten hard and swift against his chest as his eyes filled with tears, because by then he'd understood.

He told himself to go home, go to work, do whatever he had to do to get his mind off her. But instead he'd followed her home, and as he pulled to the curb a few blocks down from her driveway, he'd experienced an overwhelming sense of déjà vu. Because he knew her house. Her street. He'd been there before.

But the other time he'd come for the child.

He ran his thumb across the glass that covered the photograph, stroking the delicate features that were as familiar to him as his own. He could still see that afternoon unfold as if it were yesterday. That sweet, lovely child racing toward him on a shiny new bicycle. A cloud of golden curls streaming behind her. And those turquoise eyes…

Eyes the exact shade of Maddy's…

And his mother's…

His heart had raced with excitement that day, too, as he got out of the car and called the child's name.

She brought the bicycle to a halt as her eyes squinted in the late afternoon sunlight filtering through the trees. "How do you know my name?"

"I'm a friend of your grandmother's."

"You know Maw-Maw?"

"Her name is Lucille, right? She sent you a present. Would you like to see it?"

The child's face was very expressive, and he could see her natural curiosity warring with her common sense and the warnings she'd surely received all her short life.

He smiled. The child could hardly contain herself. She had a natural exuberance and a mischievous glint in her eyes that he found utterly captivating. He was so enchanted that he could have watched her for hours. But that would have to come later.

She bent to scratch a mosquito bite at the back of her knee. "My birthday was yesterday. Maw-Maw already gave me a present."

"I bet she made you that pretty dress you're wearing, didn't she?"

Her eyes turned suspicious. "How did you know?"

"Because I know lots of interesting things about you, Ruby. Don't you want to see your other present?"

She hesitated, glancing behind her down the street. Then her gaze came slowly back to his. "Show it to me from there."

He nodded and opened the back door of his car, lifting the doll with curly blond hair and turquoise eyes from a white box. She resembled the little girl on the bike, but she wasn't an exact match. Not yet.

"Do you like dolls, Ruby?" he asked over his shoulder.

"I like Maw-Maw's dolls. She has thousands and thousands. Maybe even more. Sometimes she makes her own dolls."

"Yes, I know. She and I took some classes together.

But even your grandmother doesn't have a doll like this one." He straightened and turned so that the child could see what he held in his hands.

She was instantly charmed. "She looks like me!"

"That's because I made her from a photograph your grandmother gave me. She's not quite finished, though." He held the doll out to her. "Do you like her?"

The child nodded, her smile as dazzling as the sunlight.

"Come take a closer look then."

She was still torn with indecision. She turned again to search the street behind her. "I have to go home and ask Mama first."

"Why not take the doll with you? I bet your mother would love to see her. Here, let me help you...."

It happened so quickly that no one on the quiet street saw or heard anything. They never did. Not even in this day and age when people told themselves they were on guard for such things. But he was very good at what he did. And the little girls who came to his attention all had one thing in common.

They loved dolls. Almost as much as he did.

The memory drifted away and his eyes misted as he watched the house through the rain. His mother had once loved dolls, too. He wondered if she still did.

Twelve

The lawn sprinklers along St. Charles Avenue were already twitching as Claire drove in to work early the next morning. Live oaks stood like brooding sentinels at the edge of the street, their dense, spreading limbs a cool green ceiling overhead. Orange and red hibiscus lined cobblestone walkways, while climbing roses spilled over cast-iron gates, and brick walls encased magnolia trees, ginger and thick clumps of oleander.

The summer gardens were in full bloom, and the ravages from Katrina that lingered in other parts of the city were nearly invisible here. One had to be a native or an expert to notice the diminished tree canopy or the scars from severed limbs left by the chainsaws.

Claire and her mother and sister had evacuated to a cousin's house in Shreveport before the flood, and when the first reports of the compromised levees came over the news, they'd listened in horror and disbelief to the accounts of whitecaps on Canal Street. Lucille had kept wringing her hands and saying over and over that it couldn't be that bad. It just couldn't.

Weeks later, when they were finally allowed back into the city, they'd found the magnitude of the destruction overwhelming. Entire neighborhoods destroyed. Streets piled high with debris, flooded cars and uprooted trees. Doors on almost every house marked with a spray-painted X, a date, the search unit and the number of casualties found inside the building.

Claire's family had been luckier than most. Her old Uptown house and her mother's home in Faubourg Marigny had been virtually untouched by wind or water, and Charlotte's loft in the Warehouse District had suffered only broken windowpanes and minor roof damage. Despite the lack of utilities and city services, they'd moved back home as soon as possible, determined to help with the cleanup and get on with their lives. But the devastation wreaked by the storm would live on long after the physical evidence had been swept away. Decades later, when people sat out on their porches watching dusk settle over the city, the memories would still come creeping back, Claire imagined, and a soft breeze from the Gulf would always bring with it a renewed sense of foreboding.

But she didn't want to think of the past this morning, not of the storm and not of her own personal tragedy. She was anxious to get to the studio early and put in some time at her bench before the gallery opened at ten. Work had always been her salvation, and now she looked forward to having her mind occupied by something other than the doll. At least until Mignon Bujold returned on Tuesday.

And then what? Claire wondered uneasily. What would come of finding that doll? The discovery might lead to nothing, but it wasn't in her to give up. She'd waited too many years for even one small clue, and now she had two. The doll…and the missing photograph of Ruby.

After going back up to bed last night, Claire had lain awake for a long time, listening to the storm move off to the west as she tried to convince herself that she'd put the photograph away and forgotten it. She even got up and searched through her picture drawer, but it wasn't there.

Claire had no idea when or why the photo of Ruby had vanished, but she had the strangest feeling it was somehow connected to the doll. And the notion that someone might still be obsessed with her daughter after all these years sent an icy chill up her spine.

Saturdays were always busy in the gallery, and Claire spent most of the day on her feet. During lulls between customers, she stayed busy packing shipments, and late that afternoon she conducted a large tour of the hot studio, where the tourists were able to watch Ansel Ready, a master craftsman who had been blowing glass for more than forty years, go through the process step-by-step.

Afterward, when Claire led the group back into the gallery, she mingled with the out-of-towners, chit-chatting about the studio, the artists and about individual pieces that had aroused someone's curiosity. She rang up their purchases, and as the last of the tour slowly filed back out into the street, she hoped to finally have a moment to catch her breath.

But long after everyone else had cleared out, a woman in a flowing skirt and dangly earrings lingered in the showroom, her gaze fixed on a display case that featured some of Claire's pieces. Claire had noticed the woman earlier on the tour, deciding something about her demeanor had seemed a bit odd. Instead of interacting with anyone in the noisy, enthusiastic group, she'd hovered at the back, isolating herself as if she didn't quite belong.

However, she'd seemed intensely focused on the tour. Every time Claire looked up, the woman's gaze was on her. Claire had never had anyone hang on to her every word the way this woman seemed to, and after a while, the undivided attention became a little unsettling.

Claire pretended to work at the register, but her gaze kept straying to the woman. She wore a thick matte foundation on her face, and her eyes were rimmed in black kohl. But even through the heavy makeup, Claire found the woman's features strangely arresting.

She looked up, caught Claire staring and smiled.

Claire shivered and suddenly she knew why the woman's appearance was so striking. Her colorless face was reminiscent of a mannequin's or a doll's. Beautiful to look at, but not quite real. She had no emotion in her eyes, no expression in her features. And when she smiled, only her lips moved.

Taking one of Claire's pieces from the display shelf, she approached the counter. "I've decided I can't live without this," she said. Her fingers around the rippled bowl were long and tapered, and she didn't wear any rings.

As much as Claire needed the money, she had a funny feeling about the purchase, as if the woman had chosen the piece not for its beauty but because of its creator. But Claire didn't know why that would be.

Her name was not on the bowl, so this stranger couldn't know it was one of her creations.

She watched as Claire carefully wrapped the fragile glass in layers of old newspaper. "I can't help noticing the bandage on your hand," the woman said. "Do you need some help?"

"Thanks, but I can manage."

The woman's eyes held a curious glint. "I'm sorry. I know it's rude to stare, but…do I know you?"

"I don't think so," Claire said. "Although I've lived in New Orleans all my life. I suppose it's possible our paths have crossed."

"That must be it."

The woman paid for the piece in cash, and as she waited for her change, she gave Claire a hesitant smile. "I think I know why you look so familiar. It's your eyes. They're turquoise, yes? A very unusual color, but I once knew someone with eyes the exact same shade."

Claire murmured a response as the woman put away her change. Then she picked up the package from the counter and left the gallery.

Even after she was gone, Claire remained uneasy. She went over to the window to watch until the woman was out of sight, telling herself all the while that she was just tired and on edge. The past few days had been trying. The doll, the accident and the missing picture of Ruby. Any one of those incidents would have been unnerving, but to have all three occur at once was overwhelming.

Claire thought again of her grandmother, who'd always claimed that bad things came in threes. Charlotte would say that Claire was letting her imagination get the better of her. And maybe she was. But ever since she'd spotted the doll in the shop window, she couldn't shake the notion that a door to the past had been opened.

A door that might lead her someplace she had no wish to go.

At a little after five, Claire locked the front door to the gallery, then closed out the register and secured the day's receipts in the vault. After tidying up the showroom and display shelves, she walked back through the studio. The other glassblowers had already gone home, but Ansel Ready was still busy at his bench, and Claire stopped to watch him for a moment as he separated a striated bronze jar from a punty rod attached to the bottom of the glass.

"You always make that look so easy," she said.

"When you've been doing it as long as I have, it should be easy." He was a small, pleasant-looking man with a ruddy complexion and long, straight hair pulled back in a ponytail. Sweat glistened on his brow as he carefully dropped the jar onto the insulated knock-off table and then set the punty rod aside. Pulling on Kevlar gloves, he placed the piece inside the annealer, an electric oven that would keep the glass from cooling too quickly. After a few hours, the control system would slowly decrease the temperature to keep the object from shattering.

Sealing the oven door, he came back over to his bench and removed the gloves. "What's on your mind, Claire?"

"Does something have to be on my mind for me to appreciate your work?"

He put away the jacks he'd been using to open up

the lip of the jar. "You've been here, what? Almost seven years now, isn't it? Even since you took your first class from me. I think I know you pretty well. And don't forget I raised four daughters. I can tell when a woman is troubled about something."

"I'm not really troubled," Claire said. "I just wondered if you happened to notice someone in the tour group this afternoon. She was blond, thin, had on one of those long, flowy skirts."

"Kept to the back of the crowd?"

Claire nodded. "Did she seem at all familiar to you, Ansel?"

"If it's the same woman I'm thinking of, it was hard to tell what she looked like through all that makeup. I thought she had a mask on at first. Why?"

"I don't know. I can't explain it, but I have a feeling that I know her from somewhere. Or maybe that she knows me somehow. Does that make sense?"

"A lot of people come into the gallery. Maybe she's been in before."

"I don't think that's it."

Ansel grew all fatherly, his brow puckering in concern. "Did she say something to upset you?"

"No. It wasn't anything that she said or did. It wasn't even the way she looked. There was just something kind of strange about her."

"I wouldn't worry too much about it. This is New Orleans. Strange is normal for us." He nodded toward Claire's bandaged palm. "You just worry about taking care of that hand. It's mighty lonely back here without you at your bench."

"You still have Esther," Claire teased, referring to one of the other glassblowers, who had been trying to get Ansel's attention for years. Despite Ansel's dogged indifference, Esther Stark was not a woman who discouraged easily.

He merely grunted as he started to clean up around his workbench. Claire said good-night and left through the back entrance. The afternoon was warm and balmy, and at five-thirty, hours of daylight remained. She fished in her purse for her car keys, and as she glanced up, she saw a man standing in the narrow alley that ran between two neighboring buildings. She couldn't see him clearly, and experience told her that he was probably one of the city's homeless, but he seemed familiar somehow.

Claire had always felt relatively safe in the American District, but she'd lived in New Orleans all her life and knew enough not to let down her guard, no matter the area. As she hurried toward her car, she kept her eyes on the man in the alley. He didn't try to approach her, but stood back in the shadows so that she couldn't see his face.

Claire had the uneasy feeling that he was watching her, and as she opened the door and slid behind the wheel, she glanced back to keep an eye on him. But he'd already disappeared.

Thirteen

———◦⟨○⟩◦———

Sunlight danced like perch off the muddy surface of the Mississippi River as Dave drove across the Huey Long Bridge late that afternoon. He was headed into New Orleans to see JoJo Barone, the owner of the strip joint on Bourbon Street where both Nina Losier and Renee Savaria had worked. When Dave walked into the Gold Medallion a little while later, the bartender glanced up and gave him a lazy salute. He was about Dave's age, tall and lean, with bad teeth and dishwater-blond hair that fell in greasy hanks around his face.

At this time of day, the front of the bar was empty and the daylight that streamed in through the open doorway didn't quite penetrate the darker recesses of the club, where a handful of customers sat grouped around the runway watching an early floor show.

Dave walked over to the bar and sat down. "Is JoJo around?"

The bartender tipped his head toward the back of the club. "He's in his office."

"Can you tell him Dave Creasy would like to see him?"

The man scratched the mushroom cloud on his Megadeth T-shirt. "Yeah, thing is, JoJo don't like to be disturbed when he's going over the books. He'll probably be at it for another hour or two, so you might as well relax and enjoy the show. What can I get you to drink?"

"I'll take a Coke."

"You sure? It'll cost the same with or without the bourbon."

"Just the Coke."

Dave glanced toward the back, where a group of middle-aged businessmen sat with loosened ties and smoldering cigarettes, watching a redhead in a green G-string pole-dance to the hip-hop beat blasting from the sound system. A mirrored ball rotating overhead threw prisms of light on the walls and ceiling, and reflected off the crystal in the dancer's belly button. She curled a leg around the pole and slid slowly up and down the slick surface, eyes closed, head thrown back. Then, grasping the pole with both hands, she lifted herself until she hung suspended with her head only a few inches from the floor, and slowly opened her legs. A drunken college boy seated with his buddy at the end of the runway let out a loud rebel yell as he waved a fistful of bills at the dancer.

The bartender poured Dave a Coke and stuck in a spear of cherries. "No extra charge." He grinned and slid the glass across the bar.

Dave took out the cherries and put them on the napkin.

The bartender was still grinning. "You don't remember me, do you?"

"Should I?"

"Carver High School. Senior year. You split open my lip with your class ring. We both got suspended for fighting and almost didn't graduate. I still got the scar, see?" He tapped a finger against his lower lip, where a thin, raised line snaked halfway down his chin.

Dave narrowed his eyes. "Bobby Ray Taubin, right?"

"I go by Robert these days." He stuck his hand across the bar. "How the hell have you been?"

Dave shook his hand and shrugged. "So what were we fighting about?"

"Damned if I remember. Some lil ol' girl, probably. Seems like you and me share the same taste in women." He nodded toward the redhead on stage. "Not bad, huh? You want a piece of that action, I'm the guy who can hook you up."

"Thanks. I'm just here to see JoJo."

"Change your mind, let me know," he said. His eyes were dark and beady, and they shifted back and forth as he talked.

Dave sipped his Coke. "How long have you worked for JoJo?"

The bartender grabbed up a dish towel and started wiping down the counter. "Off and on for a couple of years. Ever since I got out of Angola." He threw the towel over his shoulder as he waited for Dave's reaction.

"What were you in for?"

"Liquor store holdup. The guy behind the register tried to stop me. Dude looked like he'd been put through a sausage grinder when I got through with him, but he was still coming at me when the cops got there." Taubin laughed and went back to polishing the bar. "I guess I almost killed the little bastard, but I wasn't thinking too straight back then. Had too much glass in my system. I came out of the joint clean and sober, but you won't find too many people willing to take a chance on a guy with a record like mine. JoJo was the only one who'd hire me, so I've got a soft spot for the old coot."

"Meaning?"

The bartender stuck a toothpick in his mouth as he leaned an arm on the bar. His eyes darted back and forth as he stared Dave in the face. "JoJo's got enough problems these days without the law breathing down his neck."

"I'm not a cop," Dave said.

"Then why are you here? You don't drink, you don't watch the show. I gotta think a man like you has an agenda." He moved slightly so that Dave could see the baseball bat on the shelf behind him.

"I'm not here to start any trouble. I just want to ask JoJo a few questions."

"About what?"

"That's between him and me."

"Is that right?" The bartender flicked the toothpick toward the trash. "Like I said, he'll be out in a little while. He may give you a few minutes of his time and he may not. But a word of advice, chief. I'll be right here the whole time just itching for a chance to even an old score."

Dave threw some bills on the bar as he stood. "I tell you what, Bobby Ray. You just keep right on convincing yourself you're ready to rock and roll, and when I come back, you let me know if you still want to even that score."

* * *

To kill some time, Dave walked back to Decatur and picked up a muffuletta and an icy bottle of water from the Central Grocery. Then he carried his early dinner into the square and found an empty bench in the shade.

Angelette had suggested he drop by the Hotel Monteleone later that night to meet Graydon Losier, the murdered girl's father, but Dave wanted a chance to talk to JoJo first. He'd gone over the case file several times and read through all the statements. Nina Losier had been brutally beaten, her body rolled out of a car onto the wide neutral ground on Esplanade Avenue, where she was found early the next morning.

The neighborhood had been canvassed for eyewitnesses, her friends, family and the people she worked with were interviewed, and her boyfriend, Jimmy Caisson, brought in for questioning. Caisson had a history of violence, particularly against women, but when he'd produced an alibi for the night of Nina's murder, the investigation had hit a wall.

The only angle Dave could find that hadn't been exhausted by the police was the possible connection to Renee Savaria's murder. Both women had worked at the Gold Medallion, but the murders had occurred seven years apart. The lead was a slim one at best, and probably wouldn't amount to anything more than wishful thinking on Dave's part that he could finally put some closure to one of the darkest chapters of his life. The Savaria case was a black mark against a career he'd otherwise been proud of, and what he'd done in a time of desperation still ate at him.

It wasn't that his record had been spotless before the Savaria case. Like a lot of other cops he knew, he'd

taken some liberties in the name of justice. But he'd
loved his job and believed in what he was doing. He'd
never thought of himself as the type of cop who could
be coerced or bribed, but Ruby's kidnapping had
changed everything. She'd been missing for nearly
forty-eight hours when he got the first call.

*"Don't say anything, Detective Creasy, just listen.
I know your place is crawling with cops, so if you want
your daughter back in one piece, you'll go someplace
more private. I'll call you back in ten minutes."*

Dave had been trembling by the time he hung up his
cell phone, but somehow he'd managed to keep the fear
from his face and voice as he muttered to Claire that
he needed some air. He'd walked two blocks over from
their apartment and sat down on the curb to wait for
the call. It came exactly ten minutes after the first.

"Where are you, Detective?"

"Outside. No one can hear me."

*"For your daughter's sake, I hope you're being
straight with me."*

Dave gripped the phone. *"Where is she? Let me
talk to her."*

*"She's asleep. You don't want me to wake her up,
do you? She's had a rough couple of days."*

"You son of a bitch. If you've hurt her—"

*"Save your threats, Detective. You're never going to
find me and we're wasting valuable time, so let's just
get down to business. You have something I want."*

The pounding in Dave's ears was so loud he couldn't
think straight. *"What are you talking about?"*

*"The morning before your daughter disappeared,
you had a meeting with Renee Savaria's roommate. She
gave you Renee's diary. If you ever want to see your*

daughter again, you'll do exactly as I say. One little de-
viation and she dies, is that clear?" The voice paused.
"And that would be a real shame, too, because she's
such a pretty little thing."

Dave had walked back home dripping with sweat as
he tried to figure out what to do. As he'd approached
the back gate, he saw a bloodstained hair ribbon draped
through the latch, and he knew that it had been left
there for him to find. The kidnapper had been close.
He'd probably been watching the whole time.

Dave had turned, scoured the area, as terrible
thoughts ran through his head. His little girl hurt, bleed-
ing, needing him to come for her and him not having
a clue where to look. Those thoughts had been his un-
doing, and by the time he received the next phone call,
he'd been ready to deal. He'd gone to the evidence
room, ripped out the last page of the diary and burned
it, just as the caller had instructed. And then he'd waited
for his daughter to come home.

A part of him suspected all along that he was being
played. He was a cop. He should have known better.
But he'd been so desperate and scared, so racked with
guilt, that he was willing to try anything to bring Ruby
safely home. But as days and then weeks went by with
hope ever dwindling, he'd come to the terrible realiza-
tion that Renee Savaria's murderer had used his daughter's kidnapping to manipulate him into destroying the
evidence. The cases weren't related at all. A cold-
blooded killer had simply taken advantage of a heart-
breaking situation.

Dave had never come clean about the missing diary
page. He could have gone on with his career with no one
the wiser, but he knew. And by the time he tendered his

resignation at the request of his superiors, destroying evidence in a homicide investigation had been only one of a dozen transgressions that had made him unfit to be a cop.

Renee Savaria's killer had never been caught and now another girl who'd worked at the Gold Medallion was dead. If Dave had done his job right seven years ago, Nina Losier might still be alive today.

Idly, he watched the sidewalk artists and fortune tellers lined up along Pirates Alley as he drank the cold water. Street musicians played Dixieland jazz from beneath the shade trees, while earnest young men in black pants and white shirts passed out pamphlets from a local mission. A breeze rippled through the banana trees, bringing the scent of the river and the whisper of memories, and Dave closed his eyes for a moment.

I like it here, Daddy. It's like a big party!

I like it here, too, Ruby. I wish you were with me right now.

He opened his eyes and blinked rapidly against the brightness as he watched a family of tourists stroll by. One of the little girls clutched a yellow balloon in a chubby fist, while clinging to her mother's hand with the other. She smiled shyly at Dave and turned her head to stare after him as she plodded along in her mom's wake.

Dave glanced away, not wanting to be pulled back into that dangerous nostalgia. Not here, where temptation lurked on every street corner. He loved the Quarter, but it was a place where a guy like him could get into a lot of trouble if he wasn't careful. The languid decadence that slithered along the narrow streets and beckoned from hidden courtyards spoke to a darkness that had resided in his soul for as long as he could remember.

He finished his sandwich and drink and threw the trash away, then headed back to Bourbon. The closed-off street teemed with tourists, some of whom seemed at once fascinated and repelled by what they glimpsed through the half-open doorways.

JoJo Barone waited for him in a back booth. He wore a beige linen jacket that hung limply from his stooped shoulders, and a black shirt open at the neck. An unfiltered Camel smoldered between his yellowed fingers as he stared up at Dave through the smoke.

One of Dave's uncles had died of lung cancer a few years back, and when Dave had gone to visit him in the hospital, he'd been so shocked by the man's appearance he'd barely been able to look at him. The uncle he remembered had been a big, burly man with a hearty appetite and a booming laugh, but the advanced stages of the disease had given him the skeletal face and emaciated body of a POW. JoJo Barone's sunken eyes and sallow complexion reminded Dave of his uncle.

"My barkeep tells me you were in earlier to see me," he rasped. "Do I know you?"

Dave slid onto the bench across from him. "We met seven years ago when NOPD fished one of your dancers out of the river. Her name was Renee Savaria. Ring any bells?" Before he could answer, Dave said, "Seems like your girls have a bad habit of turning up dead, JoJo."

The man watched Dave through the curling smoke. "Now I remember you. Detective Creasy, right? Took me a minute to place you. You look different than you did back then."

"A lot can happen to a guy in seven years."

"I hear that." Light sparked off a heavy gold ring on JoJo's pinky as he tipped ashes into an overflowing ashtray at his elbow. "So what can I do for you, Detective?"

"You can forget the detective part. I left the department a few years ago."

"What are you doing here, then? Something tells me you didn't come in to see the floor show."

"I'd like to ask you some questions about Nina Losier's murder."

"In what capacity? You just said you're not a cop anymore."

"Call me a friend of the family."

"No offense, Detective—"

"Dave."

"You don't look like the type of guy Graydon Losier would hire to wipe his ass, let alone invite to a Saturday soiree." JoJo took a long drag on his cigarette and turned his head to cough out the smoke. He put a handkerchief to his mouth until the hacking fit was over, and when he brought it away, Dave saw spots of blood on the white linen.

JoJo tucked the handkerchief back into his pocket and acted as if nothing had happened. "But let's say you are working for her old man. I still don't get what you're doing here. The cops already know who killed Nina."

"That's news to me," Dave said. "Last I heard, they hadn't made an arrest yet."

"Don't mean they don't know who killed her. You want a name, all you gotta do is pick up a phone and call one of your old buddies down at the station."

"I'd rather you tell me."

JoJo motioned to a passing waitress, and a few seconds later, she brought him over a drink and a fresh Coke for Dave. He could smell the whiskey in the glass and pushed it away.

"If something's wrong with your drink, I'll have my girl bring you something else."

"The drink is fine. I'm just not thirsty."

JoJo smiled for the first time. "Now that surprises me. I had you pegged for a drinking man." He gestured with his cigarette. "Something about the eyes. They always give away a man's vices." He lit a fresh cigarette from the butt in his hand. "Let me ask you something, Dave. You ever wish you could go back in time? Maybe to just one specific moment when a decision you made changed the entire course of your life?"

"All the time," Dave said.

"Lately, I find myself thinking about the summer of '62. That's when my older brother gave me my first smoke. I was eleven years old. He stood there laughing his ass off while I puked up my guts behind the smokehouse. So I decided to show him what a big man I was, and for the past forty-five years, I haven't gone more than an hour or two at a time without a cigarette in my hand. Except maybe when I'm sleeping."

"What is it? Lung cancer?"

JoJo's gray eyes showed surprise. "Most people assume emphysema. How'd you know?"

"I had an uncle who had it. I recognize the symptoms."

"Helluva a way to go, from what I hear."

"I can think of a few worse," Dave said. "At least

you made it this far. That's more of a shot than Nina Losier got."

"I didn't have anything to do with that girl's death. You're wasting my time and yours if you think I did. Like I said, the cops already know who killed her."

"And I'm still waiting for you to tell me."

JoJo propped his elbows on the table and cupped one hand over the other. "Ever hear of a little cockroach named Jimmy Caisson?"

"Nina's boyfriend?"

"He's the kind of guy that likes to smack around his women. Puts a real tingle in his joystick, I reckon. You know the type. Beats the shit out of the old lady on Saturday night, then comes crawling back on hands and knees a couple days later begging for another chance. This time Jimmy got one too many chances."

"There's a problem with your theory, JoJo. Jimmy Caisson has an airtight alibi. At least a dozen witnesses can place him in a Biloxi casino on the night Nina was murdered."

"Yeah, that's what I hear. Interesting thing about that alibi, though. Jimmy has a cousin who looks enough like him to pass for his twin. They came in here together one night, I couldn't tell the two assholes apart. And I've known Jimmy since he was knee-high to a piss ant. If those witnesses saw the cousin in that casino instead of Jimmy, it'd kind of blow a hole in his story, wouldn't it?"

"You told the police about this cousin?"

"They know. What I still can't figure out is why you're here."

Dave was starting to wonder the same thing himself. If the police were in the process of breaking Jimmy's alibi, why would Graydon Losier feel the need to hire a P.I.? And why had Angelette brought the case to Dave?

Easy answer. She was after something.

"All right, let's say Jimmy Caisson did kill Nina. Let's say the police can eventually prove it," Dave said. "That still leaves Renee Savaria."

The cigarette continued to smolder in JoJo's hand. "Ancient history."

"Not to her family. Not to me, either."

JoJo shrugged. "You got a guilty conscience about something, go talk to a priest. Leave me out of it."

"Have you ever been to an AA meeting, JoJo?"

"No, why?"

"One of the steps to recovery is to admit to God, to ourselves and to another human being the exact nature of our wrongs. Seven years ago, I destroyed evidence that may have allowed Renee Savaria's killer to go free. You're the only person I've ever admitted that to."

"What am I supposed to do? Applaud or something?"

"No, you just get to sit there and hear me out. A couple of days before my daughter was kidnapped, Renee's roommate gave me Renee's diary. Some of the last notations were a set of initials and an address on Chef Menteur Highway. The location was one of your old massage parlors, JoJo. She went out there to meet someone, didn't she?"

"Maybe she did, maybe she didn't. Seven years is a long time, and my memory's not what it used to be."

"Think hard," Dave said. "Because whoever Renee met that night turned out to be her killer. I'd put money on it. And then he used my daughter's kidnapping to coerce me into destroying evidence that could have incriminated him."

"You can't prove any of that."

"No, but I bet you can. I always suspected you were holding out on me, JoJo. I think you still are. You've been protecting Renee's killer all these years, but a guy in your condition has to ask himself, what's the point? Why not come clean while you still have the chance?"

"You think where I'm going one little confession is going to make any difference?"

Dave shrugged. "Couldn't hurt."

JoJo's hands were steady and his eyes never flinched, but Dave could see a thin film of sweat glistening above his lip. "You really believe all that bullshit they teach in Sunday school?"

"Yeah, I do."

JoJo took another long pull on his cigarette, then stabbed out the butt in the ashtray. He was silent for a moment as his gaze strayed to the runway, where a blonde who looked no more than eighteen danced in nothing but sequins and stilettos.

"There was this guy. He used to come in here a couple times a week. Big fucker with a scar all the way down the side of his face." JoJo traced a finger along his jawline. "He had a thing for Renee. He used to set up these private parties for him and his friends, and he always made sure she was one of the girls I sent out."

"What was his name?"

JoJo took out another cigarette, but didn't light up. Instead he tapped the end against his hand. "You sure you want to take the lid off this crap hole? It may be old shit down there, but you start digging around, it's still gonna stink. And nothing you do will bring that girl back."

"It won't bring her back, but maybe it'll finally give her family some peace. They've had to live with the knowledge that Renee's killer has gone free all these years. They need justice for their dead daughter and I need to make things right. I think you do, too."

JoJo stared out at the crowd, then slowly ran his gaze back to Dave. "Does the name Clive Nettle mean anything to you?"

A memory clicked and a cold wave of dread washed over Dave. "He's a cop."

"Yeah, that's right. They were all cops at those parties, and some of them wore some pretty heavy-metal brass on their chests. And for obvious reasons, they were mighty particular about who they let in."

"Who are we talking about, JoJo? Give me some names."

He took a sip of his drink. Condensation ran off the bottom of the glass and dripped onto the tabletop. "I can't give you any names. Nettle was the only one I ever had any dealings with. He always made the arrangements, sometimes for cash, sometimes in exchange for looking the other way if my liquor license wasn't exactly in order."

"Where did these parties take place?"

"Motel rooms, mostly. One or two times at an old farmhouse off the highway. Somebody I used to know owned it."

"What about your massage parlors?"

"If the money was right."

"Was the money right the night Renee was murdered?"

JoJo licked his lips. "Put it this way. An offer was made I couldn't refuse."

"What happened?"

"Nettle wanted more than a lap dance that night and things got a little rough. When Renee fought back, he lost control. Most of the brass ran for the bushes when the screaming started, but a couple of the cops stayed behind to clean up the mess. They hustled me out of my own joint, and the next thing I know, Renee's being fished out of the drink."

"And you just kept your mouth shut."

His eyes met Dave's across the table. "What was I supposed to do? I open my trap, next thing I know some trigger-happy cop is outside my back door with a sawed-off shotgun pressed against my temple." He gestured with the unlit cigarette. "Besides, those bastards had it all figured out. It'd be their word against mine. And anyway, who'd give a shit about a dead stripper? Girls like Renee are a dime a dozen in this town. In a week's time, nobody would've even remembered her name. But then you got put on the case, and you didn't go looking for the easy answer. You kept digging and digging until that diary turned up. If somebody hadn't gone and snatched your little girl, they would've found another way to stop you."

Dave's hands clenched into fists underneath the table. "Was Nettle the one who made those calls to me?"

"He never struck me as the type of guy who could think too fast on his feet."

"Then who did?"

JoJo shrugged. "I've told you everything I know. We're squared now, right?"

"As far as I'm concerned we are." Dave struck a match and lit JoJo's cigarette, then shook out the flame. "But my absolution isn't exactly the one you need to worry about, JoJo."

Fourteen

Dave walked back to his truck, but instead of climbing in, he headed down Decatur to a little corner restaurant named Dessie's.

Odessa Birdsong was known city-wide for her fried chicken, smothered pork chops and dirty rice, but it wasn't the menu that drew Dave to her place that day. He and Dessie's son, Titus, had once been partners, and Dave still remembered some of Titus's old habits. Every day as soon as his watch ended, he'd stop by the restaurant to check on his aging mother. Sometimes he'd stick around and help out if she needed him; other days he'd take off after only a few minutes. But he never failed to go by and see her. Dave figured this would be a good time of day to catch him there, though the way their partnership had ended, he wasn't so sure Titus would want to see him.

Someone had painted Dessie's name in bright green letters across the plate glass window and replaced the apostrophe with a smiling red crawfish. As Dave pushed open the door, the scent of frying meat engulfed him. The place was small, with a wall of booths on one side and a few rickety tables jammed together in the center. Ancient wooden fans stirred a perpetual cloud of grease smoke that hovered near the tin ceiling, and Dave could hear a radio playing somewhere in the back.

He glanced around. At lunchtime the place always had a line out the door, but now the only patrons were two elderly black men seated in one of the booths eating catfish and hush puppies, and a younger man at a table by the window, with a bucket of crawfish and a layer of newspaper spread in front of him. They all glanced up when Dave walked in, then went right back to their meals.

The girl who stood behind the register looked to be about fifteen or sixteen. She was slim and beautiful, with a cloud of wiry curls brushing her shoulders and a complexion the color of milk chocolate. She'd been reading a magazine, but greeted Dave with a bored smile.

He didn't recognize her at first. Last time he'd seen Titus's youngest daughter, she'd been a little kid, only a year or so older than Ruby, and now here she was, all grown up. Dave's chest tightened as he smiled back at her.

She tucked a bunch of stray curls behind one ear. "You want a table?"

"I was hoping I might catch your dad here. You're Melaswane, aren't you? Titus's youngest?"

"Depends on who's asking," she drawled, and propped an elbow on the counter.

Dave couldn't help smiling again. "You don't remember me?"

"Nope."

"I'm Dave. I used to work with your dad. We were partners once."

She shrugged, as if the name meant less than nothing to her.

"Is Titus around?"

She traced a lazy pattern on the counter with her fingertip. "He's in the kitchen pinching crawfish with Gran'maman."

"Do you think you could go back there and tell him I'm here to see him?"

"I guess." She got up from the stool she'd been perched on, and as she pushed open the kitchen door, another cloud of smoke wafted out. "Daddy! There's some man out here wants to see you."

Dave could hear loud talking in the back and then Melaswane said petulantly, "I don't know. Dave or somebody."

The door closed behind her as she stepped into the kitchen, and a few moments later Titus came out, wiping his hands on the stained butcher's apron he wore.

He paused with his shoulder against the door. "Well, I'll be damned."

At fifty-five, Titus Birdsong was still an impressive-looking man. He stood at least six-three, with broad shoulders, bulging forearms and fists the size of small hams. Ten years ago, when Dave moved into Homicide, Titus had already been a legend. One of only two black detectives in a division of twenty-four, he'd been about as welcome as a fur coat at a PETA rally in the early days of his career. He'd had to contend with slashed tires and racial slurs, and someone had even stuffed dog feces in his desk drawer one time. But eventually his outstanding arrest record got noticed by the brass, and he became one of the hottest detectives in the department to watch. In time, he'd even managed to win over most—but not all—of his colleagues with his old-fashioned courtesy and good humor.

By the time Dave came along, Titus had already burned himself out. His passion and drive for the job was a thing of the past, but Dave had never really minded his partner's low-key approach to their investigations. Titus's ego was also a thing of the past, and Dave had learned a lot from the older detective. But more than that, he liked and respected Titus as a person. Their amiable working relationship had forged a strong bond between the two men, and now Dave felt a twinge of guilt that he'd been the one to betray their friendship.

He walked over to the counter and sat down. "Long time no see."

Titus let the door swing closed behind him. "You up and disappear for God knows how long and you got nuthin' else to say for yourself?"

"The last few years have been pretty rough," Dave said. "I wasn't exactly in a sociable mood. And all that flack you caught from the crap I pulled before I left…I didn't want to cause you any more grief."

"Then why you come here now?"

"I need your help with something."

Titus cocked his head. "Now, don't that just beat all?" But in spite of the disdain dripping from his voice, a glint of curiosity appeared in his green eyes, and Dave knew he had him hooked.

"Have you got a few minutes? This won't take long."

"Grab yourself a cold drink and go on outside. It's

cooler out there than it is in here. I'll be out directly, soon as I get the crawdad juice washed off my hands."

He disappeared back into the kitchen, and Dave walked over to the old soft drink cooler near the register and took out an icy Coke. Then he went out the side door and down the steps to the patio, which was just a small pad of cracked concrete shaded by a live oak. The sun was starting to dip, and the light that drifted down through the branches shimmered like specks of gold across the tabletop. A breeze ruffled the elephant ears that grew along the wooden fence, and the scent of barbecuing meat hung heavy and succulent on the afternoon heat.

Dave sat down in the shade to wait for Titus. He came out a few minutes later with water droplets still clinging to his thick, graying hair. He'd put on a fresh shirt and the cotton looked as stiff as a cardboard box. His wife, Addie, had always had a thing about starch. Titus used to say his shirts were so rigid they were like wearing straitjackets. Dave always wondered if Titus's laundry was somehow a metaphor for his marriage.

He sat down across from Dave at the picnic table, his gaze dropping to the Coke. "Got some longnecks over there in an ice chest."

"I'm sticking with soda these days."

Titus squinted against the splashes of sunlight. "How's that working out for you?"

"Some days better than others," Dave said.

"You mind if I have a cold one?"

"Knock yourself out."

Titus got up and went over to the cooler at the bottom of the steps. The bottle he removed from the chipped ice looked cold and dark, and when he unscrewed the cap, a breath of frost rose up from the neck. "I still ain't believing you're here," he said as he came back to the table. "I thought sure you'd be catfish bait by now."

"You and me both," Dave said. "I'm doing okay, though. I've still got my P.I. license and I'm working out of Morgan City nowadays. I do a lot of workmen's comp claims for the oil and gas industry, and a couple of attorneys I know use me for surveillance and research, stuff like that. Not exactly stimulating work."

"It keeps you in the game, though." Titus took a thirsty swig of his beer.

"That's about it."

"You ever think about coming back to the show?"

"Too late for that, Titus. I burned too many bridges when I left."

"You never can tell. We're shorthanded these days. Somebody put in a good word for you, it might make a difference."

"I couldn't ask you to do that. Besides, I'm not here about my old job. I want to talk to you about the Nina Losier case. I heard the investigation has hit a dead end and Graydon Losier is looking to hire a P.I."

Titus flicked the beer cap toward a trash can at the bottom of the steps. "Who told you that?"

"Doesn't matter. That's just what I heard. Then I get to New Orleans and I find out that NOPD is about two seconds away from busting a guy named Jimmy Caisson for Nina's murder. Now I don't know what to think."

"Sounds to me like somebody's yanking your chain, kid. Who you been talking to?"

"I heard it from Angelette Lapierre."

The beer bottle froze in midair, then came down with a hard thud against the table. "Oh, hell, no. Tell me you ain't all up in that shit again. Dave, what's the matter with you? That woman ain't caused you enough grief by now?"

"I can't lay my problems at Angelette's doorstep, Titus. She never held a gun to my head."

"Everything but. You're only human and Angelette Lapierre is like a bitch in heat. Ain't too many men I know who'd walk away from that kind of action."

"It still doesn't excuse my behavior. I did what I did and now I have to own it. But Angelette and me, we're through. Whatever we had is finished."

"Don't sound that away to me."

"It's over, trust me." Dave traced the scar above his left eye. "I hadn't even seen her since I moved to Morgan City. Then she called me up the other day and wanted to meet at the Crescent City Bar over on Bourbon Street."

"Jubal Roach's place?"

Dave grinned at Titus's expression. "Jubal was on his best behavior, even without you having my back."

"Maybe he's mellowed in his old age."

"Or maybe I have. Anyway, that's when Angelette told me that Graydon Losier was unhappy with the progress of the investigation and wanted to hire a P.I. She even said she mentioned my name to him."

"And you believed her? Damn, boy, when you gonna catch a clue? Graydon Losier's got more clout in Baton Rouge than Jesus Christ himself. If he had a problem with the investigation, he wouldn't need to hire a P.I. He'd just call up one of his buddies in the statehouse to lean on the superintendent."

"That's the way I see it, too," Dave said. "But what

I can't figure out is why Angelette came to me in the first place."

"Maybe she wanted an excuse to see you."

"I don't think so. I think she has another agenda." Dave paused, his gaze going to a set of tiny handprints at the edge of the concrete slab. "Titus, how well do you remember the Renee Savaria case?"

"Well enough that I don't like where I think this conversation is headed."

"Angelette made it out that the police were ignoring a possible connection between the Losier investigation and Renee Savaria's murder."

Titus shook his head. "You still don't see it, do you? She's playing you, Dave. She's chumming the waters with all this Savaria mess, and now she's got you chasing after her hook like a big 'ol suckerfish. If you really want shed of that trouble, do yourself a favor and haul ass out of N'awlins tonight. Forget you ever heard of Angelette Lapierre."

"I wish I could, but it's not that simple."

"It never is with you, kid."

He tried not to wince at the older man's tone. "I talked to JoJo Barone right before I came over here. He told me something I can't walk away from."

Titus put a matchstick in his mouth and sat back, as if trying to distance himself from Dave and his problems. "JoJo Barone is a low-life scumbag who'd sell his mama's soul to cover his own ass. He ain't exactly what I'd call a reliable source."

"Did you know he's got lung cancer?"

"I knew he had something. Looks like a walking corpse these days. I figured it was a bad case of the boogie-woogie flu, but whatever the hell he got, don't expect me to get all choked up about it. You find yourself getting sentimental over a guy like that, maybe you need to stop and ask yourself how you'd feel if it was your daughter he been pimping out of the back room of that dump on Bourbon Street."

Dave flinched and glanced away.

"Shit, man."

"It's okay."

"No, it's not." Titus sat slumped over the table, his expression contrite. "I hate like hell I said something like that to you."

"Forget it. You're right about JoJo. He is slime, but he's also dying, and I think he was being straight with me this time. Titus…he told me a cop killed Renee Savaria."

The older man's gaze swept the yard and patio before coming back to rest on Dave. "I didn't hear that."

"Titus—"

"I'm serious. Don't drag me into this shit, Dave, not this time. You need to believe a creep like JoJo Barone, that's on you, but I don't want no part of it."

"You're already in it, Titus. The Savaria case was ours, and you and me both dropped the ball. I know what happened to me after Ruby went missing, but where were you? What happened to Renee's file once I resigned? You just shuffle it to the bottom of the pile and call it a day?"

Titus's eyes sparked with anger. "You sure you want to start throwing around accusations like that? 'Cause if that's the game you're looking to play, let's have at it."

"I screwed up," Dave said. "I admit that. It took me awhile, but I'm finally on the right track. And I'm trying to right some old wrongs that have been eating at me for too damn long. But it's not just about me. That girl's family needs justice, Titus. We owe them that."

"Maybe what they need is a little peace. You ever stop and consider that?"

"Renee Savaria was killed at a private party by a cop named Clive Nettle."

Titus started shaking his head, but Dave just kept right on talking.

"There were other cops at that party and they helped cover up what he did. And then I destroyed evidence that probably kept him out of prison."

"Don't say no more, Dave. I don't need to hear this."

"Yes, you do. We were partners. I should have been straight with you years ago about Renee Savaria's diary."

Titus put his hands on the table. His fingers were large and blunt and his nails were clipped almost down to the quick. "You don't need to say anything more because I already know what you did."

Dave stared at him in shock.

Titus nodded. "Like you said before, we were partners. I knew you better than you knew yourself back then."

"But you never even looked at that diary. You weren't interested. You thought it wouldn't lead to anything."

"But you did. And once you started looking like a man with a noose around his neck, I figured there had to be a reason why."

"Why didn't you ever let on?"

"You were a good cop, Dave. You had integrity and, for the most part, you played by the rules. I always respected that. If you tampered with evidence, I knew there had to be a damn good reason behind it."

Dave glanced down at his own hands. His nails were short, too, but the ends had been chewed off instead of clipped. "They told me they had Ruby."

"I figured it was something like that. What'd they say?"

"After she disappeared, I got some calls from someone claming to be her kidnapper. He told me if I didn't destroy the last page of entries in Renee's diary, he'd kill her. So I did what he said. I burned the evidence, because I wanted to believe Ruby was still alive and that, if I did what he said, he'd let her go. I was stupid and scared and I did something that went against everything I believed in as a cop."

Titus's voice softened. "You were trying to save your baby girl. Any father would have done the same thing in your place."

"Maybe. But I wasn't just a father, I was a cop. I should have known better."

"You were out of your head with worry and grief."

"I'm all out of excuses, Titus. Once I knew they didn't have Ruby, I should have come clean about what I did. It wasn't too late. I knew that diary page by heart. We could have leaned on JoJo Barone—"

"Wouldn't have done any good and you know it. We didn't have anything on him, and without leverage, no way in hell he would've talked. You're not looking at this thing objectively, Dave. You're too emotionally invested to see the big picture. Without JoJo's cooperation, Renee's diary didn't mean shit and they knew it. A few initials with an address. Big deal. It wasn't the diary they were worried about, it was you. They knew you'd keep digging, so they had to find a way to take you out of the equation. They turned you into a dirty cop. When you destroyed that evidence, your credibility was shot, and anything else you turned up against them would have been tainted."

A dirty cop. Dave glanced away. "I can't change what I did. The only thing I can do now is try to make amends. But I can't do that without your help."

Titus was silent for a moment. "I'm ten months shy of having my thirty years in. You're asking me to get involved in something that could mess up my pension. That's all me and Addie got to live on in our old age. We were born dirt poor and that ain't the way I want us to die."

"I swear your name won't come into it. All I need is someone to help with the surveillance. As soon as I make some phone calls, I figure the rats will start crawling out of the sewers. I need you to keep an eye on Nettle. Tell me where he goes and who he sees. That's it."

Titus gazed off toward the fence. "You knew I'd do it when you came here, so I figure there ain't no use in drawing this thing out. But I want you to be straight with me about your motives, and for once in your life, you need to be honest with yourself. Justice for a dead woman's family is all well and good, but that ain't why you're doing this. You lost your little girl, and then your wife walked out on you. That's a big dose of grief for any man to swallow, but for the past seven years, you numbed it with Jack Daniel's. Now that you're sober, all that guilt is rising back up from wherever you had it buried."

He stared boldly into Dave's face. "Everybody has

to pay the piper, Dave. All you did was put it off. You think if you can find out who killed Renee Savaria and bring some peace to her family, maybe you'll have earned a little karma for yourself. But it don't work that way. Nothing you do is ever going to bring back your little girl."

Dave looked over at the handprints in the concrete. Titus had told him once they were Melaswane's, and it was hard for Dave to reconcile the tiny impressions with the teenager he'd seen behind the register earlier.

Ruby would have been fourteen years old last month, no longer a child, but a girl on the cusp of womanhood. Dave would never see her grow up. Never see her fall in love, walk her down the aisle or hold his and Claire's grandchildren in his arms. And suddenly the loss of what he'd never even known was almost as painful as the memories of what he'd once had.

He glanced back at Titus, and the older man's smile was sad. "I'm glad you stopped by, Dave. I had you on my mind just the other day and I wondered if I'd ever see you again. But I got to be honest with you. Having you back in N'awlins feels a little like having a time bomb strapped to my chest."

It was still too early to show up at the Hotel Monteleone, so Dave walked aimlessly through the Quarter, deciding if he wanted to wait and talk to Angelette or head back home. Ever since his conversation with Titus, he'd felt a strange apprehension creeping over him. As twilight settled across the city, the music and laughter blaring from the bars and clubs became the beckoning song of a very dangerous siren, and Dave knew better than to linger so close to temptation.

He walked back up St. Peters to the square and sat down to watch the sidewalk artists pack up their paints and easels for the night. The crowds of tourists had thinned, and Dave had a little corner of the park to himself. It was a pleasant evening, warm and fragrant. The pink glow on the horizon faded to gray and a breeze blew in off the water.

He sat for the longest time, trying to organize his thoughts into neat little compartments, but his mind was too jumbled. He was tired and depressed, and felt himself drifting into one of those black moods he'd been battling for as long as he could remember.

He wished he could blame all his problems on Angelette the way Titus had earlier, but the truth of the matter was he'd been his own worst enemy long before he'd ever laid eyes on Angelette Lapierre.

From the time his father had ended a four-day bender by running his car off the Atchafayla Basin Bridge when Dave was just fifteen, he'd had a tendency to self-destruct. To this day, he couldn't say why he'd felt the need to escape his old man's death by tying one on with his buddies after the funeral. It wasn't as if he'd been racked with grief. He barely even knew his father.

But after a few snorts of whiskey chased by a couple of six-packs, Dave had discovered he didn't give a shit about much of anything. Not school. Not work. Certainly not about a mother who, after a few weeks of hysterical weeping, spent the bulk of their life insurance check on a new wardrobe and a second-hand Cadillac that she drove out to a honky-tonk near the airport every night.

At first, she made a point of introducing the men she brought home, as if that somehow sanctified her behavior. But after Dave took a swing at one of her dates, she started making sure he wasn't home when she entertained. Sometimes he'd go stay with Marsilius, but most of the time he hung out all night drinking and getting into fistfights with anyone who looked at him the wrong way.

And then Claire came into his life. They lived in the same neighborhood and had been friends as kids. But as they got older, Dave had started keeping his distance. Claire was the kind of girl who got noticed by a lot of guys, and Dave had considered her out of his league. Not in social standing, but because he never thought she'd look twice at someone with his reputation.

Then one night he'd stopped in for a burger and fries at the corner restaurant where she worked part-time. He'd looked up from the menu to find her smiling down at him, and that had been it for him.

Marrying Claire had been the best thing that ever happened to him. Because of her, he'd managed to turn his life around, and things had been good for a lot of years before the old restlessness stole back over him when he wasn't looking. He'd started having a beer with lunch and a couple of drinks after work, just to take the edge off his day. For a long time he'd been able to keep his drinking under control, but then Ruby disappeared and he hadn't bothered anymore. The beer with lunch became four or five, and he started keeping a bottle in a desk drawer at work.

After he was suspended, he would start drinking as soon as he got up, and keep going until well after dark. Then he'd take his gun and go out looking for Ruby. He'd walk up and down the street, knocking on doors, accusing their friends and neighbors, people he'd known for years, of keeping something from him. Everyone understood his desperation at first, but they eventually got fed up with the harassment, and a couple of times the police were called. The responding officers were always polite and sympathetic, and instead of running him in, would take him home and help Claire put him to bed.

When he got up the next day, the cycle would start all over again, until Claire finally had enough. He'd found a note propped against the sugar bowl one morning, saying she'd gone over to stay with her grandmother while he looked for another place to live because it was over between them.

He had packed his bags and moved out that same day, and he hadn't seen Claire again until he'd gone down to sign the divorce papers in her attorney's office. He hadn't known what to say to her that day, how to tell her how sorry he was for all the hurt and humiliation he'd caused her, so he hadn't said anything at all. When their gazes finally met, he'd smiled and shrugged and watched her eyes fill up with tears.

Afterward, she'd told him that she just couldn't stand by and watch while he hit rock bottom. Dave had thought at the time it was a strange thing for her to say, because it should have been plain to anyone that he'd already bottomed out. He had nowhere to go but up.

But Claire knew him better than he knew himself. What came after the divorce were periods of sobriety followed by weeks and weeks of hard drinking, where one day faded into the next. Where he would wake up in a strange place, smelling of sweat and vomit and stale whiskey, and not knowing where he was or how he'd gotten there. He would promise himself each time that it was over. That was it. Rock bottom. But somehow there was always a greater depth of hell that he could plumb.

Finally, Marsilius had dragged him to an AA meeting. Dave never even knew his uncle drank, let alone had a problem, but evidently it was a Creasy family affliction. Marsilius had been lucky enough to get some help early on or else he would have been right there in the gutter alongside Dave, he'd said.

With his uncle's support, Dave had been sober for eight months now, and before his last lapse, he'd had two years of sobriety. Most days lately he felt stronger and steadier than he had in a long time, but tonight, with the scent of magnolias heavy in the air and the echo of a trumpet drifting on the breeze, he knew he was heading into rough waters.

Fifteen

~~⟨೧⟩~~

The temperature dropped in the early evening and the French doors in the ballroom at the Hotel Monteleone were thrown open to allow the crowd to spill out into the courtyard. The well-heeled throng that had assembled to help reelect the Orleans Parish district attorney was an incestuous mix of New Orleans royalty, old-time politicos and a greedy new breed of power brokers that had swarmed into the city after the flood.

A zydeco band played from a dais at one end of the ballroom as white-coated waiters moved through the glittering crowd with trays of champagne and hors d'oeuvres. It was a semiformal event. Most of the men wore suits and ties, but some were more casual, and Dave blended in well enough in the sports coat and pants he'd brought to change into.

The party was not his kind of thing, but some of the faces looked familiar. He'd lived in New Orleans for most of his life and he recognized the local politicians and some of the old-guard movers and shakers that had been brokering backroom deals for decades. Louisiana politics was serious business, always had been, and the passion cut across all social and economic boundaries. Dave could remember the way his old man would lay out drunk for weeks at a time, but come election day, he always managed to sober up long enough to drag his ass to the polls. He'd cast his ballot for the incumbent because, like so many other Louisianans, he didn't much cotton to change.

The mood of the crowd tonight was clearly jubilant. With the band playing a rousing rendition of "Poor Man's Two-Step" and a banner overhead proclaiming *Laissez Les Bons Temps Rouler,* no one seemed particularly concerned about past corruption or the tenuous future of a city that could very well be poised on the brink of another disaster. Tonight was a time to celebrate. A new star from one of the oldest political families in New Orleans was on the rise, and the crowd had come to bask in the glow of his charisma. Lee Elliot was the complete package—charming, handsome, and with enough money backing him that he didn't have to grovel for handouts. The contributions just kept pouring in.

What Dave couldn't figure out was where Angelette fit into the picture. He couldn't see a man with Elliot's aspirations getting seriously involved with a woman who had the kind of baggage Angelette did. Her mother had died when Angelette was ten, and she'd been raised by an aunt who made her living as a prostitute. Dave always wondered if that's why Angelette had such a cavalier attitude about accepting payoffs and bribes. You did somebody a favor, you got a little something under the table in return. It was the American way, she always said. Or at least, it was the way things were done in New Orleans.

Dave searched the room for her now. He'd been watching the crowd for nearly an hour and hadn't caught so much as a glimpse of her dark hair. One more pass around the room and then he'd head for home, he decided.

As he turned to leave, the crowd shifted and Dave's breath stalled in his chest. For a moment, the room went completely still, and the thought crossed his mind that he might be having some sort of hallucination—the kind he used to get as he lay semiconscious on the bathroom floor, when he thought from time to time that he could hear his now-dead mother calling him in to supper. Or when he'd wake up with the shakes in the middle of the night, his body covered in sweat and the need for alcohol like a raging fever in his bloodstream, and he'd see Ruby's face floating over his bed. Would even think her teardrops were falling onto his cheeks, before he realized they were his own....

Dave knew only too well what a terrible longing could conjure. But this was no vision. It was her. It was Claire.

The passage of time and ravages of grief had taken a toll. Not that she wasn't still beautiful. No woman in the room could hold a candle to her as far as Dave was concerned, but Ruby's disappearance had etched a permanent sadness in features that had once radiated a quiet joy. The strength and dignity that he'd always admired were still there, though, in the set of her shoulders, in the way she held her head. She came from a modest background; they both did. But Claire had always had more class and grace than any woman he'd ever known.

She wore a simple black dress with her grandmother's pearl brooch pinned to the left shoulder, and her hair was long and gleaming, falling about her shoulders just the way he'd always loved it. She'd cut it after Ruby came along because she hadn't wanted to fuss with it, and now Dave wondered if she'd grown it back out for her husband. Her second husband.

Dave braced himself, waiting for the moment when Alex Girard would appear at her elbow. Angelette had told him last Wednesday that Claire and Alex were divorcing, but considering the source, Dave didn't know whether to believe it or not. He tried to convince himself he didn't care one way or the other, but the thought of her with another man had always killed him.

There had always been something special about Claire. Everyone she met felt it, from the little old ladies who came over to quilt with her grandmother, to the kid who cut the neighbors' grass in the sweltering heat, and the grocer whose day was always made when Claire stopped in. Everyone loved her, the young and the old. She was one of those people who made you want to be near her, if only for a moment.

Dave remembered how, when they were driving home from a party once, he'd put his arm around her, pulled her up against him. "You know what everyone says about us, don't you? How'd a nice girl like Claire Doucett end up with a raging asshole like Dave Creasy?"

Claire had laughed and snuggled closer. "They don't see your sweet side like I do."

"I've got a sweet side? And here I thought I was a real Louisiana badass."

"You just think you are," she said, running her hand lightly across the top of his thigh.

As soon as they got home, they'd undressed and slipped into bed without talking. Dave could still see her like that, eyes drowsy, blond hair spilling across the pillow. She'd lifted her hand to his face, whispered how much she loved him, and the weight of his love for her had come crashing down on him. That was all it was. Just a touch, a whisper, a moment in time that slipped away unnoticed until it came back years later to haunt him on hot, sleepless nights.

Dave turned away and walked over to the bar. He ordered a Coke with bourbon and carried it out to the courtyard to a quiet corner where he could fade into the shadows. The crowd was smaller out here, and people tended to speak in hushed tones, as if afraid their voices might carry on the night air. The banana and palm trees rustled in the breeze and the scent from the gardenias floating in the fountain was heady and sweet.

Dave held the glass in his hand for the longest time. When he moved, the tinkle of ice against crystal was a little like the distant toll of a bell.

He wasn't going to drink it. He knew that. Not that he wasn't above chucking an eight-month stretch of abstinence, but it wasn't going to be tonight. Maybe he just needed to prove to himself that he was still in control, that it wasn't a foregone conclusion he would lapse back to his old ways after seeing Claire. Or that he would readily give up his sobriety the way he had thrown away every other good thing in his life.

He drew a long breath as he stared off into the darkness. He could barely remember a time he hadn't been in love with Claire. He'd loved her when they married, loved her even more after the birth of their baby, and had still loved her when his discontent first began to stir. His restlessness didn't have anything to do with her. His dark moods were never about Claire or his feelings for her. Sometimes Dave wondered if there was something inside him that just wouldn't let him be happy.

And then Ruby had been taken, and nothing else had mattered but drinking himself into oblivion.

His hand tightened around the glass and he hesitated only for a moment before tossing the contents into the bushes. Maybe tonight wasn't the best time to test himself, after all.

He felt someone come up behind him, but he didn't turn. Not until he heard her voice.

"Dave?"

He closed his eyes briefly as pain washed over him. He thought it ironic that the abuses he'd heaped upon his body for so long could heal so quickly, with hardly any scars, but the wounds inside him, even after seven years, were still raw.

He took a moment before he turned to face her. "Hello, Claire."

She stood in the shadows, but the glow from the tiny white lights that wound through the trees filtered down on her face. She looked pale, blond, serene. Almost like a dream.

Her eyes met his and he saw her lift a hand to her throat, as if she wasn't quite sure why she had approached him. "I thought I glimpsed you earlier, but I wondered if I was seeing things. This is just about the last place I expected to run into you."

Dave mustered a faint smile. "I could say the same about you."

"I came with Charlotte. She works for Lee Elliot in the D.A.'s office."

"So I heard. She always did have ambition. Give her another year and she'll be running that office."

"It wouldn't surprise me." Claire glanced away, as if she'd already run out of things to say to him. "How do you know Lee Elliot?"

"I don't. I'm not here to support his campaign. I came to meet a client. I've got my investigation business going again."

"You're back in New Orleans?"

Was that dread he heard in her voice? "No. I moved the office to Morgan City."

"Are you staying with Marsilius?"

"I've got my own place, but I'm close enough that he thinks he has to keep an eye on me."

Somebody needs to.

No one spoke the words, but Dave had a feeling they were both thinking the same thing. He looked off through the French doors to the ballroom, where the waiters continued to circulate through the crowd with their gleaming trays.

"You look good, Dave."

The compliment drew his gaze back in surprise. "So do you."

"No, I mean…you look really good."

He knew what she meant. "I've stopped drinking." He paused and shrugged. "Let me rephrase that. I'm not drinking tonight."

"One day at a time," she said softly.

"Always."

Someone laughed in the crowd behind her, and Claire turned to glance over her shoulder. When her gaze came back to Dave, she smiled, and the fist around his heart tightened. "I should go find Charlotte. She promised we wouldn't stay long, and I'm going to hold her to it."

"Good luck with that."

She smiled again, not *his* smile, but one that still tightened his chest. She lingered for a split second before giving a little head shake as if she couldn't quite believe that they were standing face-to-face. "It was good seeing you, Dave."

"You, too, Claire."

She wound her way through the crowd toward the French doors, and Dave came out of the shadows so that he could watch her until she was out of sight. She moved like the ghost she was, floating in front of him one moment, gone the next, an elusive specter banished back to the past.

Dave turned away, telling himself not to go there. What he and Claire had was over. Dead. Buried. Let it rest.

But some ghosts never went away. They lingered forever, existing on the fringes of his life, wandering in and out of his dreams, materializing now and then to remind him of what he'd lost and what he could never have again.

Some ghosts would never be exorcised no matter what he did. Especially when the ghost was the only woman he'd ever loved.

"Was that Dave I saw you with on the terrace?" Charlotte asked as she came up beside Claire. "What did he want?"

"He didn't want anything," she said a little defensively. "I glimpsed him through the crowd and I went over to say hello. And please don't start with me. I'm not in the mood."

Charlotte lifted a brow at her sister's tone. "Believe it or not, I wasn't going to say a word."

"I find that hard to believe, knowing your opinion on Dave."

"Maybe I'm feeling a little more charitable tonight," Charlotte muttered, lifting her champagne glass. She looked off across the crowd. "Did he say anything?"

"About what?"

She shrugged. "I don't know, about what he's doing these days. What's he up to?"

Claire turned. "He's reopened his P.I. office over in Morgan City, but why in the world do you care? Since when have you become so interested in Dave Creasy?"

Charlotte's gaze was still on the crowd. "I heard his name mentioned recently in conjunction with an NOPD homicide investigation. You know how territorial cops are. I wouldn't want him getting in over his head, that's all."

Claire stared at her sister for a moment. "Never mind about Dave. He can take care of himself. I want to know what's up with you."

"I don't know what you mean."

"You've been acting strange all evening. You hardly said a word when you picked me up, and then you deserted me as soon as we walked through the door. And now you actually sound worried about Dave. What's going on with you?"

Charlotte's gaze darted away, but not before Claire glimpsed a sheen of tears in her green eyes. "I guess I'm just feeling a little guilty tonight."

"About what?"

"I shouldn't have tried to discourage you about finding that doll. And then I dragged you here, after you just got out of the hospital…." She turned to Claire. "I'm a terrible sister."

"No, you're not. You've always been very supportive, and I don't blame you for having your doubts about the doll. I know how bizarre it sounds."

"Don't do that," Charlotte said almost angrily.

"Do what?"

"Excuse my behavior. You and Mama have been doing that all my life. Maybe it's time you both take off your rose-colored glasses. I'm not a good person, Claire. I'm selfish and ambitious, and when I see something I want, I go after it, without regard to the consequences."

"I don't believe that for a minute. That's not the Charlotte I know."

"That's just it," she said sadly. "You don't know me at all. And you have no idea what I'm capable of."

She walked off then, leaving Claire to stare after her. Out of the corner of her eye, she saw Dave standing just inside the terrace doorway, and when she turned, their gazes met across the room. She wondered if she should go back over to him, warn him about Charlotte's concerns. But before she could make up her mind, he turned and disappeared into the crowd.

Sixteen

After Dave left the Hotel Monteleone, he drove to a dive off Highway 90 and sat in the parking lot, watching the neon light flicker over the doorway as he tried to convince himself he could get through the night without a drink. Best thing he could do was go home and get a good night's sleep.

But he knew it wasn't going to be that easy, and when he finally pulled out of the parking lot and headed for home, he decided he'd better stop by and visit with Marsilius for a while. Dave had learned the hard way that it was never a good idea to be alone when the demons were riding him as hard as they were that night.

He drove with the window rolled down, and he could smell the sugarcane out in the fields. It was a calm, still night, with only a mild breeze to stir the willows that bowed low over the water.

Turning off the main highway, he took a back way home, past an old cemetery and a few houses perched on the edge of the bayou. Water oaks arched over the road, and the moonlight that shimmered through the heavy canopy turned the Spanish moss into silver lace.

The lights were off in his uncle's house when Dave drove by, but he hadn't heard Marsilius mention anything about taking the boat out. Like Dave, his uncle was a night owl, and even when he didn't have a late charter out to the oil rigs, he was often up until dawn. But tonight it looked as if he'd turned in early.

Dave decided it was just as well. Marsilius was a good guy, but he could be like a dog with a bone when he sensed Dave was hiding something. And the last thing he wanted tonight was an inquisition. Seeing Claire had left him edgy and morose. For a long time now he'd tried to convince himself that his feelings for her were dead and buried, but he'd only been fooling himself. Claire was still a part of him. She always would be, no matter how many years went by or how much they hurt each other. Even if she was married to someone else, he would always think of her as his wife.

As he pulled into the drive, he thought about heading down to the dock to see if the boat was still there. It was going to be a long night, and he figured it might be a good idea to take the *Sea Ray* out a few miles from shore and drop anchor, sit in the dark until the craving eased enough for him to sleep.

But come morning, he'd be right back where he'd started. All he'd done by stumbling from one drunk to the next was postpone the inevitable. And now Titus was right. It was time to pay the piper. Dave couldn't keep running away from his problems, because sooner or later he'd have no place left to go but the grave.

His truck tires crunched on the shale drive as he

parked beneath an oak tree and got out. A mild breeze stirred the wind chimes on his screened-in porch, and Dave paused on the steps to stare out at the darkness.

Past the row of pecan trees in his yard, he could see the glint of the bayou. The water was dark and still, but the night was alive with the sounds of crickets and bullfrogs, and the bushes were aglow with lightning bugs.

He watched for a moment longer before letting the screen door close behind him. Unlocking the front door, he shoved it open, then leaned out slightly to toss the key back into the flowerpot. A floorboard creaked inside the house and Dave froze for a split second as a terrible premonition flashed through his head. But the warning came too late. By the time he'd turned back to the door, a shadow was rushing through the darkness toward him.

A baseball bat swung at his face, and Dave ducked as his arm flew up to deflect the blow. The wood caught him on the side of his skull and then bounced off his right shoulder. He heard a loud pop in his ears as he stumbled backward, reaching for his gun. The bat struck him again, across the stomach this time, and everything went black as he doubled over and fell to his knees.

Bracing himself on one hand, he gulped in air. He'd been caught completely by surprise and now was too dazed to fight back. He had the impression there were two of them, but he wasn't sure why. He couldn't see anything. His mouth hung open and his eyes refused to focus as blood ran freely down the side of his face.

Hands grabbed his arms and dragged him inside the house, where he was dropped facedown on the hardwood floor. A long string of spittle and blood hung from his mouth as he tried to lift his head.

"Lay still, asshole."

A steel-toed boot connected with his rib cage, and Dave fell back to the floor. Someone straddled him and, with a fistful of hair, yanked his head back. A knife blade flashed in the moonlight a split second before he felt the edge against his throat. The man on top of him smelled of sweat and whiskey, and he was breathing heavily, not so much from the strain, Dave thought, but from excitement.

A pair of polished shoes came into Dave's view, but when he tried to look up, the blade pressed into his throat.

The man in front of him paused, lifted one foot and struck a match against the sole of his shoe. A second later, Dave smelled the acrid scent of cigarette smoke as the man exhaled noisily. Walking over to the window, he sat down in a chair and continued to smoke. From the corner of Dave's eye, he saw the glowing arc of the cigarette as the man lifted it to his mouth.

"You've got two options here, Dave. This can go fast and easy, or we can drag it out for hours. It's your call, but I know which option my boy here would choose. Seems as if he's got an ax to grind with you."

"Enough talk," a third man said from the doorway. "Just get on with it."

The command was soft and steely, but this time Dave didn't try to turn toward the voice. He kept his eyes forward and watched blood run off his cheek and drop on the hardwood floor.

"Tie him up," the man with the cigarette ordered.

Dave gritted his teeth as his wrists were wrenched

back and bound tightly with a thin cord that bit into his flesh.

"You're in some serious shit here." The smoking man spoke in a voice that was almost pleasant. "Obstruction of justice, tampering with evidence, interfering in an official investigation. Any one of those charges could get you put away for a very long time."

Dave lifted his head. "Is that why you brought a bartender with a baseball bat to help arrest me?"

The man got up from the chair and walked across the room to stand over Dave. "You think you're pretty smart, don't you? Got it all figured out. In that case, I guess there's not much point in keeping up the pretense." He knelt and, for the first time, allowed Dave to get a look at his face. He was a big, muscular guy with hair clipped down to his scalp and a scar that ran the length of his jawline. He smiled in the moonlight. "Do you know who I am?"

"Only by reputation. But the description I was given didn't do you justice, Nettle. No one mentioned how bad you stink. You smell just like a dead man walking."

"You're a funny guy, Dave. A regular comedian. But maybe what you smell is the stink of the gutter. I hear you've been spending a lot of time there."

When Dave said nothing, Nettle stood. "Yeah, that's right. I know you by reputation, too. I heard you were a real dumb-ass, and you just proved to me that you are."

"I don't like to disappoint," Dave rasped.

"As I said, this can go easy or I can let your old buddy Robert have his way with you. It's your call. But make no mistake. I'll get what I came for. One way or another. And the way I see it, when you start interfering in police business, fucking with an ongoing investigation, you gotta expect some blowback. Even a dumb shit like you should know better."

Dave wiped his mouth against his shoulder as he pushed himself up to lean against the wall. His head lolled back against the plaster. "If you're still trying to pass this off as official police business, then I think we need to reevaluate which one of us is the dumb-ass."

Nettle stared down at him. "Maybe I ought to let my boy here give you a little preview of coming attractions. Seems to me you could use an attitude adjustment."

"That sounds about right. You're used to having people clean up your messes, aren't you, Nettle?"

"That's pretty good coming from a guy like you." The detective pulled out his gun. "If you've got two brain cells left, you'll tell me what I want to know so we can end this bullshit right now. It'll only get uglier once I lose my patience."

"And here I thought we were getting along so well," Dave said.

Taubin was standing beside Dave and kicked him in the ribs again. "Show some respect, dickhead."

"Fuck you, Bobby Ray."

He laughed out loud. "You just sealed your own fate, Creasy."

"Shut up," Nettle said. "Let me handle this. Go out to the porch and keep watch."

"You're the boss," Taubin said. "But once you're done with him, you give me a holler, hear? Me and Dave got some unfinished business to settle."

Nettle squatted in front of him. "Let's try this again. You've been a lush for years, everybody knows it. You didn't just wake up from a stupor one morning and decide to start asking questions about a couple of homicides. Someone put you up to this."

"I don't know what you're talking about."

The butt of the gun slammed against the side of Dave's skull. "Wrong answer, asshole. You didn't print those police files I found in your desk off the Internet. Someone gave them to you. I want a name."

Dave kept silent. He was a dead man, anyway. He'd seen Nettle's face. No way he was getting out of this alive.

"Let's up the ante, shall we? You got an uncle that lives just down the road. Maybe we ought to get him over here and see what he knows."

Dave still said nothing.

"That the way you want to play it, fine." Nettle stood and shoved the gun into the waistband of his trousers, then reached down and yanked Dave to his feet. His wrists were still tied behind him and his head throbbed sickeningly. He needed to vomit, but he wouldn't give them the satisfaction.

Nettle shoved him toward the door and Dave stumbled out to the porch.

"Help me get him down to the water," Nettle told Taubin. "He'll talk then."

The two men dragged him off the porch, across the yard and down the steep, muddy bank to the water's edge. Dave had no idea where the third man was, but he had a feeling he was somewhere behind them. As they neared the water, the fecund scent of the swamp mingled with the smell of blood, and Dave started to wretch.

"Shit, man, are you sure about this?" Taubin asked anxiously as they waded into knee-deep water. "I ain't too crazy about the swamp. These waters gotta be full of gators."

"Don't worry," Nettle told him. "This won't take long."

As they waded out a little farther, the lily pads on the surface undulated with the movement. Dave could feel the sinewy maze of cypress roots beneath his feet and had to struggle to keep his balance.

When the water was nearly waist high, Nettle pushed Dave to his knees. He tried to get up, but slipped on the muddy bottom. Nettle clamped his hand around the back of Dave's neck and pressed his face underwater.

Dave went completely still, trying to reserve the air in his lungs, but after a few seconds, his instincts took over and he began to thrash around, slinging his head from side to side, trying to free himself from the vise-like grip that held him under.

The last of his air rushed out of his lungs and Dave's mouth opened instinctively. As water streamed into his nose and throat, he couldn't contain his panic.

Nettle jerked him to the surface, and Dave came up gasping and sputtering, his head still pulsing from the pressure. When his captors released him, his feet slid out from under him and he went down again. Quickly he surfaced, shaking his head from side to side, and Taubin laughed out loud. "Look at that dumb pecker-wood."

Dave saw Nettle smile in the moonlight. "I bet he's ready to talk now. Let's get him to the bank."

They pulled him out of the water and plopped him facedown in the mud.

"Who gave you those files?" Nettle asked calmly.

"I don't remember," Dave gasped. His heart was pounding hard and fast, and his mouth was filled with the taste of swamp water, blood and fear.

"Someone brought you into this," Nettle said. "I want a name."

"I don't know what you're talking about."

"Like I said, we could get your uncle down here, see what he knows. Or maybe we could pay a visit to your old partner. He might know something. Titus has a kid still at home, right? A girl about fourteen or fifteen. You know better than anyone how far a guy would go to protect his daughter, don't you, Dave?"

"You son of a bitch. You lay one finger on that girl, I'll kill you. If there's anything left once Titus gets through with you."

Nettle just laughed.

"Next time, I say we leave him under longer," Taubin said. "If he comes back up, we won't be able to shut him up. If he don't, we can just leave him for gator bait."

They moved toward Dave again, but this time he was ready for them. He rolled to his back and slammed his foot into Taubin's groin. The man's knees buckled and he fell to the ground in a fetal curl. He lay groaning in pain and rage for the longest moment before slowly rising to his feet, one hand pressed between his spraddled legs while the other hand pulled out his knife.

"You're a dead man," he gasped as he started toward Dave. "I'll gut you like a catfish—" A light caught him in the face and he blinked in shock. "What the hell…?"

A split second later, a bullet hit a cypress tree behind him and the bark exploded into the water. Taubin swore again as he dived for cover.

"This is private property!" Marsilius yelled from the darkness. "I already called the law so you've got about five seconds to get the hell out of here before I start blowing some head off!"

To punctuate his warning, he fired off several rounds, hitting targets so close to Taubin and Nettle that there was little doubt about his aim. If he'd wanted them dead, they already would be.

Taubin rose shakily to his feet, keeping his head low. "Let's get the hell out of here. I don't want no trouble with the local boys. You ain't paying me enough to get my head busted open by some redneck deputy with a billy club."

Nettle glanced down at Dave in the dark. "Do yourself a favor. Stay out of New Orleans and stay out of my business. Next time it won't turn out so good for you."

And then they were gone. Pain twisted inside Dave's gut and he rolled over to vomit in the mud. When he was finished, he lay weak and trembling on his side. It was all he could do to keep from blacking out.

A moment later, Marsilius knelt beside him in the mud. "How bad you hurt, son?"

"I'll live," Dave muttered. "Thanks to you."

"That head's gonna need some stitches."

"I don't think it's as bad as it looks." Dave struggled to sit up. "I'll clean it up when I get home, see how it looks."

"Don't talk crazy, son, they laid you open good. I'm taking you to the hospital. Can you walk or do I need to back the truck down here?"

"I can walk."

His uncle helped him to his feet. "You sure? You're staggering around like you been on a three-day drunk."

"I'm fine," Dave said, a split second before he passed out cold.

By the time they left the hospital, the sky had already started to lighten in the east. They'd waited hours to see a doctor. It was Saturday night and the end of a three-week rotation for some of the workers on the offshore oil rigs, so the emergency room had been packed with guys fresh in from the platforms and ready to party.

Dave had sat holding a towel to his head as he filled out the paperwork, and every time Marsilius went to ask how much longer it would be, the heavyset nurse behind the desk would glower and tell him they would just have to wait their turn like everybody else.

Finally, Dave had been taken to a cubicle and treated by a freckle-faced intern who looked barely old enough to vote. The gash on Dave's head took several stitches, but he didn't have any broken bones or ribs, and once the doctor had him patched up, he signed Dave's release papers because they were short on beds. That suited Dave fine. He wouldn't have stayed, anyway. He hated hospitals. Something about the smell, he decided as he walked outside.

He rolled down the window in Marsilius's truck and tipped his head back so the air rushed over his face. Clouds scuttled across the eastern sky where the sun hovered just below the horizon.

As Marsilius turned down the dusty road to home, he cut Dave a glance. "You ready to tell me what happened earlier?"

"I thought it was pretty obvious that I got my ass kicked." Dave watched out the window as distant heat lightning shimmered just above the treetops.

"You know what I mean. Who were those guys?"

"Just forget about it, okay? The less you know, the better off you'll be."

"Yeah, well, here's the thing. After the potshots I took over their heads, I have a feeling those bastards may not be feeling too kindly toward me. I'd at least like to know who I need to be on the lookout for."

"I guess you've got a point," Dave said. "The big guy is NOPD. His name is Clive Nettle."

Marsilius turned to look at him. "A cop? Shit fire, Dave, what are you mixed up in?"

Dave ignored the question. "The scrawny one is an ex-con named Bobby Ray Taubin. I think there was a third one, but I never got a look at him. Bobby Ray works for JoJo Barone. Evidently, he also does some side jobs for Nettle."

"What do they want with you?"

"I guess they don't like some of the questions I've been asking. Or more to the point, they don't like the answers I got from JoJo Barone."

"When did you go see JoJo?"

"Yesterday. He told me that Clive Nettle killed Renee Savaria at a private party he arranged, and the whole thing was covered up by some of the other cops who were there that night."

"Do you believe him?"

"If I didn't before, I do after tonight."

His uncle let out a long breath. "What the hell are you going to do with that information?"

Dave frowned into the darkness. "I don't know yet.

Look for the other cops who were involved, for one thing."

"You can't go this alone, son, you'll need somebody watching your back."

"Don't worry about it. I've got that part covered."

"Sure as hell didn't look that way to me. This is dangerous shit, Dave. You gotta bring somebody else in on this fast. Somebody you can trust."

"Yeah, well, that's the problem. JoJo said those parties were attended by some pretty heavy-duty brass. I don't know how far up this thing goes."

"What about the D.A.?"

Dave had thought of that, but going to Lee Elliot would be a tricky business, considering his involvement with Angelette. Dave still hadn't figured out her angle yet, and until he did, he wasn't about to put much faith in anyone she was that closely associated with.

"What makes you think I could even get in to see Lee Elliot?"

"Maybe you couldn't, but Claire's sister could."

Dave's laugh was bitter. "You're joking, right? Charlotte LeBlanc despises the ground I walk on. No way she'd hear me out."

"Then maybe you better get out of town and lie low for a while. I have a friend in Houston who owns a garage. He'd put you to work, no questions asked."

"I'm not running away. I wouldn't be able to live with myself if I did that. But I'd feel a whole lot better if you'd head on down to Houston. I don't want to see anything happen to you, old man. You're the only family I got left."

Marsilius downshifted as he turned a curve. "I can take care of myself. You're the one I'm worried about.

This ain't over, Dave. They'll be back, and next time I might not be around to pull your ass out of the wringer."

"They won't come back right away. They know I'll be ready for them now. They'll wait until they think they can catch me by surprise again."

"You seem pretty sure about that."

Dave shrugged. "It's what I'd do."

"I hope you're right, son. I truly do."

They were both silent after that, and Marsilius didn't speak again until he pulled into Dave's drive and cut the engine. He offered to come in, but Dave wasn't up for any more company, and he wanted to be alone so that he could try and figure out what his next move would be.

Inside the house, he went from room to room, securing doors and windows, but he knew the effort was futile. The glass in the back door had been broken so that someone could reach in and turn the lock. Dave wouldn't be able to get the window fixed until the next day, and he was too tired to even board up the opening for now.

He hoped what he told Marsilius held true, that Nettle wouldn't come for him again right away. But just in case, he placed his .38 on the sink while he showered, and slipped it underneath his pillow when he went to bed.

Then he lay on his back for a long time, staring at the ceiling as he thought about Claire. And Ruby.

He closed his eyes and tried to sleep. He was bone-deep weary, but he still couldn't rest. After a while, he got up and walked over to the window. He heard one of the rocking chairs on his front porch creak, but he wasn't alarmed. He knew who was down there.

He listened, heard the sound again as Marsilius shifted his weight to accommodate his bad knee. Dave stared out the window for a few minutes longer, then went downstairs to make coffee.

Seventeen

———◦◦◦———

"'*You are my sunshine, my only sunshine…*'"

The song penetrated the child's dreams, and Maddy's eyes slowly opened. "Mama?"

"Wake up, sleepyhead! Did you forget what today is?"

The child's gaze darted warily around the room. "Where's Father?"

Mama's smile was tender. "He's gone, darling. He won't be back until tomorrow. We have the day all to ourselves, and I've planned such wonderful surprises for you. Look!" She pointed to the end of the bed, where a pink ruffled dress hung from the wooden bedpost.

"Is it mine?" Maddy asked in awe.

"Yes, of course it's yours! Now go have your bath and I'll help you get dressed. Then you can open one of your presents."

The child hurried from the room and came back a few minutes later, all scrubbed and sweet smelling from the bath, blond hair curling in damp ringlets behind tiny ears.

The dress slid over thin shoulders and then Mama

turned Maddy toward the mirror. "See there! Are you not the prettiest little girl in the whole wide world?" She gave the child a brief hug. "Do you like the dress, Maddy? Does it make you happy?"

"Yes, Mama. But what if—"

She silenced the child's fear with a fingertip. "None of that now. It's your birthday. Nothing but happy thoughts today."

Maddy stared at the reflection in the mirror. The child staring back was pretty. Maddy couldn't help smiling. "I love you, Mama."

"I love you, too, my sweet. Now come with me. It's time to open one of your presents."

Maddy followed Mama into the large hallway and down the curving stairway that led into a spacious foyer. To the left of the staircase was the front parlor, decorated with heavy antiques and ornate wallpaper that looked like velvet. Normally, Maddy wasn't allowed to even set foot in the parlor, but today Mama had decorated the gloomy room with balloons and streamers, and the French doors stood wide open to allow in sunshine. Maddy stood gazing around. The room seemed so different today without Father brooding from his easy chair.

The table from Maddy's playroom had been brought down and laid with tiny porcelain dishes. A bowl of camellias rested in the center of the table and the scent hung heavy and sweet on the warm air.

Presents wrapped in bright paper and gaily colored bows were stacked around the chair at the end of the table. Maddy clapped in excitement. "Can I open them?"

"Only one for now. You can open the rest when the

*other children get here." Mama walked over and picked
up a large white box from the stack, handing it to Maddy.
The package was lovely, wrapped in white paper and
tied with a pink satin bow. Carefully, Maddy slipped off
the ribbon and then, one by one, removed the sheets of
scented tissue paper until the content of the box was revealed.*

*The child gasped in wonderment. The doll inside
was lifelike and so beautiful! More beautiful, even,
than Maddy's reflection.*

"Oh, Mama."

*She knelt on the floor, her eyes shimmering with
tears. "Do you like her?"*

*The child could barely speak. "I love her! More
than anything!"*

"She looks just like you, Maddy."

*Or at least, the way Maddy would look if the blond
curls had not been clipped so short. The doll had ringlets all the way down her back. But the blue eyes were
the same. And the nose, the tiny heart-shaped mouth…*

*The doll looked exactly the way Maddy dreamed of
looking.*

*"I had your aunt Savannah make her for you. Do you
remember Savannah? You met her once, a long time ago.
I sent her a picture. She had no idea it was you, of course,
but I think the likeness is remarkable, don't you?"*

For an answer, Maddy hugged the doll tightly.

*"She'll have to be our secret, Maddy. You can only
take her out on special occasions."*

"I know, Mama."

*"If your father…well, we won't worry about that
today, will we? Let's get you ready for your party."*

Five little girls from the neighborhood had been in-

vited over, and Mama had organized some games. After they were through playing, they took their places around the table. Maddy's gaze lingered on each one of them, studying their features for a long, long time so that the memory of this day would last forever. Mama took pictures, but no photograph would ever be as vivid as Maddy's memory.

And then someone mentioned Matthew, and Maddy's heart started to pound in agitation. What if they found out the secret?

But Mama covered smoothly and said that Matthew would be celebrating his birthday a little later, because boys didn't like to get all dressed up and attend tea parties. This time was just for Maddy.

The presents were opened then, and after the excitement died down, Mama served the cake, a beautiful three-layer strawberry confection with a rainbow across the top. The girls squealed in delight at the sight of the cake and then they all sang "Happy Birthday."

Just as Maddy blew out the candles, a sound came from somewhere deep in the house. A door opened and closed.

The child's gaze flew to Mama, whose face was frozen in fear. Her blue eyes darkened as a shadow filled the doorway.

"What do we have here?" a deep voice said calmly.

The pleasant tone didn't fool Maddy. The child shivered in dread of what was to come.

"Well, Katherine, it seems as if you've outdone yourself this time. This looks like quite the celebration. I can't help wondering why I wasn't invited."

Mama said nothing, but her face was so pale she looked as if she might faint.

"I think, perhaps, the party is over," Father said, still in that same deceptive voice. *"Katherine, I believe you should walk the children home. Do it now, please."*

Mama cast a glance in Maddy's direction. It was obvious she didn't want to leave the child alone, but she had no choice.

All too soon, she and the other children were gone, and the house fell deadly silent. Father walked slowly into the room, his gaze on Maddy.

"What is that you're wearing?"

Maddy said nothing.

"Answer me when I speak to you!"

Fingers dug into the child's arms as Maddy was lifted roughly from the table. *"You're an abomination and I can barely stand to look at you, but you're still my child and I won't shirk my responsibilities. I've found someone who can help you. His name is Dr. Church. I spoke to him before I left the medical convention yesterday. He's made significant strides in cases like yours, but the treatment won't work if your mother insists on turning you into a goddamn freak."*

As he said the last two words, he ripped the dress from Maddy's thin shoulders and tossed it aside in disgust. Maddy's shoes and socks came next, and then the underwear. Even at seven, Maddy hated being naked. Hated the way Father's gaze lowered, then shifted away in disgust.

With trembling hands, Maddy tried to cover the scars from all the surgeries, but Father would have none of that. He picked up the dress and underwear and shoved the clothing in Maddy's face. *"If I ever come home and find you like this again, I will take you far, far away from here. You'll never see your mother again, do you understand?"*

Maddy nodded, hoping that it was all over. Father

didn't seem as angry this time, maybe because it was Maddy's birthday.

But then his gaze lit on the doll and his handsome features contorted in rage.

He grabbed Maddy's arms and jerked the child clean off the floor. Then he walked across the room, flung open a closet door and shoved Maddy inside.

Terrified of the dark, Maddy sat naked and trembling, arms hugged around bony knees, and waited for Mama to come home.

After a few moments, when the shaking subsided, Maddy crawled over to the door and put an eye to the keyhole. Father stood where Maddy could see him, the doll in one hand and a butcher knife in the other.

"No!" Maddy screamed.

But Father lifted the knife, anyway, and chopped off all those long, glorious curls.

When Maddy's mother walked in and saw what he had done, she rushed over and tried to take the doll away from him. "Daniel! How could you!"

"How could you?" he countered. "You are to blame for this, Katherine. Can you not see the damage you've done?"

"You're the one who seems bound and determined to destroy our child. And all because of your stupid arrogance and pride." She glanced around. "Where's Maddy? What have you done to my baby?"

"Try to calm yourself, Katherine. Maddy will soon be in good hands. As will you."

"What are you talking about?"

"I've found a doctor who, God willing, can turn your little freak into a normal child. He says he can help you, too."

"No! No more doctors! When I think of the torture you've subjected that poor child to—"

She tried to grab his arm, but Father slung her away and she almost fell. He didn't seem to care.

"Dr. Church understands that you are a big part of the problem, Katherine, which is why he's agreed to treat you, as well. Of course, you'll have to be consigned to a hospital for the length of your treatment. Otherwise, you would do everything in your power to undermine Dr. Church's progress."

"You can't send me away without my consent! For God's sake, this isn't the Dark Ages. I have family, friends—"

"You have no one. No one who will listen to you, anyway. Who would believe the ravings of an unstable woman over that of a respected surgeon? Not to mention a very concerned and loving husband? No, I'm afraid you will not get your way this time, Katherine. But it's for the best. It really is."

"I won't let you do this!"

"There's nothing you can do to stop me. The arrangements have already been made."

"We'll see about that!" Mama's footsteps sounded across the hardwood floor, but then she gasped suddenly. "Let go of me! You're hurting me! Daniel, no…"

She screamed, and for what seemed an eternity, Maddy heard bad sounds outside the closet door. Father called Maddy terrible names as he raged, and Mama cried and begged him to stop. Then, after a while, Mama said nothing at all.

Maddy pressed an eye to the keyhole. An eye glared back from the other side. The child screamed and shrank away.

Father opened the door. There was blood on his suit and he held something up in one hand. For one terrible moment, Maddy thought that it was Mama. But it was the doll. She swung by her shorn hair from Father's grasp. The glassy eyes were open and staring, and the tiny lips were curled into a sweet little smile.

There was blood on the floor behind Father, but Mama was nowhere to be seen.

Maddy glanced back at the doll's tiny, sweet smile. A smile that beckoned the child into another place, a perfect place where Father could not find them.

"That's right. Take a good long look, you little faggot, because this is all that's left of your precious Maddy."

And then with one swoop of the knife, he severed the doll's head and tossed it into the child's lap.

Maddy screamed and screamed, but no one heard. And no one came to release him from his prison.

Matthew Cypher visited his father every single day. Usually he went in the afternoon, but today he had a lot to do, so he decided to go early. He parked in the back of the Oak Glen Nursing Home and used the rear entrance, hoping that he would not run into any of the staff who might want to chitchat today.

Hurrying down the dreary corridor, he kept his eyes averted from the open doorways, and ignored the groaning misery that followed him down the hallway. The smell of antiseptic and urine hung heavy on the air, but he was used to the scent by now. He hardly even noticed it.

An old woman sat alone in a wheelchair outside her room, and as he passed by her, she reached for him with a bony hand.

"Can you help me?"

Matthew paused, annoyed. "What seems to be the problem?"

"I can't find my room."

He glanced at the photograph and name mounted on the door nearest her wheelchair. "Are you Mrs. Avondale?"

"How did you know?"

"Just a wild guess." He pushed open the door. "This is your room."

"Are you sure?"

"Yes, positive."

He started to turn away, but the woman grabbed his hand. Lifting it to her face, she rubbed his knuckles against her wrinkled cheek. "You're a good son."

"I'm glad you think so. Would you like me to help you to your room now?"

"No, I'd better sit out here and wait for the bus to come. I don't want to miss it. I'm going to see my husband today. He's stationed at Fort Bragg. It'll be my first time out of Louisiana."

"Enjoy your trip," he said with a little bow, and he heard her giggle like a schoolgirl as he turned and continued down the corridor to his father's room. A nurse was just coming out and she brightened when she saw him.

"Hello Dr. Cypher. You're early today."

"I have some things to do later on, but I didn't want to miss a visit with my father. I know he looks forward to our time together."

"If only everyone's family was as thoughtful as you," she said with a weary smile.

He cocked his head and studied the young woman.

She was probably only thirty or so, but her careworn expression and slouching posture made her seem much older, as did a missing tooth when she smiled. She was a hard worker, though, and he did not envy her the dreary job.

Feeling suddenly charitable, he lingered for a little talk. "What's the matter? You don't seem yourself today."

She sighed. "My boyfriend's gone AWOL on me again, and I can't help worrying he may be in some real trouble this time."

"I'm sorry to hear that."

Desiree Choate gave a halfhearted smile as she shrugged. "Mama says it's a blessing in disguise. She ain't never had much use for Travis, even though I tell her over and over he has a good heart. He's just a little shiftless, is all."

"Not Travis McSwain?"

Her brows lifted in surprise. "Yeah, that's him. Do you know him?"

"I've seen him around. He used to do odd jobs around the house for my aunt from time to time. Her name is Savannah Sweete. He may have mentioned her. She makes dolls."

Desiree's gaze darted away, but not before he'd seen a spark of fear in her eyes.

So she knows. She's seen the doll.

He gave her a pitying smile. "Where do you think Travis has gone off to?"

"God only knows. He'll probably turn up one of these days, tail tucked between his legs like always. But just between me and you…I've been having me some real bad dreams lately. I can't help thinking maybe it's because something bad has happened to him."

"How long has he been gone?"

"A few days, I guess. He drove into New Orleans the other evening and I ain't seen him since."

"Have you gone to the police?"

"The police? Oh, Lord no. Travis would kill me if I sicced the law on his tail."

"Why? Has he done something wrong?"

"No, he just don't like cops much," she said quickly, as if realizing she might have given away too much. "It's been nice talking to you, doc, but I better get back to work."

"I wouldn't worry about Travis. If anything had happened to him, don't you think you would have heard something by now?"

"I guess so. Maybe he's just laid up drunk somewhere. Wouldn't be the first time."

"I'm sure you'll be hearing something very soon. In the meantime, perhaps this will help cheer you up."

She glanced down at the orchid he held out to her, and her eyes widened. "Oh, it's beautiful, but I couldn't take it. You brought it for your daddy."

"He won't mind. Please, I insist."

"Well, if you're sure." She lifted the delicate blossom to her nose. "Is this one of your orchids? What kind is it?"

"A cymbidium."

"Is it rare?"

"Oh, yes, extremely," he said, although it wasn't, of course. But the silly twit wouldn't know the difference.

Desiree glanced at the closed door to his father's room. "It's probably a good thing you came early today. He seems a mite restless this morning. Maybe your visit will help calm him down."

Matthew smiled. "I'll see what I can do."

He opened the door and walked through. The old man lay on his back, eyes to the ceiling, hands motionless on either side of him. His lips were parted and a stream of drool had run out one corner of his mouth and dried on his cheek.

The room stank. It always did. No matter how many times the staff came in to change and bathe the old man, he somehow managed to soil himself before their every visit. It might have been annoying if it wasn't so pathetic.

The curtained partition that separated the two beds had been slid back, and Matthew nodded to his father's roommate. Mr. Campbell was another stroke patient, paralyzed on both sides with an almost complete loss of speech. He was slightly elevated in bed, and his faded eyes watched with wary detachment as Matthew approached.

"Hello, Mr. Campbell. How are you today?"

He blinked rapidly, but Matthew didn't have a clue what that meant, so he shrugged and walked over to his father's bedside.

"Hello, Father." He bent to kiss the man's forehead. The skin beneath his lips was dry like parchment and stretched so tightly across brittle bones that his face resembled a skull. The old man was awake and conscious. His mouth moved slightly, as if he was trying to say something. Or perhaps he merely wanted to close it.

"Desiree tells me you had a restless night. I'm so sorry. I should have come sooner." He bent and lowered his voice. "Because that just won't do, Father. We can't have you causing trouble, now can we?"

He pulled a syringe from his pocket and held it up to the light. The old man's mouth moved frantically now as his eyes darted back and forth. He knew what was coming.

Smiling, Matthew placed his lips close to the old man's ear. "Tell me something, Father. How does it feel to be trapped inside that body?"

His father responded with a pathetic moan that didn't even sound human.

Matthew straightened. "Where do you want your injection today? In the thigh, underneath the arm, between the toes? So many possibilities…"

Taking a few steps toward the end of the bed, he pulled up the blanket and sheet, exposing legs that resembled brittle blue branches. Matthew uncapped the syringe, and as he jabbed the needle into his father's thigh, he glanced across the room.

The old man in the other bed lay watching him, and slowly Matthew brought his finger up to his lips.

"Shush. Don't tell."

Eighteen

A storm came up suddenly in the small hours of Tuesday morning, and Claire lay awake for a long time, listening to the rumble of thunder and the occasional car splashing by on the road in front of her house. As the lightning intensified, she got up to glance out the window, and for a moment she thought she saw someone standing across the street in the rain. But the harder she stared, the more convinced she became that what she saw was only a shadow.

She watched the rain for a while, then went back to bed, but when she finally fell asleep, her rest was fitful. She kept waking up abruptly, certain that she'd heard something in the house, only to realize that it was a branch scraping against the side of the house or rain dripping from the eaves.

She even got back up to check all the doors and windows downstairs, but she saw and heard nothing out of the ordinary. Ever since she'd discovered Ruby's picture missing, Claire worried that someone had come into her house that night. Someone had deliberately removed the photograph from the table in the sunroom, but why? Who would still want a picture of her missing daughter after all this time?

The only answer she could come up with was almost too chilling to contemplate. Ruby's kidnapper had never been caught. What if he had come back, after seven years, for some twisted reason that only he could comprehend?

She went back to bed yet again and watched the shifting patterns on the ceiling as the storm finally broke, just before dawn. The clouds moved inland and the light outside her window turned a misty violet. Claire rolled to her side and watched the sun come up. Only then did she close her eyes and sleep peacefully, until the alarm awakened her a few hours later.

By the time she headed into the Quarter, the sun was bright and the sky overhead a clear blue dome. The humidity was high after the rainstorm, and the stifling heat was like being wrapped in a wool blanket. The sidewalk artists along Pirates Alley had already opened their striped umbrellas, and the ones who were not busy sketching waved fans back and forth in front of their glistening faces.

No matter the weather, Claire loved coming to the Quarter. She'd grown up a few blocks away, in a little shotgun-style cottage in Faubourg Marigny, and the old Creole buildings with their worn facades and overhanging balconies were as familiar to her as her own backyard. Alex used to warn her about the dopers and street thugs that hung out in the area. He always said the place was a felony waiting to happen.

Claire supposed he was right. The Quarter had its share of problems, but there were other areas of the city that had much higher crime rates, and, in truth, the underlying danger had always been a part of the Quarter's appeal.

She didn't linger today, though, to enjoy the party-like atmosphere in the square. She wanted to be at the collectibles shop by the time the door opened at ten.

The neighboring shopkeeper had told Alex on Friday that Mignon Bujold would be back from her trip today, and Claire assumed that meant she would open at her regular time. Since Claire wasn't due at the gallery until one, she didn't have to rush. She could do a little window-shopping just to give the owner plenty of time to arrive at the store and open up.

But the longer Claire delayed, the more apprehensive she became. Now that a few days had gone by since she'd first seen the doll, she'd begun to second-guess herself, and had started to wonder if Charlotte might be right. The mere fact that the doll had curly blond hair and a pink ruffled dress could have been more than enough for Claire's imagination to supply the rest of her daughter's features. After all, she'd done it before. She'd been convinced dozens of times over the past seven years that she'd spotted Ruby on a playground or dashing through a crowded mall. What if this time was no different than the others?

But it *was* different. Claire had had more than a passing glimpse of the doll. The streets in the Quarter were narrow, and even when she'd stood on the corner across from the shop, her view of the display window had been unobstructed. She'd seen the doll clearly from that vantage, and she'd had an even better look as she crossed the street. The doll looked like Ruby. There was no getting away from that fact. Someone had sculpted a doll in the likeness of her missing daughter, and Claire wouldn't be able to rest until she found out why.

By the time she arrived at the shop, it was after ten, and to her disappointment, the Closed sign remained in the window, the shade was drawn and the door still locked tight.

She pressed her face to the glass and tried to peer around the edge of the shade. But this time, she detected no movement at all inside the shop, nor did she have the impression that anyone was about. To the contrary, the interior looked dark and deserted, and she drew back in frustration.

Claire had looked up the number for the shop in the directory a few days ago in order to leave a message, and now, as she stood in the doorway, she pulled out her cell phone and placed a call. She could hear the phone through the glass, and after several rings, an answering machine picked up. Once again she left her name and number, and asked that someone get in touch with her as soon as possible. Then she hung up and stood watching the midmorning traffic on the street.

The only thing she could do now was check the rear entrance. If the back door was locked, she would at least know that someone had been there since she and Alex left on Friday. If it was still open, then in all likelihood the owner hadn't yet returned from her trip.

The alley was shady and a few degrees cooler than the street, but the courtyard at the back blazed with sunlight. The pavers beneath Claire's feet were still damp and slippery from the night's rain. As she walked down the alley, the street noises faded and the only sounds she noticed were the distant trickle of a fountain and the steady click of her heels against the worn bricks.

The closer she got to the back door, the more nervous she became. She'd never laid eyes on Mignon Bujold, knew nothing about the woman's habits. There was no reason in the world that she should be concerned about a stranger, but Claire had a bad feeling that something was wrong.

She reminded herself that Alex had gone through the shop on Friday morning and found nothing. The register hadn't been tampered with, nor had there been any sign of a break-in or struggle, nothing to indicate that the owner had left the shop by any means other than of her own volition.

The shopkeeper next door hadn't even been alarmed by the unsecured premises, and there was no reason for Claire to be, either. But when the knob turned in her hand, her pulse quickened.

She glanced down the alley to the sunny street. A group of tourists strolled along in the lazy heat, but no one glanced in her direction. The gate to the courtyard was closed and nothing stirred from behind the iron fence except a mockingbird flitting through the branches of a mimosa tree. Claire was all alone in the alley.

Nothing to be afraid of, she told herself. Nothing at all.

But her palms were suddenly clammy and her heart started to pound in trepidation. As she pushed open the door, the chilly gloom seeped out into the alley. Claire stood shivering on the threshold, still hesitant to enter as her gaze darted about the dim space.

Everything inside was just as she remembered it.

Shelves stuffed with boxes and packing materials. The worktable strewn with doll parts. The kitchenette. The beaded curtain that swayed in the breeze from the vents.

It was still cold inside the building, and she wondered if the air conditioner had been running all weekend.

She took a step inside, then paused again as her hand went to her nose. She hadn't noticed a smell when she was there before, but now something unpleasant permeated the frigid air. She only caught a whiff of it now and then, and she wondered if it might be food that had been left in the trash can for days.

When she walked through the beaded curtain into the shop, the scent faded and she was able to ignore it. She'd looked through all the display cabinets on Friday, but today, without Alex to interrupt her, she conducted a more thorough search. As she knelt to examine the shelves beneath the counter, the phone beside the register rang. The jarring sound startled her so badly, she almost toppled over, and had to grab the edge of the counter to catch herself. But the structure wasn't stable, and when it shifted, she lost her balance and crashed to the floor.

By the time she'd righted herself, Mignon Bujold's greeting had played, and a woman's voice came over the speaker. "Mother? It's Lily. I've been trying to reach you all morning, but there's no answer at the house, and as usual, your cell phone is turned off. The girls are anxious to see you and I'm getting a little concerned, so please call me as soon as you get my messages." The voice paused, then added with a hint of urgency, "I hope everything is okay."

The worried tone of the caller triggered Claire's growing trepidation, and the inexplicable chill she'd felt standing outside the back door came back stronger than ever. Her every instinct told her to get out of the shop as quickly as possible.

The smell grew stronger as she walked back into the workroom, and in spite of her nerves, she paused to glance around. The odor was coming from the garbage can. She was sure of it. The owner had probably forgotten to take out the trash before she left on Thursday. That's all it was. Just the trash. Or perhaps something in the refrigerator had gone bad….

As Claire's gaze swept over the old fridge, she noticed something she hadn't seen before. Something blue was caught in the door. It looked like a swatch of fabric, so small that Claire probably wouldn't have detected it now if she hadn't been searching for the source of the bad smell.

As she focused on the fabric, gooseflesh prickled along her arms and she caught her breath, not daring to move as comprehension dawned in a flash of horror. Her mouth went dry with fear. Cold sweat misted her forehead as dread tightened in her chest. She told herself to turn and leave, go outside into the fresh air and call Alex. She didn't relish a conversation with her soon-to-be-ex-husband, but he was still a cop, and when she told him what she'd seen, what she feared, he would have to come and check out the shop for himself.

But Claire couldn't move. She couldn't tear her gaze away from that blue fabric, and it almost seemed as if she'd been hypnotized into doing something she wouldn't ordinarily do.

She found herself in front of the refrigerator, but couldn't remember walking across the room. And when her hand lifted, it was as if she were watching someone else, an impetuous stranger, reach for the handle and pull open the door. She tried to close her eyes because she didn't want to know, didn't want to see....

The body fell with a hard thud to the floor.

Claire screamed and stumbled back, nausea so thick in her throat she bent double, gagging. Drawing in desperate gulps of air, she lifted her gaze, then shuddered violently when she saw the woman's eyes. The dead, milky stare was focused on Claire, mesmerizing her with an icy penetration, and for a moment, she couldn't look away. She felt weak and sick, violated by the smell of death, her own fear and those glazed, sightless eyes.

A dozen thoughts rushed through her head. She had to call 911. She had to reach Alex. She had to get out of there before she fainted dead away.

Still, she couldn't move. She stood for what seemed an eternity, stunned and trembling, paralyzed by the kind of horror she'd known only in her nightmares.

The refrigerator had slowed decomposition and the woman's pale features were still clearly discernible. She was older, sixty perhaps, petite and slim with short, white hair. A pair of glasses dangled from a chain around her neck, the lenses frosted over, and Claire saw the flash of a sapphire-and-diamond ring on her right hand. It was Mignon Bujold. Claire was certain of it.

After a moment, when she could get her fingers to work, she took out her cell phone and called Alex's number. She tried to stay calm, but the words tumbled out in a horrified rush the moment she heard his voice.

"Claire, calm down and tell me what happened. Are you all right?"

"I'm okay. I'm…at the collectibles shop in the Quarter. Mignon Bujold is dead. It looks like…oh, God, Alex, she's been murdered."

She heard the sharp intake of his breath. "Claire, listen to me. Don't touch anything, just get the hell out of there. Go next door or down the street and wait for me. Claire? Are you listening to me?"

"Yes…"

But her gaze had gone back to the body. The last moment of Mignon Bujold's life was trapped in those frozen eyes, and a terrible thought came to Claire. What if the poor woman had been alive when she'd been imprisoned inside the refrigerator?

What if she'd been alive…and she knew no one was coming to let her out?

Claire sat in a restaurant across the street, staring at the array of emergency vehicles that had assembled outside the collectibles shop. She counted four patrol cars, their lights still flashing in the sunlight, along with an ambulance, a van from the Orleans Parish coroner's office, and oddly enough, two wreckers.

The sidewalks were clogged with patrolmen, paramedics and the usual assortment of curious onlookers. Claire could see some of the officers talking to neighboring shopkeepers, and every minute or so they would pause to jot something down on their clipboards or lift their static-filled radios.

Alex came out of the shop once, said something to one of the officers, then went back inside. He and Claire had spoken briefly when he first arrived, and then he'd sent her across the street to wait while the forensics investigator finished sweeping the crime scene.

Claire had ordered a Coke, and it sat in front of her untouched, ice melting, condensation streaming down the glass onto the table.

She couldn't stop thinking about Mignon Bujold. The notion that she'd been trapped in the refrigerator on Friday, still alive, when Claire was inside the shop, haunted her. She couldn't help wondering if the killer had committed the crime only moments before she arrived. If she'd noticed that telltale fabric caught in the refrigerator door then—if it had, in fact, been there at that time—would she have been able to save Mignon Bujold's life?

Now the woman was dead, and something told Claire that the murder was somehow connected to the doll. The register and safe hadn't been tampered with, and Mignon had still been wearing a valuable ring when Claire found her. If she'd been the victim of a random robbery, surely the assailant would have taken the jewelry. The only thing that appeared to be missing from the shop was the doll.

Claire told herself it was too early to jump to any conclusions. She needed to wait and hear what the police found inside the shop. But as much as she wanted to stay calm and rational, her mind raced and she couldn't stop shaking. She knew it would be a very long time before she would forget Mignon Bujold's sightless eyes staring up at her.

"Are you Claire?"

She turned with a start. A dark-haired woman in a trim black suit had approached the table, and Claire gave a brief nod.

The woman was slim and petite, but the high heels she wore gave her the illusion of height, and her demeanor, along with the designer bag she carried, spoke of a young sophisticated professional on her way up. She reminded Claire of Charlotte.

Her gaze was cool and detached as she stared down at Claire. "One of the detectives told me I could find you here. My name is Lily Devereaux. I'm Mignon Bujold's daughter."

Claire started to rise, but the woman said quickly, "No, please. I don't mean to disturb you, but could we talk for a moment?"

"Of course."

She sat down across from Claire, and when the waitress appeared, ordered hot tea in spite of the sweltering heat outside. As they waited for her drink, Claire realized that her initial assessment of the woman had been wrong. What she'd mistaken for cool detachment was, in fact, a valiant effort on Lily Devereaux's part to hang on to her shattered composure. Her face was nearly colorless, and when she had the tea in front of her, she wrapped her hands around the cup, clinging to the warmth as if it were the only thing that would get her through this.

Her eyes desperately sought Claire's across the table as a lone tear ran down her cheek. She wiped it away with her napkin.

"I'm sorry," Claire said. "This must be such a terrible shock for you."

She nodded, sniffed and seemed to collect herself then. "They told me you were the one who found her."

"Yes, that's right."

"I don't mean for this to sound accusatory, but…

who are you? I don't remember Mother ever mentioning you. Were you a friend of hers?"

"No. I was a potential customer. I saw a doll in her shop window one day last week and I came back to ask about it."

The gray eyes stared unblinking at Claire. "How did you get in?"

"The back door was unlocked."

"So you just walked in?"

Regardless of what she said, her tone was most definitely suspicious, Claire decided. "I know that sounds bad, but I found the rear entrance unlocked when I was there on Friday. Someone next door was supposed to get in touch with your mother and make sure that the premises were secured. I was curious to see if anyone had been there since I left. When I saw that the door was still unlocked, I became concerned."

"Do the police know that you were there before?"

"Yes, of course. I've told them everything I know, which really isn't much. As I said, I only came back to ask your mother about the doll I saw."

Claire hadn't meant to sound defensive, but Lily said quickly, "I'm not implying that you were somehow responsible for Mother's death. Please don't think that. I'm just trying to make sense of what happened."

"I understand."

Lily drew in a ragged breath. "I have two little girls. They both adored Mother. I don't know how I'm going to tell them...." She lifted a trembling hand to her mouth. "When I drove up and saw all the police cars out front, I knew something had happened. But I never dreamed...I just still can't believe it. Even after I identified the body."

"I'm sorry you had to go through that," Claire said.

The woman didn't seem to hear her. "They told me I would have to wait outside until the crime scene had been cleared. I didn't know what to do or where to go. I couldn't seem to think... I guess that's why one of the detectives told me that I should come over here and wait with you."

Claire watched, mesmerized, as Lily lifted the cup to her lips. Her hands shook so badly, Claire had to resist the urge to offer assistance, but somehow she managed alone. She took a sip, then returned the cup to the saucer with a clatter.

"I should have checked on her sooner. The girls and I were busy all weekend and I thought Mother was out of town. She wasn't due home until last night, and when I didn't hear from her, I assumed she'd gotten in late. I didn't want to bother her...." She trailed off, her eyes filling again.

"I called her house this morning, and when she didn't answer, I told myself she was probably in the shower or outside. She liked to putter around in her garden before she left for work. I tried her cell phone, but she wasn't in the habit of turning it on. She only bought one to appease me. I thought it was a good idea because she traveled a lot."

Lily's gaze dropped to her cup, and she stared for a long time into the tea, as if trying to divine a message in the dregs.

"I didn't mean to unload all that on you," she finally said. "I guess I can't stop talking about it because it's just so hard for me to comprehend. Who would do such a terrible thing to someone as kind and gentle as my mother? And why? I don't understand how something like this could happen…." She bowed her head then and her slim shoulders shook as she began to weep quietly into her napkin.

Claire reached over and touched her hand. "Is there someone you want me to call? You shouldn't have to face this alone."

Lily wiped her nose and eyes and straightened her shoulders. "I've already called a friend. He should be here soon. I probably shouldn't ask this of you. I've already imposed on you long enough. But…would you mind sitting with me until he gets here?"

"Of course not."

She turned back to the window, staring out at the commotion across the street. "I'm not usually like this. I never lose control."

"It's understandable under the circumstances." Claire wished she knew what to say to the woman, what words she could offer that might bring some comfort. But grief was an intensely personal emotion. Others could sympathize, but no one else, no matter their own experience, could ever fully comprehend.

The woman bit her bottom lip to stop the tremor. "I should have called the police when I couldn't reach her."

"You had no way of knowing she was in trouble."

"I know, but I should have done *something*."

"It's easy to think in hindsight of everything we might or should have done, but it doesn't help, and you can let yourself slide into a very dark place if you aren't careful."

"I know you're right. Still…"

She continued to look out the window, and Claire knew that wasn't a good thing because they would be bringing out the body soon. "Maybe it would help if we talked about something else," she said.

The woman's gaze finally moved away from the window. She took another sip of her tea as she mustered her shaky poise. "Why don't you tell me about the doll you came to ask about? Are you a collector?"

"My mother is. My sister and I were shopping for a birthday present for her when I saw the doll in the window. I was involved in an accident that day or I would have gone in and asked about her then. When I came back on Friday, the shop was closed and the doll was gone from the window."

A note of desperation in Claire's voice seemed to filter through Lily Devereaux's grief, and she looked up with a frown. "Which doll was it?"

"She had curly blond hair and beautiful turquoise eyes. She seemed so lifelike I had to look twice to make sure she wasn't real." Claire paused, fighting back her own rush of emotions. "This may sound strange, but she looks exactly like...my daughter."

For the first time, Lily smiled. "It doesn't sound strange to me at all. I had a twin doll when I was little. Mother still has her in her collection. You must have seen the Savannah Sweete doll. Mother only got her a few days ago and was over the moon about the purchase. If you know anything about doll collecting, you'll understand why."

Claire's heart had started to beat an erratic tattoo inside her chest, but she tried to keep the excitement from her voice. She didn't want to say or do anything that might alarm Lily Devereaux, because the poor woman had already been through enough. "The little I do know, I've picked up from my mother. I've heard her mention Savannah Sweete. I think she even took some classes from her at one time."

"It's quite possible. Savannah used to teach doll making classes here in New Orleans and in Houma, which is close to where she lives. But she had a terrible accident a few years ago that confined her to a wheel-chair, and I understand she's been almost a recluse since then. I don't know much else about her except that she's regarded as one of the finest doll artists in the country. That's why Mother was so elated when a man brought one into the shop. As I said, portrait dolls rarely come on the market and you almost never see a Savannah Sweete."

"Did your mother happen to mention the man's name?"

"I don't think she knew him. He wasn't a collector or dealer, just someone who had a doll for sale. She said he mentioned that a child had died and the reminder was just too painful. That's why he needed to get rid of the doll."

Claire turned to the window, her own eyes filling with tears. *A child had died and the reminder was just too painful.*

Outside, the wind picked up, and she watched a paper cup roll across the street and into the gutter. In her mind she saw a bright yellow kite skim low over the surf as Ruby ran laughing behind it.

"Are you okay?"

The woman's concerned voice drew Claire's attention back to the table, and she had to swallow past a sudden knot in her throat. "I don't want to bother you at a time like this, but…it's very important to me that I find this doll. Do you have any idea what happened to her? Did your mother say anything about selling her?"

Curiosity sparked in Lily Devereaux's eyes, but she shook her head. "The last time I talked to her was on Thursday morning. She said the doll had generated a lot of interest and she was anticipating a fairly heated bidding war. The piece was that spectacular."

"Did you see the doll yourself?"

"No, but I feel as if I did after the way Mother went on and on about her. She said the attention to detail was extraordinary. The eyes, the mouth, the nose…everything exquisitely sculpted and painted. She even had a tiny strawberry birthmark on her left arm…."

Lily's voice faded and everything inside Claire stilled as her mind slipped back in time. She could see Ruby so clearly. The two of them were sitting on the porch swing, waiting for Dave to come home.

"Why do I have this red bump on my arm, Mama?"

"It's a birthmark, Ruby. You were born with it."

"Maw-Maw says it's where an angel kissed me. But Daddy has one just like it. Does that mean an angel kissed him, too?"

"Somehow I kind of doubt that, honey."

Claire's chest tightened, and for the longest time, she could hardly breathe.

Nineteen

The crime scene was crawling with cops. Uniformed officers were stationed at the front and rear entrances of the shop in order to limit access, and another half-dozen or so milled around in the showroom and on the street outside the front door.

John Gilby, the heavyset coroner's investigator, squatted near the body, while Patrice Petty, the crime scene investigator, collected and bagged forensic samples. She wore faded jeans and paper covers over her sneakers, and her red hair was pulled back into a tight, sleek ponytail that glistened like copper. She and Alex Girard had worked together on dozens of crime scenes, and when she caught his eye, she gave him a smile and a slight nod. They'd had a flirtation going for years, and had even gone out a few times after he and Claire first split up. But nothing had come of it. Alex had told Patrice that he wasn't ready for anything serious, and that was the truth. He also didn't see any reason to complicate a working relationship that could be advantageous for both of them.

Two homicide detectives had been sent over by the division commander, and they stood directly across from Alex, both staring down at the body. Tony Maddox had his hands shoved deep into his pockets, jangling his keys as he rocked back and forth on his heels. He was a few years younger than Alex, maybe thirty-one or thirty-two, with dark brown hair and piercing blue eyes. He was a good detective, but there had always been something about him that rubbed Alex the wrong way. Sometimes his intensity and his dogged approach to an investigation reminded Alex a little too much of Dave Creasy.

Tony's partner, Remi Broussard, was the exact opposite, a good-natured Cajun with thick, black hair he kept clipped close to his scalp, and a brush mustache that hid the scar over his lip where a suspect had sliced him open one night during an arrest.

Like Alex, both men were dressed in lightweight summer suits that were already rumpled from the heat. Maddox had gum in his mouth, and his jaw worked fiercely as he watched the coroner's investigator finish his examination.

Alex's gaze moved to the open refrigerator. The wire shelves that had been removed to accommodate the body had been slid behind the refrigerator, against the wall. Unnoticeable, unless you were looking for them. If the woman's dress hadn't been caught in the door, compromising the seal and allowing the smell to seep out, it might have been days before anyone found her.

Good idea, but sloppy execution, Alex thought. Especially from a killer who'd gone out of his way to keep the crime scene immaculate. Something or someone must have spooked him in the act, and Alex's mind went back to Friday morning, when Claire had insisted that she'd seen someone inside the shop.

He'd dismissed the claim as her imagination, and when he'd had a look around the shop and alley to appease her, he hadn't been as thorough or concerned as he should have. But he also knew that if the fabric had been visible then, he would have seen it. Which suggested to him that Mignon Bujold had either been killed at a later time or in a different location, her body then brought back to the collectibles shop and stuffed inside the appliance.

Or a third possibility. The killer had gone back to the body for some reason after Alex and Claire had left the shop.

Logical explanations aside, Alex could too easily imagine how all that would play out in the press, a body going undiscovered by a seasoned detective. The last thing he needed was to come off looking incompetent—or worse, a laughingstock—when his career was finally gathering some steam.

John Gilby rose with a grunt, hitched up his pants and mopped his face with a white cotton handkerchief. It was as cold as a meat locker inside the shop, but his shirt was stained underneath his arms and the bald spot at the back of his head glistened with sweat. As always, he looked a mess. His ill-fitting brown trousers were threadbare at the knees and seat, and his shirttail hung out in the back. He had on a tie, but it was loosely knotted around his neck and fell several inches short of his burgeoning waistline.

"What's the word, Gilby?" Maddox asked impatiently, his jaw still working the gum. "Can you give us time of death?"

"You're kidding, right?" Gilby peeled off his latex gloves and tossed them aside. "We won't know anything until she's opened up and we get a look at the stomach and bowels. Maybe not even then."

"What about cause?" Remi asked.

"'Fraid I can't help you boys out much there, either. I can tell you this, though. She's got no visible wounds on the body that I could see, and she doesn't appear to have been sexually assaulted. The only thing I did find was a small mark at the side of her neck."

Alex glanced up. "Stun gun?"

"Looks like a needle track. We'll have to order a full toxicology screen with the postmortem." He mopped his face again, then returned the crumpled handkerchief to his pocket. "I'm done with her. Y'all can have 'em take her out whenever you're ready."

Alex nodded absently as he snapped on a pair of gloves and knelt beside the body. Turning the victim's head slightly, he moved in closer to get a look at the tiny puncture wound at the side of her neck. It was barely visible. Anyone else might have overlooked it, but Gilby was a lot more astute than his slovenly appearance suggested.

So who killed you? Alex wondered as he stared down at the body. *And why?*

Maddox squatted on the other side of the corpse and rubbed a thumb across his bottom lip. "Looks like the son of a bitch must have shot her up with something to incapacitate her, then stuffed her in the icebox so she wouldn't be found for a while. He knew she wouldn't last long in this heat."

"Motive?"

Maddox shrugged. "An old woman alone in a shop

isn't exactly an unusual target in New Orleans. Some crunkhead strolls by, spots her through the front window and decides right then and there to knock over the place."

He and Alex both straightened as Remi Broussard said in his deep, quiet voice, "I'm not so sure I buy that explanation. Don't make sense a junkie taking the time to hide the body when he won't care who finds her or when, so long as he gets his fix. And he's not going to leave a nice ring like that on her finger, either, or cash in the register. Not when he's got a mess of spiders crawling around inside his head."

He was right, Alex thought. Someone else had wanted Mignon Bujold dead, and as much as he didn't want to go there, he couldn't stop thinking about that missing doll.

He left Remi and Maddox with the body and walked into the other room to glance out the window. He couldn't see Claire in the restaurant across the street, but knew she was still there, waiting for him to come and tell her what he'd found.

Alex wished to hell she'd never spotted that damn doll, because he had a bad feeling now that Pandora's box was about to be opened.

"Hey, Lieutenant, you got a minute?"

He turned as the crime scene investigator approached him. "What's up, Patty? You find something?"

"Oh, I found plenty. We got prints and fibers all over the damn place, but the question is, do any of them belong to the killer?"

"You tell me."

"That's what I wanted to ask you about. You running this thing or am I going to have deal with that asshole, Maddox?"

Alex grinned at her bluntness. "I guess we'll have to let the captain sort that out."

"I was afraid you'd say that."

"What else did you find?"

"Come take a look." She motioned for him to follow her over to the counter. The surface was sooty where she'd dusted for prints. "See that mark on the floor? The counter's been scooted out of place about half an inch. I figured this might be where he took her down, so I went over the area a few times. I found this shoved up underneath the counter." She held up an evidence bag that had already been numbered and labeled.

"What is it?"

"It's a photograph of a kid. Looks to be six or seven. Maybe somebody dropped it and it got slid under there by mistake. Could have been there for years. Then again…" She shrugged. "You never know."

Alex took the bag from her hand and glanced down at the photograph. Recognition shot through him like an icy needle and his chest tightened painfully. For a moment, he thought he might be having a heart attack, but a split second later, he realized what he felt was panic.

Because the child in the photograph was Claire's daughter, Ruby.

A few minutes later, Alex stood outside on the sidewalk in front of the shop, wondering what the hell he was going to do about that picture. He'd told Patrice Petty that he would show the photograph to Mignon Bujold's daughter to see if she recognized it, and then he'd slipped the bag into his pocket and walked off.

It was almost noon and the sun shone down on the street like a brilliant spotlight. Alex fished in his pocket for his sunglasses and put them on. After being inside the air-conditioned shop for the better part of an hour, he found the heat outside stifling. But the sweat that broke out across his forehead was cold and clammy. A nerve twitched at his temple, and he put his hand over the spot, trying to massage away the tic.

Yet no matter what he did, he couldn't stop thinking about the photograph. It was like an iron weight in his pocket. He wanted to believe that he'd been mistaken. The kid in the picture only resembled Ruby Creasy. All that talk about a look-alike doll had planted ideas in his head. That's all it was.

But as much as Alex wanted to believe this was just some bizarre coincidence, he couldn't completely discount the possibility that Claire had been right all along. Somehow the doll she'd seen in the shop window was linked to her missing daughter. And now a woman who had come into possession of that doll was dead.

He ran his thumb and forefinger along the corners of his mouth as he stared out at the crowd that had gathered on the street. A couple of reporters were there, too, and the minute they spotted him, they pressed forward, shouting questions in his direction even as he deliberately turned away. The last thing he needed was for the media to get wind of that photograph.

One of the uniforms came over and said something to him. Alex nodded even though he barely heard the man's comments. His attention was on the restaurant across the street. Claire had just come outside, and when she spotted Alex through the crowd, she hurried toward him.

She was stopped briefly by the officer guarding the perimeter, but as soon as he recognized her, he held up the tape and let her pass.

"Alex, I have to talk to you," she said urgently as she came up beside him.

"I need to talk to you, too, but it'll have to wait. Right now I need to get back inside."

She caught his arm. "This can't wait. It's about Mignon Bujold's killer."

The officer standing next to Alex heard her and glanced curiously in their direction. The two reporters were standing farther away, but Alex wasn't about to take a chance on being overheard. He'd been burned by the press before.

He took Claire's arm and guided her around to the side of the building and underneath the crime scene tape that barricaded the alley from the sidewalk. When they were far enough away from the street, he turned with a frown. "What's so important that you couldn't wait five minutes for me to finish up?"

"I just had a long talk with Lily Devereaux about the doll I saw in the window the other day. Alex, she said a man Mignon didn't know brought that doll into the shop. He told her that a child had died, and he wanted to get rid of the doll because it was too painful a reminder."

Alex felt the ache in his chest sharpen. "You think he was talking about Ruby?"

"I don't know. But I'm convinced the doll is connected to her kidnapping and now to Mignon Bujold's murder. Lily told me that the doll had been sculpted by an artist named Savannah Sweete. She specializes in portrait dolls and her work is very detailed. Lily said the doll I saw in the window that day had a tiny strawberry birthmark painted on her left arm, just like the one Ruby had. That can't be a coincidence, Alex. Even you have to see that now."

"It still doesn't prove that the doll is connected to Mignon Bujold's murder. You're jumping to an awful lot of conclusions. And I don't deal in coincidences when I investigate a crime, I deal in facts."

"Okay, fact one—that doll looks exactly like Ruby, right down to the birthmark on her arm and the dress she was wearing when she disappeared. Fact two—nobody could have sculpted and painted her so perfectly from a picture. The birthmark was too tiny to show up in a photograph. Whoever made that doll had to have seen Ruby in person at some time or another. And three—a few days after Mignon Bujold bought that doll from a stranger, she turns up dead. There's a pattern here, Alex. An undeniable connection. You have to reopen Ruby's case."

"For your information, Ruby's case has never been closed. As far as NOPD is concerned, it's still an ongoing investigation."

"Then put some manpower on it," Claire said desperately. "I know you have the clout to do it."

Alex massaged his pounding forehead. "Go home, Claire. Go home and let me do my job."

"But that's just it. Will you do your job?"

"What's that supposed to mean?"

"You never wanted to believe that the doll looked like Ruby. You never wanted to believe there was a connection to her kidnapping. Even now, after everything I just told you, you still don't want to believe me. You refuse to keep an open mind, and I have to wonder if you're the best person to investigate this case."

"That's not for you to decide. And thanks for your faith in me, by the way."

"I'm not trying to insult you. I know you're a good cop. I don't think you would deliberately do anything to sabotage an investigation, but I also know you don't want to see me hurt. I'm afraid of what you might do to protect me. But you don't need to worry about me. I can handle the truth. What I can't deal with is you keeping something from me."

His gaze broke from hers and he looked off down the alley toward the street. A hush fell over the crowd gathered in front of the shop as the coroner's assistants wheeled the portable gurney through the front door and loaded the body into the back of a van.

If they were lucky, the autopsy would tell them how Mignon Bujold had died and approximately when. But it was the *why* that worried Alex. Why had she become a target? Because the doll had crossed her path?

His gaze moved back to Claire. Her eyes looked very blue even in the shade, and her lips—lips that he had kissed over and over in a desperate attempt to obliterate her past—trembled ever so slightly with emotion. He couldn't look her in the eye so he glanced away again.

"You need to go home," he said.

"I can't."

"This is a police matter. You'll just get in the way if you stay here."

"What about the doll?"

"What about it?"

"Do you believe me now?"

"What I believe is that you're so desperate, you've convinced yourself that a doll is somehow the answer to all your prayers. You need to let it go. If there's a connection, we'll find it."

"I'm not giving up on this," she said stubbornly. "I don't care what you say."

He hardened his voice. "Then I'm going to give you fair warning. If you interfere in any way in this investigation, I'll treat you just like I would anyone else. I'll toss your ass in jail and throw away the key."

Claire lifted her shoulders. "You do what you have to do, Alex. Because that's what I intend to do, too."

She turned and started walking back toward the street. Alex called after her, but she kept going. He wanted to stop her, but he couldn't. The weight of the photograph—and his own guilt—held him back. He leaned heavily against the wall and let his head drop back against the smooth, worn brick.

Twenty

❧❧❧

Water lilies undulated in the *Sea Ray*'s wake as Dave cut back the engines and drifted toward the dock where Marsilius sat in a lawn chair, his face shielded by the brim of a straw hat. Dave had taken the boat out just after lunch and stayed until almost sunset.

Dropping anchor a few miles from shore, he'd set the rods and spun out the lines, then sat under a cloudless sky and waited for the fish to bite. After a couple of hours, the ice bins were lined with spotted bass, crappie and bream, all gutted and cleaned and waiting for the frying pan or the freezer. After he put away the rods, he'd cranked up the engines and made a run down to Vermillion Bay. The afternoon had been hot and sunny, the water as calm as a mirror, but by the time he headed back, clouds were already gathering in the west and he could smell the rain.

Tossing a line to Marsilius, Dave took the other and slipped the loop over a metal cleat bolted into the wooden dock. He was shirtless and he could feel the prickle of sunburn along his back and shoulders as he bent to his work.

"Someone's waiting up at the house to see you," Marsilius told him once they had the boat secured.

Dave jumped up on the dock. "Who is it, a client?"

"It's Claire."

Even after seeing her the other night, Dave found the sound of her name came as a shock. He turned and stared at the water, his heart pounding.

On the other side of the bayou, an old black man sat under a willow tree, fishing off the bank with a cane pole. Two little boys threw rocks and shells into the water nearby, scaring off the bream that had come to the surface to feed near the water lilies. The old man didn't seem to mind. He sat puffing on a pipe, his eyes glued to the cork bobber floating among the lily pads.

"Dave, did you hear me?"

"I heard you, old man. What does she want?"

Marsilius shrugged, but his eyes were curious beneath the brim of his straw hat. "She didn't say, I didn't ask."

"She must have told you something."

He took off the hat and fanned his face. "All I know is she came into the bait shop looking for you. I told her you took the boat out, but I expected you back directly. She asked if I thought it would be okay for her to wait at your place. I said sure, didn't see no harm in that."

"Did you let her in?"

"I offered to, but she said she'd just as soon wait outside. But she must be getting pretty hot up there on that porch, Dave. You better go on up there and see what she wants."

Dave resisted the urge to glance over his shoulder at the house. It was a strange feeling knowing that Claire was up there waiting for him. He had a picture in his mind of her in a yellow dress, sitting in the swing on her grandmother's front porch. "There you are," she'd say breathlessly as he slowly climbed the porch steps. "I was beginning to worry you weren't coming."

"You weren't worried. You're not the kind of girl who gets stood up."

"Why do you say that?"

"Because a guy'd have to be crazy to leave you sitting out here all alone. Especially in that yellow dress."

She'd cock her head, smile in that way she had. "And you're not crazy, are you, Dave?"

"Nope. What I am," he'd say softly, bending to brush his lips against hers, "is just about the luckiest son of a bitch in the whole wide world."

Dave turned off the conversation in his head as he glanced at Marsilius. "I'll go up in a minute. I need to clean out the ice chests first and hose off the boat."

"I'll take care of that. You go on now, don't keep her waiting any longer."

But when Dave turned toward the house, Marsilius called him back, frowning. "Look here, son. I don't know what she's got on her mind, but I could tell something was bothering her. You go easy on her, hear?"

"What do you think I'm going to do? Throw her off my porch?"

"You've always been bad to hold a grudge, Dave, don't claim you ain't. She married somebody else and that didn't sit well with you. I reckon you made that plain enough. But something's going on with that girl and there's no sense in you going up there making her feel any worse about it."

Dave just shook his head. "You don't give me much credit for anything, do you?"

"I speak my mind, if that's what you mean."

Dave left without another word and walked up to the house through the oak and pecan trees that ringed his property. The breeze picked up, scattering leaves across the path in front of him, and the sky took on a greenish tint.

He paused at the edge of the yard to slip on his shirt before striding down the dirt pathway to his house. A moment later, he drew back the screen door and stepped up on the porch.

Even when she turned, when he saw her full on, she didn't seem real to him. It was like he'd awakened from a deep sleep, a dream still hovering at the edges of his consciousness, and in that fleeting moment he couldn't tell if what he saw and heard and felt was real or only a vision.

The screen door snapped shut behind him, and as their eyes met, a smile died on her lips. Her gaze moved over his face, taking inventory of the bruises and the stitch marks near his scalp. "What happened to you?"

"Let's just say I had a difference of opinion with someone, and leave it at that."

Their eyes met again and she looked away. "You never change, do you, Dave? You always did have a talent for trouble."

"According to Marsilius, it's one of the few things I was ever any good at."

She didn't return his smile, but instead glanced

around. "I like your place. It's nice here. Peaceful with all the trees."

He accepted the compliment with a shrug. "It's not much to look at, but it's home."

"Home," she said softly, turning to stare out at the yard, making a point not to look at him.

Dave watched her standing there, and a lump rose in his throat. She wore a white cotton skirt and sandals, with a blue camisole that matched the turquoise of her eyes. Her hair was clipped up in back so that he could see the fine, glistening hairs at her nape.

He swallowed, tore his gaze away. "Marsilius said you wanted to see me about something."

She turned, and what she saw in his eyes seemed to take her aback for a moment. Her hand fluttered to her throat, covering the pattern of freckles on her chest that he had once traced with his fingertip.

"I've come to see you about a professional matter. If you have the time," she added hesitantly.

"Sure. Just give me a minute to get cleaned up. I've been out on the water all afternoon." His hands trembled as he took the key out of the flowerpot and unlocked the front door, but he managed to say evenly, "You want to come inside where it's cooler?"

She glanced at the door, then shook her head.

"Suit yourself. How about something cold to drink?"

"I'm fine. Don't worry about me."

"Okay. I'll be back in a minute."

Dave closed the door between them and stood for a moment, eyes closed, the sound of his heartbeat loud and uneven in his ears. Someone had once told him that the past, more than DNA or fingerprints, was what made each human being unique. A person was shaped by the places he'd been and the things he'd done and seen. For Dave, it was what he had lost.

He didn't know why Claire had come to see him, but he told himself it didn't matter. He couldn't let himself get drawn back into her orbit. He couldn't let himself wish for something that was never going to be, because there was no going back, ever.

There was no changing the past or the person he had become because of it.

A little while later, he climbed out of the shower, dressed quickly and ran a comb through his wet hair before going back downstairs. He took a pitcher of tea from the refrigerator, filled two glasses with ice and carried a tray out to the front porch, where he set it on a small table between the two rockers.

"How about some tea? I don't know about you, but I'm parched." He handed one to Claire.

She thanked him and took a sip. "It's good," she said in surprise. "Sweet, but still with a bite. It reminds me of Mama's tea."

"I'll take that as a compliment," Dave said. "How is Lucille?"

"She's fine. But I expect you already know that, don't you?" When he didn't say anything, Claire smiled. "I know you keep in touch with her. She let it slip once."

Dave shrugged. "She was always good to me. I never saw any reason to cut her out of my life just because you and I split up."

"She thought the world of you." Claire paused, glancing out the screen at the rose bush that grew at the corner of the porch. Dave saw the pain that flickered in her eyes before she could hide it.

"Why are you here, Claire?"

She set down the glass and pressed her hands against the sides of her skirt. "You said the other night that you'd moved your office down here. You're doing P.I. work again."

"That's right."

"I'd like to hire you. I need you to find something for me." Her face was calm, but her voice shook a little as her gaze met his in the fading light.

"You want me to find something for you," Dave said, his voice flat, hollow. "Does this have something to do with the divorce?"

"Did Mama tell you about that?" She sounded surprised.

"Lucille never mentioned it. I heard it from someone else. Is it true?"

"Yes. Alex and I are divorcing, but that's not why I'm here. And I should probably tell you up front that I don't have much money. I'm hoping when you hear me out, that won't be a factor."

Dave sat down in one of the rockers and took a drink of his tea. "You have my attention. What is it you want me to find?"

The twilight softened her features. She looked pale and serene standing by the screen, but when she spoke, her voice was edged with anxiety. "I want you to find a doll for me."

"A doll." He almost laughed, but he saw that her expression was serious when she came over and sat down beside him. "What happened? Did Lucille get robbed or something?"

"This isn't about Mama, either." Claire's eyes searched his face. "I think the doll I'm looking for was sculpted by a local artist named Savannah Sweete. She lives somewhere in Terrebonne Parish. Her specialty is portrait dolls."

"If she lives that close, she shouldn't be too hard to locate. Did you try looking her up in the phone book or on the Internet?"

"She has an unlisted number and I couldn't find an official Web site. She's been wheelchair bound since an accident a few years ago, and I've heard that she's a recluse. Even if we find her, it may not be that easy to get in to see her."

Dave scratched his sunburned neck. "You want me to drive over to Terrebonne Parish and ask around about her?"

"Yes…but there's more to it. I told you that she makes portrait dolls. The doll I want you to find looks exactly like Ruby."

Dave didn't say anything for a moment. His first thought was that it was some sort of bizarre joke, but Claire, of all people, would never be that cruel. And besides, he had only to see the shimmer in her eyes to know that she was emotional about this.

"Are you telling me that you had someone, this Savannah Sweete person, make a doll that looks like Ruby?"

"No. Not me. But someone did. I saw her in a window in the Quarter when I was shopping with Charlotte. The eyes, the mouth…everything about her was exactly like Ruby. Right down to the dress she had on when she went missing." Claire paused, put a hand to her mouth as if holding back her emotions. When she lifted her gaze, he saw that the shimmer was gone, replaced by something that might have been fear.

A chill crawled up Dave's spine. What the hell was she talking about? A doll that looked like Ruby? It made no sense.

"Claire, this all sounds pretty damn weird."

"I know how it sounds."

"Are you sure she looked that much like Ruby?"

"She was the spitting image."

"Did you go into the shop and ask about her?"

"I wanted to. But I couldn't that day. I was involved in a traffic accident. You probably already know about that, too, don't you?"

"Lucille may have mentioned it."

"But she didn't say anything about the doll?"

"Not a word. This is the first I've heard of it."

"She probably didn't want to say anything because she doesn't believe me. No one does. But I'm telling you the truth. I saw the doll clearly that day and it looked so much like Ruby, I couldn't take my eyes off it. But by the time I was able to get back to the shop the next day, the doll was gone."

"Someone bought her?"

"I don't know. The shop was closed. Someone next door told me that the owner was out of town and wouldn't be back until today. So I went back to the shop this morning and I found her. The owner, I mean. She was dead."

That same chill was crawling up and down Dave's spine again. "How did she die?"

Claire drew a deep, shuddering breath. "Someone stuffed her body in a refrigerator."

"Good God…"

"I know. I can't begin to imagine who would do such a thing."

"What did the police say? Do they have a suspect or a motive?"

"Not that they've shared with me. But I think the motive was the doll. She's the only thing missing from the shop."

"How do you know that?"

"The cash register and the safe hadn't been tampered with, and there was no sign of a forced entry. And the owner was still wearing an expensive ring on her finger when I found her, so I don't think it was a random robbery. I think she was killed because of that doll."

"That's a pretty big conclusion to jump to, from what you've told me."

"No, it's not," Claire said desperately. "It's the only conclusion that makes any sense. The owner's daughter told me that a strange man had brought the doll into the shop and offered her for sale. He said a child had died and he needed to get rid of the doll because it was too painful a reminder." Her lips trembled, but this time she didn't try to quell the emotion. "You see what this means, don't you? The doll and Ruby's kidnapping have to be connected."

"Claire, you can't know that for sure. The doll could have been made before Ruby went missing."

"By whom?"

"Maybe Lucille had one made and forgot about it."

"She would have remembered something like that. Besides, it's expensive to commission a portrait doll, especially from an artist as talented as Savannah Sweete. Mama didn't have that kind of money. Dave, whoever made that doll had to have seen Ruby in person at some point."

"Why do you say that?"

"Because she has a tiny birthmark painted on her left arm."

Their gazes dropped to Dave's arm, to the red strawberry mark he had been born with and passed on to their daughter.

"Claire, are you saying that this doll artist had something to do with Ruby's kidnapping?"

"I don't think she's the one who did it. But she may have been in contact with the person who did."

Dave got up and went over to stare out at the bayou. The light outside was fading, and he heard the hoot of an owl from one of the oak trees. The call was eerie, lonely. A sound from his past.

He realized that his hands had started to tremble again, and he stuffed them in his pockets as he turned. "What do you expect me to do with this information?"

"I told you. I want you to find that doll for me."

"And then what?"

She looked up at him, her eyes troubled. "What do you mean?"

"Our daughter is dead. It took me a long time to accept it, but now that I finally have, I'm not so sure it's a good idea to go digging up the past. I've spent a lot of time in some very dark places since Ruby disappeared. Places that look and feel a little too much like hell. I'm not that anxious to go back."

She stood slowly. "What are you saying? You're not going to help me?"

"What if you're just using that doll as a smoke-screen, Claire?"

"What do you mean?"

"Maybe it's your subconscious way of dealing with the divorce."

"You think I'm making all this up to take my mind off my broken marriage?" Her tone was incredulous, her blue eyes angry and dark.

Dave turned back to stare out at the twilight.

Behind him, he heard Claire take a breath. "I should have known better than to come here. You weren't there for our daughter seven years ago, and I don't know why I thought anything would be different now. It's always been about you, hasn't it, Dave? What's best for you?"

"You're right," he said wearily. "This is all about me."

"Don't do that." She grabbed his arm, made him face her. "Don't shut down like that. Not this time. This is too important, and some of us don't have the luxury of running away when things get too tough."

Her tone surprised him. "Is that what you think I did?"

"That's what I know you did. All those nights when you were drinking yourself into one stupor after another, I was looking for our daughter…making phone calls, passing out flyers, connecting with all the national databanks. I did whatever I could, because running away wasn't an option for me."

"You don't think I looked for Ruby? You don't think I did everything humanly possible to find her?" He turned, stormed into the house and started grabbing up the boxes piled against one wall. He carried them out to the porch one by one and dropped them at Claire's feet. "It's all there. A paper trail of every lead I followed, no matter how small. And every time I came to a dead end, I had my heart ripped out all over again. So maybe you'll cut me some slack if I'm not anxious to put you through that same torture."

She lifted her chin, but her eyes were gleaming with tears. "That's not your decision to make."

"Maybe not. But I don't have to be around when you get gutted."

Her eyes looked stricken as she stared up at him. "I never should have come here."

"No, you probably shouldn't have. But you did, and now let's just get this over with. All these years, you've blamed me for Ruby's kidnapping, and now here's your chance to finally get it off your chest. Come on, Claire. Just say it. I know you want to."

"That's not true. I never blamed you. I'm the one who was at the house when she was taken. I'm the one who let her ride her bicycle on the sidewalk that day."

"And I'm the one who didn't come home when he was supposed to. I'm the one who wasn't there to protect her. You might as well say it, Claire, because it's right there in your eyes. It has been from day one. And it's not anything I haven't told myself at least a million times since it happened."

"You want me to say it, then here it is. You should have come home that day. You should have been there to protect our little girl, but instead you were with *her*."

The bitterness in Claire's voice was like a slap in the face. Dave took a step back. "I always figured you knew. Who told you?"

"*She* did."

Dave closed his eyes briefly.

"That's right," Claire said. "That's the kind of woman

you took up with. You chose her over your own wife and child. And it wasn't enough that my daughter was missing and I had to go through the worst kind of agony a mother could ever face. She had to call me up and tell me where you were at the exact moment Ruby was taken."

"God, Claire…" Dave couldn't bear to look at her. "I'm sorry."

"Yeah, so am I."

"Not that this justifies what I did, but it didn't mean anything—"

"Why do men always say that?" she asked in disgust. "It doesn't make it better. It makes it so much worse, knowing that you were willing to throw away what we had over something that didn't even mean anything to you. What kind of person does that?"

Dave didn't answer, because he didn't know what to say. Nothing was ever going to erase what he'd done. And nothing was ever going to change how Claire felt about him.

"You chose her over Ruby and me that day," Claire said quietly.

"It wasn't like that. It wasn't a conscious choice—"

"Did she hold a gun to your head?"

"Claire—"

"Then you made a choice. It's as simple as that."

"I made another choice that day, too. I left her to come back home to you."

"But it was too late, wasn't it? Ruby was already gone."

He sat down heavily in the rocking chair and stared straight ahead. "I don't know what to say to you. I could tell you that I've paid dearly for my mistakes, but somehow I don't think that would make much difference."

She shook her head sadly. "No, it wouldn't. There's nothing that will ever make things right. But even after everything I've said to you, I know deep down that Ruby's kidnapping wasn't your fault. No more than it was mine. Maybe you were right," she said. "Maybe it is a mistake to start digging up the past. Because it seems like whatever you and I buried seven years ago still has the power to destroy us."

Twenty-One

❧⤙⤜❧

The cooling air smelled like flowers and wet dirt as Dave stood at the screen door and watched Claire's car head down the gravel road toward the highway.

Her taillights flashed briefly as she neared a bend in the road, and then the sound of the engine faded in the twilight.

He told himself he should go after her, that he couldn't leave things this way between them. He even went out to his truck, got in, turned on the ignition and backed out of the driveway. But instead of trying to catch Claire before she reached the highway, he turned in the opposite direction, and a few minutes later pulled into the parking lot of a dilapidated icehouse that sat on the edge of the bayou.

The place was dark and seedy and nearly empty. A country and western song played on the jukebox as a few customers sat at the tables, smoking and drinking, their faces reflecting a strange, bluish glow from the neon light that flashed outside the window.

Dave walked over to the bar and sat down.

"What'll you have?"

"Give me a draft and a couple of bourbon shots. And here." Dave fished in his pocket for his keys. "Take these and don't give them back to me no matter what I say."

The bartender tossed them into an old shoe box he kept underneath the bar. "Is there somebody you want me to call so you don't have to walk home?"

"Don't worry about that. I'll see that he gets home okay."

Dave turned at the sound of the husky voice at his ear. Angelette sat down next to him, her dark eyes smiling, knowing. She wore a low-cut red dress that showed the tops of her breasts when she leaned over. Her lips curved when she saw Dave stare, but then he deliberately glanced away.

She tossed her dark hair over one shoulder as she turned to the bartender. "I'll have what he's having. And looks like you better keep 'em coming. I have a feeling it's going to be a long night."

When the drinks were in front of them, Dave drained one shot of whiskey, then took a long drink of his beer. Funny how natural it felt sitting in a smoky dive with the flicker of neon light reflecting in Angelette's dark eyes. Dave could smell her perfume, a thick, musky scent that seemed to emanate from her hair and from her smooth, suntanned skin.

"You're awfully quiet tonight, Dave. What's the matter, cat got your tongue?"

He stared straight ahead, cradling his beer in both hands. "What are you doing here?"

"I came by your place earlier. I saw a car in the drive

and figured you had company. So I came over here to kill a little time."

Dave finished the second shot, and closed his eyes as the fire took hold in his belly. His fingertips and scalp tingled, and he could feel the warmth of the whiskey on his face. And already he wanted another drink.

Angelette was way ahead of him. She ordered another round, then grabbed his arm, tried to pull him up off the stool. "Come on," she said. "Let's take this party outside."

"I'm not going anywhere with you." But he grabbed his beer and reluctantly followed her out the door.

The music drifted outside and Angelette hummed to herself as she pulled out a chair and sat down. "At least we can hear ourselves think out here."

A waitress brought out the fresh round, and Dave picked up a shot, drained it and picked up the next one.

Angelette stared at him through the deepening twilight. "That's some hard-core drinking, baby doll. What brought it on?"

Dave shrugged and downed the fourth shot. The moon was just starting to rise over the bayou and he could hear the cicadas and the bullfrogs over the music. But it was all becoming a bit hazy. Angelette's perfume mingled with the jasmine that grew around the deck, and the sounds of the swamp became indistinguishable from the murmur of voices inside the bar. It was all just noise inside Dave's head.

A car pulled into the parking lot and a high beam caught him square in the face. He squinted and put up a hand to shield his eyes until the lights went out. A door slammed and a woman's soft laughter drifted through the darkness.

By the time he had a few more shots, Dave started to relax. He was on familiar turf now. He'd spent more nights like this than he could remember, in icehouses and bars all up and down Highway 90. The buzz inside his head was like the comfortable chatter of an old friend.

"Dave?"

"Yeah?"

"That was Claire's car I saw at your house, wasn't it?"

"I'm not going to talk about Claire with you."

He saw her smile tighten in the half-light. "All right."

He gazed off at the water. "Why'd you do it, Angie?"

"Do what, Dave?"

"Why did you tell her about us?"

She picked up her beer and shrugged. "Because they say the wife's always the last to find out. I thought she had a right to know."

"Bullshit."

Angelette drew back from the table, anger flashing in her eyes. "You walked out on me. You left me in that dump like some cheap whore that you'd bought and paid for and didn't give a damn about. What did you think, Dave? That I was one of those women who liked being treated like shit?"

"So you took it out on Claire? A woman who never did anything to you?"

"She had it coming."

Anger shot through the alcohol fog inside his brain, and Dave clenched his fists. "How do you figure that?"

"She had you. That was enough to make me hate her."

Angelette laughed, but the sound was bitter and hollow as she fished in her purse for a cigarette. "What can I say? I was young and foolish and I thought I was in love."

"That's no excuse. You went out of your way to hurt a woman who was already grieving for her missing child. I knew you had a cold heart," Dave said. "I never thought you were vicious."

"Turns out there's a lot about me you don't know." She lit her cigarette and shook out the match.

"Yeah, I guess I'm starting to find that out."

She sat smoking quietly, one arm folded over her middle as she stared at him across the table.

"You knew when you approached me about the Losier case that NOPD had a viable suspect and was close to making an arrest, didn't you? It was all a setup."

She flicked ashes into the dark.

"You never even talked to Gordon Losier about me, did you? Why say that you did?"

"Because I wanted to make sure I could get you interested in the Savaria case again. I figured the best way to do that was to convince you there was a connection between those two dead girls. I don't get it, though. What has you so upset, Dave? Are you mad that I played you? So what if I did? I'm not the first and I probably won't be the last, but in the end, you got what you wanted, didn't you?"

"What do you mean?"

"You've tortured yourself all these years about who made those phone calls to you after Ruby disappeared. Now you know it was a cop."

He stared at her for a moment. "How did you know about that?"

She shrugged and kept silent.

"Were you there the night Renee Savaria was murdered? Were you in on the cover-up?"

She laughed as she tossed her cigarette into the darkness. "Come on, Dave. Those parties were for the good ol' boys. You think they'd invite a female cop into their inner sanctum?"

"Then how did you know about Renee Savaria, much less about those phone calls?"

She leaned forward, smiling. "Use your imagination. What do you think I was doing all those nights when you were crying in your beer over Claire? You think you were the only cop who had the hots for me back then? I had plenty of guys after me, and they weren't like you, Dave. They didn't get all quiet and moody and remorseful after we did it. Some of them got pretty talkative afterward, especially after a few drinks."

"Why didn't you ever say anything? You knew what Nettle did to that poor girl. You knew about the cover-up and you didn't say a word."

"What was I supposed to do? I spill the juice on a bunch of my brothers, you know as well as I do what would happen. Career over, that's what. I'd be lucky if I didn't get a bullet in the face."

"So why are you forcing the issue now?"

She ran a finger around the rim of her beer mug. "Because things are different. A lot's changed since you left the department. That glass ceiling isn't quite as bulletproof as it used to be, and I'd like to take advantage of some new opportunities. But as it turns out, the guys who covered up what Nettle did seven years ago are the same assholes standing in my way now. That's where you come in."

"I do the dirty work, is that it? I get rid of Nettle and the others and you don't get popped for snitching on a fellow cop. This isn't about justice, is it, Angie? It's about your ambition."

Angelette smiled and lifted her drink. "What can I say? We can't all be martyrs like you, Dave."

Dave woke up the next morning to the smell of coffee and frying bacon. His body recoiled from the scent and he stumbled into the bathroom to throw up.

After he'd emptied his stomach, he sat with his head against the porcelain for at least ten minutes before he felt strong enough to get up. He didn't want to look at himself in the mirror so he kept his eyes averted as he tried to brush his teeth, but he couldn't even manage that. He sank to his knees and hung his head over the toilet once again.

When he rose this time, weak and shaking, he stripped off his underwear and climbed into the shower. He stood under the spray for a long time, hoping the water would help beat back the demons.

When he finally got out, he brushed his teeth again and then took a quick look at his reflection. His face was still bruised and battered from where he'd been worked over the other night, and now he also had bags under his eyes and a sickly yellow tinge to his skin.

He glanced away quickly, not liking what he saw— and hating what he'd done. Eight months of sobriety down the toilet along with last night's dinner. At that moment, Dave didn't even want to contemplate what lay ahead of him. As soon as he could, he had to get himself back to an AA meeting.

He went into the bedroom and pulled on a pair of

jeans, then walked downstairs buttoning his shirt. He figured Marsilius had come over this morning and let himself in, but instead it was Angelette he found at the stove. She had on the same red dress she'd worn the night before, but now she was barefoot, her dark hair tangled from sleep.

She looked up with a grin as she turned the bacon. "Morning, sunshine."

He leaned a shoulder against the door frame and folded his arms. "What are you doing here?"

Her smile faded. "Are you telling me you don't remember last night? I'm hurt, Dave."

"Angie—"

She laughed at his scowl. "Relax, hotshot, nothing happened. I drove you home, helped you to bed and then spent the night on the couch. See?" She pointed with the spatula, and he glanced over his shoulder, saw a blanket folded at the end of the couch, and let out a slow breath.

"Sit down," she said. "Breakfast is almost ready."

"I don't think I can eat."

"Yeah, you don't look so good. But you'll feel better when you get something in your stomach."

Somehow Dave doubted that, but he sat down and watched as she dished up a plate of scrambled eggs and bacon, and carried it over to the table.

He forced himself to pick up the fork and take a few bites. "It's good. Thanks."

She sat down at the table with him, but she only had coffee.

"You're not hungry?"

"I'll have something later. Right now, I'm more concerned with what you plan to do about Nettle."

"I don't know yet."

"It's not going to be easy taking him down, Dave. If he feels cornered, he'll come out fighting."

He gave a brittle laugh. "No shit."

"He did that to you? I wondered."

But didn't care enough to ask, Dave thought. "He already thinks I'm working with someone. If you want to keep your name out of this, you better keep your distance from now on."

She studied him for a moment, as if trying to figure something out. When she spoke, her voice was cool and detached, and she rose from the table without looking at him. "That's good advice, Dave."

Walking over to the couch, she picked up her purse and hooked the strap over her shoulder. "You take care of yourself, hear? I have a feeling that from here on out, me and you won't be seeing much of one another."

Dave waited until he heard Angelette's car pull out of the drive, then got up and carried his dishes into the kitchen. Dumping the rest of the food into the garbage, he stacked his plate and cup in the sink, then went outside to the porch.

The day was already hot and humid, and he could feel sweat collect at the back of his neck and run down his spine. His hands and legs were shaking. It was all he could do not to walk over to Marsilius's place, take a longneck from the cooler and pop it open.

Instead, he went back inside, poured a tall glass of iced tea and swallowed some aspirin. He carried the drink to the porch and sank down in one of the rockers. It had been a long time since he'd felt this sick and weak. He didn't know what he was going to do about Nettle, because right now he couldn't think beyond the moment. He didn't know how he'd get through the next hour without a drink, much less the rest of the day, the rest of his life.

He stared out at the sun shimmering off the bayou, but what he saw instead was the long, dark road that lay ahead of him.

The phone started ringing inside the house, and Dave's first inclination was to ignore it. He didn't want to talk to anybody right now, least of all Marsilius, who was probably calling to check up on him. But if he didn't pick up, his uncle was apt to show up on his doorstep, and Dave sure as hell didn't want that.

He went inside to answer.

"Dave, it's Titus."

"I was beginning to think you'd just blown me off," Dave said.

"Don't think I didn't consider it. Listen up. I followed your boy Nettle out here to a dive off Airline Drive." He gave Dave the address. "You better get your ass down here quick 'cause you ain't gonna believe who just showed up to meet him."

When Dave walked into the Gold Medallion that afternoon, Bobby Ray Taubin was stacking beer cases behind the bar. He tried to bolt for the back, but Dave slid over the counter, caught him by the collar and slung him back into the glass shelves on the wall. Taubin went crashing to the floor amid an array of broken glass and spilled liquor.

Before he could get up, Dave was on him. He grabbed a broken whiskey bottle and shoved it under the bartender's chin. "Nobody here but you and me now, Bobby Ray."

Taubin's eyes shifted back and forth as blood ran down the side of his face.

"I'm going to give you two choices, just like you gave me the other night," Dave. "You either do as I say, or I give your parole officer a call, fill him in on what you been up to since you got off the farm. My guess is he'll give you a one-way ticket back to West Feliciana Parish."

"What do you want from me?" Taubin asked sullenly, lifting a hand to wipe the blood out of his eyes.

"It's real simple." Dave tossed the whiskey bottle aside and dragged Taubin to his feet. "You're gonna help me nail Clive Nettle's hide to the wall."

Twenty-Two

❦

Mist settled over the bayou as Matthew guided his pirogue through the cattails and lily pads that grew thick against the bank. Night had fallen and the half-submerged cypress trees were black against the starlit sky. A bullfrog croaked nearby, and he could see the gleam of beady eyes in the darkness, the twinkle of lightning bugs through the bushes. His oars dipped rhythmically in the water as he moved deeper into the swamp.

Rounding a sharp bend, he saw a light on the water up ahead. His pulse quickened as his gaze dropped to the bundle at his feet, and he saw that the blanket had shifted, exposing a tiny, pale hand in the moonlight.

Careful.

His very presence in the swamp at this hour could arouse suspicions, and if anyone saw what he had in his boat, let alone if they followed him to his destination...

Don't worry, no one will see us. No one will ever know.

He pulled the blanket over the hand and straightened. The light was getting closer and the sound of laughter drifted over the dark water. Turning the boat, he paddled back toward the bank, carefully maneuvering the bow through a maze of cypress knees and rotting logs. Spanish moss hung like layers of silk from the trees, the lacy tendrils skimming the water's surface, undulating gently in the current.

He drifted under one of the curtains and used his oar to steady the pirogue as he waited. The other boat was so near now he could hear the individual voices, even make out snatches of conversation. He held his breath as a light flashed over the area where he was hidden.

"There!" one of the voices said excitedly. "Did you see it?"

"Got it! Big ole fat one, too."

He let out a quick breath. *Nothing to worry about.* It was just some kids out frog-gigging. Not his forte, but to each his own, he always said.

Still, he didn't want them to see him, so he remained hidden until the voices faded in the mist. When he was sure they were gone, he paddled back out into deeper water. A sinewy ribbon skimmed across the surface in the moonlight and he shivered, all too aware of the dangers in the swamp.

Another turn and he was there. The dilapidated shack was perched at the water's edge, the porch sagging and the roof caved in from rot and decades of Gulf Coast storms.

Drifting up to the bank, he looped a rope over a cypress knee, then jumped over the side of the boat into ankle-deep water. He reached for the bundle and cradled it carefully in his arms as he entered the shack.

Once inside, he turned on his flashlight and

skimmed the beam over the dusty walls and corners. Cobwebs glimmered in the light and something small scurried across the floor at his feet.

The cabin was haunted by his past. The memories were so overwhelming that he started to tremble. If he listened closely, he could hear the beat of all those silenced hearts, feel the accusing stare of all those sightless eyes. He didn't like coming here, but there was no other way.

Setting the flashlight aside, he pried up a loose board and then removed the blanket from the silent bundle beside him. Long dark hair splayed across the filthy floorboards. Eyes shimmered in the moonlight spilling in through a broken window.

He touched her cold cheek and shuddered.

The doll was nearly perfect. He had outdone himself this time. Each step of the process had been inspired. Sculpting the clay, making the plaster mold, firing the porcelain and painting the delicate features— the end result, a work of art.

He had tested the limits of his talent...but still he'd fallen short.

He wanted to weep in frustration. No matter how many times he tried, no matter how hard he worked, he could not capture the essence of the child with only his hands and a block of clay. There was only one way to truly do her justice. His special way.

Quickly, he placed the doll—another failure—inside the hole with the others, turning his head so that he wouldn't have to see all those gleaming eyes and taunting smiles. Settling the board back in place, he stood for a moment, letting out a long shaky breath as he waited for his nerves to steady.

Then he returned to the pirogue, unfastened the rope and paddled away from the cabin without looking back.

He never looked back when he came here. He was too afraid of what he might see.

Twenty-Three

By Thursday, Claire's hand was so much better that she decided to stay on after the gallery closed, and make up for lost time in the studio. The other glass-blowers left one by one, until by nine she had the place to herself. Normally, she loved working alone, but tonight she found herself jumping at every little sound. Which was to be expected, she supposed, after everything that had happened in the past week.

Perspiration gathered at the back of her neck and along her spine as she rolled the pliable glass across the steel marver to smooth and shape the surface. She hadn't slept well the night before, and the heat in the studio was quickly sapping her energy. She'd gone to bed early, but every time she closed her eyes, she saw Mignon Bujold's pale face staring up at her. And when Claire finally dozed off, she dreamed of being trapped in a cold, dark place, unable to move, unable to scream for help. She'd awakened struggling for breath, her heart pounding in terror until she realized it was only a nightmare. But she hadn't been able to fall back asleep for hours.

Luckily, the gallery had been so busy all day that she hadn't had time to dwell on the gruesome aspects of the shopkeeper's death. But now, in the quiet of the studio, the horror came rushing back, and with it, Claire's mounting frustration. It was obvious to her that a connection existed between the woman's murder and the doll, but why would no one believe her? Her desperation had finally driven her to Dave, and when he'd refused to help her, Claire's disappointment had been crushing, even though she'd tried to tell herself the outcome was to be expected. When had she ever been able to count on Dave Creasy for anything?

But a part of her had wanted to believe that he'd changed, and that when he heard about the doll, he'd be the one person who would believe her, who would be willing to move heaven and earth to help her.

Instead, he'd turned everything back to him and his needs, and Claire didn't know why that had surprised her. She'd once loved him deeply, but when she looked back now, she realized that their relationship had always been about him. The dark moods, the drinking, even his betrayal. He'd slept with another woman not because he loved her, but because Angelette Lapierre had offered something he wanted and needed that Claire couldn't give him. And because he was Dave, he'd taken it.

Sometimes Claire still wondered if the devastating hurt and humiliation of his betrayal, perhaps even more than her grief over Ruby's disappearance, had been the catalyst that pushed her into Alex's arms. And then once there, she hadn't wanted to admit that she'd made a terrible mistake.

Now her second marriage had dissolved, too. Lucille thought it was because Claire had never gotten over Dave, but if seeing him again had proved anything to her, it was that her decision to walk out on him seven years ago had probably been the smartest thing she'd ever done. On most days, it was all she could do to battle her own demons, much less his.

As Claire continued to mold the glass, she tried to clear her mind, but tonight work wasn't as therapeutic as she had hoped it would be. She couldn't seem to concentrate, and found herself going through the steps automatically, reheating the glass, attaching the punty rod to the bottom, removing the blowpipe from the lip. Someone had borrowed her tools earlier and left them on her workbench. As she reached for the jacks, her hand stilled and a shiver crept over her. For a moment, she could have sworn someone was watching her.

She glanced at the row of windows, then turned to scan the space behind her. The studio was well-lit and she could see the whole room from where she was sitting. The door to the gallery was closed and locked, as was the rear entrance. Claire had worked alone in the studio dozens of times, and the solitude had never spooked her before. She didn't know what had triggered her apprehension now, but suddenly she had the same premonition she'd experienced standing outside the back door of the collectibles shop. And as she turned, her gaze moving slowly over every inch of the studio, her heart began to hammer against her rib cage.

This is crazy.

She'd been in the studio since the gallery closed at five, and she'd made sure to lock both outside doors when everyone else left. No one had come in or out since she'd been at her workbench, so there was nothing to worry about.

But for some reason, Claire's mind flashed to the woman who had taken the tour of the studio on Saturday. Even though she'd stayed at the back of the crowd, Claire had noticed her because of her unusual appearance. She hadn't thought much about her since that day, but now Claire found herself remembering the woman's strange behavior.

But there was no way that woman—or anyone else—could get inside the studio without Claire knowing it. She was letting her imagination get the better of her. Taking a deep breath, she went back to work.

When she finally had the piece inside the annealer oven, where the glass would gradually cool until morning, she removed her Kevlar gloves and started to clean up around her workbench. Then she went to get her purse and keys, and recheck the gallery door before letting herself out the back way.

As soon as she opened the door, she saw the white box. It was tied with a pink ribbon and placed on the pavement where she wouldn't miss it when she left.

Claire glanced up and scanned the parking area.

A security light had recently been installed at the back of the warehouse for nights when one of the glassblowers stayed late and had to leave the building alone. Her car was the only one left. No one else was around. No one that she could see, anyway.

She picked up the box and stepped back into the studio, closing and locking the door and turning the lights back on.

Adrenaline was suddenly pumping through her veins and her hands were trembling. She tried to calm her racing pulse, tried to tell herself there was no reason to panic. She didn't even know if the box had been left for her. There was no name on the package. Maybe she should just leave it until morning and see if it belonged to one of the other glassblowers.

But even as the notion flitted through her head, she was already removing the lid, her hands fumbling with the layers of tissue paper until the contents were revealed.

It was the picture of Ruby that had been taken from Claire's home a few nights ago. The original wooden frame had been replaced by one cut from cardboard and decorated with spray paint and glitter. The kind of frame a child might make in school for a Mother's Day gift or Christmas present.

Claire's stomach churned with dread as she turned the picture over and read the inscription on the back. Icy fingers stroked up and down her spine.

The childish scrawl read simply: "To Mama."

Claire was still shaking when she pulled into her driveway a few minutes later. Dave's truck was parked at the curb, and she had no idea why he was there. She supposed she should be grateful that she wouldn't have to enter her dark house alone, but mostly what she felt was isolated and helpless. No one had believed her about the doll. Why would the photograph be any different?

Shivering, she got out of her car and walked across the yard to the porch. At some point during the evening, someone had stood outside the door of the studio while she worked, had perhaps even watched her through a window. Someone had left the picture for her to find, but who would do such a thing? And, for God's sake, *why?*

She'd run out of the studio in a panic after opening the box, barely taking the time to lock the door before bolting across the parking lot to her car. Claire could see herself in her mind's eye, and her overwrought reaction shamed her a little. And then she grew angry.

Someone had deliberately used a photograph of her daughter to frighten her. Was it not enough that Ruby had been taken from her? Did her memories have to be tainted now, as well?

As Claire climbed the porch steps, she could see Dave sitting in one of the rockers, but neither of them spoke until she reached the top. He rose then, his face still in shadows.

"Hello, Claire."

"Hello." Her voice sounded strained and shaky, and she didn't want him to get the wrong idea of why she was upset. "What are you doing here?"

"Waiting for you."

She clutched her purse close to her side as their eyes met in the darkness. It was all she could do not to blurt out her discovery, but she'd swallowed her pride and gone to him once for help. He'd turned her away, and she had no reason to believe that she could count on him now. She couldn't count on anyone. Not Dave, not Alex, not her family. Claire had been on her own ever since she'd first seen the doll in Mignon Bujold's window, and the only thing she had any control over was her fear. She couldn't let it overwhelm her. If she wanted to find out the truth, she had to remain strong.

"Are you okay?" Dave asked with a frown.

"I guess I'm just surprised to see you."

"Are you sure that's all it is?"

"Yes, of course." She drew a long breath. "What do you want?"

He took a step toward her, his eyes catching the moonlight. "I need to talk to you."

"Why? I think you pretty much told me everything I needed to know on Tuesday, and I'm tired tonight. I want to get inside."

"I owe you an apology."

Claire had moved to the front door, keys in hand, but now she stood motionless. "You didn't need to come all the way to New Orleans for that. We both said things we shouldn't have."

"I'm not talking about our conversation the other day, although you're right. I do regret the way things ended." He hesitated. "I came to tell you that I'm sorry for what I did seven years ago. I'm sorry about everything."

Claire felt something deep inside give way, but she clung to the last vestiges of her strength. It had been a long day. She was tired, she was scared and she was in no frame of mind to have an emotional conversation with her ex-husband. "So what is this? Step five or nine? I forget."

She saw him flinch. "I'm just trying to do what's right these days. I know an apology doesn't make up for what I did, but I needed to say it anyway."

She turned, a taste like metal in her mouth as her anger flared. "And it's always about what you need, isn't it? Did it ever once occur to you that maybe I don't want to hear your apology? Maybe what I need is just to leave things alone. Forget it ever happened."

"But have you forgotten? I know I haven't. Even after all this time, it kills me that I cheated on you. And I still don't even know why I did it."

"You know, you're right, Dave. I did need to hear that. I feel so much better now."

"Claire…"

She sighed, letting the anger slip out of her. "You may find this hard to believe, but I have more on my mind these days than your betrayal. Go home, Dave. Go home and leave me alone, because nothing you say can change what happened."

"Just let me come in for a minute. Please, Claire." He held his hands out in supplication. "I don't expect one apology to change how you feel about me, but at least hear me out. If you want me to help you find that doll, we need to clear the air about some things. It's important."

Her gaze lifted. "You've changed your mind about helping me?"

"Let's go inside and we'll talk about it."

His face was still in shadows. Claire couldn't see his expression, but something in his voice made her shiver. "All I want to know is if you believe me."

"Yes," he said quietly. "I believe you saw a doll that looks like Ruby. What it means, I have no idea. But I do believe you. Can I come inside so that we can talk?"

She gave a reluctant nod even as she tried to quell the rush of relief inside her. She opened the door and reached inside to flip the light switch. But when she glanced back, he was still standing in the same spot, staring out at the street.

"What's wrong? I thought you wanted to come in."

"I do. But something just struck me."

"What?"

"I was just standing here thinking about the way I used to drive by all the time, hoping to catch a glimpse of you."

Claire's chest tightened. "You mean when my grandmother lived here?"

He hesitated. "Yeah."

"That was a long time ago."

"Kind of seemed like yesterday until I drove through the old neighborhood on my way over here. That little burger joint where you used to work on weekends is a quick mart now."

"I know. It has been for years."

"I guess I hadn't noticed." He turned with a shrug. "Anyway, it made me think of the first time I ever stopped in there. Do you remember?"

"Of course I remember. You were in one of your moods. You looked as if you were ready to kill somebody when you came in the door."

"And then there you were, smiling at me. I couldn't take my eyes off you. I'd known you most of my life, but something just clicked in my head that day. It was like I was seeing you for the first time. It was only a moment, over in a heartbeat. But that's when I knew."

A car pulled into the drive next door, the headlights reflecting in Dave's eyes as he stared down at Claire. She tried to look away, but couldn't.

"Ever since you left my place the other day, I've been trying to think of the exact instant when things went so wrong for us. If there was a moment when it started, there had to be a moment when it ended. But I didn't see it. It passed by and I didn't even notice."

"Because you weren't looking," Claire said softly. She hugged her arms around her middle. "It wasn't just a moment, it was a lot of them. It was your job and the drinking. The dark moods. There was a part of your life, a part of yourself, that you couldn't or wouldn't share with me. I wanted to understand, but you shut me out, and sometimes you made me feel as if I were trespassing on something private. Something that wasn't any of my business. There were times, especially toward the end, when I felt like an outsider in my own marriage."

"Why didn't you tell me you felt that way?"

"I did tell you. You just weren't listening. And anyway, it really doesn't matter anymore."

"It does to me."

Claire swallowed. "That's because you're still living in the past. But the rest of us have moved on." She walked quickly into the house.

A moment later, she heard the door close behind him as he followed her inside. "You've moved on, huh. Is that why you want me to help you find a doll that looks like Ruby?"

"That's different. The doll exists, whether you believe me or not. It's not a smokescreen or my imagination or anything else. The doll is real and so is this." She removed the photograph from her purse and handed it to him.

He glanced up with a puzzled frown.

"I found it tonight as I was leaving work. Someone put it in a box and left it outside the door." Claire nodded toward the picture. "Turn it over and read the back."

He flipped it over, and as he read the inscription aloud, Claire shuddered. "To Mama."

"Ruby didn't write that," she said. "I'm pretty sure it's the same photograph that was stolen from here a few nights ago, and it didn't have anything written on the back then."

"Someone broke in here?"

"I think Mama left a window open. It was one night last week when we had one of those sudden thunderstorms. I was already in bed and I heard glass breaking. When I came downstairs, I saw that a vase had fallen in the sunroom and shattered on the floor. The window was open. I assumed the curtain had swept it off the table. Then I realized a picture of Ruby was missing from the same table."

"Why didn't you tell me about this before?"

"You didn't believe me about the doll...." She shrugged and trailed off.

"Did you tell anyone?"

"I didn't know who to tell. I didn't want to worry Mama, and besides, I wasn't even sure that the picture was really missing then. I thought I might have forgotten that I'd put it away. And now it turns up outside the studio, on a night when I'm working alone."

"Did you see or hear anything unusual tonight? Have you noticed anyone suspicious hanging around the studio or gallery in the past few days?"

"A woman came in last Saturday. I thought she was part of a group that toured the studio that afternoon, but she didn't leave with everyone else. She stood in front of a display case for a long time, staring at one of my pieces. Maybe she was just trying to make up her mind, because she did eventually buy it. But there was something about her that made me uneasy. I don't even know how to explain it. She had on thick makeup that made her look...I don't know...unnatural somehow. Now that I think back about it, I can't help wondering if she was deliberately trying to conceal her real identity. But I guess that sounds a little paranoid. Or maybe just plain crazy."

"I was a cop in this town for nearly ten years. Nothing much sounds crazy to me anymore."

"Not even a doll that looks exactly like our missing daughter?"

He glanced back down at the photograph in his hand. "Did you have the picture displayed like this when it was taken?"

"No, it was in a wooden frame. I saved almost all of Ruby's school projects. They're put away in boxes in the attic. I've never seen that before." Claire rubbed her hands up and down her arms. "This is going to sound a little crazy, too, but I think someone is trying to send me a message."

"Or maybe someone's just trying to mess with your head," he said slowly.

"What do you mean?"

"I've seen this kind of thing before. Some sick creep latches on to a story and tries to make himself a part of it."

"After seven years?"

Dave handed the picture back to her. "Can you think of anyone who might have a grudge against you? Anyone who might want to upset or hurt you?"

"No, not like this."

"Are you sure?"

"Yes, of course I'm sure."

His tone made Claire nervous. He was getting at something, but before she could ask him what he meant, his cell phone rang. He took it out of his pocket, glanced at the display and frowned. "I'm sorry. I have to take this. Do you mind?"

Claire watched as he opened the door and stepped out on the porch. She could hear him talking softly to the caller, and she told herself to tune out the conversation. Whatever was going on was none of her business.

Then she heard Ruby's name, and followed him out to the porch. "Dave?"

His gaze met hers in the dark. "I'll see you in a little while," he said into the phone, then snapped it closed.

"What's going on?" Claire asked nervously. "Who was that?"

"It's a case I'm working on."

"But I heard you say something about Ruby."

"It's not what you think. I've been making some inquiries about that doll maker you mentioned. I don't have time to get into it now, but I'll come back when I'm finished, if it's not too late, and tell you everything I found out. Right now, though, I have to go."

"Tell me now. You can't make me wait!"

"She lives about thirty miles south of Houma. I swear, Claire, that's all I know."

Dave started down the steps, but she caught his arm. "Are you going to see her?"

"Right now? No. This doesn't have anything to do with her."

Claire's grip tightened on his arm. "If you're keeping something from me—"

"I already told you, I don't know anything more about that doll than you do."

"But you know *something*. I can see it in your eyes."

"Claire, for your own sake, don't push this."

She drew back in fear. "What does that mean?"

"It means I'm in a hurry. I meant what I said a minute ago. I'll come back later and we can talk more about Savannah Sweete. But now is not the time."

"Dave?"

He half turned as he clambered down the stairs. "What is it?"

"Let me come with you."

"That's not a good idea. For a lot of reasons."

"I'll just follow you in my car if you don't let me come."

He turned. "I'll lose you in five minutes."

"Probably. But if this is about Ruby, I have a right to be there. You know I do."

He searched the street for a moment, then scrubbed his hand down his face. "Maybe you do. Maybe you have more right to this truth than anyone else."

"What's that supposed to mean?"

"No more questions," he said. "Let's just get going."

Claire stared out the window of Dave's truck as they drove across the Huey Long and headed south on old Highway 90. Moonlight shimmered on the river as the willow trees that grew along the bank swayed in a mild breeze. Neon lights flashed above a honky-tonk set back from the road. The parking lot was full even on a Thursday night, though there wasn't much traffic on the road.

"How much farther?" Claire finally asked.

"We're almost at the turnoff. There's a fishing cabin on a bayou just up the road. That's where we're going."

"You still won't tell me why we're going there?"

"We're meeting some people. You'll find out the rest soon enough." The lights of a passing car caught Dave in the face and he squinted. "I do need to tell you something before we get there, though. It's something I should have told you a long time ago."

Her heart quickened as she stared at his profile. "What is it?"

She saw his hands tighten on the steering wheel. "Two days after Ruby disappeared, I received a phone call from someone claiming to be her kidnapper."

Claire felt the blood drain from her face. Another car passed them on the road before she was able to speak. "Why didn't you tell me?"

"I couldn't. That was one of the demands. I wasn't to tell anyone. Not the police or the FBI. Not even you."

She lifted a quivering hand to her mouth. "You were in contact with our daughter's kidnapper and you didn't tell me? How could you keep that from me?"

"I was trying to save Ruby's life. Claire, please try to understand. I was terrified of what they might do to her. I couldn't take a chance on telling you. You were on the verge of a breakdown. I was afraid you might let something slip to the police."

"But the FBI told us that if we were contacted, the worst thing we could do was try to deal with the kidnapper on our own. You were a cop. You knew that."

"Somehow none of that matters when your own kid's involved."

Claire closed her eyes. "What happened?"

"I agreed to their demands. They wanted something from me and I gave it to them."

"What did they want?" She was almost afraid to ask.

"Do you remember the homicide case I was working at the time of the kidnapping? The victim's name was Renee Savaria."

"I remember. Her body was found in the river. She was just a kid, eighteen or nineteen, I think. You never liked to talk about your cases, but I knew that one kept you awake at night. I'd sometimes hear you pacing in the other room, and I would lie in bed thinking about her poor parents and what they were going through. If you were that deeply affected, I couldn't even imagine what it was like for them, wondering how their child had suffered before she died." Claire turned to stare out the window. "A few weeks later, Ruby disappeared."

Dave was quiet for a long time. "I worked on that case for weeks without any real leads or suspects. And then I got my hands on Renee's diary. The last entry was the location and date of a private party that she had been hired to work. According to a witness, Renee was killed at that party by a cop named Clive Nettle. The other cops there that night helped cover it up."

Claire stared at him in shock. "Why would they do that?"

"Self-preservation. If word had gotten out about a cop party involving teenage prostitutes, a lot of careers would have been ruined. Not to mention the fear of prosecution once Renee turned up dead."

"How did you find out?"

"A deathbed confession of sorts. Someone who was there that night recently told me what happened."

"If you know all this, why hasn't Nettle been arrested?"

"I'm working on that." Dave slowed as they came to an intersection, then made a right turn onto another two-lane road. A convenience store with gas pumps sat on the left side, and to the right was nothing but rice fields.

"I don't understand what any of this has to do with Ruby's kidnapping," Claire said.

"It doesn't. But I was made to think that it did."

"How?"

"The ransom demand was that I destroy the last page of Renee Savaria's diary."

The truck tires thudded over the metal grid of a bridge, and Claire waited until they were across before she spoke. "Did you do it?"

His face looked pale in the dash lights. "Yeah, I did it."

"You destroyed evidence that could have proved that girl was killed by a cop. Because of what you did, Nettle got away with murder."

"That's exactly right." Dave's voice was hard and cold and empty.

"And you did it for Ruby." Claire's lip started to tremble and she looked away from him.

"I would have done anything to bring her back, Claire. You have to know that."

"Why didn't you tell me?"

"I couldn't. I was too afraid to tell anybody, and I wanted to spare you as much as I could. After it was over, I was too ashamed."

"Ashamed of trying to save your daughter?"

"Ashamed of letting myself be duped. Ashamed of going against everything I believed in as a cop."

"Is that why you resigned?"

"Partly, I guess. And partly because I just didn't give a shit about anything. After Ruby disappeared, nothing made sense anymore. Not even you and me."

Twenty-Four

Claire laid her head against the back of the seat as she turned to stare out at the passing scenery. They crossed another bridge over a bayou, and she could see the reflection of the cypress trees in the water. The air blowing in through Dave's open window was scented with honeysuckle and magnolias. Claire closed her eyes, his words echoing in her head. *After Ruby disappeared, nothing made sense anymore. Not even you and me.*

"Where we're going tonight has something to do with those phone calls seven years ago," she said. "That's why you were talking about Ruby earlier, isn't it?"

"I shouldn't have let you come with me," he said. "What you see and hear in that cabin probably won't sit too well on your conscience."

She turned her head to look at him. "Meaning?"

"I'm going to do whatever is necessary to find out who made those calls."

"Good."

He shot her a surprised glance. "You may not think that later."

She was silent for a moment. "What's going to happen once we get to the cabin?"

"I told you, we're meeting some people."

"Who?"

"Titus for one."

"Titus Birdsong? I didn't even know the two of you were still friends."

"He's risking a lot by helping me out. I'm never going to be able to pay him back for this."

"For what?" Claire asked worriedly. "You're starting to scare me a little. What is it that you're planning to do?"

"Only what I have to. Try to remember that."

She shivered at his ominous tone. "Who else is there?"

"Clive Nettle."

She stared at him in shock. "Clive Nettle is at the cabin?"

"Don't worry," Dave said. "In his present condition, he won't pose much of a threat."

"I'm not worried about that. It's just that…now I think I understand what you meant when you said you were willing to do whatever was necessary to get at the truth."

"And that scares you."

"A little," she admitted.

"Do you want to go back?"

She shook her head. "No."

As they left the rice fields behind, the area became more wooded, and Claire saw the glimmer of another bayou through the trees. The longer they were on the road, the more apprehensive she became. Her stomach was in knots, her nerve endings vibrating like a plucked guitar string. And when she lifted her hand to her cheek, the skin on her face felt cold and clammy.

Dave made another turn, onto a dirt road, and she saw a light just ahead.

"That's it," he said, and a moment later, he pulled up next to a light-colored sedan and parked.

They both got out of the truck, and as they walked up to the cabin, Claire glanced around. They were in the middle of nowhere. The place was isolated and, except for the presence of the other car and the flicker of light in the broken window, appeared completely deserted.

Dave knocked once, then said in a low voice, "It's me."

The door was drawn open and a large silhouette filled the opening. Claire hadn't seen Titus Birdsong in years, and it took her a moment to recognize him.

Light spilled out from the doorway and she could see him staring down at her. Quickly, he dropped his gun to his side. "Claire?"

"Hello, Titus."

"Claire? What are you doing here?" His gaze shot to Dave.

"It's okay. She knows about the phone calls and she knows we've got Nettle inside."

Titus shook his head. "Don't matter to me what she knows, she ain't got no business being out here. This ain't no place for a woman."

"I appreciate the sentiment, Titus, but you don't need to protect me. I have a right to know who made those phone calls to Dave. Ruby was my daughter, too."

For a moment Claire thought Titus was going to refuse to let her come in, but then he stepped back with a loud sigh. "I hope you know what you're doing," he muttered to Dave.

Claire followed them inside, and for a moment, Dave blocked her view of the room. She had a brief impression of rough-hewn walls and bare floorboards, a rusted tin roof, and she could smell kerosene from the lamp that provided the light. Then Dave moved out of the way and she saw Clive Nettle.

He was almost as large as Titus, with close-cropped dark hair, black stubble and a scar that ran down the side of his face. He sat bound and gagged in a ladder-back chair, one eye nearly swollen shut and blood drying at his temple. His head lolled forward, chin on chest, and Claire thought at first that he was unconscious. Then he lifted his head and looked directly into her eyes.

A shudder ripped through Claire and she took a step back. She thought she'd been prepared, but the sight of that battered face turned her stomach. Nausea rose in her throat, and she pressed her hand to her mouth.

"You okay?" Dave asked. "Maybe you should wait outside."

She shook her head, but it took her a moment to speak. "What did you do to him?"

"What I had to."

"He's…okay?"

"He'll live. At least until he gets to Angola."

Claire nodded, drawing a breath.

Dave walked over to Nettle and yanked the gag out of his mouth. "You weren't very cooperative when I was here earlier. Let's see if you've changed your tune now that you've had a little time to ponder your situation."

"I already told you, I got nothing to say to you. And

don't think this won't come back on both you assholes."
He nodded toward Titus. "Your career is over, you dumb
shit. You chose the wrong side. And as for you…" He
turned his head slowly to Dave. "You're as good as
dead."

"Is that so? Because I feel pretty good at the moment. As a matter of fact, I'm liking my odds more and
more these days. You, on the other hand…can't say I'd
want to be in your shoes when all this goes down."

"Do I look worried?"

"You should be. You're a pathetic excuse for a man,
Nettle, much less a cop."

"Up yours, pal. Last time I checked, I still have a
badge and you don't."

"Tell me what happened that night with Renee. She
tried to fight you off, didn't she? Probably made her
sick to her stomach just to look at you, let alone have
you put your filthy hands on her."

Nettle's smile became a sneer as he glanced at
Claire. "You know better than anyone what a man will
risk for a little poon tang on the side, don't you, Dave?"

Dave's fist caught the cop squarely on the jaw, knocking the chair backward. It crashed into the wall, collapsed, and Nettle hit the floor with a loud thud. Dave bent
over him and grabbed a fistful of his shirt. "You murder-
ing bastard. I ought to finish you off right here and now."

The chair was broken in several pieces around Nettle, but his hands and ankles were still bound. He tried
to scoot away, but Dave dragged him back and clamped
a hand around his throat, squeezed until the man's face
turned red and his eyes fluttered and rolled back in his head.

"Dave, for God's sake!" Claire cried.

"Ease up, partner," Titus said softly.

Dave released Nettle and straightened. "Maybe now you're ready to talk."

"Fuck you," Nettle wheezed, and spat blood on the floor at Dave's feet.

Dave leaned against the wall and folded his arms. He suddenly looked as comfortable and relaxed as a man chatting with a neighbor at a backyard barbecue. "Let me tell you how I see this all playing out, Nettle. JoJo Barone is going to finger you and every other cop who was there at that party the night you killed Renee. He's a dying man, so he doesn't have a lot to lose, and I seriously doubt he'll want to spend the rest of his days worrying about how to pick up the soap in the shower without bending over. The D.A. leans on him hard enough, he'll roll. We both know he will."

"That's it? That's all you got? The word of a two-bit greaser like JoJo Barone?" Nettle laughed, a low, nasty sound that made Claire's skin crawl.

"That's all we need," Dave said. "Because when JoJo starts naming names, you're going to find out real fast who your friends are. Bobby Ray already sold you out. That's why you're here. My guess is, your old buddies in the department won't be much different. When they get wind of what the D.A. has in mind, they'll hightail it to the nearest attorney and try to cop a plea that'll keep their asses out of prison. You don't have that option. You're going to do hard time, no question about that. But if you want to stay off death row, you better make your deal while you still have something to offer. And the only way to get to the D.A. is through me."

Nettle laughed again. "Do I look that stupid to you? Lee Elliot wouldn't give a guy like you the time of day, let alone buy into this drunkard's fantasy you're trying to peddle. Here's a news flash, chief. Your cred's kinda shaky these days."

Dave shrugged. "I guess you'll have to ask Elliot yourself when he gets here."

"Oh, he's on his way here, is he? You really are delusional. Kind of pathetic, really. I heard you were a pretty good cop before you turned into a lush. Now you sound just plain crazy. If you had anything on me, I'd be in lockup right now instead of cooling my heels out here with you two fucks."

"Maybe Elliot wanted to make sure you'd stay alive long enough to give him a statement."

Claire saw something flash in Nettle's eyes.

"Think about it," Dave said. "It's an election year and this kind of case is a wet dream for an ambitious prosecutor like Lee Elliot. Murder. Conspiracy. Police corruption. He plays it just right, he could ride this horse all the way to the governor's mansion. If you don't cooperate, he'll just move on down the line to the next guy on JoJo Barone's list."

"I still say this is nothing but one big bluff."

"It's not," Claire said, and she felt Dave's gaze on her as she took a step toward Nettle. "My sister is an assistant D.A. Her name is Charlotte LeBlanc. She was handpicked by Lee Elliot to be on his team. They're very close. I can get her on the phone right now to verify everything Dave just told you."

Dave straightened as he glanced at his watch. "Clock's ticking, Nettle, so here's the deal. You want to talk to Elliot, you'll have to agree to my terms. Otherwise, when he gets here, he'll find nothing but an empty cabin. A day or two from now, when he's already made a deal with someone else, Titus here will march you into headquarters in handcuffs and leg irons. That won't look so good on TV. That's the kind of image that sticks in a prospective juror's head."

"No shit," Titus said with a grin. "And no offense, but you ain't exactly got what I'd call a sympathetic mug to begin with. You don't want your veins pickled up there at the farm, you best hear the man out."

"All you have to do is give me a name," Dave said. "You tell me who placed those calls to my cell phone after my little girl disappeared, and you and me are done. You make your deal with Lee Elliot. I'll stay out of it."

Nettle turned his head and looked at Claire. "You sure you want her in here for this?"

"I'm not leaving," she said, but her hands were sweaty and her heart had suddenly started to race.

He nodded toward Dave. "Why don't you ask him why he brought you out here? I'm beginning to think this little dog-and-pony show he put together was just for your benefit." He glanced up. "Ain't that right, chief?"

"You're a piece of shit, Nettle."

The man laughed, his grinning face grotesque in the flickering lamplight. He cut his gaze back to Claire and lowered his voice. "You really want to know who made those phone calls?"

Claire nodded, her mouth suddenly so dry she couldn't speak.

Nettle gave her a look that was half amused, half pitying. "It was your old man. Yeah, that's right," he said with a grin when Claire reacted. "Alex Girard made those calls. He thought it all up on his own. Said the kid was already dead, might as well use the kidnapping to our advantage."

Claire felt as if she'd just been punched in the chest. She leaned against the wall, her breath suspended painfully in her lungs. And then her gaze went to Dave, and she could tell from the look on his face that Nettle was right. He'd already known about Alex. He just hadn't had the guts to tell her himself.

Lee Elliot knew how to work a crowd, even the small group of cops that had gathered outside the cabin door to watch Clive Nettle's perp walk to the nearest squad car. In his light-colored suit and silk tie, the Orleans Parish D.A. looked as if he'd just come from a Garden District soiree rather than a lengthy meeting with a cold-blooded killer. He had the charm and charisma of a natural-born politician, the breeding and manners of an old-fashioned Southern gentlemen, the lazy drawl of a pickup-truck redneck. In short, he was everything to everybody.

After Nettle was loaded into the back of the squad car, Elliot came over and clapped Titus on the back. Angelette was with him, but she didn't say a word. She'd been keeping a low profile ever since she arrived. However, as she stood next to Elliot, Dave could feel her gaze, burning with its usual intensity.

"I appreciate that you boys wanted me out here to make sure everything went down by the book, but you would have made my job a lot easier if you hadn't been quite so zealous in your pursuit of justice. Looks like you used Nettle for a punching bag. That won't sit well with his defense attorney."

"He resisted arrest," Titus said.

"And you won't have a problem swearing to that under oath, I don't suppose."

"No problem at all. You got a Bible on you, I'll swear to it right now."

"I don't think we need to go that far." Elliot's gaze shifted to Dave. "And let me guess. You just happened to be in the neighborhood and offered your assistance."

"Something like that."

Elliot's blue eyes twinkled in the flashing light from the nearest squad car. "You know, you're a pretty impressive guy, Dave. I like how you operate. We could use a good investigator like you in the D.A.'s office. Have you ever thought about coming back to the force? The commissioner is a second cousin of mine. I could put in a good word for you."

"Thanks, but I've burned too many bridges in New Orleans. I like it just fine where I am."

"You ever change your mind, give me a call."

He moved on then, and Dave looked around to find that Titus had also disappeared. He was left standing alone with Angelette. She wore a short black skirt and turquoise blouse that clung to her curves, and her black hair was pinned up, highlighting her long, smooth neck. When she caught his eyes, she gave him a slow smile.

Dave wanted to look around and see where Claire was, but he thought that might be a little too obvious.

"What's the matter, Dave? You look a little nervous."

"It's been a helluva night."

"Hasn't it, though? And I guess congratulations are in order. Took you seven years, but you finally nailed Renee Savaria's killer."

"Not without your help. If you hadn't been able to

persuade Elliot to come out here tonight, I might have had to take matters into my own hands."

"Nah, you wouldn't do that. You might have roughed him up a little more, but you wouldn't have inflicted any serious damage."

"What makes you think that?"

Her smile gently mocked him. "You may be fucked up in the head, but you're still basically a good guy."

"And just when did you come to that conclusion?"

"Oh, I always knew it. You just used to piss me off so bad I never wanted to admit it." She twirled a strand of dark hair around her fingertip. No one but Angelette could make such a simple gesture seem so suggestive.

Dave cleared his throat. "Let me ask you something, and I want you to tell me the truth. Whose idea was it to get me involved in all this? Yours or Elliot's?"

Angelette leaned back against one of the cars and folded her arms. "What difference does it make? You got what you wanted. We all did. Why not just enjoy the moment?"

"I don't like being played, that's all."

"Poor baby. Lee's right, you know. Now that the herd at NOPD is about to be thinned, you could get your old job back if you wanted it. Be like old times."

"I meant what I said, Angie. I burned my bridges in New Orleans. I'm not coming back."

She looked on the verge of saying something, then changed her mind. "In that case, I guess all you've got left to do is figure out what to do about her."

Dave turned his head in the direction of Angelette's nod. He saw Claire then. She was standing in front of one of the squad cars, talking to Lee Elliot. In the harsh glare of the headlights, she looked pale and shocked, like the victim of a bad car crash. Dave's chest tightened as he watched her, and for a moment, he had the strangest sensation of having just awakened from a dream.

"You're never going to get over her, are you?" Angelette said softly.

"It doesn't matter," Dave said. "What we had is in the past."

"I guess we are, too." She reached up and brushed the back of her hand against his cheek. "So long, Dave."

He waited until she was gone, and then he turned, his gaze meeting Claire's. She quickly glanced away.

Another moment went by and then he went over to her. Even when he came up beside her, she didn't turn, wouldn't meet his eyes.

"I was just offering Claire a ride back to town," Elliot said. "In fact, I insist. Charlotte would never let me hear the end of it if I didn't see her sister safely home."

Dave stared down at Claire. "Is that what you want?"

"It's fine. There's no sense in you having to make a special trip back to New Orleans."

"I don't mind the drive."

"There's really no point."

"Okay, if that's what you want. I'll call you tomorrow about Savannah Sweete." He turned and started walking toward his truck.

A moment later, Claire caught up with him.

"Dave?"

He turned.

She put a hand to her mouth, as if she wasn't quite certain what had possessed her to follow him. "I just have to know one thing."

He braced himself. "What is it?"

The wind lifted her hair, and for a moment it was all Dave could do not to reach out and smooth the soft strands with his hand.

"Did you really know who Nettle was going to name when you brought me out here?"

"I suspected. I didn't know."

Her eyes searched his face. "Why didn't you tell me?"

"Would you have believed me?"

"I don't know." She looked off toward the cabin, as if still having a difficult time accepting what had happened. "Is it possible he made it all up? Maybe he just said what he knew you wanted to hear."

"I don't think so, Claire. Titus followed Nettle to a bar on Airline Drive yesterday. A little while later, Alex showed up, and they were together for a long time. It seemed as if they had a lot to discuss."

She shuddered, and then without warning, she reached up, lightly touched the cut on his forehead. Her fingers were cool and soft, but the feel of them against his skin was like an electric jolt. Dave didn't move, could barely even breathe. After a brief moment, she took her hand away.

"Did Nettle do that to you?"

"He had a little help from a creep named Bobby Ray Taubin."

"What about Alex? Did he have anything to do with it?"

"I don't know. A third man was there that night, but I never got a look at his face."

Claire bit her lip. "Is that why you set all this up?"

"I set this up because I wanted justice served," Dave said. "It's not revenge, if that's what you're asking."

"I'm sorry. I didn't mean to imply that it was. It's just…I hardly know what to think anymore. All those years that Alex and I were married…all the times we were together…I had no idea what he'd done. I thought he was a good man, someone I could love and respect."

Dave looked down at his hand. His knuckles were swollen and one had split open against Nettle's jaw. But the pain was nothing compared to the ache inside his chest. "None of this is on you, Claire. He was your husband. You wanted to believe the best about him. No one can fault you for that."

She drew a long breath and released it. "Do you ever wonder why things happen the way they do?"

"All the time," he said. "But it doesn't do any good."

"It's like someone opened a door to our past and now all this pain just keeps rushing out."

"I don't think there's any grand design here, Claire. If I hadn't been drinking for all those years, this mess would have been settled a long time ago. The clues were there, I just wasn't in any shape to know what they meant."

She brushed a shaky hand across her face. "What's going to happen to Alex now?"

"If all this sticks, he's facing some pretty serious charges. Accessory to murder, conspiracy. I guess it all depends on how good his lawyer is. I'm sorry."

"Don't be sorry. If he used Ruby's kidnapping to cover up that girl's murder, then I don't care what happens to him."

Dave could see her lips trembling, and when she bowed her head, moonlight glinted in her hair, turning the gold highlights to silver.

As he watched her struggle with her emotions, he

felt something tear loose inside him. He had only just started learning to live with the past, and now it was the future that scared him. Because the road ahead had no glimmers of light to guide him, no fleeting images of happiness such as he saw when he looked behind him.

No matter what happened from this night forward, Claire would fade back into his past, a moment, a memory, an elusive ghost that would always be there to haunt him.

Twenty-Five

Alex Girard swore at the persistent ring of the door-bell as he came out of the bedroom. Pulling on his shirt, he walked over and checked the peephole. Then he drew open the door in surprise.

"Claire? What are you doing here at this hour?"

"I need to talk to you."

He glanced over his shoulder as he propped an arm against the door frame. "It's late and I've had a long day. Whatever it is, can't it wait until morning?"

"No, it can't." She brushed past him before he could stop her.

He closed the door and turned, noticing for the first time how agitated she seemed. She wore a denim skirt and white tank top, and her hair was damp, as if she'd just come from the shower.

Down the hallway, the bedroom door closed softly, but Alex didn't think Claire heard it. She was too distracted.

"What's wrong? You look upset."

"I am upset. I found out something tonight that was very disturbing."

Alex's gaze shot to the bedroom door before he could stop himself. "And what might that be?"

Claire paused. "Does the name Renee Savaria mean anything to you?"

Outwardly, he managed to remain calm, but his lungs felt crushed all of a sudden, as if someone had placed a very heavy weight on his chest. He'd had an inkling something like this might be coming. Dave Creasy had been asking too many questions lately, and something was bound to surface. Whatever he'd dug up he'd evidently passed along to Claire. And now here she was.

He walked into the kitchen to fix himself a drink. "The name rings a faint bell," he said over his shoulder. His voice sounded normal, but his hand trembled as he got out the glasses. "You want a drink?"

She shook her head.

He poured himself a whiskey, then came back into the living room and sat on the arm of the couch. "What's this all about?"

"Renee Savaria was murdered by a cop seven years ago."

He swirled the liquid in his glass as he thought about that for a minute. "I have a vague recollection of the case," he said, "But I don't remember anything about a cop. I think you got that part all wrong."

"Don't lie, Alex. You have more than a vague recollection. You were there the night she was murdered and you helped cover it up. You even used Ruby's kidnapping to manipulate Dave into destroying incriminating evidence." She pushed back her damp hair with a trembling hand. "How could you do such a thing? How could you marry me, knowing what you'd done? What kind of person are you?"

"Those are some ugly accusations." His hand tightened around the glass as he forced himself to meet her gaze. "Who put you up to this?"

"Nobody. I came here on my own."

"I don't think so. This isn't you talking. Somebody's put a bug in your ear and I've a pretty good idea who it was." He set the drink aside and slowly stood. "How long have you been seeing him?"

"I don't know what you're talking about."

"Sure you do, Claire. Was it before we separated?" His mouth tightened. "For the life of me, I can't figure out what you see in that guy. He's had a serious sauce problem for years, and yet you still can't get over him. I wish you would tell me what the fascination is because I would truly love to know."

"Don't change the subject. This is about you, Alex, and what you did seven years ago. I don't know how you can stand there and look me in the eyes after what you've done."

"So that's it? You have me all tried and convicted on Dave Creasy's word? You're not even going to consider the possibility that he could be making the whole thing up just to make me look bad? It's the kind of thing he'd do, Claire, and you know it."

"You seem to be missing something here. Dave isn't the one who told me about your involvement. I heard it from Clive Nettle."

Alex felt his hands go cold, and for a moment, it was as if the earth had opened up beneath his feet. He sat down hard on the couch arm, the color draining from his face.

"I see that name does ring a bell," she said softly.

Claire studied him, and what she saw in his eyes devastated her. She hadn't realized until that moment how badly she'd wanted to believe it was all some terrible mistake. Their marriage was over, but she still cared about him, had once loved him. How could she not have known what he was capable of?

He said nothing for a long time, and then his gaze slowly lifted to hers. "Why are you doing this? What are you trying to prove?"

"It's all true, isn't it? I can see it in your eyes. Now I understand why you didn't want to believe me about the doll and the connection to Mignon Bujold's murder. You were afraid if Ruby's case was reopened, all this would come out."

"Claire, I didn't have anything to do with her kidnapping. You have to believe that."

"You didn't take her. I believe that. But you weren't above using her disappearance to cover up a murder. You made those calls to Dave, knowing that he would do anything to bring his daughter home. You used his grief and desperation to protect a cold-blooded killer, and now you're going to have to pay for what you did. You won't be able to lie or charm your way out of this. It's all coming out. Nettle has already talked to the D.A., so you may as well admit to me what you did."

He glanced down at his drink, seemed to consider for a moment what he wanted to say to her before he spoke. "Even if I was there the night Renee Savaria was killed, that doesn't mean I had anything to do with her death. I would never lay a hand on a woman, Claire, you know that. But that wouldn't have mattered to the press. Every cop there would have been crucified. What good would have come from wasting all those careers?"

Claire felt something inside her go dark as she

looked at him. It was like turning the light off in a roomful of memories. The man before her was a complete stranger.

"Nothing I did changed anything," he said. "Ruby was already dead. You know the statistics as well as I do. Twenty-four to forty-eight hours, Claire. I did everything I could to find her, but she was already dead."

"You don't know that! She could have still been alive when you placed those phone calls. Dave might have been able to find her if you hadn't made him think her kidnapping was connected to Renee Savaria's murder."

"You still don't see it, do you?" Alex's smile was sad. "This isn't about me. It's about Dave. It's always been about him."

Claire shook her head. "You're wrong."

"You're still trying to make him the good guy so it justifies your feelings for him. He is what he is, Claire, and one of these days you're finally going to have to accept that Dave Creasy is your cross to bear. Just like Renee Savaria is mine."

Claire didn't slam the door behind her, but somehow the soft click of the latch seemed even more final to Alex. She hadn't been angry when she left. There had been no emotion in her exit at all, just that one brief click and it was over. Done. Claire Doucett was no longer a part of his life.

He told himself to get up, finish dressing and plan a course of action. If Nettle had already talked to the D.A., then Alex probably had a day or two at the most to find a good attorney to get him out of this mess.

Instead, he remained on the arm of the couch, ice melting in his drink, as he stared out the window.

He sensed a presence in the hallway, and he turned to find Charlotte leaning against the door, arms folded, as she watched him. She was fully dressed, looking exactly the way she had when she'd walked through his door a few hours ago. Except for her hair. It was still mussed from the pillow.

"Is it true?"

He mustered up a vague denial as he drained his glass. "Don't believe everything you hear. You know how Claire is. She has a vivid imagination."

"I didn't hear you deny her allegations."

"You didn't hear me admit to anything, either, did you?"

"I heard enough to draw some pretty damning conclusions."

"Conclusions don't mean much in court. And somehow I don't think you want to get on that witness stand and subject yourself to a hostile cross-examination. Could get pretty nasty with Claire in the courtroom."

"I doubt it will come to that." Charlotte gave him a faint smile as she held up her cell phone. "I just spoke to Lee Elliot. He corroborated everything Claire said here tonight. You'd better find yourself a damn good lawyer, Alex, because you are in some serious trouble."

"I wouldn't be so quick to judge if I were you. Every story has two sides."

"So I've been told."

"What I told Claire was right, you know. Nothing I did changed anything."

Now it was Charlotte who gave him a pitying smile. "You're wrong about that. It changed you, Alex. It turned you into someone that Claire could never fall in love with. And somehow I think that might be the most fitting punishment of all for you."

She left the apartment as silently as her sister had, and still Alex didn't move. Through a break in the buildings outside his window, he could see the shimmer of lights on a barge on the river, and he listened for the foghorns that he could sometimes hear at night before he drifted off. The plaintive sound always left him lonely and longing for something that seemed just out of his reach. He'd always thought it was Claire he missed, but now he knew that what he'd really been searching for all these years was his soul.

When had he become one of the bad guys? Alex wondered. The transformation had been so subtle, he hadn't seen it coming. One bribe, one payoff, the first time he'd agreed to look the other way. When had his ambition convinced him that in the scheme of things, none of that really mattered? The bigger picture was all that counted.

And then, as the years went by, it became about survival—covering his ass. One thing led to another until he hadn't worried so much about right and wrong anymore, and somewhere along the way, he'd started to think of himself as immune, untouchable.

And now the sins of his past were all catching up with him.

The barge disappeared and the sounds of traffic outside his window faded. He got up to turn off the light, then went back to his place on the couch, a strange lightness in his limbs. The apartment was empty and silent, and for the first time in years, Alex Girard sat alone in the dark with his conscience.

* * *

Dave had been home for a long time, but he hadn't felt like going up to bed yet. When he first got in, he'd fixed himself something to eat and turned on the television, watched a movie straight through and then the news. When he started nodding off, he carried his plate into the kitchen, rinsed it off in the sink, then went upstairs to shower.

Crawling into bed, he stretched out his legs, trying to relax, but it took a long time for the tension to drain out of him. He'd just managed to drift off when the sound of a car in his drive startled him awake. He got up and went over to the window to see who it was.

He recognized the car, and he watched as the door opened and Claire got out. She looked up at the house, but Dave didn't think she could see him in the window. He hadn't turned on the light. Pulling on a pair of jeans, he went downstairs to let her in.

She was still coming across the yard when he stepped out on the porch. She heard the door and faltered. "Dave?"

"Yeah, it's me."

Moonlight flooded the yard and a mild breeze drifted through the trees. He could see the gleam of her hair, hear the swish of her skirt as she started toward the porch.

He reached over and unlatched the screen, realizing suddenly that he was nervous. "Are you okay?"

"I guess so." She climbed the steps and Dave held the door open for her, but she hesitated. "I got you out of bed, didn't I? I'm sorry."

"I wasn't asleep. What brings you out here at this hour?"

She smiled apologetically as she stepped up on the porch. "I couldn't sleep, either."

It was a warm night, but Dave thought he could see her shiver. "You want to come inside?"

"Could we just sit out here for a while?"

"Sure."

But she didn't sit. Instead she walked to the end of the porch and stared out at the bayou. Dave was behind her, but he made sure he didn't cramp her space as he watched her in the darkness. She'd changed clothes since she left the cabin earlier, and he thought he could smell her shampoo in the breeze. It was sweet, like honeysuckle.

"I went to see Alex tonight." She turned, and their eyes met briefly before she glanced away.

"Do you want to talk about it?"

She lifted a hand to the back of her neck. "No. That's not why I came all the way out here. I want you to tell me about Savannah Sweete."

"I would have called you in the morning."

"I know, but I didn't want to wait. I don't want to think about anything else right now. I just want to find that doll."

"I'll tell you what I know, but it's not much. Like I said earlier, she lives about thirty miles south of Houma, near Tiber. I drove by her place yesterday, but I couldn't get in to see her. The gate across the property was locked, so I went back to town and asked around about her. Your information seems to be pretty accurate. She's an artist who specializes in portrait dolls, and they can run as high as two or three thousand dollars."

"Is that all the information you could get?"

"Pretty much. You were right about the accident,

too. She's confined to a wheelchair and hardly ever leaves her house. The people I talked to seemed pretty protective of her, but when I explained the situation to the parish sheriff, he said he'd have a word with her nephew, see about getting us in to meet her. He even offered to drive out there with us if we need him to."

Clare glanced up at him. "We?"

"I'd like to be there when you talk to her. If that's okay with you."

"I don't know, Dave. I'm not so sure that's a good idea anymore."

"Isn't that why you came to me in the first place? You wanted me to help you find the doll. What's changed?"

She paused, glanced out at the darkness, and said softly, "We've changed."

He looked at her standing there, and suddenly he couldn't breathe.

She turned away, but he could still see her profile. Her face looked pale and fragile, but her backbone was ramrod straight as she gazed out at the trees. Her hair was pinned up in back and the moonlight glistened along her creamy skin. And at that moment, Dave would have cut off his arm with a butter knife for one brief touch of that smooth neck.

"I lied," she said softly. "I didn't come out here to talk about Savannah Sweete. The truth is, I don't know why I came."

He swallowed. "It doesn't matter. I'm glad you're here."

"Dave…"

The way she said his name sent a shiver down his backbone. He stood silently, a strange humming inside him. It was as if every nerve ending in his body had suddenly come to life after years of lying dormant. He reached up, brushed the softness of her cheek with his fingertips, and she trembled.

Afterward, she went into the bathroom to dress. She came back out wearing only her shirt and panties, and as she perched on the edge of the bed, Dave reached out and drew his finger down her backbone. She was so beautiful to look at, and her skin was like warm silk. Her hair had fallen loose from the pins and hung in tangled curls about her shoulders.

She shivered at his touch and glanced at him over her shoulder. "Believe it or not, I didn't come out here with that in mind."

He sat up in bed and propped himself against a pillow. "Sadly, I do believe that."

She smiled. "I should probably finish getting dressed and go home now."

"It's late and it's a long drive back to New Orleans. You're here now. You may as well spend the night."

"I don't think that's such a good idea, do you?"

"It's a fine idea. You crawl back into bed and I'll go downstairs and sleep on the couch."

"You'd do that for me?"

"After all the shit I've put you through, I'd say a good night's sleep is the least I owe you."

She lay down on the bed facing him. He brushed the hair from her shoulders and slid his hand down her arm. Her body had changed in seven years. She was thinner than he remembered, and her skin was so pale, as if she no longer spent any time in the sun. But her subtle curves fascinated him. She was an intriguing stranger who had once been his wife.

She watched him for a moment. "I feel as if I should say something."

"There's really no need."

"Maybe there is. I don't mean to be blunt, but I'm not looking to start anything back up with you, Dave."

He tried not to wince. "I never thought you were."

She pillowed her head on one arm. "I've been married more than half my life. I think it's time I try being alone for a while."

"Take it from me, being alone isn't all it's cracked up to be."

"You seem to be doing okay."

"I'm always just one bad day away from another bender. We both know that."

"Dave—"

"I put you through hell when we were married, Claire. I'm not delusional. I wouldn't wish me on my worst enemy."

"I guess I wouldn't, either." Her eyes were sober, and then she smiled and leaned over to kiss him gently on the mouth. "But you do have your moments."

Twenty-Six

‿‿✦‿‿

Matthew opened his bedroom door and crept into the hallway. The wooden floor in his aunt's old house creaked beneath his bare feet, and he froze, breathless and terrified that she had heard him.

After a moment, when nothing happened, he continued down the corridor toward the stairway. Her bedroom was at the top of the stairs, and as he stole past her door, he heard the murmur of voices coming from inside.

That wasn't unusual. In the weeks since Father had brought Matthew here to live with Savannah, she'd had a number of nighttime visitors. Matthew could always tell when company was on the way because she would make him go up to his room for the rest of the evening. He hadn't minded at first. The house was old and creepy, and he had begun to think of his room as a haven. But he soon grew restless and bored with the few toys that Father had packed for him, and he longed for someone his own age to play with. But what he wanted more than anything was for Mama to come and take him away from here. He'd prayed every single night for that to happen, but he was beginning to lose faith. It had been so long now since she'd gone away.

The floor creaked and he paused again outside his aunt's room. This time, he thought she surely must have heard him, but instead of coming to the door, she raised her voice in anger. Matthew thought at first she was yelling at him, but then he realized her rage was directed at someone in her room. The voices were so loud, he couldn't help but overhear.

"...gives me the creeps the way he skulks around at all hours. How much longer do you expect me to keep him here?"

"Until I find a house and get settled in my new position. It won't be that much longer. Where's your compassion? He's your sister's child, your own flesh and blood."

Matthew went completely still, his veins icing as he recognized the other voice. Father! He hadn't been back since he'd dropped Matthew off weeks ago. That was the only good thing about being here. Father did not come home every night.

"My dear sister stole you away from me. And now I'm supposed to raise her brat while she's in the nuthouse?"

"I told you, it's just until I get settled. As soon as I can set up Matthew's sessions with Dr. Church, I'll come and get him."

"Tell me something, Daniel. Since when does a seven-year-old kid need a shrink? What's wrong with that boy?"

Father hesitated. "He's confused about things."

"His gender?"

"Why would you ask such a thing?"

"Because he's lived in my house for the past two months. I've noticed things."

"What kind of things?"

"He's not a normal boy, Daniel. He's not rowdy or disruptive and he never wants to go outside. The only thing that seems to interest him are my dolls."

"You don't let him into your studio." Father's voice sharpened.

"Not on purpose, no. But I've caught him in there once or twice. I didn't see any harm in letting him look around. He wasn't bothering anything. I don't think he even touched the dolls. He just wanted to sit there and...watch them."

"I don't care what he was doing, you need to keep him out of there. He might ruin some of your work."

"You really think he'd do that?"

"Perhaps not intentionally, but he is just a boy. And it's not unusual for a child that age to act out when he loses his mother."

"You make it sound like she's dead."

He paused for a long time before answering. Then he said slowly, *"She might as well be."*

His lengthy hesitation made Matthew think of the terrible argument on Maddy's birthday. Matthew hadn't wanted to think about all the terrible things Father had said to Mama, or the blood he'd seen on the floor and on Father's coat. When Matthew thought of Maddy's birthday, he tried to remember it as a happy day. But he hadn't seen his mother since then, and even at his tender age, he knew that, without her, any future celebrations would never be the same.

He suddenly realized that he didn't want to hear the

rest of the conversation. He was afraid, but for some reason, he couldn't make himself turn away, even when the voices fell silent. Even when, a few minutes later, the noises coming from inside the room were soft moans and deep grunts.

Matthew didn't understand what was going on inside his aunt's bedroom, but he knew that it was something bad. He knew that it was somehow a betrayal of his mother, and he angrily turned and ran down the stairs as fast as he could. His aunt's studio was down a long corridor that led to the back of the house. Matthew opened the door and stepped quickly inside.

Moonlight flooded through the wall of windows, so he didn't have to turn on a light. He stood glancing around at the pedestals on which some of his aunt's favorite dolls were displayed. He took them down one by one, stroking cool cheeks, running his hand down gleaming hair.

Then he went over to the unfinished sculpture that she had left on her worktable. A picture of a little girl was mounted on the wall behind the table, and as Matthew studied the sculpted face, he could already see a resemblance to the child in the photograph. She reminded him a little of Maddy, but the mouth was all wrong. He climbed up on a stool and sat looking at the clay face for a long, long time. Then he reached for one of the shapers and began to mold the mouth into Maddy's.

"What are you doing?"

The voice seemed to awaken him from a deep trance. Sunlight flooded through the windows and he blinked. He had been sitting there all night. He hadn't been sleeping, though. The clay face before him had been completely transformed.

"What have you done?"

His aunt's voice was cold with fury. He glanced up, saw her contorted features and cringed. Quickly, he turned back to the clay face, hoping to catch a glimpse of Maddy, but she was gone. His aunt had scared her away.

She came over to where he still sat, grabbed his arm and jerked him off the stool. "You just destroyed two days worth of work. What do you have to say for yourself?"

"I wanted to find Maddy."

"Who the hell is Maddy?"

Matthew clamped his lips shut. Shush. Mustn't tell, a little voice warned him.

His aunt's hand tightened on his arm. "I asked you a question. Who is Maddy?" When he still didn't answer, she started to laugh. "I get it. She's you, isn't she? All right, then. You want to find Maddy? You go look for her in here." She grabbed up the clay and dragged Matthew across the room by his arm. She opened a door to a small storeroom, shoved him inside, then threw the clay at his feet.

"That'll give you something to do while you sit in there and think about what you did."

The door closed behind her, and Matthew was all alone in the dim little room. Hands trembling, he took out the old Polaroid picture he kept hidden away in his pocket. He could barely see the faces in the photograph, but it didn't matter. He knew them by heart. Six little girls seated at a table. Maddy was at the end, her face aglow with happiness. And in the window behind her, if Matthew looked hard enough, he could see Mama's reflection in the glass.

It was a perfect picture. A perfect reminder of a perfect day.

Wiping the tears from his cheeks, Matthew slid down to the floor and reached for the clay. He closed his eyes for a moment and imagined what he wanted to see.

"You're in there," he whispered. "I can feel you."

And one of these days, he would find a way to let her out.

Matthew sat at the dressing table in his aunt's bedroom and stared at his reflection. Savannah's clothes were laid out on the chaise by the window, and all he had to do now was finish her makeup. The wig would come next, cut and styled just the way she liked it. His aunt was very particular about the way she wore her hair. For as long as Matthew had known her, she'd been fastidious about her appearance. He supposed it was an admirable trait, especially after the accident, when even the smallest tasks had taken a monumental effort on her part. She was a strong woman, though. Matthew was constantly amazed by her constitution.

He got up from the dressing table and went over to the bed to stare down at her. She wore a white cotton nightgown that clung to her thin frame. Her hair had gone completely gray, and the skin on her face was pulled so tight across her skull it almost appeared transparent.

She lay on her back, staring up at the ceiling, but when she sensed Matthew's presence, her gaze cut to him and her eyes widened. Something that might have been anger glinted in the pale depths, and Matthew laughed softly.

"You've still got some fire, don't you?"

A telltale frown appeared on her brow before she could relax it.

"I saw that," he said with another laugh. "Your medicine is wearing off. I guess I'll have to increase the dosage. Can't have you grunting like a pig while our guests are here."

She stared at him, unblinking.

"I did tell you that we're having company this morning, didn't I? A Sheriff Granger called a little while ago. He's sending a couple out here later who are interested in a doll they think you may have sculpted. They say it looks like their missing daughter. Have you ever heard anything so ridiculous in your life?"

He sat down on the edge of the bed and reached for the medicine vial he kept nearby. He also had a supply of hypodermic needles in her bedside stand. He'd made sure when he first came to take care of her after the accident that everything he needed was right at his fingertips. That was back when she had still wanted his help, of course.

Matthew drew his knuckles lightly down her cheek. It really was a pity that it had come to this. His aunt was a gifted artist, and he hated that her talents could no longer be utilized. But she had only herself to blame for her current misfortune. She shouldn't have stuck her nose into Matthew's business.

When he'd first come back to the area several years ago, he and Savannah had gotten on just fine. He'd been willing to let bygones be bygones, and she'd been flattered by his interest in doll making, had taught him almost everything she knew. Then she'd started to ask too many questions. The accident had curbed her curiosity for a long time, because she'd needed Matthew then. She hadn't wanted to do or say anything to drive him away.

As time went on, however, she'd grown more and more independent. Eventually, the questions had started up again, and somehow she'd found out that Matthew had dropped out of medical school a few weeks after the family fortune had come under his control, and she'd threatened to expose the fact that he wasn't a licensed physician. He might have been able to talk his way out of that one, but then another child had disappeared and her curiosity had turned into suspicion. Matthew had to take matters into his own hands, as he had learned very early on to do.

He drew aside the blanket and quickly gave her the injection in her left hip. Then he threw the needle away, pulled the covers up to her chin and leaned down to kiss her forehead.

Walking over to the window, he stared out across the lawn, down to the gate and to the gravel road beyond. It might have been his imagination, but he thought he could see a trail of dust in the distance, and his heart quickened with excitement.

She's coming!

After all these years, Mama was finally coming back for him.

He felt moisture on his face and he quickly wiped it away. No time for tears. He had to be ready when she got here.

Twenty-Seven

❧❦❧

By ten o'clock that morning, Dave and Claire had crossed into Terrebonne Parish, and from Houma, they headed south on Highway 53, deep into bayou country. The sunlight that shone through the oak and willow trees was soft and dappled, and hot enough out over the bayou to melt all but a ribbon of morning mist. The water was dark green with algae and duckweed, and along the banks, lily pads grew thick and tangled and bursting with yellow blossoms.

Near the tiny town of Tiber, they took a side road that ran through acres and acres of sugarcane fields. The area was rural and impoverished, the houses they passed along the way little more than shotgun shanties with dirty yards and outdoor privies. From open windows and dilapidated porches, dark eyes watched with wary curiosity, and only an occasional hand lifted in greeting.

Claire had lived in Louisiana all her life, but she was still a stranger to the traditions and superstitions that permeated the bayou country. Voodoo had been a profitable tourist attraction for decades, but was still a serious practice in the Acadian swamps. It wasn't unusual to see a dime tied around an ankle or a gris-gris hanging from a dusky neck to ward off bad luck.

As they drove into the countryside, Claire's uneasiness deepened, but she tried to hide her trepidation from Dave. They'd spoken very little on the trip, neither of them ready to talk about what had happened the night before. And as they drew ever closer to their destination, Claire suspected that his apprehension was as great as her own. He stared straight ahead, jaw set, hands gripping the steering wheel. And when they rounded a bend in the road and could see glimpses of the house through the trees, he said tightly, "That's it."

Savannah Sweete lived at the end of a gravel road in a white-pillared plantation house surrounded by a wrought-iron fence. Magnolia trees and crepe myrtle bushes lined the winding drive, and when Claire rolled down her window, she could smell honeysuckle mingling with the earthier scent of the swamp.

The gates were closed across the drive, but the parish sheriff who had arranged the meeting told Dave that Savannah would be expecting them. All he had to do was tap his horn and she would use her remote to let them in.

She must have been watching for them because the gates swung open before Dave sounded the horn, and they were able to drive straight through. The house sat on a slight incline, in deep shade, surrounded on three sides by towering oak and pecan trees and on the east side by the bayou. The lawn sloped down to the water's edge, and Claire could see a pirogue tied up at a wooden dock.

Dave parked in the gravel drive, and as they got out of the truck, Claire lifted a hand to her eyes. White wicker rockers on the front porch were cooled by ceiling fans. Hollyhocks grew in the sun, blue hydrangeas in the shade, and as she climbed the porch steps, Claire could hear the drone of bees swarming a bottlebrush bush at the corner of the house.

She waited nervously while Dave rapped on the door with the big brass knocker. When the lock clicked open, seemingly of its own accord, Claire said, "How did that happen?"

"It must be on a remote like the gate." He pushed open the door and stepped inside.

The foyer was dim and smelled musty and damp, as if no one had lived in the house for years. The ravages of time and neglect were clearly visible in the faded wallpaper, the peeling woodwork and the water-stained ceilings.

An oak staircase curved up to a shadowy gallery, but the parlor to the right of the front hall was filled with sunlight. To the left of the foyer, an elevator with an ornate grille had been installed to accommodate Savannah's wheelchair.

Dave walked over to the stairs and called up. "Hello? Anyone home?"

Everything was silent except for the gold-and-walnut grandfather clock ticking in the foyer. A moment later, floorboards creaked overhead. A woman's voice said from the shadows, "Yes?"

"I'm Dave Creasy and this is Claire Doucett. We're here to see Savannah Sweete. She's expecting us."

"Of course. Sheriff Granger called and said you were on your way. There's a pitcher of sweet tea in the parlor. Please make yourselves at home. I'll be down in a moment."

They walked through the wide opening into the parlor, and Claire glanced around. Despite the sun shining in through the long windows, the room was dreary, furnished with heavy draperies and dark velvet divans. Windows looked out on an enclosed terrace, and beyond the garden, she could see a white, lattice summerhouse down by the bayou.

But what caught her attention more than anything were the dolls. They were everywhere. Peering down from the walls. Peeking playfully around curtains. Having tea at a tiny table set for two. And all of them so lifelike that Claire found herself having to look twice.

"Holy cow," Dave muttered. He rubbed the back of his neck as if the hair there was suddenly standing on end. "Why do I feel as if we've just landed in some sort of freak show?"

"They are a little unnerving," Claire agreed. "But wouldn't Mama get a kick out of this place?"

A few minutes later, they heard the elevator descend. The iron gate swung open and Savannah Sweete's wheelchair rolled smoothly onto the hardwood floor.

She was slim and attractive, her face unlined, the skin at her throat still smooth and supple. Her gray hair was cut short and fringed at the ends, and her smile, when she entered the room, seemed genuine and friendly. She was much younger than Claire would have guessed, or else she was very adept at concealing her years. She was beautifully made up—eyes, lips, cheeks all dusted with soft colors that complemented her pale skin. She was as perfect as her dolls.

She wore a black pleated skirt that fell over her

knees and a silk lavender blouse draped with a matching sweater. There were pearls at her throat and in her lobes, and it was obvious to Claire that she still took a great deal of pride in her appearance. Even her hands and nails were perfectly groomed.

"I'm Savannah," she said, and held out her hand first to Claire and then to Dave. Her drawl was very pronounced, her demeanor pure Old South. "Won't you sit down?"

When they were settled on one of the divans, she rolled over to the coffee table to pour the tea. "I understand you have some questions about one of my dolls. Sheriff Granger said something about a resemblance to a missing child?"

Claire glanced at Dave and he nodded, indicating she should explain. "This may sound strange, but a few days ago, I saw a doll in a French Quarter shop that looked exactly like our little girl. She was kidnapped seven years ago."

"Oh, my dear." Savannah's hand went to the pearls around her neck. "I don't know what to say. What a terrible ordeal you've lived through all these years."

Claire's throat knotted at the woman's compassion. "Thank you," she murmured.

"And then to see your child's face on a doll. The shock must have been devastating."

"Yes, it was."

"You believe the doll you saw was one of mine?"

"I'm almost certain of it."

"But surely you don't think I had anything to do with your daughter's kidnapping."

"We don't think you had anything to do with her disappearance," Dave said. "But we think the person who took her may have commissioned you to make a doll in her likeness. The kidnapper may have even brought Ruby to see you."

"Oh, I sincerely doubt that. I always work from photographs. And seven years ago, I was already confined to this chair. I rarely saw callers apart from my nephew. If anyone had brought a child to see me, I'm sure I would have remembered."

"If you only use photographs, how do you manage to get the details of your subjects so perfectly?" Claire asked. "I'm told that the doll I saw had a tiny birthmark on her left arm, exactly where our daughter had a birthmark. I don't think it would have even shown up in a photograph."

"My clients are required to fill out a questionnaire before I'll even touch the clay. I ask them to describe things like birthmarks, freckles and even scars."

Claire opened her purse and removed a picture of Ruby. She passed it to Savannah. "Do you recognize her?"

"Oh, my. Would you look at that precious face." Savannah glanced up, her eyes soft. "What a perfectly beautiful little girl."

Claire leaned forward. "Have you ever seen her before? Or a photograph of her?"

Savannah Sweete studied the picture a moment longer before handing it back to Claire. "I'm sorry. Over the years, I must have received hundreds of photographs, and at my age, I can't possibly remember them all."

"My mother is a collector," Claire said. "She took one of your classes several years ago in New Orleans. She said that some of your students were fairly adept at copying your style. Were any of them good enough to make a doll that could have been mistaken for one of yours?"

"Most of the people who signed up for my classes were dabblers. Bored housewives or retirees looking for a new hobby. Once in a blue moon someone truly talented came along. To answer your question, I suppose it's possible. If I could see the doll, I would be able to tell you definitively if it's one of mine. I have a certain technique I use that, so far as I know, has never been duplicated by any other doll maker. I won't bore you with the details, but it's all in the making of the mold. The method I've perfected is what makes my dolls appear so lifelike."

"What do you do with the questionnaires once the doll is finished?" Dave asked.

"I have a file for each project. Everything goes into a folder."

"Including the photographs?"

"Unless the client requests they be returned."

"Where do you keep your files?"

"My nephew helps me out with the paperwork. I used to keep everything in the attic, but he was afraid all those boxes might catch fire and I would be trapped in the house. So he rented a storage place in town and keeps everything there."

"Would it be possible for us to go through some of those files?" Dave asked.

"I'm sure that could be arranged, but I would need to speak to Matthew about it first. We're very close. He lived with me for a while as a child, and he's still very protective of me. If he thought you were trying to somehow implicate me in a kidnapping, I'm afraid he wouldn't be very cooperative. So I think it's best if I smooth the way. Besides, I don't even have a key to the place. And I should probably warn you that without a name or a date, you'll be searching for a needle in a haystack."

"It's still worth a try," Claire said.

Savannah nodded. "I can see how important this is to you, so I'll speak to my nephew as soon as possible. I don't know if the sheriff told you or not, but Matthew is the town doctor. He's cut back on his office hours, though, so he may even have time to go through some of the boxes himself."

Claire stood. "We'll appreciate anything you can do. Thank you so much for agreeing to see us this morning."

"Oh, my dear, there's no need to thank me. As I mentioned, I rarely receive visitors, but when I heard a missing child was involved…what else could I do?"

She followed them into the foyer. "I do hope you find out something soon. And I must say, you've aroused my curiosity about that doll."

Dave handed her his card. "As soon as you hear from your nephew, please give me a call at that number so we can set up a time to meet."

Claire scribbled her home number on the back of one of the gallery's cards and gave it to Savannah, as well. "In case you can't get in touch with one of us right away, you can leave a message and we'll call you back."

The woman took both cards and rolled to the door to see them out.

At the bottom of the steps, Clare glanced back. Savannah Sweete was still in the doorway and lifted her hand to wave goodbye. She stared after them for a long time, then closed the door.

* * *

A little while later, Dave stood on his porch steps as Claire drove away. The car disappeared around a bend, the sound of the engine faded through the trees, but he remained motionless as the dust settled on the dirt road. Then he turned and went inside the house, fixed a glass of soda over ice and carried it into his office.

He hadn't talked to Titus since the night before, and now he was anxious to find out how news of Clive Nettle's arrest was hitting the police department. He picked up the phone, then set it back down when he heard a car pull up in his driveway.

Thinking it might be Claire returning for some reason, he got up and went out to the porch. But the rusted-out Camaro parked beneath the oak tree wasn't her car, and the scrawny woman who climbed out was most definitely not Claire. She strode across the yard, cigarette dangling from her mouth and flip-flops slapping against her feet.

She wore jeans and a blue tank top that dipped low over a sunken chest. Her skin was deeply tanned and she wore no makeup on a face that was too hard, too thin and too grim. Her hair was straight and dirty blond, and she wore it parted in the middle and tucked behind her ears.

Dave opened the screen door and stepped out. "Can I help you?"

She took the cigarette out of her mouth and Dave noticed she was missing a tooth. "Are you Dave Creasy?"

"Yeah, that's me. Who are you?"

She flicked ashes into the dirt. "My name's Desiree Choate. Are you the guy that's been asking around about a doll?"

"Yeah, that's right."

"My cousin owns the gas station in Tiber. He said you came by the other day and left your card. That's how I knew where to find you."

"What can I do for you, Ms. Choate?"

"Desiree." She brushed a strand of hair from her face. She was probably no more than thirty, but she had the haggard demeanor and defeated eyes of a woman who had never caught a decent break. Dave had known women like her all his life. "It said on your card that you're a private investigator."

"That's right."

"The way I heard it, you're trying to locate a doll that looks like a missing kid." She paused, her gaze meeting his. "Do you look for people, too?"

He smiled. "Most of the time, yeah."

She exhaled smoke into the light that spangled down through the oak trees. "You're trying to find a doll. I'm trying to track down my old man. Maybe we can help each other out."

"You know something about the doll I'm looking for?"

"I've seen it. But that's all I'm saying until you agree to help me."

"Maybe you'd better come inside then." Dave opened the screen door and moved back so that she could step up on the porch. She followed him into the house and he motioned toward the office. "Go in and take a seat. Would you like something to drink?"

She looked hot and thirsty, but she shook her head. The cigarette still smoldered between her fingers, and she looked around for a place to put it out. Dave shoved an ashtray in front of her. She ground out the butt, then tried to wave away the smoke with her hand. "Sorry about that."

"No problem." He sat down behind the desk. "Where did you see the doll and how do you know it's the one I'm looking for?"

"I'll tell you everything just as soon as I'm satisfied you'll help me out with Travis."

"Who's Travis?"

"The guy I live with."

"Is he missing?"

"I don't know if he's missing or just laid up drunk somewhere. That's what I need you to find out for me."

Dave nodded. "All right. I'll do what I can. I'll need to ask you some questions, but first you tell me what you know about the doll."

"Like I said before, I think I've seen the one you're looking for. Curly blond hair. Blue eyes. Looks damn near like a real kid."

"Where did you see it?"

"One night last week. I worked a double shift at the nursing home, and when I got off, Travis kept asking me if I knew anything about dolls, the kind people collect and pay a lot of money for. I told him the only doll I ever owned was an old Barbie that my mama bought for me at a yard sale one time. So Travis gets on the Internet and starts looking up some stuff. People don't give him much credit, but he's pretty smart that way. Anyway, he copies down all these names and addresses of shops in New Orleans where he thinks he can sell this doll."

"Did he say where he got the doll?"

"No, but knowing Travis the way I do, I'm pretty sure *how* he got it. He's real bad to steal. It's like he can't help himself or something. I'm not making excuses for him, that's just the way he is."

"What did he do with the doll after he showed it to you?"

"He shoved it under the bed, and you know what? After a while, I got to thinking that I could hear that damn thing's heartbeat, that's how bad it creeped me out. I can't explain it except that it was just so real-looking. After a while, it started getting to Travis, too. Kind of took the wind out of his sails that night, if you know what I mean. By the time he left for New Orleans the next day, we were both jumpy as all get-out."

"Did he tell you where he sold it?"

"No, that's just it. It's been more than a week since he left, and I haven't seen him since. He lays out every once in a while, but not like this. He's never stayed gone this long before. I'm starting to worry that something might really have happened to him this time."

"Have you reported him missing to the authorities?"

"I didn't think that was such a hot idea, him being in possession of stolen property and all. That's why I came here to see you."

"What's his full name and what kind of car does he drive?"

"Travis Lee McSwain and he drives an old white T-bird that my daddy let him have."

"Do you know the year and license plate number?"

"No, but I can get it for you."

"I'll need a recent photo as well."

She chewed her bottom lip. "You think you'll be able to find him?"

"I've got a buddy who's a cop in New Orleans. I'll

have him run the plates, see if the car has been impounded or involved in an accident. He can check the hospitals, too." And the morgue, Dave thought.

She nodded. "Since you're going to all this trouble for me, maybe I've got something more that will help you out." She opened her purse, removed a snapshot and slid it across the desk to Dave. "This was pinned to the doll's dress. Sounds a little strange, but one of the little girls in the picture looks a lot like that doll. Is that the kid you're looking for?"

Dave's heart stopped for a split second as he picked up the photograph. But he saw almost at once that none of the children in the picture was his daughter. Six little girls were seated at a table, and the one at the end bore a striking resemblance to Ruby. Same hair, same features.

"There's some writing on the back," Desiree informed him. "It's a date and a Baton Rouge address. I guess that's where the picture was taken."

As Dave studied the photograph, gooseflesh rose on his nape. What were the odds of another child looking that much like his daughter? It could happen, he guessed. Everyone was supposed to have a twin somewhere. The little girl in the photo looked to be about seven, the same age as Ruby when she'd disappeared. But if the date on the back was accurate, the picture was nearly thirty years old. It had been taken more than two decades before Ruby had even been born.

Was it possible the doll Claire saw in the shop window had been made to resemble this child rather than Ruby?

A thought came to Dave suddenly, and the hand holding the photograph started to tremble. What if his daughter had been kidnapped because of her resemblance to the little girl in the picture? What if someone had been trying to replace a child that had been lost twenty-some years before Ruby had even been conceived?

Twenty-Eight

Late that afternoon, Dave drove into Baton Rouge and located the address on the back of the photograph that Desiree Choate had given him. The house was only a few blocks from Louisiana State University, in an historical neighborhood that reminded him of the Garden District in New Orleans. A live oak canopy covered the streets, and the homes were a mix of colonial, Victorian and Greek Revival, most with tall chimneys and wraparound galleries.

He pulled to the curb in front of a stately redbrick colonial with dark green shutters and tall, white columns in the front. It was cool and shady beneath the trees, and he sat for a moment, enjoying the breeze through his open window. When he got out of the truck, he saw a woman in a straw hat next door, down on her knees weeding a flower bed. She looked up when she heard his door slam, gazed at him curiously for a moment, then went back to her work.

Dave stood on the sidewalk in front of the house. A wrought-iron gate was set in the garden wall, and he could see orange and yellow hibiscus blazing through the pikes.

The trim on the house looked freshly painted and the lawn was cut and watered. As he contemplated going up to knock on the door, the woman in the straw hat came to the edge of her yard and hollered over to him.

"If you're looking for the new owners, they haven't moved in yet."

Dave turned and walked over to join her. She was in her late fifties or early sixties, slim and handsome in bright orange capris and a white cotton blouse tied at the waist. Her cheeks were red from the heat, but she still managed to have the fresh, crisp look of a woman who came from a world of good breeding, good manners and good connections. She'd been weeding her own flower beds, not because she had to, but because she liked to, Dave surmised.

"I'm not looking for the new owners," he said, taking out his identification and P.I. license. "My name is Dave Creasy. I'm a private investigator. I'm trying to locate a family who used to live here."

She glanced at his I.D., then her gaze lifted to his bruised face, a glint of curiosity in her eyes. "I'm Doatsy Benoit. I've lived here for nearly forty years so if you can tell me a name, I may be able to help you."

"The only thing I have is a photograph." He took the snapshot from his pocket and handed it to her. "Do you recognize any of these children?"

The woman held the picture out in front of her. "Well, I certainly do. The little girl in the yellow dress is my niece, Annie. And the others used to live in this neighborhood. I've known most of them all their lives. They're grown up now and scattered across the country."

"Can you tell me who the child is at the end of the table?"

"That's Maddy Cypher. This must have been taken at her seventh birthday party. It was a long time ago, but I remember because Annie was visiting from Monroe that week. Maddy's mother, Katherine, saw us outside one day and came over to ask Annie to the party." The woman paused, smiling. "Now you have to understand, Annie was a real tomboy. She hated dress-up parties, and I all but had to hog-tie her to get her to go. But I thought it was the neighborly thing to do, and besides, I always felt so sorry for poor Katherine. She just seemed so lost and lonely, bless her heart. Not a single friend in the neighborhood, and you hardly ever saw her out and about."

"When did the family move away?"

The woman thought for a moment. "My goodness, it must have been thirty years ago. In fact…they left rather abruptly the night after Maddy's party. I never saw any of them again."

"Do you have any idea why they left so suddenly?"

Her eyes darkened. "Why are you looking for the Cyphers?"

"I'm working on a case involving a missing child. I have reason to believe the little girl in this photo may somehow be connected."

Doatsy Benoit's brows lifted as her gaze flashed to the house next door. She put a hand to her throat. "Oh, dear. In that case, maybe you'd better come in. If you want to know about the Cyphers, this could take awhile."

A few minutes later, Dave was seated across from Doatsy Benoit on her sunporch, a glass of iced tea in front of him and a plate of lemon cookies between them. She'd taken off her straw hat when they came inside, and her short, blond hair was mussed on top, like a child's after a nap.

She was one of those women who appeared completely comfortable in her own skin, with the kind of confidence that belonged to the very wealthy or the very beautiful. Dave suspected that Doatsy Benoit had once been both.

"There were two of them," she said. "A girl and a boy. Maddy and Matthew. They were the same age and looked almost identical."

Dave frowned. Savannah Sweete had said her nephew's name was Matthew. "Were they twins?"

"That's what I thought." Doatsy glanced out the window, her eyes softening. "Maddy was such a beautiful, charming little girl. To look at her, you'd never know anything was wrong with her."

"What *was* wrong with her?"

Doatsy hesitated, her gaze dropping to the cookie plate. "According to her mother, she had asthma that was aggravated by severe allergies. That's why you would never see her outside playing with the other children."

"What about the boy?"

"Matthew? The complete opposite. He was a sad, solemn little thing. One of those unfortunate children who seem to be born with an old soul. I used to see him outside quite a bit, but he was always by himself and it was almost always when his father was home. I think the poor little thing was trying to avoid him. Daniel Cypher was a fairly well-known surgeon, one of those brilliant, handsome men who casts a big shadow. The kind, I suspect, who would have a lot of expectations for his children, especially his son."

"How well did you know the Cyphers?"

"Not well at all, I'm afraid. But they were right next door and I couldn't help noticing some things."

"What kind of things?"

She sighed. "The kind of things that should have been confronted."

"Like abuse?"

Her mouth tightened. "I don't know that for sure. I never saw him lay a hand on them. It was just a feeling I got from some of the things Katherine said. She and Daniel were so secretive and stand-offish. I knew something had to be going on inside that house."

"Did they have any other family in the area?"

"Not that I know of. Although I do seem to recall her mentioning something about a sister once. She didn't say much about her, but I had the impression they weren't close."

Doatsy paused, then nodded toward the photograph that lay on the table between them. "I'll tell you what I do remember. On the day of that party, Daniel came home unexpectedly and he sent all the children home early. I was working in my garden when Annie got back, and a little while later, I heard loud voices coming from next door. I knew Katherine and Daniel had to be fighting, and I was afraid of what he might do to her. He seemed to have a terrible temper. So I walked over and rang the bell.

"Katherine answered the door, pale and trembling. She said she was fine, just had a little dizzy spell. Later that night, I saw Daniel and Matthew come out of the house carrying suitcases. Not the kind of overnight bags you might take to the hospital or on a brief trip, but several large bags. Daniel put the luggage in the trunk while Matthew climbed into the back seat. Then Daniel got in and they drove off. As I said, I never saw any of them again."

"What about the mother and the little girl?"

Doatsy's gaze went back to the window, where she had a view of the house next door. "They didn't leave with Daniel and Matthew that night, but I never saw them again either."

"What did you think happened to them?"

"It was awhile before I found out," Doatsy said mysteriously. "My sister used to be a nurse and she worked at the same hospital as Dr. Cypher. I mentioned to her one day that I was worried about Katherine and Maddy. She knew we were neighbors, but she would never gossip about Dr. Cypher while he was still on staff. That day she told me that Dr. and Mrs. Cypher didn't even have a daughter. They had only one child and he was a son."

"So who was the little girl?"

"There was no little girl." Doatsy's gaze met Dave's and she nodded. "That's right. Maddy and Matthew were one and the same child. Nowadays, the proper term for someone like Matthew is intersexual. Babies born with ambiguous gender. My sister was on duty the night he was delivered, and she said Dr. Cypher was beside himself. He was almost in a fit of rage."

"Directed at whom?"

"His poor wife, I suspect. Or maybe God."

"What about Matthew?"

"This was back in the early seventies, and my sister said that surgery on intersexed babies was still routinely ordered by the attending physician, and often requested by the parents. You would assume that most did so out of love. No parent would want to see their child shunned and stigmatized for being different. But Daniel Cypher?" She said his name in disgust. "I've known powerful men like him all my life. He probably considered a child like Matthew as an affront to his own masculinity. So he ordered reassignment."

"Meaning surgery."

"A very complicated and painful surgery with more to come as the child grew older. And then injections of hormones when he hit puberty." She put a hand to her mouth as she shook her head sadly. "Can you imagine how confused that little boy must have been? A cold, domineering father set on having a son, and a loving mother who indulged the child's natural inclinations when they were alone. I later heard that Katherine had suffered a complete psychotic breakdown and had to be permanently institutionalized. I shudder to think what Matthew's life must have been like with Daniel as his sole influence."

"And you say you never heard from any of them again?"

"No, but something strange happened a few months ago. It was right after the house next door had been put on the market. I saw the same car drive by every night for about a week."

"Did you happen to notice the make or model?"

"It was a black sedan—that's all I could tell. But a few minutes after I saw the car go by one night, I noticed a man out walking on the street. It was raining and he had his shoulders hunched over. But he stopped in front of the house and just stood there staring up at it for a long time. And when he turned, and the streetlight caught him just right, something about him reminded me of Matthew."

* * *

Charlotte was sitting on Claire's front porch when she got home from work that day. Her sister wore a light gray silk suit and heels, and Claire figured she must have come straight over from the office. She had on sunglasses, but she slipped them off as Claire climbed the steps.

She rose, hands on hips. "I tried to call you I don't know how many times last night. Where on earth were you?"

"I went for a drive." Claire got out her keys to unlock the door.

"I was worried sick about you!"

"Why?"

"You were gone for hours." Charlotte followed her inside and closed the door. "That's not like you."

"A lot's happened lately. I just needed some time to sort things through." Claire wasn't about to admit to her sister that she'd spent the night with Dave. She wasn't ashamed of what she'd done, but she didn't feel like having to justify her actions. And besides, what she and Dave had shared was a very private thing. She wasn't ready to have it brought out in the open and analyzed.

"Why were you trying to reach me?" Claire asked. "Was anything wrong?"

Charlotte dropped her purse on the couch and turned, but her gaze didn't quite meet Claire's. "I need to talk to you about Alex."

"Oh." Claire tossed her keys into a basket on her desk. "I already know what you're going to say."

Charlotte lifted her brows in surprise. "He told you?"

"Reluctantly. He didn't want to, but he didn't have a choice. When I went to confront him, I already knew what he'd done, but I wanted to hear it from him. And even then, I still had a hard time believing he could do such a thing. What kind of man would use a little girl's kidnapping to cover up a murder?"

Charlotte quickly looked away. "I know, Claire. I can't believe it, either. I'm so sorry. I keep thinking about all those times I tried to get you to reconcile with him. I thought he was the perfect guy. And now to find out what he did…" She closed her eyes. "I feel like such a fool."

"But you didn't know. He fooled me, too."

Charlotte rubbed her temples with her fingertips. "He's in a lot of trouble, Claire."

"He should be."

"Don't you even want to know what kind of charges he could be facing?"

Claire walked over to the window, glanced out, then turned back to Charlotte. "Right now, I don't really care what happens to him."

"That doesn't sound like you. You've always been the most forgiving person I know."

"Forgiving?" She gave a bitter laugh. "You don't know me as well as you think you do. I'm capable of carrying around hate and anger for years. Just ask Dave."

"You've forgiven him now, though, haven't you?"

Claire glanced back out at the street. "I don't know. I'm not sure what I feel for Dave these days."

Charlotte came over to stand beside her at the window. "Sometimes I think you're still in love with him. You're just too afraid to admit it."

"Maybe I am. Maybe I always will be. But it's not enough. Not with Dave. Being with him is too hard. It's like waiting for a bomb to go off. You know disaster is coming and so you constantly brace yourself for it. You go through each day with your stomach in knots, expecting the worst. I don't know why anybody would want to go back to that."

"Maybe because he's changed," Charlotte said softly. "And maybe because you've never been happy without him."

A little while later, Charlotte sent Claire upstairs for a long, hot shower while she went into the kitchen to see about dinner. By the time Claire came back down, she could smell spaghetti sauce simmering on the stove. She poked her head into the kitchen to see if she could help. Charlotte stood at the sink, washing greens for a salad.

"I've got everything under control. You just go sit down and relax." When she didn't hear the door close, Charlotte glanced over her shoulder. "You do remember how to relax, don't you?"

"Vaguely."

Claire was still standing there watching her when Charlotte turned from the sink. "What?"

She shook her head. "I still can't figure you out. First you take up for Dave, and now this. I can't help thinking something's going on with you."

"I didn't exactly take up for Dave. I said it's possible that he might have changed." Charlotte wiped her hands on a dishtowel. "I'm just trying to do something nice for you. Don't make me regret it."

Claire smiled. "Now that sounds more like you."

She poured Claire a glass of wine, put it in her hand and gave her a little push toward the living room. "Go away, you're making me nervous. I'll let you know when dinner's ready."

There was nothing for Claire to do but sit down and put her feet up. She closed her eyes and might have drifted off if the phone hadn't rung.

"I'll get it," Charlotte called from the kitchen.

A moment later, she came through the doorway, palming the receiver. "Do you know someone named Savannah Sweete?"

Claire sat up, her fatigue suddenly forgotten, and reached for the phone. "This is Claire," she said anxiously.

"I hope I'm not calling at a bad time," the woman drawled. "But I've come across something that I thought you should know about."

"What is it?"

"It may not be anything of consequence, so I don't want you to get your hopes up. But after you left this morning, I kept thinking about that picture of your daughter. I couldn't get her little face out of my mind, and I started to wonder if maybe I *had* seen her before. Or at least her photograph. So I called my nephew and had him bring over some of the file boxes I told you about. I've been sitting here going through them all day, and I finally found something you might find helpful. It's a photograph of a little blond girl."

"Is it Ruby?"

"It looks an awful lot like that picture you showed me this morning, but I can't be certain. I think it would be best if you came out here and took a look at it yourself. I tried calling Mr. Creasy at the number he left, but there's no answer."

"I'm glad you called me," Claire said. "When can I come see this picture?"

"How about tomorrow morning?"

Her grip on the phone tightened. "I don't mean to sound pushy, but could I come this evening? I really don't want to wait until morning."

"Are you sure you want to make such a long drive this late in the day?"

"I'm only an hour away," Claire said. "I really would like to come now. If I don't, I'll be worried about that photograph all night."

"I understand. You just come on then. I'll be here waiting for you."

"Thanks. And thank you so much for going through those files so quickly. You don't know how much this means to me."

"Oh, it was nothing. I was happy to do it," she said. "I'll see you in an hour."

Charlotte had stood there listening the whole time, and as Claire set the phone aside, she said curiously, "Who on earth is Savannah Sweete?"

"You've never heard Mama mention her? She's a doll maker who lives over in Terrebonne Parish. It's possible she may have made the doll I saw in the shop window last week. She's gone through some of her files, and she thinks she may have found a picture of Ruby."

"That's great, I guess. But why not wait until morning to drive down there?"

"Because I waited to go back to the collectibles shop after I saw the doll, remember? It was gone by the time I got back. I'm not taking a chance like that again."

"What about dinner?"

Claire grabbed her purse and keys. "Save it for me. If I leave now, I can be back by dark."

Charlotte followed her out to the porch. "You want me to come with you?"

"No, you stay. If Dave gets her message, he may call here. You can tell him that I've already gone down there to look at the picture."

"Okay, but Claire…"

She turned at the bottom of the steps. Charlotte stood on the porch, staring down at her.

"Be careful, okay?"

"I'll be fine. Savannah Sweete is a perfectly lovely woman. There's really no need to worry about me at all."

The phone rang while Charlotte was putting the spaghetti sauce away. She cradled the receiver against her shoulder as she sealed the lid on the storage container and opened the refrigerator door.

"Claire?"

"No, this is Charlotte. Who's this?"

"Dave Creasy. Could I speak to Claire, please?"

Charlotte couldn't blame him for his guarded tone. She hadn't exactly been cordial the last few times she'd seen him. "Claire isn't here, but she said you might call if you got Savannah Sweete's message."

"What message?"

"She phoned here earlier and said that she'd found a photo of Ruby. Or at least, she thinks it could be Ruby. I guess she tried to get in touch with you first. Anyway, Claire wanted you to know that she's on her way down there to look at the photograph."

"She's on her way there *now?*"

Charlotte frowned at his tone. "She left a few minutes ago. Is something wrong?"

Dave hesitated. "I'm not sure. I found out some things today that concern me a little. I don't know yet if there's a connection to Savannah Sweete, but I'd rather Claire not go down there alone."

"What is going on?" Charlotte demanded. "You're making me very nervous."

His hesitation was slight, but enough to put her on alert. "It's probably nothing. I'll head down that way myself, but I just left Baton Rouge. I'm at least an hour and a half away, and that's without traffic."

"Claire just left fifteen minutes ago, determined to find out about that doll. If I can't reach her by phone, I'll try to catch up with her on the road. Do you have directions to this place?"

Charlotte grabbed a pen and jotted the information Dave gave her on the back of an envelope.

"Highway 53 from Houma, then a right just before I get to Tiber."

"There'll be a gas station on your right," Dave said. "The road's not marked so you'll have to watch for it."

"I don't plan on having to go that far. As soon as I hit Highway 90, I'll catch her."

"If you do end up going all the way to the house and something doesn't seem right, just get Claire out of there, okay?"

Charlotte bit her lip. "You're worried about her, aren't you? I can hear it in your voice."

"I'm concerned," Dave said. "Like I said, I'd feel a lot better if she wasn't going down there alone."

"She won't be for long. I'm headed out right now. Here, let me give you my cell number in case you need to call me."

They exchanged phone numbers and then Charlotte

grabbed her purse and ran out the door. She wouldn't let herself think about that note of anxiety in Dave's voice.

Claire would be fine. She had to be. Because Charlotte couldn't bear to think otherwise.

Twenty-Nine

The light was fading by the time Claire made the turn at Tiber and headed down the gravel road toward Savanna Sweete's house. The sky was lavender, and the pink clouds in the west were gilded. The sun was setting, but the air was still hot. She'd run the air conditioner for most of the way, but now she rolled her window down and the wind that rushed in was thick with the scent of the honeysuckle that grew along the fencerows. She could smell the bayou, too, and as she pulled up outside the gates, mimosa and magnolia.

She tapped her horn, and the gates swung open so quickly she found herself wondering again if Savannah had been watching for her from an upstairs window.

Claire drove through, and as she glanced in her rearview mirror, she saw the gates slowly close behind her. She didn't know why, but she suddenly felt a prickle of apprehension as she pulled up to the house and parked.

She climbed the porch steps, knocked on the door,

and almost immediately the lock clicked open, just as it had earlier that day. Claire stepped inside and glanced around. As the sun sank behind the trees, the light through the windows in the parlor turned golden, but the foyer and stairs lay in deep shadow.

She stood at the bottom of the stairs and called up. "Ms. Sweete? It's Claire Doucett. We spoke on the phone a little while ago."

The house remained silent.

Claire climbed a couple of steps and called up again. "Ms. Sweete? Are you up there?"

When the woman still didn't answer, Claire stepped back down into the foyer. She was expected. She had made it clear on the phone that she was on her way there, and it seemed doubtful that the older woman would have gone out after they'd spoken.

Claire started into the parlor, but a sound from upstairs stopped her cold. Her heart thudded as she slowly turned, her gaze going to the top of the steps.

"Hello? Is someone up there?"

The sound came again, a feral grunt that lifted the hair on Claire's neck and sent a shiver down her spine.

"Hello?" Slowly, she climbed the stairs. "Ms. Sweete? Are you up here? It's Claire Doucett. I'm coming up. I just want to make sure you're okay."

There was light at the top of the stairs from a window, and as Claire moved onto the landing, she saw her.

The woman lay on the floor, her back to the stairs, one clawlike hand extended toward the elevator. The animal sounds coming from her throat chilled Claire to her core, and she found herself hesitating for a moment before she rushed to the woman's side and bent to touch her shoulder.

The sounds grew louder and more agitated, and Claire realized she'd frightened the poor woman. She quickly drew back her hand. "I'm sorry. I didn't mean to scare you. I want to help you."

She moved around to the other side so that Savannah could see her. The older woman's face was so thin and drawn, her eyes sunken so far back into the sockets that she looked nearly skeletal. She smelled of vomit, urine and decay. Claire put a hand to her mouth, trying to stifle a gag.

"What happened to you?" she asked in shock.

The woman grunted in response, her eyes darting back and forth as if she couldn't focus. She wasn't Savannah Sweete. She was much older than the woman Claire had met that morning. But who was she? And what was wrong with her?

Claire was almost afraid to touch her again. Her limbs looked as if they might snap as easily as dried twigs with even the slightest of pressure. She wore only a thin cotton nightgown, and the legs protruding from the hem were bruised and mottled.

"My God," Claire muttered.

She started to rise, but the woman seemed to grow even more frantic, and the hand outstretched toward the elevator lifted slightly off the floor and brushed against Claire's leg.

A tremor shot through her. "It's okay. I won't leave you here alone. I'll call for help and stay with you until someone comes."

The woman was still on her side, lower legs curved behind her and one arm beneath her. Claire wanted to turn her to make her more comfortable, but she didn't dare.

"I'm going to call someone, okay?"

The woman's eyes rounded with distress and her mouth opened and closed, but no sound at all came out now. She was obviously trying to form a word, but her jaw flapped uselessly.

She finally managed a single syllable, but her voice was so weak Claire could barely hear her. She moved in closer, and the woman's eye movements became frantic.

"Ra...ra...ra..."

"I'm sorry," Claire murmured. "I don't know what you're trying to tell me."

She started to move away, but the sound grew steadily louder and more desperate, as if it were being ripped from the woman's very soul.

"Ra...ra...ra..."

And then Claire realized it wasn't just a random syllable or inane noise. It was a warning.

Run!

Heart pounding, she rose shakily to her feet, her mind on one thing only. She had to get help. Something had obviously frightened the poor woman terribly, and Claire could feel her own panic starting to churn to the surface. But that wouldn't do anyone any good. If Savannah Sweete was still in the house, she might need help, too. Claire had to remain calm. She had to stay in control.

Phone!

She had to call for help, had to get an ambulance out here immediately. But the woman seemed terrified to be left alone even for a moment. Calire pulled out her cell phone, realized that it was off and turned it on. While she waited for a signal, she heard the creak of the elevator cables.

The cage rattled to a stop on the second floor, and as the grid swung open, Claire saw a man inside. His head was bowed, as if in prayer or deep contemplation. Then he looked up, and as his gaze met hers, Claire's mouth went dry with fear. There was something familiar about his eyes, something terrifying about the way he smiled at her.

He was average height, but extremely thin, with prominent cheekbones and a wide forehead. His clothing was nondescript—khaki trousers, light blue shirt, wire-rimmed glasses. There was nothing at all frightening about his appearance, but Claire started to tremble.

"Who are you?" she said.

"I'm Matthew. Savannah's nephew." His gaze lit on the old woman on the floor and he clucked his tongue. "What are you doing out of bed?"

"She's hurt," Claire said. "We need to call a doctor."

"I am a doctor. Didn't my aunt tell you that this morning?"

"Then you have to help her. She seems very sick."

He walked out of the elevator, but instead of kneeling by the woman on the floor, he stepped over her and moved toward Claire.

"What are you doing? You have to help her!"

"I have to help you first."

"There's nothing wrong with me." She saw then that he had a syringe in his right hand, and fear flushed through her system. "What are you doing?"

"It's okay. It won't hurt."

He smiled again, and with the slowness of a nightmare, Claire registered the color of his eyes. They were like turquoise, the same color as the doll's eyes. The same color as Ruby's eyes.

Dear God, it's him.

It was Ruby's kidnapper. The person who had made the doll in the likeness of her daughter.

Claire tried to stay calm, but her heartbeat drummed in her ears and her breath quickened. She took another step away from him, felt the railing behind her back and realized there was nowhere to go but down.

Her cell phone was still in her hand, and she tried to press the buttons. If she could speed-dial Charlotte or 911—

"Please don't make me hurt you." There was a strange pleading note in his voice, an almost childlike quality to the way he stared at her.

"I won't," she said. "Just put the needle down."

"I can't do that."

"Yes, you can," Claire said. "You don't want to hurt me."

She lunged for the stairs then, but he tackled her from behind and they both went crashing to the floor. The phone flew out of her hand as she hit the hard surface. Blood exploded in her mouth as she bit down on her tongue. He plunged the needle into her neck, the sharp prick like the sting of an angry hornet.

Claire's muscles jerked uncontrollably, and then she went almost completely still. Her vision blurred and she thought for a moment she would pass out. Then everything came back into sharp focus as he rolled her onto her back.

Her mouth sagged open, but the scream died in her throat. Panic dropped like a cold, black wave.

Get up! Get up and run!

She tried to muster her strength to crawl to the top of the stairs, but she couldn't even lift her hand.

His eyes seemed to dance with madness as he knelt beside her and stroked his palm down her cheek. "See there?" he said gently. "It doesn't hurt, does it? The worst is already over."

He bent and grasped her feet, turning her so that he could pull her across the floor to the elevator. He dragged her inside, closed the gate, and a second later, Claire could tell they were descending. She could hear the clang of the cage and the rattle of the cable, but she couldn't feel the floor beneath her back. She couldn't feel his hands on her, either, but she knew they were there because she could see his fingers coiled around her ankles.

The elevator jolted to a stop and he pushed open the gate. He pulled her off the car and then was towing her again, this time down a long dim corridor. Claire had no idea where he was taking her. He released her once to open another door, and then they were on the move again.

Once inside the room, he placed her feet gently on the floor and stood looking down at her for the longest time. Then he turned, disappeared from her line of sight, and a moment later, Claire heard the door close and the lock click.

And she was all alone in her prison.

Charlotte's skirt caught on a metal spike as she scrambled over the fence, and she heard the fabric rip as she jerked it free. "Damn it!"

The suit had cost nearly a month's salary, way more than she could afford, and she swore again as she tossed her high heels to the ground and then jumped. Maybe she should have just waited in her car and laid down on the horn until someone opened the gate to let her in. She'd honked a couple of times, had even tried to find a way to open the gate herself. Finally, she'd given up, taken off her shoes, hiked up her skirt and climbed the fence. She was lucky it wasn't electric, she silently grumbled, grabbing one of the metal rods to brace herself while she put her shoes back on.

Her heels sank in the soft earth as she plodded across the yard to the driveway. The light was fading, and in another hour, twilight would fall. Charlotte tried to fight the urgency that had been clawing at her gut ever since Dave's phone call, but she couldn't shake the feeling that something was wrong.

She'd hoped to catch up to Claire before she got here, but Charlotte had overshot the turnoff at Tiber and lost at least another ten minutes backtracking, which meant that her sister had probably been here for nearly half an hour.

You're just being paranoid, Charlotte scolded herself as she started up the driveway. Claire was fine. Savannah Sweete was a doll maker, for goodness sake, and Charlotte had met enough of those characters through her mother to know the type. There was no reason to worry.

When she saw Claire's car parked beneath an oak tree, she sighed in relief. *See?* Nothing was wrong. Dave had just been overcautious and caused her to panic a little.

Still, as Charlotte climbed the porch steps, an odd shiver raced up her backbone and she quickly glanced around, feeling as if someone might have come up behind her. But no one was there, and she again let out a breath.

She turned back to the door and rapped several times

with the knocker. When no one answered, she knocked again, and this time she heard a loud click as the door popped open about an inch.

"Hello?"

Charlotte waited, thinking that someone would open the door and invite her in, but nothing happened. She reached out and gave the door a nudge. It swung open and she called out again. "Hello? Is anyone here? Claire?" She stepped inside. "It's Charlotte."

She closed the door and took a few steps across the foyer. "Where is everybody?"

"In here, dear."

Charlotte jumped at the unexpected voice, then followed it into a large parlor. A woman in a wheelchair sat in front of the windows, backlit by the fading rays of the sunset. She had short gray hair and thin shoulders, and she sat with a shawl draped over her legs. Charlotte's initial impression of the woman was fleeting, because the moment she walked into the parlor, her attention was caught by all the dolls.

She turned, glanced around. They were everywhere.

"They are a bit much, aren't they?" the woman said with a soft laugh. "I can't bear to part with them, though. They've become a part of my family."

"I can see why. They're very lifelike." Eerily so. Charlotte gave the woman an apologetic smile. "I'm sorry to barge in like this, but I'm looking for Claire Doucett. She's my sister."

"Oh, yes. My name is Savannah Sweete."

"You're the doll maker."

She smiled. "Yes."

Claire hadn't mentioned that the woman was in a wheelchair. Not that it mattered, of course, but Charlotte was caught a little off guard. "Is Claire still here? I saw her car in the driveway."

"She went upstairs to bring down some files. Won't you sit down while you wait for her?"

"Maybe I should just run up and let her know I'm here." Charlotte was already half turned toward the doorway. She heard the wheelchair squeak, and when she swung back around, she saw the shawl fall from Savannah Sweete's lap as the woman stood. Then she lifted her hand and slowly removed the wig from her head.

It took only an instant for Charlotte to process the strange tableau, and then cold fear shot through her bloodstream.

"Who are you?"

He smiled. "I'm the Dollmaker."

Everything hit Charlotte at once, in a sudden flash of comprehension. The Dollmaker…the one who had created a doll that looked like Ruby. Charlotte didn't know how she could be so certain, but she knew without a doubt that she was staring into the eyes of Ruby's kidnapper. Her killer.

Terror twisted like a rope in Charlotte's chest. "Where's Claire?"

He was still smiling as he walked toward her.

Charlotte turned and lunged across the foyer, but the door had locked behind her. Frantically, she tried to find the release, then whirled, searching for another way out. She was too late. He'd had plenty of time to come up behind her, but he didn't attack. He just stood there still smiling.

Up close, his face was thin and delicate, and seemed frozen in place, like a piece of clay. His body beneath the khaki trousers and light blue shirt was gaunt, and he had high cheekbones, a wide forehead, eyes the color of turquoise. Like Ruby's.

And like Claire's.

Charlotte forced herself to breathe slowly, deeply. She had to keep her panic under control. Her life depended on it, and so might Claire's. "You took her, didn't you? You're the one who kidnapped Ruby."

His smile was taunting, and chilled Charlotte's blood, even as her rage exploded. Something snapped inside her and she flew at him, pounding his face and chest with her fists.

"Where's Claire? What have you done to her, you sick bastard?"

She kept hitting him, and he stumbled back against the wall. He didn't struggle, didn't fight back, didn't do anything except stand there absorbing her punches.

A warning went off in Charlotte's brain a split second before she felt a hard pressure in her abdomen, a searing pain, as if her insides were being ripped out with a hot poker. She staggered back, glanced down and saw a red stain seeping through the silk of her suit.

She still didn't know what had happened until she looked up and saw the dripping blade in the Dollmaker's hand.

Thirty

The table was set with Maddy's favorite tea set, and the Dollmaker smiled as he sat cross-legged on the floor, admiring all the pretty packages. Now that he had everything cleaned up, he could relax for a while and enjoy the party.

His gaze went around the table. Maddy was at the end, of course, because the party was in her honor. Like Maddy, the other children were attired in their prettiest party dresses, their smooth, painted faces aglow in the light from the candles on the cake. Everything was perfect. Just like the photograph. Just like his memories.

The only difference this time was the flowers. Instead of camellias, he'd placed one of his orchids in the pretty glass bowl he'd purchased at the gallery from *her*. He didn't like saying her name, even to himself. He didn't like thinking about her other life. She was his now. She was everything he needed to make his perfect little world safe and happy and complete.

The child sat quietly at the end of the table. She didn't

say a word, but her solemn little eyes watched his every move. She didn't ask to go home anymore. They all stopped asking at some point, and that's when the eyes became empty, the face a blank canvas. That's when he knew it was time.

Actually, it was past time. He should have had the sixth doll completed by now, but his loneliness had caused him to delay the process longer than he normally would have. He'd put himself needlessly at risk, but it didn't matter now. Everything would soon be perfect once again.

Rising, he went over to the mirror and smiled at the reflection. Fingers gently stroked the long, golden curls, a hand brushed across the smooth, pink-tinted cheeks. The turquoise eyes twinkled as the mouth curved into a delighted smile. Maddy's smile.

"There you are," a childish voice whispered. "I told you I would find you, didn't I?"

Turning, he walked over to his worktable and smiled at the woman who gazed up at him. Her eyes widened and she tried to speak, but nothing came out of her mouth.

"Don't be afraid." He took her hand and squeezed it. "It's me, Mama. Don't you recognize me?"

The Dollmaker coated tiny strips of paper with plaster of paris, and one by one, placed them on her face, pressing and kneading with his fingertips so that when the plaster hardened, the mold would be a perfect replica of her bone structure.

A surreal sense of horror gripped Claire as she stared up at the long, golden curls, the painted cheeks on a smooth, pale face. Fear crawled through her veins.

She'd been afraid as she lay alone earlier, but now she realized a terror that seemed to have no bounds.

She tried to move her arms and legs, but couldn't muster the strength to even flutter her eyelids.

He worked quickly, almost frantically, pressing layer upon layer against her face. He covered her eyes so that she was in total darkness, and then her nose and mouth. As the plaster began to harden, Claire had to struggle for breath. In another few moments, she would suffocate, slip slowly into a cold, terrifying blackness.

"Mama?"

"I'm so scared, Ruby. And I'm so sorry you had to feel this. I would give anything if I could have saved you."

"I love you, Mama."

"I love you, too, baby. More than anything in the world..."

"Claire!"

Dave tore at the mask on her face. The plaster had started to harden, but it was still pliable enough to remove with his fingers. His hands were shaking by the time he had it all stripped away, and his blood went cold when he saw her face. She was so pale. He couldn't tell if she was still breathing....

And then her eyes fluttered open and she stared up at him in terror. Her throat moved convulsively, but she couldn't speak.

"It's okay," he whispered. "I'm taking you out of here."

She blinked rapidly, and Dave realized a split second too late that she was trying to warn him. He turned, saw the man behind him, and swung his arm up reflexively to deflect the weapon. The blade caught him across the forearm, and Dave staggered back, momentarily stunned by the pain.

He came at Dave again, but this time he was ready. His fist swung up and caught the man beneath his left eye. The bone popped like the crack of a rifle, and his head snapped as he went sprawling backward. The blade flew from his hand, and Dave kicked it out of the way as a crimson rage exploded within him.

He lunged forward, and the man's face contorted with terror as he tried to scramble away. His eyes were watery with shock and pain, and he cradled his head as Dave reached down and grabbed him by the throat. He hauled him to his feet, and for one split second, let himself stare into the eyes of his daughter's killer. And then his hand tightened slowly. The muscles in his arm quivered as he pressed against the windpipe, and he could feel blood dripping from the fingertips of his other hand.

The man slapped at him, tried to claw his grip loose from his throat, but still Dave held on. The blue eyes were wide with fear and confusion. He looked like a child being punished for something he didn't understand. And in those quivering lips, deep inside those terrified eyes, Dave glimpsed a child who had been heartlessly shunned by his own father.

And even then Dave could have killed him without a drop of remorse. The temptation to exact his own justice was almost overwhelming. Then he saw a pale little face peering at him from the far corner of the room, and for a moment, Dave thought it was Ruby.

It couldn't be, of course. Ruby would have been much older by now. His daughter was dead. Nothing he did here today would ever bring her back.

But as Dave stared at the child across the room, he saw the same innocence in her, and he did not want her to have this memory.

He released his grip on the man's throat and shoved him away. The Dollmaker collapsed to the floor and curled himself into a fetal position, burying his face in his hands as he whimpered like a wounded kitten.

Claire had been dreaming about Ruby, and when she awakened, it took her a moment to realize where she was. Then it all came back to her. She was in the hospital, and Charlotte was just down the hall from her. Her sister had made it through surgery and was expected to make a full recovery.

Lucille was sitting in a chair by the bed, and when she saw that Claire was awake, she got up and came over to her side.

"How are you feeling?"

Claire lifted a hand and flexed her fingers. They were still weak, but the muscles were responsive. "Almost back to normal. I don't need to be in the hospital, Mama."

"You let the doctors decide that, honey." Lucille brushed a strand of hair from her daughter's face.

"How's Charlotte?"

"I just came from her room a few minutes ago. She's still out, but she seems to be resting comfortably. They've got her all doped up, so she's not in any pain."

"Why don't you go back and sit with her, Mama? I really am fine."

"I will in a minute."

"Have you heard anything about the little girl?" Claire asked softly.

"Her family's on their way from Alabama to pick her up. I can't even begin to imagine what they must be feeling tonight."

Claire was silent for a moment. "She must have been so scared."

Tears flooded Lucille's eyes as she lifted Claire's hand to her cheek.

"I can't help thinking about what she went through," Claire said. "How she must have wanted to cry out for me, but couldn't. She must have thought I would come and get her, but I never did. I couldn't save her, Mama. My own daughter."

"You couldn't save Ruby, honey, but another little girl's life has been spared. Be thankful that another mother doesn't have to go through what you did. And Ruby's safe now, Claire. She's safe and warm and Maw-Maw is there to look after her. You can rest easy now, baby."

"I love you, Mama."

"I love you, too, Claire."

After a while, she drifted off again, and when she woke up, the chair beside her bed was empty. Her mother had gone back to Charlotte's room, and Claire lay there for a while, staring into the darkness. Then she turned her head and saw someone at the window.

"Dave?"

"I'm here, Claire."

**New York Times
bestselling author**

HEATHER GRAHAM

On a weekend vacation, Beth Anderson is unnerved when a stroll on the beach reveals what appears to be a human skull. As a stranger approaches, Beth panics and covers the evidence. But when she later returns to the beach, the skull is gone.

Determined to find solid evidence to bring to the police, Beth digs deeper into the mystery—and everywhere she goes, Keith Henson, the stranger from the beach, seems to appear. Then a body washes ashore, and Beth begins to think she needs more help than she bargained for....

THE ISLAND

"Another top-notch thriller
from romance icon Graham."
—*Publishers Weekly*

*Available the first week
of March 2007, wherever
paperbacks are sold!*

MIRA®

www.MIRABooks.com

New York Times bestselling author

CARLA NEGGERS

The largest uncut diamond in the world, the Minstrel's Rough is little more than legend. Brought into the Pepperkamp Family in 1548, it has been handed down to one keeper in each generation. Juliana Fall has inherited its splendor from her uncle—and, unwittingly, its legacy of danger.

There are others who seek the Minstrel's Rough: a U.S. senator, a Nazi collaborator and a Vietnam war-hero-turned-journalist, among them. Now Juliana has only two choices: uncover the past before they do...or cut and run.

"No one does romantic suspense better!"
—*New York Times* bestselling author
Janet Evanovich

*Available the first week of March 2007,
wherever paperbacks are sold!*

MIRA®

www.MIRABooks.com   MCN2419

New York Times
and *USA TODAY*
bestselling author

DINAH MCCALL

When a passenger plane goes
down in the Appalachians, rescue
teams start looking for survivors
and discover that a five-year-old
boy and a woman are missing.
Twenty miles from the crash site,
Deborah Sanborn has a vision
of two survivors, cold, hurting
and scared. Over the years she
has learned to trust her gift, and
she senses these strangers are
in terrible danger. She sees a
hunter, moving in for the kill....

THE
SURVIVORS

"Intense, fast-paced,
and cleverly crafted..."
—*Library Journal*
on *Storm Warning*

*Available the first week
of March 2007, wherever
paperbacks are sold!*

USA TODAY bestselling author

LAURIE BRETON

Everyone assumes that successful Boston Realtor Kaye Winslow
has it all. Until the day she goes out to show an expensive new
listing and vanishes into thin air, leaving behind her credit cards,
her BlackBerry and an unidentified male corpse.

Turns out a lot of people don't like Kaye, and many of them have
a beef with her. But until the not-so-lovely Kaye Winslow is located,
people close to her are just a little bit twitchy—because any one of
them could be accused of murder.

POINT
OF
DEPARTURE

"Only seasoned armchair sleuths will guess the killer's identity."
—*Romantic Times BOOKreviews* on *Lethal Lies*

Available the first week of March 2007, wherever paperbacks are sold!

REQUEST YOUR FREE BOOKS!

2 FREE NOVELS
FROM THE ROMANCE/SUSPENSE
COLLECTION PLUS 2 FREE GIFTS!

YES! Please send me 2 FREE novels from the Romance/Suspense Collection and my 2 FREE gifts. After receiving them, if I don't wish to receive any more books, I can return the shipping statement marked "cancel." If I don't cancel, I will receive 4 brand-new novels every month and be billed just $5.49 per book in the U.S., or $5.99 per book in Canada, plus 25¢ shipping and handling per book plus applicable taxes, if any*. That's a savings of at least 20% off the cover price! I understand that accepting the 2 free books and gifts places me under no obligation to buy anything. I can always return a shipment and cancel at any time. Even if I never buy another book from the Reader Service, the two free books and gifts are mine to keep forever.

185 MDN EF5Y   385 MDN EF6C

Name   (PLEASE PRINT)

Address   Apt. #

City   State/Prov.   Zip/Postal Code

Signature (if under 18, a parent or guardian must sign)

Mail to **The Reader Service:**
IN U.S.A.: P.O. Box 1867, Buffalo, NY 14240-1867
IN CANADA: P.O. Box 609, Fort Erie, Ontario L2A 5X3

Not valid to current subscribers to the Romance Collection,
the Suspense Collection or the Romance/Suspense Collection.

Want to try two free books from another line?
Call 1-800-873-8635 or visit www.morefreebooks.com.

* Terms and prices subject to change without notice. NY residents add applicable sales tax. Canadian residents will be charged applicable provincial taxes and GST. This offer is limited to one order per household. All orders subject to approval. Credit or debit balances in a customer's account(s) may be offset by any other outstanding balance owed by or to the customer. Please allow 4 to 6 weeks for delivery.

Your Privacy: Harlequin is committed to protecting your privacy. Our Privacy Policy is available online at www.eHarlequin.com or upon request from the Reader Service. From time to time we make our lists of customers available to reputable firms who may have a product or service of interest to you. If you would prefer we not share your name and address, please check here. ☐

BOB07

USA TODAY bestselling author

JENNIFER ARMINTROUT

In the two months since I was attacked in the hospital morgue and turned into a vampire, I've killed my evil sire Cyrus, fallen in love with my new sire, Nathan, and have even gotten used to drinking blood. Just when things are finally returning to normal, Nathan becomes possessed by one of the most powerful and wicked vampires alive—the Soul Eater. And then he slaughters an innocent human. With the Soul Eater and my possessed sire on the loose, I have a lot to fear. Including being killed. Again.

blood ties book two: POSSESSION

"This fast, furious novel is a squirm-inducing treat."
—*Publishers Weekly* on *The Turning*

*Available the first week of February 2007
wherever paperbacks are sold!*

MIRA®

www.MIRABooks.com

MJA2418